PRAISE FOR

VELVET WAS THE NIGHT

"[*Velvet Was the Night*] is a noir with a heart of gold, and it's a narrative in which the empathy we feel for its characters ultimately reveals an important truth: That [Silvia] Moreno-Garcia is not only a talented storyteller but also an incredibly versatile one."

—NPR

"An absolute flex . . . [*Velvet Was the Night*] left me marveling at what kind of sorceress Moreno-Garcia must be as she reworks genre after genre, weaving in Mexican history and culture, satisfying familiar cravings without resorting to mere pastiche. The most tantalizing suspense of all comes with wondering what she'll do next." —*Slate*

"An adrenalized, darkly romantic journey." —*The Washington Post*

"*Velvet Was the Night* is a rollicking work of historical noir with a vivid sense of time and place and an unforgettable cast. Moreno-Garcia made me care deeply about her characters and their dangerous, riveting misadventures. This is a stylish, hard-boiled novel painted in shades of gray, with a whole lot of heart."

—Steph Cha, author of *Your House Will Pay*

"Silvia Moreno-Garcia takes you into the gritty underworld noir of 1970s Mexico City with a propulsive read where no one and nothing is as it seems."

—Isabella Maldonado, bestselling author of *The Cipher*

"Silvia Moreno-Garcia's *Velvet Was the Night* is a treat to be savored, a dizzying combination of American and Mexican noir written in the most individual of voices."

—BARRY FORSHAW, crime critic for *Financial Times*

"*Velvet Was the Night* is a delicious, twisted treat for lovers of noir. Silvia Moreno-Garcia is a masterful writer who pulls you into her dark world and never lets you go. From the suspenseful, slow-burn plot to the crisp, desperate characters, you will be obsessed."

—SIMONE ST. JAMES, *New York Times* bestselling author of *The Sun Down Motel*

"Moreno-Garcia proves her prowess as a historical fiction powerhouse again."

—*BuzzFeed*

"Immensely satisfying, refreshingly new and gloriously written . . . Moreno-Garcia mashes up Anglocentric genres with mid-century Mexican history, resulting in a brew flavored with love, heartbreak, violence, music and unsettling dread. . . . The gift of this book, and Moreno-Garcia's storytelling, is how it imbues this well-worn genre with added strength, grace and even musicality."

—*The New York Times Book Review*, Editors' Choice

"An enthralling tale that's as fun as it is mysterious . . . The characters are fascinating, the tone lush and romantic, and it's all wrapped up in a mystery with twists and turns one likely won't see coming. . . . [Silvia Moreno-Garcia is] the sort of author whose works automatically end up on your 'must-read' list."

—*USA Today*

"The author's previous novel, *Mexican Gothic*, turned the screw on the traditional ghost story; here she gleefully pries hard-boiled noir from the cold, white hands of Chandler and Hammett."

—*Oprah Daily*

"A lush, magnificent trip into a world of danger and discovery . . . not to be missed!"

—S. A. Cosby, author of *Blacktop Wasteland* and *Razorblade Tears*

"A rich novel with an engrossing plot, distinctive characters, and a pleasing touch of romance . . . Readers won't be able to put it down."

—*Publishers Weekly* (starred review)

"Fans of Moreno-Garcia's other novels will relish this title, as will noir aficionados and readers who like stories about everymen and -women rising to the occasion."

—*Library Journal* (starred review)

"It's hard to describe how much fun this novel is—Moreno-Garcia, whose *Mexican Gothic* (2020) gripped readers last year, proves to be just as good at noir as she is at horror. The novel features memorable characters, taut pacing, an intricate plot, and antiheroes you can't help but root for. A noir masterpiece."

—*Kirkus Reviews* (starred review)

"Moreno-Garcia . . . returns to noir crime fiction with a winner that brings together a romance-fiction-obsessed secretary and a lovelorn enforcer during the brutally suppressed student riots in 1970s Mexico City."

—*Booklist* (starred review)

By Silvia Moreno-Garcia

The Beautiful Ones

Certain Dark Things

Signal to Noise

Gods of Jade and Shadow

Untamed Shore

Mexican Gothic

Velvet Was the Night

VELVET WAS THE NIGHT

VELVET WAS THE NIGHT

SILVIA MORENO-GARCIA

New York

Velvet Was the Night is a work of fiction. Names, places, and incidents either are products of the author's imagination or are used fictitiously. Any resemblance to actual events, locales, or persons, living or dead, is entirely coincidental.

2022 Del Rey Trade Paperback Edition

Published in the United States by Del Rey, an imprint of Random House, a division of Penguin Random House LLC, New York.

Del Rey and the Circle colophon are registered trademarks of Penguin Random House LLC.

Originally published in hardcover in the United States by Del Rey, an imprint of Random House, a division of Penguin Random House LLC, in 2021.

This book contains an excerpt from the forthcoming book *The Daughter of Doctor Moreau* by Silvia Moreno-Garcia. This excerpt has been set for this edition only and may not reflect the final content of the forthcoming edition.

LIBRARY OF CONGRESS CATALOGING-IN-PUBLICATION DATA

Names: Moreno-Garcia, Silvia, author.
Title: Velvet was the night / Silvia Moreno-Garcia.
Description: New York: Del Rey, [2021]
Identifiers: LCCN 2021005283 (print) | LCCN 2021005284 (ebook) |
ISBN 9780593356845 (paperback) | ISBN 9780593356838 (ebook) |
ISBN 9780593359808 (international edition)
Classification: LCC PR9199.4.M656174 V45 2021 (print) |
LCC PR9199.4.M656174 (ebook) | DDC 813/.6—dc23
LC record available at https://lccn.loc.gov/2021005283
LC ebook record available at https://lccn.loc.gov/2021005284

Printed in the United States of America on acid-free paper

randomhousebooks.com

2 4 6 8 9 7 5 3 1

Text design by Fritz Metsch

Gracias por la música, padre

It is well established that the Hawks are an officially financed, organized, trained and armed repressive group, the main purpose of which since its founding in September 1968 has been the control of leftist and anti-government students.

—United States Department of State, confidential telegram, June 1971

VELVET WAS THE NIGHT

1

June 10, 1971

HE DIDN'T LIKE beating people.

El Elvis realized this was ironic considering his line of work. Imagine that: a thug who wanted to hold his punches. Then again, life is full of such ironies. Consider Ritchie Valens, who was afraid of flying and died the first time he set foot on an airplane. Damn shame that, and the other dudes who died, Buddy Holly and "The Big Bopper" Richardson; they weren't half bad either. Or there was that playwright Aeschylus. He was afraid of being killed inside his house, and then he steps outside and wham, an eagle tosses a tortoise at him, cracking his head open. Murdered, right there in the most stupid way possible.

Often life doesn't make sense, and if Elvis had a motto it was that: life's a mess. That's probably why he loved music and factoids. They helped him construct a more organized world. When he wasn't listening to his records, he was poring over the dictionary, trying to memorize a new word, or plowing through one of those almanacs full of stats.

No, sir. Elvis wasn't like some of the perverts he worked with, who got excited smashing a dude's kidneys. He would have been happy solving crosswords and sipping coffee like their boss, El Mago, and maybe one day he would be an accomplished man of that sort, but for now there was work to be done, and this time Elvis was actually eager to beat a few motherfuckers up.

He hadn't developed a sudden taste for blood and cracking bones, no, but El Güero had been at him again.

El Güero was a policeman before he joined up with Elvis's

group, and that made him cocky, made him want to throw his weight around. In practice being a poli meant shit because El Mago was the egalitarian sort who didn't care where his recruits came from—ex-cops, ex-military, porros, and juvenile delinquents were welcome as long as they worked right. But the thing was El Güero was twenty-five, getting long in the tooth, and that was making him anxious. Soon enough he'd have to move on.

The chief requirement of a Hawk was he needed to look like a student so he could inform on the activities of the annoying reds infesting the universities—Trotskos, Maoists, Espartacos; there were so many flavors of dissidents Elvis could barely keep track of all their organizations—and also, if necessary, fuck up a few of them. Sure, there were important fossils, like El Fish, who was twenty-seven. But El Fish had been in one political shenanigan or another since he was a wee first-year chemistry student; he was as professional as porros got. El Güero hadn't achieved nearly as much. Elvis had just turned twenty-one, and El Güero felt the weight of his age and eyed the younger man with distrust, suspecting El Mago was going to pick El Elvis for a plum position.

Lately El Güero had been making snide remarks about how Elvis was a marshmallow, how he never went on any of the heavy assignments and instead he was picking locks and taking pictures. Elvis did what El Mago asked, and if El Mago wanted him to pick the locks and snap photos, who was Elvis to protest? But that didn't sway El Güero, who had taken to impugning Elvis's masculinity in veiled and irritating ways.

"A man who spends so much time running a comb through his hair isn't a man at all," El Güero would say. "The real Elvis Presley is a hip-shaking girlie-man."

"What you getting at?" Elvis asked, and El Güero smiled. "What you saying 'bout me now?"

"Didn't mean *you*, of course."

"Who'd you mean, then?"

"Presley, like I said. The fucking weirdo you like so much."

"Presley's the king. Ain't nothin' wrong in liking him."

"Yankee garbage," El Güero said smugly.

And then, when it wasn't that, El Güero decided to use an assortment of nicknames to refer to Elvis, none of which were his code name. He had a fondness for calling him La Cucaracha, but also Tribilín, on account of his teeth.

In short, Elvis was in dire need of asserting himself, of showing his teammates that he wasn't no fucking marshmallow. He wanted to get dirty, to put all those fighting techniques El Mago made them learn to good use, to show he was as capable as any of the other guys, especially as capable as El Güero, who looked like a fucking extra in a Nazi movie, and Elvis had no doubts that his dear papa had been saying "heil" real merrily until he boarded a boat and moved his stupid family to Mexico. Yeah, El Güero looked like a Nazi and not any Nazi but a gigantic, beefy motherfucking Nazi, and that's probably why he was so pissed off, because when you look like a blond Frankenstein it's not that easy to blend in with no one, and it's much better to be a shorter, slimmer, little dark-haired fucker like Elvis. That's why El Mago kept El Güero for kidney-smashing and he left the lock picking, the infiltrating, the tailing, to Elvis or El Gazpacho.

El Gazpacho was a guy who'd come from Spain when he was six and still spoke with a little bit of an accent, and it goes to show that you can be all European and pretty much fine because that dude was as nice as could be, while El Güero was a sadist and a bully with an inferiority complex a mile wide.

Fucking son of an Irma Grese and a Heinrich Himmler! Fucker.

But facts were facts, and Elvis, only two years with this group, knew that as the most junior of the lot he had to assert himself somehow or risk being sidelined. One thing was clear: there was no fucking way he was headed back to Tepito.

Therefore, it's no surprise that Elvis was a bit nervous. They'd gone over the plan, and the instructions were clear: his little unit was to focus on snatching cameras from journalists who would be covering the demonstration. Elvis wasn't sure how many Hawks would be coming in and he wasn't quite sure what the other units would be doing, and really, it wasn't like he was supposed to *ask* questions, but he figured this was a big deal.

Students were heading toward El Monumento a la Revolución, chanting slogans and holding up signs. From the apartment where Elvis and his group were sitting they could see them streaming toward them. It was a holy day, the feast of Corpus Christi, and he wondered if he shouldn't go get communion after his work was over. He was a lapsed Catholic, but sometimes he had bouts of piousness.

Elvis smoked a cigarette and checked his watch. It was still early, not even five o'clock. He went over the word of the day. He did that to keep his mind sharp. They'd kicked him out of school when he was thirteen, but Elvis hadn't lost his appreciation for certain types of learning, courtesy of his *Illustrated Larousse*.

The word of the day was *gladius*. He'd picked it because it was fitting. After all, the Hawks were organized in groups of a hundred, and they called the leaders of those groups "the centurions." But there were smaller units. More specialized sub-groups. Elvis belonged to one of those; a little goon squad of a dozen men headed by El Mago, further subdivided into three smaller groups with four men each.

Gladius, then. A little sword. Elvis wished he had a sword. Guns seemed less impressive now, even if he'd felt like a cowboy back when he first held one. He tried to picture himself as one of those samurais in the movies, swinging their katanas. Now wasn't that something!

Elvis hadn't known anything about katanas until he joined the Hawks and met El Gazpacho. El Gazpacho was all over the Japanese stuff. He introduced Elvis to Zatoichi, a super fighter who looked like a harmless blind man but who could defeat dozens of enemies with his expert moves. Elvis thought maybe he was a bit like Zatoichi because he wasn't quite what he appeared to be and also because Zatoichi had spent some time hanging out with the yakuza, who were these crazy dangerous Japanese criminals.

Gladius. Elvis mouthed the word.

"What're you learning today?" El Gazpacho asked. He had his binoculars around his neck, and he was wedged by an open window and didn't look nervous at all.

"Roman shit. Hey, you know any decent flicks with Romans?"

"*Spartacus* is pretty okay. The director filmed *2001: A Space Odyssey*. It's cool, takes place aboard a spaceship. 'Also Sprach Zarathustra.' "

Elvis had no idea what El Gazpacho had said, but he nodded and held out his cigarette. El Gazpacho grinned and took a drag before returning it to him. El Gazpacho grabbed his binoculars and looked out the window, then he checked his watch.

The students were singing the Mexican anthem and the Antelope was mocking them by singing it with them. In a corner, El Güero looked bored as he cleaned his teeth with a toothpick. The others—members of their sister unit, another little group of four—looked tense. Tito Farolito in particular had resorted to telling bad jokes to lighten things up because the word was there were ten thousand protesters, and that was no small amount. Ten thousand is the kind of number that makes a man think twice about this whole line of work, even if he's drawing 100 pesos a day and twice as much if he's with El Mago. Again, Elvis wondered how many Hawks would be at the demonstration.

The Hawks began to stream into the rally, carrying signs with the face of Che plastered on them and chanting slogans like "Freedom for the political prisoners!" It was a ruse, a way to allow them to get close to the protesters.

It worked.

Just when the students were walking in front of the Cosmos movie theater there came the first shots. It was time to rock and roll. Elvis put out his cigarette. His unit hurried down the stairs and exited the apartment building.

Some of the Hawks carried kendo sticks, others shot into the air, hoping to scare the students that way, but Elvis used his fists. El Mago had been clear about the basics: grab any journalists, take their cameras, rough them up if they get stubborn. People with cameras and journalists only. They weren't to waste their time and energy beating any random nobody who didn't have film with him. No killing, either, though they could rough 'em up nicely.

Elvis had to give it to the protesters because in the beginning, when the fighting started, they weren't doing half bad, but then the shooting was no longer bullets in the air, and the students began to panic, began to lose it, and the Hawks were prepared, streaming in from different sides.

"It's blanks!" a young man yelled. "It's not real bullets, it's just blanks. Don't run away, comrades!"

Elvis shook his head, wondering what kind of stupid dumbfuck you had to be to think those were blanks. Did they assume this was an episode of *Bonanza*? That a sheriff with a tin star pinned to his vest was going to ride in before the commercials, and it would be fine?

Others were clearly not as optimistic as that guy urging everyone to stay put. Doors and windows were slamming closed along the avenue and the nearby streets, and shopkeepers pulled down their rolling steel shutters.

Meanwhile, the granaderos and the cops were sitting pretty. There were plenty of men with thick anti-bullet vests and heavy helmets on their heads and shields in their hands, but they were forming a sort of perimeter around the area and none of them intervened in one way or the other.

Elvis grabbed a journalist who had an ID clipped to his vest, and when the journalist squirmed and tried to hold on to his camera, Elvis told him if he didn't let go he was going to break his teeth, and the journalist relented. He could see El Güero wasn't being so polite. El Güero had another photographer on the ground and was kicking him in the ribs.

Elvis exposed the film of the camera he'd grabbed and then tossed the camera away.

People with cameras were easy to spot, but El Mago had also told them to give all journalists in general a scare, not only the photographers—'cause all journalists could use a lesson about who was boss, these days—and it was a bit harder to figure out who the print and radio journalists were. But the Antelope knew all their faces and names, and he pointed them out when he saw them; that was his role. The other thing to keep in mind was that they couldn't let themselves be photographed, so Elvis spent half his time trying to spot cameras, trying to watch out for a flash, lest some eager little fucker get a good picture of him.

Nevertheless, it was all going pretty much as expected until the sound of a machine gun blasted the air, and Elvis turned to look around.

What the fuck? Bullets were one thing, but were the Hawks now shooting with *machine guns*? Was it even their own people? Maybe a clever student had brought firepower. Elvis raised his head and looked at the rooftops, at the apartment buildings, trying to figure out where the hail of bullets was coming from. It was hard to tell, with all the people running to and fro, and the screaming, and someone on a loudspeaker saying that people should retire to their homes. Retire to your homes, now!

The ambulances were coming, he could hear them wailing, heading down Amado Nervo. They were pressing forward and the machine gun had ceased, but bullets were still flying, and Elvis hoped no trigger-happy idiot hit the wrong target. The majority of the Hawks had their hair cut short, and they wore white shirts and sneakers to help identify them, but Elvis's group also sported denim jackets and red bandanas because they were part of one of the elite teams; because this was the dress code for El Mago's boys.

"Grab that son of a bitch," El Gazpacho said, pointing to a dude who held a tape recorder in his hands.

"Got it," Elvis said.

The dude looked old, but he was surprisingly nimble and managed to run a few blocks before Elvis caught up with him. He was screaming outside the back door of an apartment building, begging to be let in, when Elvis yanked him back and told him to hand over his equipment. The man looked down at his hands as though he didn't remember he had been lugging that around, and maybe he didn't. Elvis took the recorder.

"Get lost," he ordered the man.

Elvis turned around, ready to go find his teammates, when El Gazpacho stumbled into the side street where Elvis was standing. Blood dripped down his chin. He stared at Elvis and raised his arms in the air and tried to speak, but the only sound was the bubbling of blood.

Elvis rushed forward and caught him before he tripped and fell. A minute later El Güero and the Antelope rounded the corner.

"What the fuck happened?" Elvis asked.

"No idea," the Antelope said. "Maybe one of those students, maybe—"

"We gotta drive him to the doctor."

"Fuck no," El Güero said, shaking his head. "You know the rules: we wait until one of the cars swings by and then we load him into that. No driving him ourselves. We still have work to do. There's a cameraman from NBC hiding in a taco shop, and we've got to grab that prick."

El Gazpacho was gurgling like a baby, spitting more blood. Elvis tried to prop him up and glared at his teammates. "Fuck that, help me get him to the car."

"The car's too far. Wait for an ambulance or one of the vans to swing by."

Yeah, yeah. But the problem was Elvis didn't see no ambulance or no van swinging by right then and everyone was busy as fuck. It could take nothing for El Gazpacho to be rolled into a vehicle, or it could take a while.

"Motherfucker, it'll be five minutes, and then you can go figure out what's up with the cameraman."

El Güero and the Antelope didn't look very convinced, and

Elvis couldn't hold poor Gazpacho forever and he couldn't carry him nowhere. He wasn't that strong; he was quick and wily and could kick and punch courtesy of the personal defense lessons El Mago had given them. The strong one, that was El Güero, a fucking Samson who could probably lift an elephant in his arms.

"El Mago ain't going to be happy if his right-hand man bites the dust," Elvis said, and at last that seemed to rattle the Antelope enough, because the Antelope was deadly afraid of El Mago, and El Güero was a subservient snake when El Mago was around, sliding on his belly for crumbs, so some preservation instinct must have activated inside his dull brain.

"Let's get him to the car," El Güero said, and he lifted El Gazpacho, who was no small man, as though he were a baby, and they ran the few blocks necessary to reach the alleyway to find that someone had torched their car.

"Who the fuck!" yelled Elvis, and he spun around, furious. He couldn't believe it! Those little fuckers! It must have been one of the protesters who'd singled out the vehicle due to its lack of plates.

"Well, your plan's fucked now," El Güero told him, and the sadistic motherfucker looked a bit giddy. Elvis didn't know if it was because things weren't going well for Elvis or because he hated El Gazpacho.

Elvis looked around at the lonely alleyway strewn with garbage. The smoke made his eyes water, and the scent of gunpowder clogged his nostrils. He pointed to the other end of the alleyway.

"Come on," he said.

"I'm heading back. We got work to do," El Güero said, and he was putting El Gazpacho down. Just dumping him down on the ground like a sack of flour, leaving him there atop a damn pile of rotten lettuce. "We gotta get that cameraman."

"Don't you fucking dare, you son of a bitch," Elvis said. "El Mago, he'll have your balls if you don't help us."

"Up your ass. He'll be pissed we were a bunch of pussies and didn't finish the job. If you want to play nurse, do it alone."

That was that. El Güero was walking away. The Antelope didn't seem to have made up his mind about what to do. Elvis couldn't believe this crap. He wasn't no softie, but you didn't leave one of your teammates to bleed out in a stinking alleyway like that. It wasn't right. And this was El Gazpacho! Elvis would rather have a foot amputated than leave El Gazpacho behind.

"Come on, help me here. What? You lost your dick?" Elvis asked the Antelope.

"What the fuck's my dick—"

"Only a limp, dickless shit would be standing there rubbing his hands. Grab him by the shoulders."

The Antelope grunted and complained, but he obeyed. The three of them made it to the end of the alleyway and down the street. There was a blue Datsun parked there, and Elvis shattered the glass of the passenger's window with a bottle he found on the ground. He slid into the car.

"What you gonna do?" the Antelope asked.

"What's it look like?" Elvis replied as he frantically looked inside his backpack until he fished out the screwdriver. Handy thing, that. It was an old habit of his to carry it from back in the day when he'd been a juvenile delinquent. The cops would give you a massive beating if they found you carrying a knife and then arrest you for having a concealed weapon, but a screwdriver was no knife. The other thing he liked to carry were two little pieces of metal that he used to pick locks when he didn't have his full kit.

"You can't hotwire it like that," the Antelope said, but the Antelope liked to complain about everything.

Elvis jammed the screwdriver in place, but it wouldn't go. He bit his lip, trying to calm the fuck down. You can't pick a lock if you're shivering; same with starting a car. *Gladius.*

"Man, can't you hurry it?"

Gladius, gladius, gladius. Finally! He got the motor running and motioned for the Antelope to get in the car. The Antelope started protesting.

"The mission still needs to be completed, and what about El

Güero and the others and that cameraman from the American network?" he asked, sounding a little breathless.

"Jump in," Elvis ordered. He couldn't afford to have a panicked operative, and he kept his voice level.

"We can't take off."

"He's gonna bleed to death if you don't press against his wound," Elvis continued in that same level tone he'd learned from El Mago. "You gotta get in the car and press hard."

The Antelope relented and pushed El Gazpacho into the car and climbed in next to him. Elvis took off his denim jacket and handed it to the Antelope. "Use that."

"I think he's gonna die anyway," the Antelope said, but he did press the jacket against El Gazpacho's chest as instructed.

Elvis's hands were slick with El Gazpacho's blood as he took the steering wheel. The gunshots had started again.

2

THE STREET SMELLED of fritangas and oil, a far cry from the scent of frangipani and roses and island paradises, which she'd tried to conjure the previous evening, spraying cheap perfume around her apartment and playing "Strangers in the Night." The conjuring had failed. Instead, she hadn't slept well and had a headache.

Maite attempted to pick up the pace. The alarm clock hadn't gone off, and she was going to be late, but she had to stop at the newsstand. Would Jorge Luis's surgery go according to plan? The question had gnawed at her mind for days now.

She was hoping there would be no one ahead of her, but two men were standing in line. Maite bit her lips and clutched her purse. The papers were all talking about the confrontation that had taken place on Thursday. "The president is willing to listen to everyone," declared *Excélsior*. She hardly paid attention to the headlines. Sure, she'd heard chatter about the student demonstration, but politics seemed terribly dull.

Love, frail as gossamer, stitched together from a thousand songs and a thousand comic books, made of the dialogue spoken in films and the posters designed by ad agencies: love was what she lived for.

The young man ahead of her was buying cigarettes and chatting with the owner of the newspaper stand. Maite stood on her tiptoes desperately trying to signal to the newspaper stand owner, hoping he might send the man on his way. Finally, after another five minutes, it was her turn.

"Do you have the latest *Secret Romance*?" she asked.

"It hasn't come in yet," the newspaper stand man said. "There's some kind of problem over at the printer. But I've got *Lágrimas y Risas*."

Maite frowned. It wasn't that she didn't like *Lágrimas y Risas.* She had loved the adventures of the Gypsy girl Yesenia, the exotic world of Geisha, and the suffering of the humble maid María Isabel. Most of all, she had been taken by the evil ways of Rubí, the antiheroine who was desired by all men, a seductive, dangerous devourer of hearts. But the current story at *Lágrimas y Risas* hadn't caught her fancy. This stand didn't carry *Susy: Secretos del Corazón*, and frankly she was addicted to *Secret Romance*. The drawings were top-notch, and the writing was excellent. She wouldn't even consider one of the Western comic books dangling from clothespins or the raunchy ones that featured naked women.

In the end, Maite ended up deciding against buying an issue of *Cosmopolitan* for the romance story in the back and purchased a bag of Japanese peanuts and indulged herself in the latest *Lágrimas y Risas,* which was cheaper than glossy magazines. She was supposed to be saving money, anyway. She had to pay the mechanic. A year before she had bought a car. Her mother warned her against such an expensive purchase, but Maite stubbornly plunked down the money for a secondhand Caprice.

It was a huge mistake. It broke down after the first two months, then she was in a collision, and now it was back with the mechanic. Mechanic! Armed robbers, that's what those men were. They took advantage of an unmarried woman and charged more than they would have if they'd been dealing with a man, and there was nothing she could do about it.

A man. That's why she was fearing Friday. It was Maite's birthday. She would be turning thirty. Thirty was the age of an old maid, the point of no return, and her mother would no doubt remind her about that, insisting that she knew some young man or another who would be perfect for Maite and couldn't she be less picky? Maite's sister would agree with her mother, and the whole evening would be ruined.

To make things worse, Friday was also the day she contributed to the savings pool. It was company policy. Well, not really. But Laura, who was the most senior of the secretaries, maintained a monthly office pool which everyone had to contribute to so that at the end of the year they received a lump sum. The one time Maite had declined to participate in the "voluntary" office pool, Laura had been incensed. The next time, she tendered the money.

It was a racket. Laura said the savings pool helped people keep their money safe, so the greedy banks couldn't get their claws on it and they didn't have to pay the fees on an account, but Maite was certain Laura dipped into the pool during the year. Besides, if they'd had a real savings account, that would generate interest, wouldn't it? But no. They had to have this ridiculous cushion of money sitting in someone else's lap, and if Maite dared to ask for her share early in the year Laura would have a fit.

Friday and that silly racket, and then her birthday to top it off.

Maite could already picture the cake and the pink icing spelling out in big letters "Maite, Happy Birthday." She didn't want to be reminded about her age. Earlier that month, she'd found a gray hair. She couldn't be graying yet. She couldn't possibly be thirty. She didn't know where her twenties had gone. She could not recall what she'd done in that time. Maite couldn't name a single worthy accomplishment.

Maite rolled the comic book up and tucked it in her purse, walking at a faster clip. Rather than waiting for the elevator, she braved the four flights of stairs up to Garza Abogados S.C. She was ten minutes late; thank goodness most of the lawyers hadn't streamed in yet. When she was a young girl, just out of secretarial school, Maite had thought working for lawyers would be exciting. Perhaps she would meet an interesting, handsome client. They would elope. But there was nothing exciting about her line of work. Maite didn't even have a window that opened and the plants she brought to liven up her desk kept dying.

Around ten a.m. the woman with the coffee trolley and sweet breads rolled in, but Maite remembered that she was supposed to be on a budget and shook her head. Then Diana came up to her desk to tell her that the boss was in a mood.

"How come?" Maite asked. Her desk was far from the green door with the name "Licenciado Fernando Garza" emblazoned on it. Instead she worked for Archibaldo Costa, who was a distracted, bald man. The other secretaries said the reason Archibaldo remained on the payroll was that he had been old man Garza's best friend, and Maite could believe that. His spelling was atrocious, his writing was worse, and Maite did the real bulk of redacting acts and certificates.

"The Corpus thing with those students. He was railing about professional agitators, about commies."

"He thinks it was communists?" replied Yolanda, who sat at the desk next to Maite's.

"Sure. He says they're trying to make President Echeverría look bad."

"I heard it was some sort of foreign plot. Russians."

"Same thing, isn't it? Reds are reds."

"It's refried Tlatelolco."

More secretaries joined the conversation, expounding on what they'd read in *Novedades* and *El Sol de México*, with a couple of them questioning the accuracy of those newspapers, saying they'd read *El Heraldo de México* and a journalist from *that* paper said thugs had beat him up. This comment earned them an angry "pinko" from another secretary. Maite didn't know who was right, only that people were talking about Hawks and conspiracies and it was all a little bit much. She had been running errands for Costa the previous Friday and hadn't gone into the office, so she had missed the chatter about what happened Thursday afternoon in San Cosme. She hadn't paid much attention to the news over the weekend and had assumed it would have all blown over by Monday morning and she needn't bother disentangling the politics at play. Maybe she ought to have bought the paper that morning, if it was going to become something everyone was discussing. Maite never knew what was important and what wasn't. But then, before she could ask for more information, Fernando Garza himself walked by, and the women returned to their seats.

"Hey, girlie, get me a pair of socks during your lunch hour, will you?" he told her as he headed toward the elevator.

Maite frowned. They'd had an office boy who did such chores, but he'd left for a better job, and the lawyers hadn't seen fit to find a replacement. Now most of the errands he'd performed fell onto Maite or Yolanda.

Maite tried to tell herself it was better if she didn't really have much time for lunch, because that way she wouldn't be tempted to spend her money at a decent restaurant, but the fact that she had to waste half an hour of her lunchtime standing in line and paying for a pair of socks irritated her.

"It's because his feet are smelly," Diana told her when they were leaving the office. "He could put on talcum powder, but he forgets at least once a week. Whenever he takes off his shoes, the stench is unbearable. I've got to tell you, old man Garza would never have taken off his shoes in the office."

It had been six months since Fernando Garza's father had retired, and Diana was still talking about how the old man would have never done this thing or another. She obviously missed the wrinkled bastard. Maite didn't think she'd miss Archibaldo if he retired. Not that she wanted him to leave. She'd spent five years at Garza precisely because she wasn't built to withstand change.

Maite didn't like her job, but she refused to look for something else. Her office, not far from the Chinese clock at Bucareli, wasn't the finest one in the city by far, but the pay was steady, and she had learned to gauge the temperament of the workers there and comply with the expectations of the bosses. A few times a year, especially during the rainy season, she would grow restless, and instead of solving her daily crossword puzzle, she surveyed the help wanted ads in the paper and circled a few of them with a red pen, but she never phoned. What was the point? Before Garza she'd worked for another lawyer, and it was much of the same.

"What do you think, should we get together this Friday to celebrate your birthday?" Diana asked.

"Don't remind me about that," Maite said. "I'm supposed to visit my mother, and my sister will probably make an appearance."

"Go to see her, and then we can have dinner. My sister is serving ate con queso for dessert."

"I don't know," Maite said, shrugging.

Diana was three years older than Maite, more outgoing, less nervous. She knitted on the bus and lived with her two older sisters, mother, and grandmother in a cavernous casona that was damp and dark. The women all looked like each other, one a little more weathered than the next. Diana's grandmother had no teeth and spent her days napping in the living room under two blankets. Maite knew that in a few years Diana would sit in that chair, that her face would be the withered face of the grandmother, her hands hidden under the heavy blankets.

Maite imagined herself older, as old as her friend's grandmother. She wasn't beautiful, not even pretty, and the thought of her meager charms disappearing filled her with dread. Maite's mother had probably been right all along, about marriage. About Gaspar. But he'd been so dull, and Maite had still been filled with hope, with expectations, and despite her mother's nagging she wanted more than a man who didn't inspire the least bit of sentiment in her.

Most of her acquaintances had married and had children by now. They didn't have much spare time to spend with her anymore and a simple arrangement to go to the movies became a monumental task because they had to find someone to take care of their babies. Diana, however, was a stalwart presence there. Diana was the one person she truly liked at Garza.

She wondered what she'd do if Diana also abandoned her, if she married and stopped working at the office, and once again she felt miserable and old.

She should have married Gaspar. She would have if it hadn't been for Cristóbal.

Cristóbal. Cristóbalito. Her first love. Her one love.

As the most junior of the secretaries at a newly inaugurated law firm, Maite's duties had been simple: sorting letters, opening correspondence, and addressing envelopes, among other tasks. It was only her second job. Before that she'd worked at a department store, but she'd quit that to attend secretarial school in the hope of bettering herself. The secretarial classes had lasted for a year, during which she learned some typing and a little about the world.

That spring of 1961, Maite was nineteen, and when a young man smiled at her in the elevator she blushed. It turned out they sometimes boarded the elevator around the same time in the morning, and Maite began to time her arrival so it always coincided with his. After a few of these coincidences he introduced himself: he said he was Cristóbal, but she could call him Cristóbalito. He was an accountant working on the floor above hers.

She stopped responding to Gaspar's phone calls and instead focused her attention on Cristóbal.

At first their interactions were limited to having an ice cream or watching a movie, and all the things young couples are supposed to do. Eventually, though, he wanted more than handholding or the quick squeezing of her leg at the cinema. He arranged for them to visit cheap hotels for quick fucks. Maite, who was afraid of sinning, cringed each and every time they walked into one of those places, but once he was kissing her and taking off her clothes it was another story.

In between lovemaking sessions she told him about her passion for music, her many records, her acquisition of classic books, her vocabulary lessons by mail. She wrote him love notes and bad poetry. She could not express her feelings, nor render the beating of her heart upon a page; she poured herself into every smile and every touch, attempting to clutch an ocean of passion between her hands for him.

He did not understand a single thing she told him.

It lasted almost a whole year, their relationship. He dumped her near Christmastime for a different secretary on a different floor because Maite had begun to talk marriage, and quite frankly Cristóbalito found her a boring fuck.

Maite quit the job. She pretended she was sick so she could stay home, and then she really felt sick and spent most of the summer and quite a bit of the autumn of 1962 dragging her feet around her mother's apartment, without a purpose nor much thought. Eventually her mother forced her to get a job at an office supply store, which she loathed. And eventually, too, she stumbled upon an issue of *Lágrimas y Risas*. Before that, she had read *Susy: Secretos del Corazón*, which contained many romantic stories, but it was *Lágrimas y Risas* that enraptured her. Then came her current obsession: *Secret Romance*.

The latest storyline concerned Beatriz, a young nurse sent to a distant tropical island to care for an ailing old woman, who is torn between her passion for two brothers, Jorge Luis, a chivalrous doctor, and Pablo Palomo, a dissolute playboy nursing a broken heart.

She lived for those stories. She woke up, fed her parakeet, went to work, came back, put on music, and pored over each panel in the comic books; she gnawed at each word like a starving woman. She loved the characters she found between the printed pages, and she suffered bitterly with them, and somehow that suffering was like a sweet balm erasing the memory of Cristóbalito.

And now Jorge Luis had been in an accident and must have surgery. It almost didn't matter, her upcoming birthday, compared to that. The car, still at the repair shop, didn't matter. She concentrated on the problem of injured Jorge Luis, on trying to imagine whether Beatriz would learn the truth about his disappearance or Jorge Luis's evil mother would keep his medical condition a secret. The story was a pink cloud that blotted reality away.

Until Friday. On Friday the rains came and scrubbed clean the pastel colors that had intoxicated her. Friday, and the next issue of the magazine was finally there, finally between her hands. She saved her reading for the evenings, when she could sit in her old green chair and play Bobby Darin, Frank Sinatra, or Nat King Cole. She had bought a set of records to teach herself English and dissect the lyrics of songs but couldn't be bothered with them. If she really wanted, she could have bought the Spanish language covers that were much more affordable and easy to find, although in many cases she realized these didn't resemble the original lyrics by a long shot. She didn't mind the mystery the songs posed. In the end, she liked the music even if she couldn't understand the words. Sometimes, she penned lyrics to go with the tunes. The *Illustrated Larousse* was handy, helping her find new words she could rhyme with "love" and synonyms for "misery" to sprinkle inside spiral notebooks.

Maite was so nervous she made an exception that morning, and she read through *Secret Romance* before lunch, leafing through it while the other secretaries were busy typing or proofing documents.

On page twenty-five Jorge Luis fell into a coma. Maite was aghast. She rushed to the bathroom, locking herself in one of the stalls, and went over the last pages again. But there it was. Jorge Luis was in a coma! There was no mistake.

Maite wasn't sure how long she stayed in the bathroom, but by the time she walked back into the office, the secretaries were putting their money in the collection box. She stared at Laura as she held up the box and shook it in her face.

"Laura, I forgot."

"Maite, you *always* forget. This is not how it works," the woman said, and the other secretaries shook their heads.

"Fine," Maite muttered. She found a bill and tossed it in the box.

After work she dashed down the stairs instead of waiting for Diana like she normally did. She had eaten nothing that day and had a headache again. She wanted to go home and go to sleep, but her mother was expecting her.

Maite glanced at the phone booth ahead of her, but if she didn't show up her mother was liable to pop by her apartment to check up on her. She still didn't agree that a woman should live on her own. Women didn't leave home until they were married, but two years before, Maite had grown tired of the limits of her mother's home and decamped for her place at the Escandón. She knew she didn't really earn enough to afford the apartment, which was located close to the edge of the elegant Condesa and therefore commanded a higher price than if she'd been living at the edge of Tacubaya. That, the furniture she'd acquired, the car, and her proclivity for buying LPs, books, and magazines torpedoed her budget.

Maite made it to her mother's place in the Colonia Doctores. The area had been for many years lower middle class, but these days it was leaning toward lower despite the names of the illustrious physicians that had given the area its moniker. Even if she'd had her car, she wouldn't have brought it to her mother's place. They stole anything with four wheels there and also picked pockets. Cheap motels and rowdy bars further provided the area with an air of seediness. When Maite was growing up, she had lied and told her classmates that she lived in the posher Roma.

Maite wished she had been born in Monaco or New York. Most of the girls in the comic books she read looked like they'd never set a foot in places like the Doctores. If they had toiled in poverty, then they had been lifted to a higher plane by the fat wallet of their beloved. Cinderellas, dreaming. Maite dreamed too, but nothing came of it.

Thirty. She was thirty and her hair was beginning to sprout gray strands. Her body betrayed her.

When she walked into the combination kitchen–dining room, the first thing Maite's mother did was chide her for being all wet from the rain.

"I mopped today," her mother said.

"Sorry."

"Sit down. Manuela should be here soon."

Maite shuffled into the living room and turned on the radio. She had hoped the rain would keep her sister away. Manuela was two years younger than Maite and had been married for five years already. She had two annoying kids and an equally annoying husband who was going prematurely bald and was never home. Maite's mother watched over the children in the afternoons. If they weren't in the apartment already, it meant they were on their way, soon to interrupt the blessed sound of the music in the living room—"Can't Take My Eyes Off You" was playing. In her purse, *Secret Romance* weighed heavily. She wanted to read it again. To make sure that she hadn't read it wrong.

Manuela walked in then with her children. The kids proceeded to ignore Maite and immediately turned to their grandmother, demanding cake.

"Very well," Maite's mother said, and they went to the kitchen-dining room. She took out the cake she'd baked that day while Manuela found a package with candles.

"It's chocolate," Maite said, eyeing the cake.

"So?"

"I don't like chocolate."

"Everyone else likes chocolate. Besides, it has cherries too. You like cherries."

"Manuela likes cherries, Mama. No, not that. I don't want candles," she protested.

"You can't have a cake without candles," her mother said as she began systematically placing each candle.

"You don't have to put them *all* on the cake."

"Nonsense, Maite. Thirty years and thirty candles."

Maite crossed her arms and stared at the chocolate-and-cherry cake.

"I got the promotion, by the way," Manuela said at the point when their mother had counted to twenty candles. "And the boss gave me a new fountain pen. Look, isn't it lovely?"

"That's beautiful. Look, how pretty!" their mother said, and she put the candles down, now cooing over the new fountain pen that Manuela was flashing before them.

Manuela hadn't even wanted to go to secretarial school. She had merely copied Maite. When they were kids she hoped to become an airplane stewardess. Now she worked at a bigger and better firm than Maite, one where they apparently gave their employees fancy fountain pens.

Maite wondered if she could swipe the pen without her sister noticing, but she hadn't stolen from her since they were teenagers. Now she limited herself to stealing small things from the tenants in her building and occasional items from the drugstore or department stores.

Maite's mother recounted the candles and found a box of matches.

"Ask for a wish," Manuela said.

Maite stared at the tiny flames and couldn't think of a proper wish. The children began to complain, calling out for cake. Maite's mother warned her she'd get wax all over the cake, and Maite finally blew out the candles without wishing for anything. Maite's mother cut the cake, serving the children first, then Manuela.

"You know I'm watching my figure," Manuela said, making a face. Her sister was skinny, but she liked to make a show of everything.

"Come on, you must have a little."

Maite's mother pleaded with Manuela, who finally agreed to have a thin slice of cake. Finally, Maite was handed a slice, almost as an afterthought. She was hungry, but toyed with the cherries on her plate, rolling them from one side of the plate to the other, unwilling to eat any of it.

Manuela liked chocolate-and-cherry cake. Maite should have known their mother would cater to her, even on this day. She wished she had waited for Diana and taken her up on her dinner offer. Now it was too late.

Maite thought of Jorge Luis, and she started to convince herself that his accident hadn't really happened. Next episode there would be an explanation. Maybe it had been a bad dream. Yes, that was it. Beatriz would wake up, the sound of the drums playing in the distance . . .

The jungle, yes. How she loved the jungle they drew in *Secret Romance.* The flowers, unnaturally large and lush; monkeys and exotic birds taking refuge in the foliage. Jaguars, waiting in the dark, and the night made of cheap ink; pinpricks of stars and the round moon festooning the sky. Lovers holding hands, lovers swimming in a waterhole.

One of Manuela's kids was walking around with his hands filled with cake. He placed his hands on Maite's jacket, which was hanging from the back of her chair, smearing chocolate over it. Manuela chuckled, caught the kid, and wiped his hands clean with a napkin.

"I'll have to dry clean that," Maite said, staring at her sister pointedly.

"Scrub it with a bit of soap."

"It's not washable. You're supposed to dry clean it."

"Don't be silly. Go wash it. It'll take a minute. Go."

Maite grabbed the jacket. She went into the bathroom and furiously scrubbed the stain, but it did no good. It was firmly set in place. When she came out, her mother and her sister were giddily talking about a cousin of theirs. Manuela had lit a cigarette. Her sister's brand of cigarettes gave Maite a headache and Manuela knew it.

"Can you smoke somewhere else?" Maite asked.

"Maite, sit and eat your cake," her mother said.

"I should get going," she announced.

Neither her mother nor her sister replied. Manuela's youngest child had started crying. Maite fetched her handbag and left without another word.

Back at her apartment, Maite turned on the lights and said hello to the green-and-yellow parakeet she kept in a cage by the living room window. Then she went into the kitchen and made herself a ham-and-cheese sandwich. She ate it quickly, then unrolled the magazine she had been carrying around all day and looked at the panels again.

There was a knock at the door. She ignored it, but then came another knock. Maite sighed and opened the door.

It was the art student from the apartment across the hallway. Sometimes Maite saw her walking up the stairs carrying a canvas under her arm. She didn't know her, but she knew her type: modern, free, young, a member of a new generation who didn't have to pay their respect to their fussy mothers and their irritating sisters, instead happily drinking, smoking, living it up.

"Sorry, I hope it's not too late," the girl said. She was wearing a poncho with exuberant floral designs. Maite was still dressed for the office, in her white blouse with the frilly high collar and her tan skirt, though she had taken off the soiled jacket. Next to this girl, she looked like a school matron.

"It's fine."

"I'm Leonora. I live across the hall from you."

"Oh, yeah. I know," Maite said. The girl had been in the building for six months. Maite had timed it. She kept good track of the tenants in the building.

"I'm sorry if I haven't introduced myself, you know how it is. Anyway, I was talking with the building's super, and she said you take care of pets sometimes."

The building's super, a tiny, gossipy old woman called Doña Elvira who lived on the first floor, was allergic to both cats and dogs. This turned out to be a small boon for Maite, since she offered her services to her neighbors when they needed a pet sitter, a job that might ordinarily have been filled by the super.

"I do. Do you need me to watch a pet for you?"

"Yes, my cat," Leonora said. "It would be for a couple of days. I'm going to Cuernavaca tonight, and I'll be back by . . . well, Sunday night. Monday morning, tops. Would you be able to do it? I know it's last minute, but I'd appreciate it. The super says you are reliable."

The super had complained that the girl had men over and they were *loud*. She said it with a raised eyebrow that left no doubt about the source of the noise. Maite wondered if Leonora was going to meet with one of those men, preferably in a location where the neighbors didn't mind the operatic lovemaking. She bet the girl had an impressive number of boyfriends. She was beautiful. She looked like the girls in the comic books, with her green eyes and her chestnut hair. But she wasn't weeping. Many of the girls on the covers were either weeping or kissing a man.

"What do you say?" the girl asked. Her smile was both pleasant and nervous, like watching a butterfly flutter around. Maite shrugged.

"I'm usually booked for more than a handful of days. It's hardly worth the effort if it's anything less than a week, you know?" she lied, wondering how much she could charge without the girl bolting away. The earrings in Leonora's lobes looked like real gold, not the fake stuff they hawked downtown and that turned green after a few days. Maite sniffed money.

"Oh, please, I don't want to take off without knowing someone's watching the cat. Animals might get into all sorts of trouble when you're not around. I had a dog that ate a box of chocolates and died."

"I know. No responsible pet owner leaves an animal without someone around, and I can see you're in a hurry. Very well, let me think," Maite said and quoted the girl a higher rate than usual, which Leonora agreed to, grateful for Maite's kindness.

Leonora handed Maite her apartment keys.

"Would you mind if I get your phone number?" the girl asked. "I . . . in case . . . the cat, you know. In case I need to communicate with you about the cat."

So she was that kind of pet owner, the type who fussed about their little angel, calling them baby and darling and dressing them in ridiculous outfits. Maite had never particularly liked pets, except for her parakeet. Taking care of them simply gave her an extra source of income and allowed her the chance to purloin the personal items of their owners.

As she wrote down her number, Maite wondered what would be the first thing she'd steal from Leonora. She took great care in choosing her loot. It was never anything extravagant, anything people would notice, but it must always be something interesting.

The girl, still nervous about the cat, detained Maite with an explanation about the spot where she kept the cat food before departing.

Maite went back to the kitchen and grabbed her magazine. There was no doubt about it. Jorge Luis would be back; he'd wake up in an issue or two. Cheered by this thought, she walked into the spare room and looked through her records. She played Bobby Darin and let herself imagine that a dream lover was waiting for her.

That night Maite dreamed of drums in the jade-green jungle. But in the morning the view from her living room was still of a gray city, rooftops crammed with TV antennas, and there was no lover for her, no matter how much she hoped and prayed.

3

LAY LOW, THAT'S what El Mago said when he phoned. Elvis was utterly willing to comply, considering the big fuss people were making over the night of June tenth. Officially, nobody tied to the government was willing to admit there was such a thing as the Hawks, and some newspapers that toed the government line had pointed out the students were all commie agitators, which should have been enough to quiet the bitching. But other newspapers, and some folks—stupid protesters and their friends, and even a columnist or two who didn't know how to keep his mouth shut—were wagging their tongues, talking about brutes who had chased them down and even shot at them. It was getting messy.

To be honest, Elvis hadn't expected this sort of attention. The Hawks regularly roughed up activists and dissolved suspicious small student meetings. The previous month a few Hawks had gone into a public high school and vandalized the library. No one really said a peep, or if they did, folks felt free to ignore the altercations.

But now it was all very delicate. People were printing names in clandestine circulars. Names like Alfonso Martínez Domínguez. Imagine that. He was the fucking regent of the city, not some low punk people could badmouth without consequence, but a fucking *regent*. President Echeverría kept saying he didn't know anything, and overall Elvis had the impression the whole damn thing had turned into a disaster. Too many people were asking too many fucking questions.

No wonder that El Mago had ordered them to stay inside the apartment as much as possible. This would have pleased El Elvis quite a bit normally, since it gave him a chance to go through his Larousse dictionary and listen to his records, but with El Gazpacho out of commission and in another location, it was El Güero and the Antelope keeping him company, which was the same as having two vultures watching over his shoulder.

They were salivating, those motherfuckers, waiting to whine and tell El Mago all the ways El Elvis had fucked up the other day. El Elvis, as a result, decided to put on his headphones and attempt to muffle his worries away with a bit of Bobby Darin; he was sticky sweet, but Elvis didn't mind a crooner with a good set of pipes. Who didn't fucking like "Beyond the Sea"?

Elvis wasn't going back to Tepito. He wasn't. Tepito was a bottomless pit, a fucking cesspool. There was no future there for him.

He'd left home at the age of fifteen. Two years before that, he had been expelled from school. For no good reason, either. Elvis liked to learn and he liked to read, but when it came to writing words down he often switched letters around, his handwriting was poor, and it took him a long time to get assignments done. It was as if the words all clogged inside his head and he had to carefully fish them out one by one.

Well, his teachers didn't think too much of him. When Elvis vandalized a lavatory, it was deemed enough to kick him out, even though he knew that other kids did far worse and they never got expelled. It was just that his teachers were wanting to be rid of one of the "dumber" kids in the class. Real nice of them.

He didn't enroll in another school after that. His mother had four children to look after and no patience for him, so she hit him with the mop and told him to find a job. Elvis couldn't find a gig that was better than bagging groceries, so he fell in with one of the little gangs in the area for pocket money and for kicks. Everyone in this gang was about his age, and they didn't do anything that was real bad, limiting themselves to harassing the maids when they did their shopping rounds. For cash, they threatened to throw rocks at the windows of shop owners in the area. Most of them paid up.

There was one exception: the owner of the Andorra Pharmacy had a son a few years older and a few centimeters taller than the kids in the gang, and he warned them he'd get his uncle—supposedly a policeman—involved if they tried anything. He also beat a couple of them when they hung out too close to his precious pharmacy.

It hadn't been Elvis's idea to retaliate. God knew he had better stuff to do than pick fights. But one of the kids in their gang was real pissy because the pharmacist's son had given him a black eye, and he wanted revenge. So they banded together, waited for the kid to walk home one night, and beat him up. He was big, but against the combined power of half a dozen teenagers it was a tough fight, and tougher still when it turned out that the boy with the black eye had somehow seen fit to bring a rusty old piece of metal to the fight and stabbed the pharmacist's son.

Fortunately, the pharmacist's son didn't die. Unfortunately, it turned out that his warnings about his policeman uncle were real. Within a day or two the word was out that the cops were looking for every little fucker who had participated in the attack.

Elvis wasn't eager to go to jail or reformatory school or any fucking place with an angry policeman, so he hightailed it out of the city. He was fifteen and had little understanding of the world, but he had heard from another teen that San Miguel de Allende was full of tourists who wanted to get laid, and he thought what the hell.

He was right about the tourists, though getting laid was a bit more difficult since most of the gringitas in the town were looking for buff, big-dicked men to fuck, and Elvis was a slim teenager, not a dude cut out for pornos and horny girls' fantasies. But if he managed to look forlorn they usually threw him a few pesos, and he scraped by.

When he met Sally things improved. She was an American

lady who they said had a thing for youngsters and some sort of fetish for "authentic" Mexican culture. Elvis was in need of a place to stay and hot meals, so he traded his shoes for huaraches to tickle her brown meat fantasy. For a while it was fine. He did errands for her, took care of the plants in the house she rented, ate her pussy when she demanded it. In return, he had full access to her record collection and a room, a bathroom, and a TV, though no pocket money.

The record collection was the best part, truth be told. That's how he'd picked the name Elvis, after listening to several records from the King. He thought there was a certain resemblance between the young Elvis and himself, so he bought a black leather jacket like the one the singer wore in one of his flicks. His real name was lousy, anyway, and he began playing a guitar Sally had hanging in the living room and never touched.

He liked Sally, which is why it came as a bit of a shock when he discovered she'd picked up some other guy—a little older than Elvis, but not much—who must have had a bigger cock or licked pussy better, then kicked Elvis out. Just like that, from one day to the next. Elvis had no problem calling it quits with the dame, but only after he sneaked back into the house, stole the money he knew she kept in a box, and also absconded with six vinyl records.

He did what any dumb kid with sudden riches would do: spend it at the pool halls around Guadalajara, which was his new home. Outside an ice cream parlor, while eating a nieve de mamey, he met Cristina, a girl about his age who ended up getting him involved with a weird little religious cult near Tlaquepaque.

Elvis was a fool for pretty women, and Cristina pulled him in like a damn vortex with her soft, soft voice and her even softer glances. By the point when she asked him if he didn't want to go hang out with her friends in Tlaquepaque, Elvis couldn't have cared if she went around Guadalajara suckering in and recruiting guys on the regular, which he later figured out she actually did.

Cristina led him to a shabby house with funny folks who dressed in white and talked about magic mushrooms, auras, and healing crystals. Many of them had come from Mexico City, where they met doing yoga around Parque Hundido, and they'd spent time at Real de Catorce and Huautla, like any middle-class wannabe hippie did, before they stumbled onto Jalisco. Their leader did nothing but fuck the pretty young women in the congregation, while the uglies and the men were sent to work around the farm the cult used as a base of operations.

It turned out their leader didn't like modern music very much, insisting on playing records featuring wind chimes and gongs, which was the last straw. Elvis liked Cristina, maybe he even loved her, but not enough to stay around watching another dude plow her from behind while Elvis had to feed the chickens or shovel manure, all without the comfort of even a rock 'n' roll song or two.

He was seventeen by the time he stumbled back into Tepito, back into his mother's apartment with no money and no prospects. His mother looked none too pleased to see him. He didn't really feel like joining a gang again, though he half-heartedly hung out with his old friends and spent his days bored out of his skull for about two months until the afternoon when he stole the *Illustrated Larousse* from a Porrúa bookstore. He'd known a classmate who'd owned one of those, and he'd found it fascinating. It was a big, bulky book to steal, but he managed it and thought that maybe his future lay in books.

Books! He, who couldn't spell when he was stressed, the letters still jumbled in his head. But he did like to read, and having stolen one gigantic book he figured he could steal more, then resell them through the vendors along Donceles. He quickly got to stealing, reading, and reselling. Then, realizing that the used bookstores and those pricks from Donceles paid him a pittance and made a huge profit, he installed himself in an alleyway near Palacio de Minería. A few vendors brought folding tables; others simply set their books on flat pieces of cardboard. Elvis brought a tablecloth and stacked his wares.

After a little while he figured out the most profitable line of commerce: textbooks. University students would come around, ask if he had something, and he'd promise to obtain it for them. This meant he'd steal it from whatever bookstore was easiest and then sell it to the student.

Thieving turned out to be Elvis's talent. After a couple of weeks he decided to augment his book sales with vinyl records, which was a sensible choice. He had aspirations to open up his own little shop, down in Donceles, and sit behind a cash register, book in hand and his Presley records playing.

That didn't happen, because one day a bunch of fuckers appeared in his alleyway and started beating the vendors. Elvis had heard of things like this happening around the city, with cops, or other motherfuckers who must work for cops, chasing away the street sellers and beggars. They wanted to clean up the city for the Olympics.

But despite simmering violence, Elvis had been lucky. Well, not anymore. Everyone began to grab their wares and run away. Elvis began picking up his wares too, intent on simply making a quick exit with no fuss, but then an asshole decided to smash the copy of "Jailhouse Rock" Elvis had been proudly displaying, and he lost it.

Though he wasn't terribly strong, though he wasn't really a fighter, Elvis grabbed a thick tome of Rousseau and started beating the son of a bitch in the face with it. Within a few minutes some of the guy's buddies realized what was going on and intervened, treating Elvis like a human piñata, until after several punches and spitting, he heard an older man speak.

"Let him be," he said.

The thugs holding Elvis stopped punching him. He sat down, out of breath. The older man stood in front of Elvis. He was dressed impeccably, with a suit jacket, a burgundy tie, and shiny shoes. He looked at Elvis curiously.

"You put up quite a fight," the man said, reaching into his pocket and holding out a handkerchief.

Elvis stared at the man's hand. The man waved the handkerchief again, and Elvis slowly grabbed it and pressed it against his mouth, wiping the blood away.

"If it'd been fair I would've messed up that guy real good," Elvis said.

"I know. You are fast. Good reflexes."

"I guess," Elvis said, not wanting to specify that stealing requires good reflexes and the ability to pick up speed in case an employee catches you in the act and you have to sprint your way to safety.

"Is this your merchandise?" the man asked, leaning down and grabbing a book: *20,000 Leagues under the Sea*.

"Aha," Elvis said.

The man ran his hands down the spine. He glanced at Elvis again. "How old are you, boy? Eighteen? Nineteen?"

"Almost eighteen, yup," he said. "But what's it to you?"

"A job, maybe," the man said. "They call me El Mago. You know why? Because I can get people out of tight situations, like Houdini. And I can also make things appear and disappear."

"And these guys," Elvis said, pointing at the thugs who were shooing away the last remaining street sellers, "are these the people who help you pull rabbits out of hats?"

"Every magician needs an assistant, does he not? Maybe you have the chops for it."

"I wouldn't look too good in leotards or being sawed in half, mister."

El Mago smiled. He had a treacherous smile. It was warm and made you think he was your best friend in the world, even when he was watching a guy get his kidneys ground into nothing by one of his men, as Elvis would later find out. But right then he didn't know better, and he thought it was a pleasant smile.

El Mago gave Elvis a card with his phone number and told him to call him if he wanted to stop fooling around and make real cash. Elvis made an appointment to meet with El Mago. He hadn't been too confident anything would come of it, but he remembered that Colonel Tom Parker had discovered Presley and plucked him from the shadows to turn him into a superstar. So obviously weird shit like that did happen sometimes. Maybe El Mago was the real deal, an important man, or maybe he was nothing. But Elvis needed to find out. He went to El Mago's apartment, curious and unsure of what to expect.

It was a great apartment. El Mago had bookshelf after bookshelf lined with fancy tomes and an amazing stereo console. Interesting records too. Not rock or anything Elvis had heard about, but jazz. He had a bar cart, with a decanter and matching glasses and a cocktail shaker. When he asked Elvis if he wanted a smoke, he took out a silver cigarette case.

Cash. Yeah, Elvis smelled cash, but more than anything he was enchanted by El Mago's way of life. This is exactly what he wanted: to have an apartment with high ceilings and bookcases going all the way up, the hardwood floors and the coffee table of glass and polished metal.

El Mago was kingly. Elvis had never seen anything like it, such assurance in manner, such *class*. He was a gentleman. Elvis had never met a gentleman; he had grown up with scum and shitheads, and here was this man, extending his hand—and it felt to him it was the hand of god, that's how impressed he was—and lifting him from the muck.

The only thing that Elvis had ever won in his life were the plastic Hanna-Barbera figurines that came in Tuinkys. This was like finding a damn diamond inside the snack.

Of course Elvis accepted El Mago's job offer and joined the Hawks. He became one of Mago's boys. That's what he called them: my boys.

It hadn't been easy, all the training and the rules. The Hawks were run military style, and since a bunch of the members had been lowlife assholes like himself, picking up routines and following commands wasn't first nature. But he persevered through the drills, mastered the tactics they were taught: how to bug a room, how to tail someone without being found out, the works. Apparently some of the Hawks had even been trained by the CIA, who didn't want commies in Latin America and were assisting the Mexican government, which meant that Elvis received a top-notch education.

After a few months of initial prep he'd been assigned to a group, then reassigned to the one led by El Gazpacho, with El Mago overseeing them. His training didn't end, but slowly he was given more and more assignments. Two years of that unit and he thought he had the whole thing figured out, that it would be an easy climb. Until now.

No sense in getting spooked, though. Not yet, Elvis told himself. Right. That meant more music—Mr. Sinatra was always a sure bet, and no one could belt "Fly Me to the Moon" like he did—and checking out his dictionary. He tried to learn a word each day, and when he really liked a word he wrote it out on a little notepad, cherishing it that way. It'd been three days since the operation had gone down and Elvis was trying to maintain his routine. His push-ups, his music, timely meals, the word of the day.

Boys need routines, that's what El Mago told them. But Mago hadn't showed his face around the apartment, and all he'd said when he phoned was that everyone was to stay put. Elvis limited himself to buying the papers and cigarettes, eyeing the city wearily.

Three days now.

Eclectic. He looked at the dictionary. *E-clek-tik.* Elvis tried the word, whispering it to himself, then saying it louder. When he was done memorizing the word he put on a Beatles record and adjusted his headphones. Not everyone liked The Beatles, especially in his line of work. Other Hawks grumbled that this rock shit was dangerous, it smelled like communism. But Elvis didn't see any harm in music, and El Gazpacho secretly loved Lennon's voice.

He tilted his head, regarded himself in the mirror, and when Lennon said the line about better running for your life, he made a motion with his hands and pretended to shoot himself in the mirror.

He didn't speak English but he knew a few phrases. El Gazpacho had gladly translated lyrics for him, and Elvis had a decent memory.

Elvis kept thinking about how El Gazpacho loved all those Japanese movies and the time they'd gone to see a Godzilla film and pelted the screen with popcorn.

How was El Gazpacho? Would he return soon?

He frowned, reached for his sunglasses, and put them on, pushing them up the bridge of his nose. He made the motion with his hands again, pretended he was holding up a pistol, then let his arms fall to his sides.

He could have gone to El Gazpacho's room and grabbed a real gun, but he didn't dare walk in there.

Around seven El Mago showed up, summoning them to the living room. El Güero immediately launched into an explanation about how Elvis was a dipshit and not much could ever be expected from a lowlife who hailed from Tepito, while the Antelope mostly nodded and added a loud "aha!" here and there.

"If you allow me, sir, if I may be completely honest, El Elvis is sorta a fag," El Güero said, sounding like a professor who was giving a very important lecture on nuclear physics or some shit like that. "You can't trust him to do anything right. What did you call him, Antelope?"

"A wimp," the Antelope said.

"No, the other thing."

"Chamaco baboso."

"No. A shit-flinging chimpanzee from the dirtiest cage in Chapultepec. No offense to the real monkeys. And he listens to all that propaganda, like a fucking degenerate anarchist," El Güero said.

"What propaganda?" El Mago asked. He sounded more curious than concerned.

"That rock music. The president said it ought to be censored, that it leads to anarchy. I for one agree. They closed the singing cafés, but what good does that do if people can still listen to this shit as they please?" El Güero said, and Elvis thought if El Güero could, he would have wrapped himself in the Mexican flag and rolled around the floor to emphasize his point.

Yeah, they'd closed a harmless bunch of singing cafés like the Pau Pau where all they did was play silly cover songs. You couldn't even *dance* at a fucking café, and still the cops went and pulled people out of there when they felt like it.

He didn't think anyone should get ruffled about a few songs; it wasn't no sign of anarchy. He'd looked up that word one time and there was nothing, but nothing, that applied to Elvis. Besides, everyone knew that the rich kids in Las Lomas hired bands like Three Souls in My Mind to play at their private parties and they listened to whatever the fuck they wanted while sipping their rum-and-Cokes, so it didn't seem fair to him that a few got cake and others got shit. But no one paid him to speak his opinions, so Elvis stood, hands deep in his pockets, all quiet.

He'd steeled himself for this all day long, filling his head with words and songs and facts—the guitar on Elvis Presley's first album was a Martin D-28; a haruspex was an ancient priestess who examined the entrails of animals—and he didn't interrupt El Güero, not one single time.

He'd get his turn before El Mago, and he didn't want to spoil it with theatrics.

"Boy, let us go for a walk," El Mago said after a while, and Elvis simply nodded and obeyed.

El Güero looked positively giddy at that command. Elvis didn't bother grabbing his jacket; he simply followed El Mago down the stairs.

"I want you to explain why you disobeyed my orders," El Mago said when they reached the street. "You were supposed to wait for a van to pick you up if someone was injured."

"He would've died if we'd waited, sir. He was banged up real bad."

"But that is not the reason why you stole a car and drove him to a doctor."

"What do you mean?"

"I am trying to determine your motive. Was it because El Gazpacho is your friend? Because you thought I would be upset if a unit member died? Or because you did not think my reaction would matter? Explain yourself."

Elvis didn't know what El Mago expected him to say. It seemed to him that when you've been sharing meals and assignments with a dude for months on end that you owe it to the guy to at least try and get him some help and not let him die like a dog in the street.

El Gazpacho called Elvis "brother," and sure, maybe it was a quick endearment, but it also meant a little something. Bro, you know.

My bro.

Comrades in arms and all that, except that sounded maybe a bit commie, and El Mago didn't like no commies. So he frowned, thinking hard as they walked slowly, rounding the corner.

"You gotta have some loyalty in this world," Elvis said at last. He was looking straight ahead so he couldn't see El Mago's expression when he spoke; he didn't want to see it lest he spot something nasty behind his eyes. Elvis was trying to stay cool, but he felt nervous.

"Loyalty."

"Seems to me."

El Mago was quiet. "You never quite cease surprising me, Elvis," he said. "Loyalty. A valuable commodity. It seems in short supply these days."

Elvis raised his head at that, despite his nerves, and glanced at the older man. He thought there was something melancholic about El Mago right then. He'd only seen him like this a couple of times. He kept his secrets, El Mago. He had to, Elvis supposed. You couldn't go around spilling everything, showing each and every emotion.

They had stopped next to a newspaper stand. El Mago turned toward the magazines and papers, staring at the photos and the headlines.

"The operation got out of hand the other day. Your unit did not, in fact, muck up too much. But other units and their leaders lost control. In a day or two the president is going to order a public investigation into what happened."

"What'll happen?"

"Some people will have to go. The chief of police and the mayor will not last beyond next week, I am sure of it. Public relations, you know? There might be some reorganizing of the units. Everyone is jumpy, fingers are being pointed. It is a dangerous time."

Elvis nodded. He didn't know where that left him, but he didn't dare ask. Then, as if reading his mind, El Mago turned to him.

"You will stay with El Güero and the Antelope. I want you to remain at the apartment and keep a low profile, as you have been doing for the past few days."

"El Tunas and the others . . . they'll also come around?" Elvis asked, because his unit was normally bigger than just them. They cooperated with the two other little groups. The twelve of them together.

"It is just the three of you. The others are needed elsewhere. For now, if there is an assignment, you will be the leader."

He'd dreamed of leading a unit and the perks that came with that, like the car and having your own gun. Not that he was particularly a weapons guy, but it seemed pretty cool to have a good handgun to strap to your waist—it's not like you could get a sword and call yourself a samurai, even if he'd like that better. Plus, if you wanted to climb up, if you wanted to make anything of yourself, you had to be a unit leader.

It was the first step to becoming someone like El Mago.

However, the senior operative was El Güero, and one would have expected him to take the lead.

Elvis opened his mouth, wishing to point this out, and then quickly closed it, self-preservation wisely urging him to shut up. If El Mago had made up his mind about him, there was no point in asking for explanations, plus he was simply glad he had not been dismissed from the Hawks.

El Mago turned around, and they began walking back to the apartment. "You have a question?" El Mago said, and the smirk on his face made Elvis realize that he knew exactly what he'd been thinking.

Elvis slid his hands out of his pockets and grabbed the crumpled pack of cigarettes in the back pocket of his jeans.

"Uh . . . El Gazpacho, how's he doing?" he asked, both because he genuinely wanted to know and because asking about El Güero's seniority would have been stupid.

El Mago frowned. "He is injured."

"Yeah, but how's he feelin'?"

"He is in bed with a bullet in his gut, how do you think he feels?"

"Just wonderin'."

"Well, do not," El Mago said curtly. "Head back, boy."

Elvis nodded. He took out a cigarette, lit it, and crossed the street toward the apartment while El Mago went in the opposite direction. He hoped he hadn't fucked things up by inquiring about El Gazpacho. But that night El Mago phoned and officially informed El Güero and the Antelope that their new unit leader was El Elvis. Elvis celebrated quietly. With his headphones on, he listened to "Eleanor Rigby" and drank Fanta.

4

ROUTINES PROVIDE MEANING, that's what Maite believed; therefore she tried to stick to her own patterns. Monday through Friday routines were fairly easy since work dictated her behavior. The weekends, however, were wide open. There were plenty of chances to flounder, to sink into tedium.

Saturdays she got up an hour later than usual, fixed herself a cup of coffee, and drank it in the company of her parakeet. Around eleven she stepped out to buy the groceries at the tianguis that popped up in a nearby park. There she ate a bite at one of the food stands before dragging her market bag, now filled with vegetables and fruit, back home and buying a newspaper.

That day, however, she hurried her purchases, eager to return to the apartment building. She had spent half the night awake, imagining what her neighbor's apartment would look like. She could have headed there at the crack of dawn, but she knew how much better it was to stretch out the moment, to let it linger on the palate. As she shopped she wondered about the color of the drapes, the type of furniture she'd find. Between the stalls with ripe bananas and tomatoes, she daydreamed.

After tucking away the groceries, she finally allowed herself the chance to turn the key and walk into Leonora's apartment, slowly closing the door behind her. She absorbed the place, just standing in the living room, her hands pressed against her stomach.

The curtains were blue, made of denim, and they were drawn closed. Maite flicked on a light. A paper lampshade bathed the furniture with a soft, yellow glow. Leonora had less furniture than Maite, but she could tell it was of a better quality than her own. In a corner there was a peacock rattan chair piled with canvases and the couch was covered with a long, tasseled cloth stamped with a butterfly pattern. A low table and two couches served as the dining room. Canvases were also propped against the walls.

Maite looked at the paintings and found them dull: splashes of red with no possible meaning. She was more interested by the photos on a shelf. Leonora and her friends appeared in a variety of poses. There was one shot where she was draped over a man's lap, a cigarette in her hand, her head thrown back. Maite stared long and hard at that photo, lingering on the man's handsome face.

A fat tabby rubbed against Maite's legs, and she shooed it away, irritated by the animal. She wished to finish exploring before getting down to the mundane tasks of feeding the animal and cleaning up its shit.

She went into the bedroom and saw that Leonora kept her mattress on the floor. The red silk bedsheets were crumpled and balled up in the center of the bed, and on the floor there was an ashtray. There was booze too, bottles of expensive wine, and a pair of dirty glasses forgotten in a corner. A ceramic Buddha and a plate with half-burnt incense sticks had been arranged atop a pile of books, but for all the Bohemian décor you could smell the money. It was visible in a very modern glass-and-brass table, the quality of the glasses and dishes, the finely carved wooden box where Leonora kept colorful pills, a bag filled with marijuana, and another one with mushrooms. Gold bangles and designer sunglasses were carelessly scattered around the floor, along with cheap bracelets with wooden beads.

The apartment reeked of money and pot, of pricey wine bottles left open and spoiling, souring the air.

Maite riffled through Leonora's closet, pressing a green velvet jacket against her waist and glancing at the tall mirror with a silver frame leaning against the wall. A long, cream dress with embroidered flowers, completely unlike anything Maite owned, mesmerized her, and she also pressed that against her body, sliding her hands across the delicate fabric. She looked at the label and decided it must command an exorbitant price. But she couldn't take clothes. Once she had stolen an earring from a tenant on the second floor, but only one, so that the woman would think she had simply misplaced it. Clothes and jewelry were too conspicuous. Besides, Leonora and Maite were not the same size.

She put the jacket and the dress back in the closet and walked into the bathroom. Leonora's bathroom mirror had a white plaster frame with tiny white flowers. Maite grabbed the vintage silver hairbrush resting on the sink and carefully brushed her hair. On a shelf above the toilet she found a jar of face cream and several tubes of lipstick. She tried one on.

It was a gaudy pink, meant for a younger girl. It aged Maite, added years to her face, and she wiped her mouth clean with a Kleenex, disgusted by the sight of it.

She ventured back into the living room and crossed her arms, again looking at Leonora's pictures, again fixing her eyes on that one shot where the young woman had her head thrown back. The man in the picture was wearing a tie and the corners of his mouth were crooked into a charming smile. Now *that* was a handsome man. He even looked a bit like Jorge Luis, if Jorge Luis hadn't been a black-and-white drawing. Leonora might have gone away with that man, or another equally good-looking one, for the weekend. She must be throwing her head back and laughing now.

Maite spun around.

There wasn't anything she wished to take. Sometimes it was like this, a struggle. Other times she would walk into a room and she would know at once what she wanted. It had to be something personal, something that reminded her of that particular apartment, so that later she might easily conjure the space in her mind. That was the key.

She had stolen before, stolen from department stores and shabby corner stores, but it had never given her joy. It was a mere compulsion that left her restless and unsatisfied. It had taken her a while to figure out that what she sought was not the object in question, but the thrill of possessing a secret. As if she had been able to peer into the most intimate recesses of a person's mind and pulled open a hidden compartment.

She'd stolen an old Italian lace fan from the lady with the blind dog on the fifth floor and a broken violin bow from the busy mother on the third floor who was always chasing after one of her children. At one point they'd all asked her to water their plants or feed their goldfish, and she'd slipped into their homes quiet and smiling, trying on their shoes, using their shampoo, eating one of the bonbons in a box. The stolen item was the punctuating mark at the end of her adventure, the flourish on a signature.

The cat was meowing. Maite walked into the kitchen. She found the cat food tins next to the stove and opened one, distractedly dumping it into the cat's bowl. Leonora had left a cardboard box above the garbage can. She peered inside it, found nothing but old newspapers, and moved the box aside so she could throw the tin away. When she was putting the lid back on the bin she noticed something white in the corner.

Maite moved the garbage can away. It was a small plaster statuette of San Judas Tadeo. It had a crack running down its side, and the girl had taped the bottom of it with yellow masking tape. It was rubbish that she'd forgotten to throw out, like the old newspapers.

Maite held up the statuette, running her fingers over the smooth hair of the saint.

She wrapped the statuette in a newspaper and walked out of the apartment, careful to lock the door and ensure the cat didn't follow her.

Back in her home she put on music. The Beatles played as she unwrapped her new treasure and placed it in the little brown chest in the bottom drawer of her dresser where she kept all the items she'd stolen. Everything felt right. It had been a good day.

Sunday, she went to the movies, which was a mistake. She preferred romances and comedies, but it seemed to her these were in small supply these days. She wound up watching a Japanese action film as a couple next to her kissed each other, oblivious to the world. The popcorn she'd bought tasted stale, and someone smoked in the row in front of her while a samurai faced off against a one-armed foe on the big screen. She shifted in her uncomfortable seat. By the time she stepped out of the theater it was raining, and she crossed her arms and hurried across the street, trying to protect her head with a newspaper but giving up after a few blocks.

After the high of the previous evening she could already feel herself sinking into an unpleasant low. It went like that for her, up and down like a roller coaster. Why did the world have to be like this, she wondered as she waited for her bus. Gray, unpleasant. In the comic books everything had a certain cheer, even if the pages were all in black-and-white. And the next day was Monday. The thought of the office with the dull clacking of the typewriters made her grimace. Two days of rest were not enough to wash away the tedium of her work week.

Maybe she should look for another job. Check the help wanted ads, actually make it to interviews. There were better firms out there. She didn't even have to limit herself to working for a law office. Perhaps there was a more exciting position available somewhere else. A publishing company. That sounded classy. Surely all her reading would come in handy there. True, she mostly read comics, but they counted as something, and she did have several classics from the Sepan Cuantos collection. Furthermore, she had gleaned enough about sophisticated fashions from the magazines that she wouldn't stand out in such an environment. Oh, she'd chuck away the sensible shoes and the brown jackets for something with a little more pizzazz. At a place like that some glamour wouldn't be unexpected, would it? Just a smidgen of it.

Or she would look at those *Learn English at Home* records she hadn't touched in a while and really get into the lessons this time. She could be a bilingual secretary and command more money. She might even work for a diplomat. An ambassador! Weren't all the nice embassies in Polanco? This, too, would require sophistication and perhaps even a bit of travel, but Maite was willing to fly wherever she was needed to support the important work of her bosses.

Wouldn't her sister die of envy then?

She was eager to put her plan into action. As soon as she got home she checked the paper for suitable jobs, but after a little while she grew discouraged by the many times the phrase "twenty to twenty-eight years old" appeared. Even when she was within the specified age range, all the very best jobs seemed to want more than she had to offer, and there was that other phrase too: "excellent presentation."

Pretty. That's what they meant. Everyone wanted pretty girls, or at the very least, put-together girls. It wasn't that Maite looked like a slob, but her clothes never quite fit her right. Her mother said it was because she didn't have proper undergarments and explained that in her day you wore a good quality long-leg girdle, not just pantyhose. But it wasn't that. It was that the clothes were cheap, they weren't tailored for her, a seam came apart here and there, and the colors were wrong. But she never seemed to be able to pick the right thing. Like that time she'd saved and saved and bought the cream-colored blouse with the frilly high collar at the neck only to get home and realize that she looked ridiculous, like a no-neck monster.

That was the problem. Maite was ridiculous and worse. She was pusillanimous, dull, utterly mediocre. Once you added all that together coupled with her lack of initiative, there really wasn't any reason to consider another job.

She stared out the window as the rain fell.

She should make herself a cup of coffee, that's what she should do. She should read her old comic books and listen to tangos. Play Carlos Gardel and songs about love and heartbreak. But as Maite sat there, with the rain falling, crumpling the newspaper in her hands, she felt no desire to do any of that.

Maite grabbed her coat and decided to go out. She'd walk.

That's what was best. Go for a walk, flee her hideous little apartment. The air was stale in this room, and she didn't want to think about jobs or requirements or anything of the sort.

As soon as she stepped into the hallway she saw the man standing in front of Leonora's door. He turned his head quickly and looked at her. She recognized him as the man in the picture she had been admiring before, but his hair was a little longer and he was wearing a red jacket.

"Oh, it's you," she blurted out stupidly, and the man frowned.

"Have we met?" he asked, looking surprised.

"No, no," she said quickly shaking her head, trying to fix her blunder. "I've seen you in a picture with Leonora."

"You know Leonora?"

"Sort of. I'm watching her cat for her. She'll be back tomorrow. Were you looking for her?"

He nodded.

Well, of course he is, you dummy, she thought. *Why else would he be here?*

She wondered who had let him in. The tenants were supposed to be careful about letting strangers into the building, and there was the superintendent on the first floor who gossiped about everyone, but she supposed someone must have been lax about the entrance policy. People were always doing that, holding doors open even if they shouldn't.

"She said she'd be around."

"I don't think she'll be back today," Maite said, reaching into her purse, pretending to look for her keys so she could lock her door. She looked slowly, as if she couldn't find them, hoping he'd say something else.

He did.

"If you're watching her cat then you must have the key to her apartment. I was supposed to pick something up from her. I think she left it inside for me."

"You really should ask the super about that."

"She borrowed my camera, and it must be inside her apartment. Maybe you could open the door for me? It would take a minute."

"Well . . ."

"Forty-five seconds. If it's not on the table I'll zip right out. You can come in with me if you want." There was an edge of anxiety to his words, but also a heavy dose of charm.

"I don't even know your name," Maite said, and congratulated herself on being crafty enough to come up with that line.

The man smiled. He stretched out a hand. "Emilio Lomelí."

"I'm Maite."

"I realize you were headed somewhere, but it would take a minute."

"I'm not in a rush."

She took out Leonora's keys and opened the door, and they walked into the apartment. He seemed to know his way around the place and went into the bedroom, opening the drawer of a tall white dresser. Leonora observed him from the doorway, trying to think of something else she might say, something witty and interesting.

"What type of camera is it?"

"It's a Canon F-1. Are you interested in photography?"

"No, not really," Maite admitted.

He nodded and opened another drawer. Maite rubbed her hands together, trying hard to imagine what else to say. A minute or two more and he would give up and step out of the apartment, but she didn't want him to leave yet. He was such a distinguished man, and she seldom had the chance to talk to someone like him.

Maite licked her lips. "Are you a photographer? I imagine you are."

"Yep."

Silence again. He had opened the bottom and last drawer. By the way he hunched his shoulders she could guess he hadn't found what he wanted.

"Do you want me to help you look?"

"No, it's fine," he said as he stood up and glanced around the room. "She keeps all the photo equipment in this dresser. If it's not there I'm not sure where it could be, and I don't want to keep you here forever."

"It's no bother," Maite said. "Do you want to look somewhere else?"

"Let's give the living room a try."

He walked past her, back into the living room. He moved a few of the canvases aside and inspected the shelf with the photographs. It all seemed to be in vain. He turned to her finally with a shrug. The yellow light in the living room accented his amber-colored eyes, making them more vivid.

"I guess she took it with her. Hey, if by any chance you find it, can you give me a ring?" he asked.

"Sure. But Leonora is coming back tomorrow."

"I don't know about that. When Leonora takes off like this she can be gone for days. She gets restless. Needs inspiration," he said, smiling again and reaching into his pocket. He took out a business card. "Here. This is my phone. Will you call me if you find the camera?"

Emilio Lomelí, Antiques. The card was embossed, the letters velvet-soft against her fingertips.

"If I see a camera, I'll phone you. Are you her boyfriend, by the way?" she asked, hoping the question sounded indifferent, casual.

"No. It's a bit hard to explain."

Explain all you like, she wanted to say, but he was already headed toward the door, checking his watch, and she imagined that he had an important place to be. Important stuff to do. She followed him and locked the door, and they were standing in the hallway again. Maite remembered she was supposed to go out, so she headed toward the stairs and he did too.

She scrambled to come up with something to say to him. She dearly wished she had been wearing something nicer. She had on a shabby, shapeless gray coat and her comfy blue shoes. If she'd known she was going to be talking to a man like this, she would have taken the time to apply a bit of mascara and pick a more flattering outfit. She remembered seeing a shearling coat inside Leonora's closet and wondered what she might look like in something like that.

"Thanks, Maite," he said when they reached the front entrance.

"No problem," she replied, ecstatic that he'd said her name. It sounded wonderful coming from a handsome man's lips.

She closed the door and pretended to fiddle with the lock, sneaking a look in the direction he had gone and seeing him walk away. He went around the corner and was gone. Maite clutched her purse tight against her chest.

She thought about following him for a moment. Not with any nefarious intention, but simply because she wondered where he was headed, simply to prolong the moment between them. But she didn't dare, afraid of what he might think if he should turn his head and see her walking behind him.

The next morning she arrived at work bright and early. She was eager to chat with Diana, but she didn't get a chance until lunchtime, when they both hurried to the coffee shop across the street.

"I met somebody," Maite said. "His name is Emilio."

"Then that's why you wouldn't have dinner with me Friday," Diana said, raising an eyebrow at her.

"Don't be silly, no. I met him yesterday. He's very handsome, very interesting. He sells antiques. Would you believe it? A mutual friend introduced us—there was a little reunion, I wasn't even going to go—and we talked for hours. We have so much in common."

"Well, that's exciting. But what about Luis?"

Maite fibbed. Never big lies. Little things. It wasn't malice. You simply couldn't go through life being frank. When someone asked what she had done during the weekend, it wasn't possible to always say "nothing." "Nothing" sounded dry and sad. Therefore, once in a while, she embroidered her life with a little lie. She took the men from the comic books she read and fashioned them into imaginary dates, boyfriends.

Besides, it was nice to have someone to share her fantasies with, to see Diana's eyes brighten with admiration when Maite regaled her with a story about her exciting weekend date. She didn't do it all the time either. It had been weeks since she'd last mentioned Luis, who was obviously patterned after the hero of *Secret Romance*. A dashing physician.

"I don't know," Maite said. "He's too quiet."

"You're terrible, Maite," Diana replied, but she spoke with admiration, and Maite felt that in the end she was doing Diana a favor by telling her these stories. They entertained both of them; they turned what might have been a gloomy lunch break into something magical.

"Are you going to see him again then?"

"I haven't decided yet."

"You have such good times."

"Well, you know, once in a while," Maite said modestly as she thought about her weekend spent doing a crossword and watching the bird in its cage.

Diana wanted more details about her new quasi-boyfriend, so Maite invented suitable interests and hobbies—he had taught himself to play the guitar and liked watching Japanese films—she even shared some of his imaginary charming comments. She eventually grew weary of the charade and was glad when they crossed the street again and returned to work.

On the way back home she felt tired, her head pressed against the window of the bus, as she watched with indifference as a couple of young men tried to pinch the ass of a teenage schoolgirl, who valiantly warded them off. She closed her eyes. She didn't want to see any of that. There was such ugliness in the world.

After making herself dinner and feeding her parakeet a treat, she knocked on Leonora's door, but no one answered. She let herself in and saw that the apartment looked just as it had the day before. The girl was not back yet. On the couch, the fat tabby lifted its head and looked at Maite. She fed the cat, guessing the girl would arrive later that night. She wanted to try on that shearling coat she'd seen in the closet, but instead she rummaged through the girl's toiletries and sprayed expensive perfume on her wrists.

She'd read that you ought to place perfume on the pulse points. She sniffed at her wrist, wondering what a lover would think of this scent.

Leonora's perfume was sickly-sweet.

Back in her apartment she read *Secret Romance*. She chewed a nail, wondering when Beatriz would realize her lover was hidden away in an isolated house, deep in the jungle. It was early, but she fell asleep on the couch.

She dreamed of it. The jungle, with tall palm trees and an errant, sensual moon. With orchids and a jasmine perfume. The beating of drums late at night and the distant music of the waves against the shore. She dreamed she was dressed in a black beaded dress that trailed behind her and that she walked through the jungle, moving closer to the place where people played the drums.

Drums like a beating heart, drums making the earth quiver.

She pushed aside the foliage to emerge onto a clearing, and in the middle of the clearing there was a stone slab, and on the stone slab there was Leonora, laid up like the victim of some ancient Aztec sacrifice as shot by a Hollywood crew, dressed all in white, her eyes fixed on the moon as she awaited the arrival of a warrior-priest with a knife.

Maite looked down at the girl, but the girl did not see her. The girl saw only the moon. She was caught in a spell, in a trance, like Jorge Luis in his coma.

Maite stepped aside; she left the drums behind, she left the girl on the stone slab, and descended toward the beach. Crabs bit her feet and stones scraped her skin, and she smelled this rich scent, like salt and sulfur and brine. The world had smelled like this in the beginning, during creation, when the ocean raged and the creatures in the water multiplied, making the ocean teem with life.

When Maite awoke it was late, and her neck ached from sleeping in a strange position. She rubbed it, dragged herself to bed, and tried to rest a little longer.

5

MAITE EXPECTED LEONORA back on Tuesday, but when she knocked the girl didn't answer. She opened the door to the apartment and fed the cat before heading to work, irritated by the thoughtlessness of her neighbor. She wondered what Leonora could be doing that was keeping her so busy. Well, she probably didn't have to guess *too* hard: partying. Since Leonora had moved into the building, Maite had heard loud music coming from her apartment late at night more than a few times. The super had complained the girl threw large get-togethers even though the building was supposed to be a "family" building.

"You know, young girls," the super said, shaking her head. "But she always pays the rent on time, which is more than I can say of certain people."

Maite had wanted to tell the super that she was also a young person, that she too could turn up the music on her console, make it play really loud and invite friends over for drinks. But that would have been a lie. So she nodded in agreement.

Maite spent most of her morning wondering if Leonora was still partying and if so how exactly. Perhaps Sunday had bled into Monday and then into Tuesday. One long, orgiastic celebration with champagne and truffles. Perhaps it was something more earthy. Pot, the strumming of a guitar, the sort of hippie nonsense university students dabbled in.

She wondered why the girl hadn't invited Emilio Lomelí to go with her. If Maite had been the girl, she would have phoned him immediately and asked him to accompany her. Perhaps Leonora had access to men who were even more interesting and good looking than Emilio Lomelí.

Some people had all the luck, didn't they? Leonora was young, beautiful, she had no money woes. Maite frowned, resenting all the precious, perfect people who went around with no care in the world and who couldn't be bothered to return to their homes, to feed their damn cats.

When Maite reached her apartment, before she had the chance to take off her shoes and put on her slippers, the phone rang.

"Hello," she said.

"Maite? It's me, Leonora."

"Leonora, I thought you said you'd be back on Sunday. Monday, at the latest."

"I was delayed," the girl said. Her voice sounded a bit odd, as though she was holding the receiver very close to her mouth. "I need to ask you for a favor. I'm not coming back for a while, and I need you to bring me a box with my things and the cat."

"Bring you?"

"Please. I can't stop by the apartment right now. The box is above the garbage can. The cat carrier is under the sink. Could you meet me in half an hour? I'll give you an address."

"I don't have a car. How do you expect me to carry a cat and a box?"

"Can you take a taxi? I'll pay for the taxi. I'll pay you triple for each day. Oh, please, please, I wouldn't ask if it wasn't important."

She could hear the girl breathing on the other end of the line. She could imagine her twisting the telephone cord between her fingers.

"I was supposed to meet my friends," Maite lied.

"I promise, I'll pay you triple. I'll pay for the extra time, the cab . . . Bring me the box and the cat. Please, I really need them."

"Well, all right. What's the address?" Maite asked, reaching for the notepad she kept by the refrigerator and scribbling down the information.

"Don't give them to anyone else. You understand?"

"Yes, yes."

"Half an hour. You'll be there?"

"Yes, fine."

After hanging up, Maite headed into Leonora's apartment and stuffed the cat in the carrier. The tabby was too fat—it barely fit inside the little metal bin. The box wasn't large, but it was still cumbersome to lug downstairs when she was dragging an overweight feline. For a moment she had thought to take the bus, to tell the girl she had called a taxi, then pocket the difference. She decided it was too much effort and opted for the taxi.

She assumed Leonora was at a friend's place, but the cab dropped her off at a printer's shop. On the windows of the shop the printer had pasted numerous posters and business cards, so it was impossible to see the inside clearly. Maite managed to pry the door open and juggle a cat and a box, shoving both in after some muttering.

There was a long counter and behind the counter all the printing equipment and paper and ink necessary to run a business like this. A young man was operating a mimeograph machine in a corner, cranking a handle.

Maite set the box on the counter and the cat on the ground. She wondered if Leonora was in the back.

The young man turned to look at Maite. He had a stylish beard and wore a t-shirt and overalls, and behind his ear he'd tucked a pencil. His hair was longish and his eyebrows were very thick, like a pair of extra furry azotadores had taken up residence above his eyes. He nodded at her, wiped his hands on a rag he carried in his pocket, and approached the counter.

"Can I help you?" he asked.

"I'm here to see Leonora."

The young man frowned. "Leonora? Why would you come to see her here?"

"She said she'd meet me at this address. I have some things for her."

"I didn't realize she'd be coming around."

"Maybe she's running late."

"What time did she say she'd meet you?"

"About right now."

The young man nodded. There were three chairs by the window. Maite sat on one of them, and she placed the cat on another. She kept the box on her lap, drumming her fingers against it. The young man went back to cranking the handle of the mimeograph. In a corner, a small metallic fan turned its blades.

After ten minutes had passed Maite began to fidget, tapping her foot against the floor. After around twenty minutes the damn cat began to meow mournfully periodically. When a whole hour had gone by, Maite stood up and approached the counter again.

"I think Duke is hungry," the young man told her. He was smiling a little.

Maite blinked. For a moment she didn't know what he meant. Then she realized he was talking about the damn cat. Of course he was hungry! Maite was hungry herself.

"Do you have any idea where I could find Leonora? I need to deliver the cat to her."

"Sorry. I mean, if she's not home . . ." The young man scratched his cheek. "Could be she's at her sister's house. It's near here."

"Do you know the phone number for her sister's house?"

"I've got the address. I've delivered flyers to her there."

"Can you give it to me?"

The young man frowned. "I'm not sure I should be giving her address to strangers."

"I'm Leonora's neighbor, okay? I live right across from her, that's how I wound up with her cat. Now I really don't want to drag the cat and that box back and forth a million times. Is her sister's home really nearby? If it is, I could stop there and ask if she's around. It sounded like she needed the papers in the box."

Maite didn't care if Leonora needed squat, but she wanted to get paid. Her car was not going to drive itself out of the mechanic's shop. With the money Leonora had promised her, she'd be able to settle her bill and get the damn car back. They were holding it hostage. The good old days when accounts could be fixed with a handshake and a verbal promise were long gone. Shops and businesses would not extend credit to a person in need. The world was hard now, and those bastards wouldn't let the car out of their sight until Maite paid every single cent owed.

Leonora had promised Maite thrice her original fee. She wasn't going to pass on that. Yes, yes, maybe Maite had overcharged the girl in the first place, which meant she was going to make out pretty well once she collected, but Maite figured Leonora could afford that and more.

"Well?" she told the young man.

"Give me a second."

The young man reached for a filing cabinet and pulled out a drawer, then found a receipt. He brought it to the counter and copied the address for Maite.

"Now look, I'll give this to you, but please tell Leonora to give me a ring when you find her, will you?" he said, holding up a scrap of paper.

"I would if I knew your name," Maite replied, irritated, snatching the address from his hand.

The magazines Maite liked to read offered tips on how to snag a boyfriend. Things such as ask him about his interests and don't smoke too much. Recently she had read something called "The Fantastic Guide to Flirting" that included the recommendation to remember that every man you meet is a potential date, so women shouldn't ruin their chances by being too rude or shy. Maite realized her harsh stare was probably not among the recommended tactics for interactions with men, but she was short on patience. Besides, even if the magazine assured her toads could turn into princes, this guy wasn't a handsome specimen that she might want to impress, like Emilio. She could afford to be less than charming and it wouldn't matter one bit.

"I'm Rubén," he said with a certain pleasant blandness that

must come with customer service, so that she felt compelled to reply in turn with a politeness that had been sorely lacking only seconds before.

"Maite. I'll tell her," she said, remembering her manners and shaking his hand. "And if you see her, can you tell her I went to her sister's place?"

"Sure."

Leonora's sister lived in the Condesa, which was great news because it meant Maite would be heading in the direction of her apartment. If it had been somewhere else, she might have rethought her strategy. But she needed the money, and she also didn't want to be stuck caring for the fat cat for days or weeks on end. Leonora had said she'd be gone for "a while," and who knew what that meant exactly, if she was finding herself, or being creative, or god knows what. Maite didn't even like cats. There wasn't enough food to feed it. It would be on its last tin that night, and Maite would be damned if she was going to also be paying for meow-meow's cuisine.

Maite finally arrived at the wrought-iron doors of a tasteful two-level house. She rang the bell and waited. A young woman opened the door. She was maybe a couple of years older than Leonora. The resemblance between the sisters was strong. She had Leonora's pretty little mouth and her cheekbones, but her hair was cut shorter.

"Yes?" the woman asked.

"Are you Cándida? Leonora's sister?"

"Yes."

"Is Leonora around? I'm her neighbor. I'm trying to get a hold of her."

"I'm not—" Nearby, a baby began crying. The woman turned her head and sighed. "Why don't you come in?" she asked. "Follow me."

Maite walked behind her. The cat, perhaps to compete with the baby, was meowing again. Maite wanted to give its carrier a good shake but contained herself.

Maite and Cándida walked into a large living room with plush sofas and a large orange-and-red rug on the floor. The house boasted a big TV and an impressive stereo console. A baby in a blue onesie was playing in its playpen in the middle of the living room. Or the baby had been playing. It was currently waving a pacifier in one hand and emitting a pitiful wail.

Cándida bent down, scooping the baby into her arms. Then she scrambled toward the television and switched it off. Maite set the box and the cat carrier on the floor with a grateful sigh.

"Sorry, you were saying you wanted to get a hold of my sister?"

"Yes. I've been watching her cat, and I need to return it to her."

"I don't think I understand."

"I was supposed to watch it until Monday, but she hasn't come home and now she wants me to bring her the cat, but I can't seem to find her. I wouldn't bother you, but she never showed up at the place where we were meeting, and that's how I wound up here."

Maite lifted the cat carrier for her to see. The woman was now patting the baby's back, and the baby was beginning to calm down.

"I thought Leonora would be home, but if she isn't that explains her phone call. Oh, Lord, I hope she hasn't done something stupid."

"What do you mean?"

"You probably already know what my sister is like."

"We talk and such, yeah. We're not great friends," Maite replied cautiously.

"I wouldn't know her friends these days," Cándida said, shaking her head. "That's the problem. I mean . . . not you. You look respectable."

Respectable. It wasn't an insult, but somehow Maite bristled at the description. Respectable meant dull. Though she supposed she did look dull in her cheap suit and her cheap shoes.

Cándida wandered toward a shelf that had pictures in silver frames. She was staring at one photo. It was Leonora and Cándida with a gray-haired man. The man looked very solemn; the women were smiling tentatively. Leonora wore a flowy pink dress and had a flower pinned to her shoulder. It might have been a high school graduation picture.

"That's our uncle Leonardo."

"Leonardo and Leonora?"

"Yes. She's named after him. This was three years ago, before she started changing. She's an artist, you do know that, yes?"

The man appeared in another picture, dressed in a military uniform, looking younger. His resemblance to Leonora and Cándida was rather striking in that photo: same eyes, most definitely. Other pictures showed a couple she assumed were the parents of the girls, and there was a bridal photo of Cándida.

"I've seen her paintings." Technically this was true, since she'd been inside Leonora's apartment.

"Our uncle never thought that was a great idea, but he still agreed to pay for her apartment and bring her here. I don't know what happened. Maybe it was . . . Mexico City is different than Monterrey, I guess. One moment she's happy, she's painting, then she's not. She's wasting all her time, going to parties, dating boy after boy. There're drugs, of course, there's alcohol, and awful, awful people.

"You know she hangs out with all those students who are always protesting and going to rallies? God, I can't remember the name of the organization she's been with lately, that stupid art collective. At any rate, I think some of them went to that rally. The one that's been in all the papers."

"Yeah, I saw some stuff about that," Maite said. She had skimmed the headlines, avoided the secretaries as they spoke about dangerous pinkos or government agents. All that talk of secret groups of hired thugs and communist plots made her nervous. Yet she had an idea of the magnitude of the altercation: Zabludovsky had interviewed the president, and the president had said those responsible for the attacks would be brought to justice. He'd said that students shouldn't demonstrate in aggressive ways, that he condemned both irresponsibility and repression. Maite understood little, but she grasped this: that beneath banal phrases and appeals to the good of the nation something dangerous simmered.

"Leonora is not bad, but sometimes she gets these silly ideas in her head and, well . . . she phoned me today in the morning asking for money. I thought maybe she wanted to bail people out. You have to understand, she's done that before. Her friends make some sort of fuss, get arrested, and she bails them out. Or . . . well, drugs and booze are another big-ticket item. But she said it wasn't for that and she said . . . she said June tenth had changed everything."

"Did you give her the money?"

"I can't," Cándida said. "It's not because I'm stingy. My husband has me on a modest allowance. I have some savings, but the last couple of times, I asked our uncle for the money. Of course, I couldn't tell him what it was for. He'd never agree to bail out a bunch of mischief-makers or pay for drugs. It's *bribe* money, really. Not *bail* money. Just so they'll let them go."

Now that the baby had been soothed and once again had a pacifier in his mouth, Cándida deposited him back in the plastic playpen and switched the TV back on, turning down the volume. The baby held on to the railing of the playpen and stared at the images. The coyote was chasing the road runner.

"She told me she was heading away for a while. Do you know who she's staying with? Maybe there's a friend I can call. She wanted her cat and her papers," Maite said. "Could she be with Emilio Lomelí?"

Maite was hoping Cándida would say that might be the case. That way she would have an excuse to phone him. But the young woman shook her head.

"I don't see why she would be. They broke up a few months ago."

"Could she be at your uncle's?"

"Uncle Leonardo pays Leonora's bills, but they don't see eye to eye lately."

"I guess I should leave the cat with you, then. I'm not sure what else to do with it."

"The cat?"

"Yes, the cat. She also promised she'd pay me for the cab I took and the days I watched over it. You could settle her account and I could leave it here," Maite asked, trying not to sound too eager. She definitely did not relish the thought of becoming the permanent nanny of that furball.

Cándida touched her throat and reached toward the box of cigarettes resting atop a glass coffee table and lit one. "Oh, never! I wouldn't be able to keep a cat. You do know what they say about cats? They asphyxiate babies."

"I don't think that's true."

"My husband wouldn't like it."

"Maybe your uncle can take it? And, you know, settle Leonora's bill?"

"I really don't want to bother him with this stuff. I told you, they don't see eye to eye. Can't you keep watching the cat?"

"I didn't agree to that."

"I'm sorry. Look, write your number down. If Leonora calls, I'll tell her you stopped by."

"Feels like I'm playing telephone tag," Maite said dryly, but she did write her number down for Cándida.

When Maite left the house she looked at the ominous sky and wondered if it would rain before she reached home. She didn't want to spend any more money on taxis, especially when she would probably have to buy the stupid cat more food. Her apartment wasn't that far. She could take a bus and hope for the best. On the other hand she was getting tired, and she still hadn't eaten a proper meal.

Maite huffed and decided to find a place to eat and then trace her route home. If only she had her damn car! But now she was never going to see it again, not without this stupid, flighty girl settling her accounts.

6

EL MAGO TELEPHONED and gave Elvis fifteen minutes to be ready. Elvis had already finished his daily exercises, so he rushed into the shower and dressed in what he called his work uniform: jeans, leather jacket, blue-and-tan shirt. El Mago arrived on the dot, as he always did, and Elvis jumped in the car. They drove to Konditori.

El Mago ordered a coffee, black. Elvis liked his coffee with milk, sweet, but he had taken to imitating El Mago and also asked for a black coffee. He did ask for a slice of black forest cake to go with it.

"You should not be having so much sugar. It is a disgrace, the way you eat."

"Come on. It's a waste to come to a place like this and sit around with a black coffee and not even one pastry," Elvis replied. "Can't be carrot juice and eggs all the time."

"It keeps you fit."

El Mago was all about keeping them fit and sharp. Sit-ups, push-ups, squats. Get your blood pumping early and fast, that's what El Mago told them. Elvis had never been much into routines until he joined the Hawks, and though he didn't mind making his bed or jumping rope, he did miss scarfing garnachas at odd hours of the day. But El Mago was strict about that too. This gave credence to the Antelope's theory that he was a military man, but Elvis wasn't too sure, and he'd never been able to figure El Mago out.

If he'd been military, he didn't mention it. Maybe it had been a while back. Besides, when El Mago wore his round, black-rimmed glasses, he looked like a retired professor. The way he spoke made Elvis suspect he was closer to a scholar than a soldier. But then, there was no way of knowing. El Mago was "El Mago," no last names and no title, just like El Gazpacho, El Güero, and the Antelope didn't have any proper names.

"Sure, it keeps you fit, but who's gonna pass on fucking cake?"

"Language and diction, Elvis," El Mago said. "What have I told you about language and diction? Are you even trying?"

"I try, sir." He did. Not just with the word of the day but by reading the papers and listening to the announcers on the radio.

"You are not a verdulero at the market, at least not when you are with me," the man said. "In any case, restraint is learned."

"I guess."

"You do not *guess*. You should know it," he said firmly, and Elvis sat very straight, like a student before a favorite teacher.

El Mago took off his glasses and placed them on the table. He looked a bit haggard that morning. Nothing terrible and no one else would have probably noticed, what with the nice suit he wore and the nice tie and his gray hair perfectly parted, but Elvis knew El Mago well enough to spot the dark circles under his eyes. Something or someone was bothering El Mago. But these days Elvis supposed everyone was being bothered.

"So, may I ask if anything has changed?" Elvis asked, trying to mind his words. "Is El Gazpacho feeling better? Are we getting back in action?"

He was praying the answer was yes. Back in action meant there would still be Hawks. He'd been having an awful feeling lately, and the Antelope didn't help, all nervous and talking about how they were going to be dissolved, and then what would they do? The Antelope was ex-military. He'd been a fucking cadet, summarily expelled. Some shit like that. There was no going back for him.

For none of them.

"There is an assignment," El Mago said, opening his briefcase and taking out a folder.

The file was thin. Elvis looked at the picture of a young and pretty woman clipped to the notes. Only one picture. It showed her with her hair pulled back, looking at the camera, her lips parted. Leonora Trejo. El Mago had written a few notes about her in his clean, neat handwriting. It was odd. This was all normally typed. There was usually a lot more.

"Who's she?"

"She is your assignment. Art student, in university. The girl has gone missing, along with a camera with important photos. I want her found and the photos too. And no harming her. It is strictly find-and-retrieve, you understand?"

"Sure. But if she's missing, where you want me to start looking?"

"Give her apartment a sweep. If you are lucky, the photos are there and half of your work is over."

"And if I don't find it there?"

"Then things are getting started for you, are they not?"

A waitress came back with their coffees and Elvis's slice of cake. She asked if they wanted anything else, but El Mago waved her away. Once the waitress was gone El Mago took out another file and handed it to Elvis. This one was substantially thicker.

Elvis flipped through it, staring at the photos of a man with glasses. A man in a black habit with a white collar. He'd never seen that before.

"It's a priest," Elvis said, glancing up at El Mago in surprise.

"A commie," he clarified.

"A commie priest?"

"A Jesuit. A member of Obra Cultural Universitaria. They are from Monterrey. They were supposed to keep students in check. Instead, some of them are preaching liberation theology and making trouble. Christ, the first communist, they say." El Mago smiled his pleasant smile. But there was something sour in it. As usual, the smile hid the fangs.

"What's he doing here if they're from Monterrey?" Elvis asked, taking a bite of his cake.

"There is a lot of nastiness going on, Elvis. These reds, they have been talking guerillas and weapons, and do not doubt it, these crazy Jesuits like this Father Villarreal, they are eager to see blood spilled. They have been waiting for a spark to light the bomb, for something to make everything go off."

"Wouldn't us beating those students have made it worse, then? That would make us the crazy ones, not them. Unless someone above wanted it to go off."

El Mago had opened his lighter and was about to light his cigarette but he stopped, staring at Elvis.

"You are too damn clever sometimes, Elvis," he said.

Elvis rubbed the back of his neck. El Mago finished lighting his cigarette, took a drag, then tapped a finger against his cup of coffee, frowning. "You are correct, that mess did not help one bit. If I had been in charge of the whole operation . . . but there are plenty of fools who do not know how to handle problems without bullets and liters of blood. That is why I am telling you right now: this operation here, *my* operation, it needs to be clean and quiet. These are dangerous times to be standing out."

"Yeah, I get it. But what's the priest got to do with the girl? She also with Obra Cultural?"

"No. This priest, he came here to make friends with all the rabble who are starting up commie associations and groups. All that garbage. The girl is part of a subversive art collective. He met her through that. Before all of this, she was a good Catholic girl. Now he is her confessor."

"Couldn't have been that good a girl if she's hanging with reds, no?" Elvis said. "Although I guess it matches the color of her lipstick."

El Mago grabbed a glass ashtray and slid it to the center of the table. "Do not be overly amusing today, Elvis."

"Sorry," he said, taking a sip of his coffee.

"Talk to him, rough him up a bit and give him the treatment. See if he knows where she is."

"Rough him? I don't know—"

"This Jesuit needs a good punch in the mouth."

"I don't want to beat no priest," Elvis said quickly.

"What, now *you* are a good Catholic boy?"

Elvis couldn't remember the last time he'd gone to mass. Long before he joined the Hawks, that's for sure. But that didn't mean he wasn't wary of messing with someone of the cloth or that he didn't make the sign of the cross when he saw an image of the Virgin of Guadalupe. Even the fools in Tlaquepaque, with their healing crystals and their chants, believed in something. You had to be a bit afraid of a superior power. Those who weren't were treading on dangerous soil.

"I'm not going to hell if that's what you're thinking," Elvis said. "I'm pretty sure you'll be toasty warm in hell if you go on hitting priests, whether they're Jesuits or whatever."

El Mago gave Elvis an icy look. The Antelope said some of the upper-level Hawks had been trained abroad, with the CIA and shit, to help keep the commies out of Mexico, out of Latin America, and they'd learned lots of interesting and useful tactics. Elvis wondered if it was those folks who'd taught El Mago to stare like that, all frost. It was like staring into an abyss.

That's what El Mago was. This damn abyss, sucking you in. This damn fucking force of nature. You didn't cross him. Not because you were afraid he'd pull out a gun and shoot you, but because he simply had that aura about him. The feeling that this was someone who devoured people, but never got his suit dirty.

The thing was, he wasn't always like that. The rest of the time, he was very much all right, even nice. Elvis liked talking to El Mago. He didn't fool himself into thinking they were friends, but he thought they might be associates. He wanted to do good work for El Mago. Hell, he wanted to make him proud. El Güero had even made fun of him about that, chuckling and saying Elvis wished El Mago would adopt him. That was a crock of shit—first of all because Elvis was a grown man, and second because he'd never particularly missed his stupid father, so why bother trying to find a second one—but it cut dangerously close to the truth.

He did think El Mago was darn cool, what with his excellent suits and fancy shoes and this very put-together image. He wanted to be like that one day. Only when El Mago looked like this, he wasn't cool anymore, and Elvis tried to recall what the fuck he was doing hanging out with him.

"You talked to me about loyalty, Elvis; well, this is what loyalty means. Do not make me think I am wrong about you," El Mago said, his voice low.

The voice of a gentleman, which was what he was.

A dangerous one.

He was Elvis's god, but a dark god. The god of the Old Testament, that, as a good Catholic boy, he'd learned to fear.

"You're not." Elvis glanced down, fixing his eyes on the ashtray. "I'll talk to him, don't you worry."

"Good. I want this done quick, you understand me?"

"Sure I do."

"You do not need to type reports. I will call you."

El Mago wiped his lips with his napkin, then tossed it on the table and stood up.

"Oh, and Elvis?" El Mago said, giving his cigarette one last drag before dumping it into the ashtray. "El Gazpacho is out of the unit."

"What do you mean out?"

"Out. Gone. He did not have what it takes," El Mago opened his wallet and tossed a couple of bills on the table. "Finish your cake and get your crew working."

7

MAITE STOPPED BY the printer's shop the next day right after work. She went because she was still holding on to the faint hope that she might get in touch with Leonora and obtain her money. If this proved to be the case, then she could hold off on asking her mother for a loan.

She couldn't take the bus anymore. It was a cesspool of depraved monsters. When Maite chanced to get a seat, then she was safe. But if she had to stand, it was an invitation for every pervert in the city to rub himself against her or try to touch her ass. Every female from the age of twelve to sixty-five had to endure the same treatment, and there was no recourse, but Maite at least had the possibility of escape. She had her car. And it was stuck with the mechanic because Maite couldn't pay her bill.

Maite had told herself that she would wait and in a month or so she would settle her account with the mechanic, but she was tired of waiting, and she couldn't be taking taxis to work. It was very simple: she needed to pay.

Either her mother or Leonora would help her accomplish that. But her mother nagged her about everything, and the mere thought of having to phone the woman upset Maite's stomach, threatening to give her an ulcer.

Maite pushed open the door of the printer's shop and walked in. She had expected to find Rubén alone, like last time, but there was an older man at the register and a teenager. Rubén was stacking boxes on an old, red dolly. He was wearing his overalls and humming a tune.

"Hi," she said, waving at the young man. "Hello."

Rubén stared at her. He put his box down and came from behind the counter. "Hello," he said. "You're back."

"Sorry to bother you like this, but I haven't been able to get a hold of Leonora. I was wondering if you had any other contact information for her. Do you know any other friends who I might talk to?"

"You mean she hasn't returned?" Rubén asked, grabbing a handkerchief that dangled from his pocket and wiping his hands with it.

"No."

"What about her sister, what did she say?"

"She said Leonora wanted money and she wouldn't give it to her, and that's the last she heard from her. Look, I wouldn't be bothering you if—"

"Rubén, I don't pay you to be meeting with your girlfriends during your shift. Get those boxes ready. Mr. Pimentel is coming in fifteen minutes," the older man said, resting both hands firmly on the counter and giving the young man a stern look.

"Yeah, one second," Rubén replied, raising a hand without looking at the shop owner. His eyes were fixed on Maite. He seemed worried. "How long has she been gone?"

"She left Friday night."

"It's Wednesday. That's six days today."

"I can count. What about that . . . that art collective of hers. Would she be there?"

"Asterisk? Why would she be there?"

"Rubén!"

"Yes, one more second," Rubén said quickly, raising his hand again. "Look, I'm real busy today, but can I drop by your apartment tomorrow night? I'll ask around Asterisk about Leonora and tell you what I find out."

"Fine. At six. I have things to do," she lied. She simply didn't want the man knocking at her door at midnight. The super was nosy, and if a man came to visit her late at night and she saw him heading up the stairs with her, she'd be subjected to an interrogation, and she didn't feel like it. Besides, he looked like a hippie, and she was wary of that. Hippies were all a bunch of losers and marijuanos who gave women venereal diseases and organized orgies; that's what the people at her office said. Though, to be fair, Maite was curious about the orgies.

"What's your apartment number?"

"I'm right across from Leonora. Three B."

"Okay."

Rubén headed behind the counter again and began pushing the dolly toward the back of the store. The older man had not shifted an inch and was still standing with his hands planted on the counter, eyeing Maite with suspicion. She clutched her purse and hurried out of the place. Good heavens, what a rude man! But, who knew what Rubén was like. With the plural "girlfriends," maybe he was always bringing women around. Was Leonora one of his girlfriends? She didn't remember seeing him in any of the pictures at the girl's apartment, but then she'd been too busy staring at Emilio Lomelí's photograph to notice any other men.

Emilio Lomelí. *What a great name that is*, she thought, as she evaded a homeless man asking for a coin and managed to board a bus that, mercifully, had an empty seat in the back. She was wedged against a woman who was trying to soothe a baby and a teenager popping gum, but it was better than the alternative.

During the bus ride home Maite pondered whether she should call Emilio. On the one hand, he was an ex-boyfriend, and there was no need to get him involved in this. But it would be a perfect excuse to talk to him again.

Maite's main concern was that she would phone and have to speak to a pesky secretary. She could visualize her easily: pencil skirt, glasses, a no-nonsense attitude. Maybe it wouldn't even be a secretary, but a personal assistant, which sounded much classier. How would she explain who she was and what she wanted to that woman? Maite supposed she could simply say she needed to speak to Emilio about a business matter, but she always got nervous when she talked on the phone, and it was impossible for her to hold a proper conversation with someone she thought was attractive.

Had she been silly when she talked to Emilio the other night? Very likely. *You always give people the wrong impression*, Maite chided herself, nibbling on a nail. She knew she should stop with the chewing of her nails, and she also knew she simply needed to speak on the phone more often, and then she would become more confident. She wished she had money to get her nails done and her hair coiffed. Other women could be confident because they had good nails and good hair, and Maite couldn't even consider getting her hair colored professionally.

Money, money.

The car.

Despite her distaste for phone conversations, Maite had to dial her mother. This was one of the rare cases where it was best for her to actually maintain some distance from the person she was conversing with.

As soon as Maite walked into her apartment, she headed for the phone. Her mother answered at the first ring, and Maite smiled. Someone had told her you could tell when someone was smiling over the phone, that it could be felt in the voice, and she was hoping to sound pleasant and polite, but she had not gotten more than a few words in before her mother interrupted her.

"I'm watching the babies, what is it?" her mother asked.

Maite felt like pointing out that her sister's kids were no longer babies. They could walk around and smear people's clothes with chocolate, after all. She contained herself, maintaining her tremulous smile.

"Listen, Mother, I have the car at the mechanic—"

"Again? I've told you a million times that you need to get rid of that piece of garbage. They took advantage of you when they sold it to you. You should have bought a sensible car, like your sister. You don't see her trying to drive anything ostentatious."

"It's not ostentatious."

"A Volkswagen lasts forever, Maite. You should have bought a Volkswagen."

"Yes, I'm sure it does. But, Mother, I need a small loan to pay off the mechanic's bill. It's almost paid off, except for the last bit. If the guy didn't charge me such high interest—"

"What about the savings box at your job? Don't you deposit money into that?"

"Yes, but they don't give us the money until December, for the holidays. It's June. You know that."

"Your sister never has any trouble making her payments."

Maite's smile faded, her face souring. Her sister was also married and their mother watched her children for free, not to mention that Maite knew for a fact she was always buying the kids toys and clothes.

"You spend too much on rent, that's the real issue. Why do you need two bedrooms? You live alone. For that matter, why must you have an apartment on that street? There're cheaper places."

"It's a central location, Ma."

"Why do you need a car if it's so central?"

"You know what, I can manage," Maite said. "I've got to go."

Her mother started to say something else, but Maite hung up. She stood in the kitchen with her hand on the phone for a couple of minutes before finally walking into the living room. Her parakeet had been happily chirping, but now that Maite approached it, the bird went quiet. The employee from the pet shop where she'd bought the parakeet had told her it could learn how to talk, but it hadn't ever said a single word.

She grabbed a jar with sunflower seeds and fed the bird a few of these through the bars of the cage. The cage was too small for the bird, and its door was kept closed with a bit of red string, but Maite couldn't buy a new one.

Maybe if she asked Diana for the money she could pay the mechanic. Maite did a couple of mental calculations, wondering how much she could push for without seeming excessive. Diana was a good friend, but most of her paycheck went toward her grandmother's care. The old lady suffered from every infirmity known to mankind.

Maite put the jar of sunflower seeds away and walked into the spare room that she whimsically liked to call her "atelier" when she had company. Not that she had much company. She hadn't dated anyone in ages, though she had fantasized more than once about dressing nicely, going to a bar, and bringing a stranger home with her. On one occasion she had put on a good pair of heels and her best coat and done precisely that, but the bar in question was half empty and no man approached her. Why would they? She was nothing to look at.

Maite grabbed an album at random and placed it on the turntable. "Smoke Gets in Your Eyes" began playing. Music and comic books. Why couldn't that be life! Why was life so dull, so gray, so bereft of any surprises?

She sat on her large chair and paged through *Secret Romance*, not really reading any of the speech bubbles, merely staring at the images, admiring Pablo's chiseled jaw and Beatriz's large, tender eyes. With Jorge Luis in his coma, far in the jungle, Pablo was making a play for Beatriz. In the last panel he held her close to him as she looked rapturously at the young man.

They were beautiful, each and every one of the drawings was of an aching perfection. And the jungle was lush and exquisite. The reason she'd bought the parakeet had been this comic book. She had wanted something from the jungle, but a parrot would have been more expensive and larger. Of course, her original idea had been to visit Cuba.

For a month or so Maite had toyed with the idea of touring the Caribbean. The island in her comic book wasn't Cuba, it was imaginary, but it was the closest analogue she could come up with. And it wouldn't be too expensive. They advertised trips to Cuba at a travel agency a few blocks from her workplace. She went as far as buying several guidebooks about the island and a pink bathing suit.

It all came to nothing in the end, like all of Maite's plans. Sure, she told herself she could save enough money if she was thrifty. But there was an unexpected expense, one thing that led to another, which eventually led to nothing.

And now Cuba was as distant as Mars, what with her outstanding mechanic's bill. Maite wished she could get a break just once.

She tried to imagine the jungle and in the sky a yellow moon hanging from the heavens. But then a car honked its horn outside and the parakeet screeched, and the colors of the jungle bled from her feverish mind.

8

ELVIS DECIDED TO tackle the girl's apartment first, in the company of the Antelope. El Güero wasn't too pleased to be left behind in the car, waiting for them, but someone had to stay outside and be ready in case they needed to leave in a hurry. Besides, El Güero was too tall and burly and noticeable to sneak with him into the building. And he was sloppier. Elvis needed to get in and get out.

Normally, Elvis would have staked out the apartment building over several days, taking time to learn what the flow of people was like. Since they didn't have that luxury, he decided to attempt to open the building's lock as quickly as possible. Luckily, a woman in the company of several children was coming out when Elvis and the Antelope approached the building. Elvis held the door open for her. The woman shot him a tired smile, and both Elvis and the Antelope made it in.

When they reached the door of the girl's apartment, the Antelope stood to the side, pretending to light a cigarette and blocking people's view of Elvis from the staircase in case someone walked by. Elvis pried the door open with deft fingers.

Elvis told the Antelope to take the kitchen and the living room, while he surveyed the bathroom and the bedroom. They had an hour for this search mission. More than that might be asking for trouble. It would also be unnecessary, since Elvis held little hope that the camera they needed was inside the apartment. If the girl they were looking for really had disappeared, then she probably had disappeared with the photos El Mago wanted. But there was no harm in being thorough.

Elvis searched under the mattress, in the big dresser and behind it, in the bathroom. He opened the medicine cabinet, looked inside the water tank, and quickly rummaged through the girl's clothes. He peered under the sink, making sure she hadn't taped the camera or film canister to the furniture, like junkies did when they were hiding drugs. He even checked the hem of the curtains. But there were nothing but dust bunnies and a cat hiding under the bed. In the kitchen, the Antelope had gone through the refrigerator and was pulling cans and jars from the cabinets. Elvis noticed someone had been feeding the cat. There was a freshly opened tin set on the floor in the kitchen, by the stove.

"Find anything?" Elvis asked.

"She eats a lot of lentils," the Antelope said, tossing a bag of them on the floor and popping a stick of bubble gum in his mouth. The Antelope chewed too much bubble gum, and he had the disgusting habit of sticking it under the arms of chairs. At least it was better than El Güero's habit of leaving his toenail clippings in the sink.

"Nothing in the bedroom either."

"Fucking boring assignment. You'd think they'd throw us something exciting once in a while."

"Like what?"

"Something where we got to use guns. I'm fucking good with guns. Hey, did you know Sam Giancana is hiding here?"

"What?"

"Giancana! You know, the fucking mobster. He was in bed with the CIA. He's hiding in Mexico and I know where. Right smack in the middle of Coyoacán; he works as a taquero. They should have us take him to the Americans. El Mago is real cozy with the Americans, you know? CIA this and CIA that."

"That's bullshit."

"He is so cozy! I'm not lying."

"I mean you're bullshitting me about Giancana. You're always talking shit. You never check anything out, flapping your mouth about whatever those potheads whisper to you," Elvis said. He wasn't wrong. A lot of the Antelope's work consisted of hanging around full-on junkies and hippies who talked about weed all day long, trying to catch whatever rumors he could. Sometimes there was some truth to the rumors, and sometimes it was stories about mobsters who were making tacos de suadero.

The Antelope shrugged. "But if it were true it would be better than this tagging shit we're doing. I'm damn good at target practice and never get to shoot anyone. Instead, there's this fucking busywork, which, frankly, should be for bitches. We're supposed to be *elite*."

"It ain't busywork. And who you gonna shoot?"

"I dunno. Giancana."

"Giancana, Giancana, like you ever shot anyone."

"I killed someone."

"Yeah, like who?"

"Some fucker," the Antelope muttered. "Problem is when you shoot the wrong fucker you end up like me."

The Antelope was quiet and stopped chewing his gum. Elvis knew, thanks to that, that he was actually serious about something, his eyes looking at a point above Elvis's shoulder. After a few seconds the Antelope resumed loudly chewing his gum and grabbed a can of angulas from a shelf.

"Man, who the fuck eats this shit? You ever had this shit?" he asked. "I think El Gazpacho eats this garbage!"

Elvis moved into the living room, to continue the search and let the Antelope keep talking to himself. In the end, the apartment yielded nothing.

It was too early to try their luck with the priest, so Elvis agreed that they should go have a bite, and the three of them stopped at a taco stand. El Güero wanted to eat at a cantina, but Elvis said no. He wasn't going to have drunk operatives messing up his assignment.

The Antelope ordered three tacos de cachete and began talking about how anyone who had half a brain and listened carefully knew that the CIA killed Marilyn Monroe by stuffing heroin pills up her ass. Ass death! Elvis didn't pay attention to the Antelope's babblings because he was always talking crazy shit. There was some truth mixed with the lies, but you don't go wading into a swimming pool filled with vomit to try to drink fresh water. Then the Antelope swore that Kennedy had been murdered by Johnson and his goons over El Chamizal, and that's when Elvis began singing "Love Me Tender" inside his head—he could sing a dozen Presley songs by heart and sounded pretty decent, like a well-trained parrot—because there was no way to stomach this bullcrap.

Around five they parked across the street from the priest's four-story building, which was close to the Alameda, and began their watch. Elvis fiddled with the screwdriver in his pocket. El Mago always said knives and fists were better than guns. He taught his men to shoot, but not needlessly.

Some guys, like the Antelope, they felt like they were real machos with a gun in their hands, and Elvis couldn't deny he had loved the idea of owning a weapon, the bullets as enticing as candy to a child. But the unit leader was the one with a firearm—though Elvis suspected that El Güero had a hidden gun somewhere in his room—and the firearm available was therefore El Gazpacho's gun, and he didn't want to grab it.

Not yet. To do so would mean he was taking El Gazpacho's place, and he couldn't accept that El Gazpacho had left the unit. He kept thinking El Mago had lied and even came up with explanations about why he'd lie, but they were all garbage excuses.

He wondered if El Gazpacho was back with his family. He knew El Gazpacho had an older sister. They were not supposed to discuss personal details, but it was hard to stay tight-lipped all the time, and although nobody dwelled on their families or previous work, you eventually learned something about everyone.

Elvis knew El Gazpacho liked strawberry milkshakes and playing dominoes, that he loved Japanese movies and smoked quality cigarettes. They had conducted many meaningless conversations, discussing what actresses they'd like to fuck—Raquel Welch topped their list—and the cities they wished to visit—for Elvis, it was obviously Memphis; for El Gazpacho it was Seville. He'd almost forgotten Spain and he wanted to go back, but God knew when he would. He spoke nostalgically about its streets and smells. Elvis didn't want to return to Tepito, but he told El Gazpacho stories about his old neighborhood.

In between all this insignificant banter there had emerged some truths and real camaraderie.

El Gazpacho had been his friend, even if Elvis had never learned his real name.

Maybe he should go to mass and light a candle for him, ask a saint to protect El Gazpacho and ensure he healed and went back to his family safely.

Mass. Elvis wasn't even sure why he was thinking about a mass when he was sitting in a car with two other men, waiting to interrogate a priest. Maybe, he decided, it would be good to stop by a church and light the candle immediately after this assignment was over. God might understand, or at least feel a little less pissed off, if Elvis showed a little contrition and placed a few bills in the collection box.

The priest didn't get home until nine, but they waited until close to eleven, when most of the lights in the building had gone off, to make their way inside. Once again, Elvis picked the appropriate locks, and they marched quietly into the priest's apartment.

There was still a light on in the bedroom. The apartment was very small, and the light spilling from the room and into the combination dining room/living room was enough that they could see their way easily. The priest had the TV on, and they heard a woman talking about how hip, young people drank Nescafé with milk and sugar.

The priest was standing in front of the bathroom sink, in his pajamas and ready to brush his teeth. Elvis was glad to find him like this. He didn't look like much of a priest when he was wearing his fancy pajamas.

"Father Villarreal—" Elvis said. And he might have said something else, because he'd thought about introducing himself all proper-like, the way El Mago might do it. Like a gentleman. But the fucking priest took one look at him and rushed out of the bathroom.

Not only that, but the fucker grabbed an old-fashioned razor that had been resting by the sink, and Elvis had mere seconds to throw himself aside for fear of being sliced in the stomach. It wasn't that the priest knew what he was doing with the razor, but that he *didn't*. He was waving his hands in front of him and spinning around like a wind-up toy, but such chaotic stupidity could be dangerous.

Elvis thought about tackling him, then reconsidered. The Antelope was equally startled and equally put off by the guy, and he didn't try to block the man's path when he stormed forward, blade in hand.

"Grab him!" Elvis yelled and ran behind the man and into the living room. For a second he feared the fool would actually make it outside.

But then El Güero's lumbering form emerged in front of the priest. The man hesitated in his flight, and that second of hesitation was enough. El Güero caught the priest's hand and twisted it. Father Villarreal yelped in pain and dropped the razor. Then El Güero punched the man in the head.

The priest fell to the floor and moaned softly.

El Güero was getting ready to kick the man in the head. "Hey, wait," Elvis said. "We're supposed to talk to him."

"Fuck it, this prick tried to cut me," El Güero complained.

"Drag him back to the bedroom."

El Güero grumbled something about pricks and marshmallows. Elvis bent down and picked up the razor and followed both of them into the bedroom.

"I don't have any money," the priest said as El Güero shoved him in the direction of the bed.

"Sit down," Elvis told Villarreal. "Antelope, check the room."

The Antelope nodded and began opening drawers. El Güero stood at the doorway, arms crossed, blocking any exit. The priest sat on the bed, clutching the covers with one hand. In a corner, a picture of an eagle looked down at Elvis, serving as the only decoration. The apartment seemed simple, but the television was new, and by the bed Elvis spotted a pair of good leather shoes. Maybe the priest didn't have cash lying around, but he had enough bills to purchase certain fancy goods. Perhaps he'd passed the contribution plate around his congregation.

"Father, where's the camera?"

"I don't know anything about a camera," Villarreal said, and he began rubbing his head and wincing, like it hurt real bad. Theatrical bastard. El Güero hadn't roughed him up *that* much, not really.

"You know something about a girl, no? Leonora? Where is she?"

The priest stared at Elvis as if Elvis had said a dirty word. "I have no idea."

"I thought you guys were friends. You going to deny you know her?"

"I know her."

"Then where's she at?"

"It doesn't mean I keep track of her every movement."

"Easy, Father. No need to get riled up. We're *dialogating*," Elvis said, trying to sound the way El Mago sounded.

"Dialogating," the priest said, practically sneering at Elvis.

Elvis didn't like this fucker's face, nor the way he was looking at Elvis. Respect. That's what El Mago said you had to instill. Not fear, respect. Though fear could be an easy shortcut to respect. Elvis didn't have all night to be talking to the priest; he couldn't hold his hand and warmly beg him to talk a bit. Not only because

El Mago was waiting to hear from them, but because El Güero was standing at the doorway, smirking at Elvis.

Elvis knew that if he did anything wrong that blond dickhead was going to tell El Mago every little detail. He didn't want to give El Güero the satisfaction. Besides, Villarreal had that smug look of a man who has never had the shit properly beaten out of him, and Elvis felt the sudden need to teach him what was what, man of the cloth or not.

Elvis slammed his fist against the priest's face, hard enough that the priest fell back on the bed with a sharp groan.

"When's the last time you saw her?" Elvis asked coolly.

The priest groaned, and Elvis repeated the question, curling his fingers into a fist again.

"Tuesday morning," Villarreal said, sitting up again, a hand pressed against his bleeding nose, his eyes glued on Elvis's fist.

"Go on," Elvis said.

"I don't know what you want me to say."

"Everything. What time she was here, how long she stayed, what the hell she was wearing."

The Antelope had opened a drawer and found a Bible in it, which he was flipping through. The priest looked at him sharply. "Don't touch that," he said. "There's nothing there."

"Hey," Elvis said snapping his fingers. The priest turned to him again. "You're talking to me, not him."

"My nose is bleeding," the priest complained.

"Let's cut him in the belly," El Güero suggested. "That'll teach him about bleeding."

"Damn right," the Antelope said, nodding.

Of course that would be El Güero's first suggestion. He probably thought turning the priest into a human pincushion would be a great idea, but that was not what Elvis was aiming for.

"Talk to me."

"I need to get gauze and rubbing alcohol. I'm bleeding all over the place," the priest insisted.

"Cut open his gullet," El Güero said.

"Go look around the living room for the fucking camera," Elvis ordered, then he turned to the priest. "You can worry about your damn gauze later."

El Güero snapped his mouth shut, but he didn't move from the doorway. The priest frowned, looking at his bloody fingers. "She stopped by late Sunday night. I was already asleep when she rang the bell," he muttered.

"What did she want?"

"Spiritual advice."

"Go on."

"Leonora found out something important, something about a politician. She was thinking of talking to a reporter but she was also scared and she was worried it would affect people she knew. She was afraid of the blowback."

"What politician?"

"She didn't quite say it, but I suspected Echeverría."

Echeverría. Motherfucking President Echeverría. Elvis frowned. "What about Echeverría?"

"She didn't *say* Echeverría. I suspected Echeverría because she stayed over . . . she was afraid of going back to her apartment and she stayed over, and Tuesday I heard her talking on the phone with someone and she mentioned the Hawks."

Elvis could feel the stares of the other men in the room. The Antelope had stopped riffling through drawers and had grown still. El Güero was still standing by the doorway.

"Where's she now?"

"I told you, I really don't know. When I realized how scared she was . . . how messed up this could get . . . I . . . I told her she couldn't stay here anymore. I told her maybe she'd be better off going over to Jackie's."

"Who's 'Yak'?"

The priest sighed. He was sitting at the edge of the bed, his hands clasped together, looking down at the floor. The priest was young. Elvis didn't know they could make priests this young. He was used to old men; wrinkled, ancient priests. This one looked like he might be Elvis's age. Fresh out of the seminary in Monterrey.

Elvis wondered why Villarreal hadn't gone to the Tec like all the other rich little boys there, instead picking the priesthood. Of course Elvis couldn't be sure the priest was a rich boy, but what he read in the file sure indicated that, and there were all the telltale details in the room. The TV, the silk pajamas, the Italian shoes. Even the way the priest talked. El Mago had taught Elvis to notice stuff like that. Okay. Maybe not rich. Upper middle class. But for sure he hadn't grown up in a vecindad.

"Jackie. Jacqueline. She's the leader of Asterisk. It's an art collective."

"How could this Jackie help her?"

"Jacqueline . . . she's into radical stuff. She advocates for armed struggles and . . . look, Jacqueline doesn't leave her house without a gun. She sleeps with it under her pillow and carries it in her purse. If Leonora was going to be safe somewhere, it was with Jackie. At least she has a weapon and I don't."

"So she's with that Jackie then?"

"I'm not . . . I don't think she is."

"Why not?"

"I'm not even supposed to get involved with this kind of shit," Villarreal said, raising his voice.

"And what are you supposed to get involved with, padrecito?" Elvis asked. *He* didn't raise his voice. Nothing good would come of that, except a screaming match, which he was trying to avoid. No, he kept his voice steady and low. "You're a commie troublemaker. And all commies want to get into some very bad shit, don't they? So tell me: why don't you think she's with Jackie, huh?"

Villarreal glared at Elvis, but he moderated his tone. "I left to run a few errands, and when I came back Leonora was gone. Then Jackie calls and asks if Leonora's around. I thought she was with her."

"She's not at her apartment, so who could she be with?"

He shrugged. "She had a boyfriend. Emilio Lomelí. And she has a sister. I really don't know."

"Did she leave anything with you?"

"No. If she had, I would tell you."

"I'm not sure I believe that."

"I don't care what you believe."

Elvis stepped forward and slowly extended his arm and the razor, inching it close to the man's face. The priest began trembling. He was indeed young. Boyish, even. Elvis could have been the priest and the priest could have been Elvis. But Elvis had come from Tepito and the priest had come from Monterrey, and they had followed entirely different trajectories.

Luck, that's what it was. Good and bad luck. El Gazpacho had carried a rabbit's foot for luck and see where it got him. El Mago was right: you made your own luck.

"You better care I believe you," Elvis said.

The priest didn't reply. He was staring at Elvis, terrified.

"You sure you don't have the camera? The pictures?"

There were tears in the priest's eyes. His incipient bravado was melting. "No, no," he mumbled. "No, I don't."

"Absolutely sure?" Elvis whispered, and the razor was now so close to the man's eye he could have sliced it clean off with a bit of pressure. Carved it out and left a bloody hole behind.

"I'm sure," the priest whispered back. "I swear on the Virgin of Guadalupe."

Elvis lowered the razor and nodded. "I believe you, and because I believe you we are going to break your teeth. But if you put up a fight or if you yell for help, we are going to kill you." He glanced at the Antelope. "Help keep him quiet. Güero, pummel him."

El Mago always said you had to watch when a man was being killed. Cowards looked away. But since this wasn't a murder, Elvis let his gaze wander toward the mirror in the bathroom, staring at his reflection while El Güero's fists connected with the priest's flesh. Despite Elvis's warning, he was sure the young man would have screamed, but the Antelope had pressed the pillow against his face.

It was quick work, at any rate, and Elvis was grateful for that. He had never taken any pleasure in torture. Grabbing a telephone directory, slamming it against a man's back, it held no appeal. Nor did any of the other tricks of the trade he'd learned about: electric shocks to the feet, wrapping someone's head in a plastic bag. This at least was relatively clean. Fists, blood.

Elvis stared into the mirror, saw his black hair parted to the side. Sometimes he looked like a darker Elvis Presley, skin tanned, and sometimes he didn't look like the musician at all. Right now, he thought for a moment he looked like El Mago. Something about the tilt of the mouth. And his eyes were all black, even if no human eye can really be black.

Elvis walked into the bathroom and opened the cabinet above the sink. He found the gauze and the rubbing alcohol and returned to the bedroom. El Güero and the Antelope had finished and were wiping their hands clean. The priest was on the bed, bleeding copiously. The pillow had been discarded at some point and tossed outside the room. On the bedspread Elvis spotted two teeth. The priest moaned and turned around, hiding his mangled face, and the teeth fell to the floor.

Elvis tossed the bottle of rubbing alcohol and the gauze onto the bed. "You don't tell anyone we were here."

On the way back to the apartment El Güero said they should stop for tacos de carnitas. Elvis ignored him. The stench of fresh blood clung to El Güero's clothes, infecting the car, even though the men had quickly tidied themselves up before stepping out of the apartment. Elvis didn't want to go sit in a food joint, holding a greasy plastic plate in one hand and a beer in another.

He fiddled with the radio, looking for a melody. And there it was, Los Apson singing a cover of "Satisfaction." Yes, baby. Let's rock, 'cause the fucking car smelled of pain.

9

SHE HAD FANTASIZED, when she moved into her own apartment, about what it would be like when she was able to organize parties and invite her friends over. She pictured cocktails, good music, charming conversation, beautiful people in attendance. But Maite seldom had anyone over. When her mother visited, she made sure to point out any new item Maite had purchased and complain it was a needless expense. Why should she buy new curtains? What was wrong with the old table? As a result, Maite tried to invite her mother to her apartment as little as possible.

As for gentlemen callers—Maite liked to refer to men as such; it sounded more dignified—she hadn't slept with anyone in ages. The last man in her apartment had been a disdainful clerk she'd brought over a couple of times and who commented on the size of her record collection, stating it seemed to him ridiculous to have so many books and records when you could simply turn on the TV. Maite had a large collection of imported records in English rather than the Spanish-language covers everyone bought at a cheaper price, but just like her mother the man couldn't understand why she'd throw away her money on them. They were different, Maite tried to tell him. And he said, what's the difference if you don't speak English? What does it matter who's singing? She said there's a difference between Badfinger singing or Los Belmonts. And the album art, she said. And the texture. And the liner notes, waiting to be deciphered one day. Besides, Los Dug Dug's sang in English even if they were from the north of Mexico. You couldn't just buy a Spanish cover of them, even though they had started out as cover artists, like everyone else.

The man had no idea what she was talking about. She said she was a collector, and collecting was like hunting, a sport. The man thought she was mad. A song was a song. You didn't need all three versions of it.

That's why Maite was ready with her purse under her arm at six p.m. When Rubén knocked, she opened the door and without any hesitation locked it behind herself and started walking down the stairs. She wasn't inviting him in for coffee so he could judge her curtains or her records. This also ensured the super wouldn't gossip about Maite. He looked too much like a hippie to be decent company.

They went to a coffee shop a block away. The walls were lemon yellow, as were the booths, and the pictures on the walls were shabby black-and-white photos of Italy. She didn't like the place, but it was better than heading into an ice cream shop, as though they were boyfriend and girlfriend.

She asked for a coffee, he ordered a Sidral Mundet. Rubén had changed from his overalls into a t-shirt and jeans. He looked more presentable this way, though he'd hardly qualify for the role of the hero in any of Maite's comic books. He had that Che Guevara style that was popular with students of the UNAM. It was unappealing.

"Then she hasn't come back?" Rubén asked, taking a sip of his soda.

Maite reached for the sugar basin, which had a crack clearly showing where it had been clumsily glued back together, and measured a spoonful of sugar. "No. Did you go to that place? The Asterisk?"

"She hasn't been there. I'm worried. I talked to Jacqueline, who sort of runs Asterisk, and she said she talked on the phone with Leonora, and Leonora told her she had information on the Hawks."

"Who exactly are the Hawks?"

"Don't you read the paper?" Rubén said, looking scandalized by her lack of knowledge.

Maite picked up her coffee cup daintily and took a sip. "Excuse me, I work all day long."

"So do I. I still find the time to glance at a paper, especially these days when we've got the government engaged in vicious repressive activities."

"I bet you're one of these people Leonora likes to bail out," she said, trying to guess how many mug shots they'd taken of him.

Rather than appearing abashed, the young man looked proud, raising his hairy chin. "Yeah, she's helped me out," Rubén said. "So what? I print leaflets with political cartoons on them. The government? They've got roving gangs of thugs beating students up. Who do you think attacked us when we were demonstrating?"

"I thought those were your anarchist buddies."

"Very funny. So you don't read the papers but you still spout the government's line? It figures. How are you even hanging out with Leonora, anyway?"

Rubén gave her a suspicious look, as though he thought maybe they were in one of those James Bond films and Maite was a spy.

"We're not best friends, if that's what you're wondering," Maite said. "We know each other from the building."

"Then why are you so interested in finding her?"

"Because I'm watching her cat. What? Do you think I'm one of your Hawks?"

"You never know," Rubén said. "But no. They're all men, and they're all thugs. They were under the command of Alfonso Martínez Domínguez, our recently ousted regent—in case you were too *busy* working to know that name. They like to sic them at us when they think we're getting out of line."

"Yes, I know what you mean now," she said, her spoon rattling against the cup as she added more sugar. The coffee was sweet enough, but she was trying to do something with her hands. This man was terribly irritating. She felt like slapping him. "But the Hawks are not supposed to be real."

"Who told you that?"

"It's what they say around my office."

"The Hawks are the ones who attacked the people outside the Cine Cosmos. *Someone* decided to massacre students. It wasn't ghosts," he said, sounding petulant.

"I didn't say it was ghosts, just that they're not supposed to be real. Anyway, Leonora had information on the Hawks. What kind of information?"

"We don't know. It was photos."

"Her ex-boyfriend was looking for her camera," Maite muttered, the memory of Emilio Lomelí burning bright in her mind. Now that was a real man, not this print shop employee moonlighting as an activist.

"Emilio?" Rubén asked. He looked pretty shocked by her words.

"He stopped by to see her, and I let him into her apartment because he wanted her camera, but he couldn't find it so he left. But it doesn't really mean anything."

"You think it's a coincidence? Leonora goes missing after she tells us she has some photos and Emilio is asking about her camera? What do you think are the odds?"

Well, when he put it like that, it didn't sound very likely, but she detested the tone he was using. As if Maite was an idiot because he bought a paper now and then.

"I don't know. He seemed like a decent guy. He left me his card, in case Leonora stopped by. If he had anything to do with her disappearance, he wouldn't have left his card."

"I bet he knows something. And it's a place to start digging. Maybe you should give him a call."

"Me?" Maite asked, the spoon slipping from her fingers. She gripped the sugar basin instead.

"You just said he gave you his card."

"Yes. But—"

"People don't go vanishing off the face of the Earth for no reason. Leonora must be in some kind of trouble, and we need to help her. Now this guy, maybe he knows something."

"Fine, let's say he does, and then let's say it's our business—"

"Of course it's our business."

"But if it's a missing person case, then the police—"

"The Hawks work for the government. The police and the army, they let the Hawks shoot at us. There were police cars all lined up nicely down the avenue with their megaphones, but they weren't there to stop them. They were there to ensure they could kill with impunity."

"But they ousted the regent over that business, didn't they? You said he was ousted."

"The president kicked him out, yeah, but it was so he could blame all this on someone. Fuck, maybe he even wanted the beatings to get out of hand precisely so he could oust Martínez Domínguez. Or maybe Martínez Domínguez fucked up, but you can bet that the president was aware of what the Hawks were going to do and he told the cops to stand down. Anyway, it's a repeat of Tlatelolco, and those pigs can't be trusted."

In the papers, columnists accused communist foreigners of corrupting Mexico's youth and attempting to destroy the nation. The cops were innocent, lawful citizens doing their jobs. Perhaps it wasn't true, but it made Maite's skin prickle with dread, because no one wanted a repeat of '68. That had been a bloody mess. People whispered snipers hired by the government had opened fire. Student riots had threatened the Olympics, and the government had quelled them by force. People whispered, and Maite tried not to listen. But still she heard things here and there. She couldn't drown out reality.

"I'm not sure I—"

"Aren't you worried about Leonora?" Rubén asked.

"The cops—"

"The cops can fuck themselves!"

"Will you let me finish a sentence?" Maite asked, shoving the sugar basin away.

They stared at each other for a minute. He looked like a child who'd had his knuckles rapped, and this gave Maite some satisfaction.

"I'm not going to contact the cops. God knows I don't want to be talking to any policeman! What I was trying to say is her family might get hold of the cops, and then it wouldn't look too good if we're nosing around. Besides, even if this is our business, why am I supposed to phone Mr. Lomelí? Why not you? You seem to know the guy."

"He'd hang up on me," Rubén said. "We don't like each other. I broke his nose."

"Why?"

"He put the moves on Leonora back when she was my girlfriend. She ended up dumping me."

Maite couldn't blame the girl for improving her love life, but it still made her uncomfortable to picture Emilio Lomelí as the kind of man who went around sweeping other men's girlfriends off their feet. It didn't square with her image of him. She had cast him in the role of the romantic hero, not the lothario, though lotharios could be fun. Take Pablo from *Secret Romance*. True, before meeting Beatriz he had been slipping in and out of the beds of countless beauties, but only because Magdalena Ibarra had perished in that dreadful scuba diving accident. Perhaps it was the same for Emilio.

"I'm sorry about that," Maite said.

Rubén shrugged. "It was a while back."

"You two study together?"

"We used to. We weren't in the same faculty, but we were both at the UNAM. I left a year ago."

"You obviously still care about her."

"We're friends now."

Maite didn't get that. People being friends after a breakup, especially a bad one like this one must have been. She could have never been friends with Cristóbalito after what happened between them. One time, two years ago, while walking down Bucareli, she'd thought she'd seen him coming in her direction, and she had been possessed by an irresistible desire to run. She dashed into an alley and promptly vomited up her guts there, on top of a pile of wet cardboard.

She had been terrified of him laying eyes on her, of seeing the disappointment in his face, her paltry charms having grown paltrier in the years since they'd been lovers. That night, at home, she pinched the flabby skin of her belly and thought about cutting it with a pair of scissors. Then she wept over an issue of *Secret Romance*.

She supposed such encounters didn't rattle men. Besides, Rubén was young. He was in his early twenties. He still had possibilities.

"Something bad has happened to Leonora. If Emilio has any idea where she is or what happened to her, then I want to know. And I think you want to know too, no?" Rubén asked.

Well, yes, obviously. There was the practical question of the money Leonora owed her, but also the fact that Maite wasn't going to be stuck eternally taking care of that cat. But she was also plain curious. She wondered what the girl was up to. Most of all, it was a great excuse to chat with Emilio Lomelí.

Maite grabbed a paper napkin and began tearing it into strips. A bored waitress behind the counter switched on a radio and Los Shain's began playing.

"What would I even tell him?"

"Tell him what you told me. That Leonora hasn't come back and you're looking for her. And don't mention me. Like I said, the guy hates me. If he thinks I'm the one looking for her, he won't say a peep. He's a spiteful bastard."

"That bad?"

"Oh, yeah. I broke his nose. Well, he ruined my car."

"How?"

"He paid someone to steal it and drive it directly into a telephone pole. I can't prove it and even if I could it wouldn't matter, but it was him."

Maite began rolling the strips and turning them into tiny balls of paper, sliding them to rest in the center of the table, and thought about Beatriz, who was desperately trying to find out what had happened to Jorge Luis, and poor Jorge Luis in a coma. It was possible something similar had happened to Leonora. She could be held by a shadowy villain in an old mansion. The idea of drifting into one of the storylines from her comic books appealed to Maite immensely.

She looked up at Rubén and shoved a ball of paper in his direction. The waitress had switched off the radio, still looking perfectly bored.

"I'll give him a call."

"That's great, thanks."

He smiled. Although he wasn't good looking and she didn't quite like him, she wondered what would happen if she asked him to walk her home to her apartment and invited him in. It was that old fantasy of behaving badly, the thought of a stranger between her thighs. She didn't know how other people did that sort of thing. But she didn't really want him. She was merely bored, and the memory of Emilio Lomelí had ignited a sharp erotic impulse that made her cheeks warm. It was similar to that feeling she got sometimes when she stood in front of the newsstand and glimpsed the adult comic books on sale there. Westerns filled with women with huge breasts. It was trash, the lot of it.

They left the coffee shop. It was raining, a drizzle, and they were walking under the awnings taking their time to reach her building. Or at least she was taking her time, and he wasn't rushing her.

"You really think the Hawks beat those students just so the president could kick the regent out?"

"I know it sounds odd, but Martínez Domínguez was Ordaz's man. When Ordaz picked Echeverría to succeed him, it was Martínez Domínguez who wrote his speeches, at least before Echeverría turned on Ordaz. It could be the other way around, that Martínez Domínguez wanted to weaken the president. The PRI is a single party but that doesn't mean it's united. Ordaz and his favorites, they're not the same as Echeverría. They're the old guard. I would say Echeverría is worse, he's sneakier. He drinks agua de chía or horchata at parties to make you think he's not one of those stiff pricks who imports brandy and champagne. But I know he mails a crate of Dom Pérignon to the director of *Novedades* every Christmas. He wears a guayabera to an official function to show that he's oh-so-Mexican, telling anyone who'll listen that he's firmly against Yankee imperialism, but he provides intel to the Americans."

"Then it's infighting."

"Sure. Unless Echeverría and Martínez Domínguez jointly decided to quash the protesters. The CIA is terrified of communists in Latin America and Mexico is dangerously close to Cuba."

"It all sounds very complicated."

"I'm not saying it's one way or another; everyone has a favorite theory."

"What's your favorite one, then?"

"Mine?" the young man said with a shrug. "They want us dead, period."

Maite wondered how someone could say such grim things and look aloof, but her companion managed it. For a second she thought about calling this whole thing quits, but with each step she took her excitement built a little. Rather than being worried, she was invigorated.

It was like in the comics. It was like her words were rendered inside speech bubbles.

"What do I do after I talk to Emilio?" Maite asked. "I'd drop by your shop again, but I don't think your boss likes it when you have visitors."

"He's a grouch. But it's a steady job. I can stop by and see you on Saturday if you're around. Lunchtime okay?"

"I don't have plans," Maite said and thought that if she wanted to ask him to come in, she could do it then. She'd have to politely dismiss him after that, though. She'd have to say, "Sorry, young man, I don't think this ought to turn serious."

She could tell Rubén what Cristóbalito had told her: We can't have a future together. But she didn't want to think about Cristóbalito. She wanted to savor this chance to lose herself in a different sort of story.

Rubén and Maite parted by her building's doorway with a polite goodbye, and she climbed the steps quickly. Once she walked into her apartment that sense of fantasy, of her atoms being suddenly composed of thousands of Ben Day dots, evaporated. It was the sight of her humdrum environment that brought her crashing down to reality. She noticed the dishes that she'd let pile in the sink and the cheap linoleum in the kitchen. In the apartment above her the neighbor's children were running around like a herd of elephants again.

God! The world was terribly ugly! Maite quickly made her way into her atelier, the sight of the books on the shelves soothing her and yet, at once, her anxiety seemed to rebound as she wondered what she'd tell Emilio Lomelí. She couldn't call him now, but in the morning she would, and she didn't want to sound like a fool.

She picked a record—"Blue Velvet," the Prysock cover. Prysock made three minutes feel like an hour—his voice slowed down time. She began scribbling a script for herself on a notepad. When the song finished, she played it again and kept on writing. Then, when she was done, she rehearsed the whole conversation three times. She wrote herself a handful of lines, but she worried about the emphasis she should put on each word.

"Good morning, I'd like to speak to Mr. Lomelí. Oh, he's not there? Could you tell him Maite Jaramillo phoned him? It's about his camera," she said.

She assumed that Lomelí would have a secretary and also that a very complicated introduction would confuse the secretary and put her off. Besides, she didn't want to be an alarmist and say, "Your ex-girlfriend is missing." No, the camera was a good enough excuse. She'd simply tell him, when he called her back, that she hadn't found the camera, and she hadn't been able to talk to Leonora either.

Maite wrote herself a few more lines. These would guide her conversation with Emilio, though the more she wrote, the more the topic diverged from Leonora. She wrote herself lines that sounded like dialogue from *Secret Romance*.

She played "Blue Velvet" a fourth time, the needle gliding across the record's surface, the volume pumped up higher, and went to get her box of treasures. She laid out all of them on top of her vanity, lining them up. The Italian lace fan, the broken violin bow, a child's tiny shoe, the plaster statuette of San Judas Tadeo.

Maite felt, in that moment, a pure, unadulterated bliss as she pressed the sheets of papers with her scribblings against her chest. All those objects upon her vanity were secrets. She had peered into the soul, the life, of another human being, and she had cut out a part of them and they'd never know it. Oh, it was bliss to be able to walk through the city and tell herself, *They think I'm an ordinary secretary, but I sneak into the homes of people and steal from them.* It was always such a delight to remember that.

But now . . . now perhaps she had more! Though Leonora's disappearance had irked Maite, it now excited her. It guaranteed an escape from boredom. Nothing like this had happened to her, after all. It was like opening a new issue of a comic book. Who were Rubén and Emilio? What role would they play in the story? What would the next panel say?

10

ELVIS DIDN'T BOTHER going to bed. He slept on the couch, knowing the call would come early. It always did when El Mago was restless. And truth be told, Elvis was restless too; he kept thinking all kinds of junk. First he thought about the priest they'd fucked up and wondered if that was a major sin or a minor one. He tried to calm himself down by considering more pleasant stuff, but ended up with Cristina stuck in his head, remembering the exact color of her hair and how soft her skin felt under the palm of his hand. She'd been so very pretty, so very delicate, like lace and moonlight.

It was no good when he got thinking about Cristina. It always led down a bad road because he began questioning whether he should have left her. Not that he'd wanted to stay with those crazy fuckers from the cult, but he could have asked her to go with him. He could have and he didn't; he took off on his own.

Normally, when Elvis was all messed up like that, anxious and sleepless, he'd talk to El Gazpacho, and they'd end up at an all-night restaurant, discussing nonsense, or they listened to music from The Beatles and talked it out over a few beers. But El Gazpacho was gone and Elvis kept waiting for the call, kept waiting for El Mago, kept hoping to fall asleep and failing.

The phone rang, and Elvis pressed the receiver against his ear.

"Fifteen minutes," El Mago said.

Elvis hadn't undressed. He ran a comb through his hair and splashed water on his face.

He grabbed his screwdriver and the two tiny pieces of metal he liked to use in a pinch to open doors. The lock pick kit was nice, but bulkier. He liked jumping back to basics sometimes too. It kept him nimble.

He headed downstairs, and the car turned the corner as he closed the door behind him.

El Mago didn't like talking over the phone. He was paranoid, thinking a line could be bugged, probably because he himself had bugged many lines before, so they talked in coffee shops. When they conversed inside El Mago's car it meant things were not going well. It was a sign, like an approaching thunderstorm, and Elvis felt nervous as soon as he got into the vehicle. If Elvis had slept a scant number of hours, it was obvious El Mago had slept less. Who knew what the fuck was happening, and Elvis couldn't go out and say, "What's wrong?" It didn't work like that with El Mago.

It was raining a little. The windshield wipers went back and forth, providing the only noise inside the car. El Mago didn't switch on the radio, and Elvis would never reach for the dial on his own, not in El Mago's car, so he tucked his hands into his jacket pockets and stared ahead. It was early enough that there was barely any traffic, and the city looked different like this, with rainbows reflected in the large oil slicks by the side of the road and the rolling metal curtains of the shops shut tight. When they passed the fountain of the Diana Cazadora, her bronze arms raised to the heavens, El Mago spoke.

"What is the word of the day?" he asked.

"I didn't pick one yet."

"You should not forget your routines."

"I won't, sir."

"What about your assignment?"

"There was no camera in the woman's apartment," Elvis said. "The priest didn't have the camera either, though the girl stopped by his place, then left. He said she had a boyfriend and a sister. So she might be with them."

"She's not with her sister, and the boyfriend is a dead end too. Don't approach them."

"But the boyfriend, you don't think—"

"Emilio Lomelí," El Mago said. "His family is not only money, but they are also PRI supporters. No, you don't go barking down that avenue."

"And the sister, she also with the PRI?"

"Something like that. Did you find anything else?"

"The girl might have gone to a place called Asterisk, an art cooperative is what the priest called it. There's a woman named Jackie there who was expecting her, but he didn't think she'd made it there. Sounds like the place to look, though, if the boyfriend and the sister are out of the question."

The cadence of the windshield wipers sliding against the glass filled the car for a few seconds as El Mago processed the information. "You will have to go to Asterisk, then, and keep tracing her steps. There is a man at the Habana who El Gazpacho worked with; his name is Justo. He has curly hair, wears glasses, and carries a cigarette behind his ear. He can get you into that place."

"Then you've heard of it?"

"Some. He will know more. A nest of pinkos, at any rate. Justo will know them all."

Elvis nodded. The Habana was notorious for that sort of crowd. Cops were always watching the place. It was almost a game; you couldn't call it government surveillance. More like an old married couple, with the cops eating tortas outside and the reds inside having coffee. A placid relationship. Asterisk might be more of the same.

"There is something else for you," El Mago said, pointing at a manila envelope that had been sitting on the dashboard this entire time but which Elvis had not touched until now, waiting for his cue.

He opened the envelope and took out the sheet of paper. Name, age, place of work, and address. No picture. It was a hastily put together file.

"This is the same building I went to," Elvis said, frowning. "Same apartment?"

"Do not be a fool. Look carefully. It is a different apartment. She is a neighbor."

"Maite Jaramillo. She know something?"

"That is for you to determine. She has been asking questions about Leonora, and she was seen at a shop that prints communist propaganda. I need you to tail her."

"How long?"

"All day, for the next few days."

Christ. That sounded like a full-blown operation. "It's gonna be difficult with only three guys and this other stuff you have me doing."

"That is what leading a squad means, Elvis. You must use your resources strategically. What do you think El Güero and the Antelope are for?"

"I know," Elvis said. "But they don't like me much."

"How did they behave when you went to see the priest?" El Mago asked.

The question was neutral, but like most everything with El Mago this was some sort of test. Elvis stuffed the page back in the envelope. "They wanted to cut him," he said, matching El Mago's tone. Also neutral. "I told them no. You didn't say nothing about gutting him."

"Ever seen a cockfight, Elvis?"

"Not my thing, sir."

"Not mine either, truth be told, but growing up in the countryside you are bound to see one at some point. With its spurs on, a rooster can be quite deadly. Yet it is not really the creature's fault, is it? They are territorial, the birds. Put two together in a palenque and they will tear each other to pieces. It is in their nature. Tell me, what do you think is El Güero's nature? Or the Antelope's?"

He thought of El Güero, who was a complete asshole, a bully, and also a bit of an idiot, and the Antelope, who was annoying and a bit too chatty but not quite so bad.

"You saying they're like roosters?"

"I am saying it is up to you to handle them. I cannot be there, asking those two to play nice. You either have the balls to lead them or they will cut your throat and I will not care."

"I get it," he said, still neutral, because El Mago was also neutral, his words impassive.

El Mago tightened his grip on the steering wheel. "You are one of many poor devils I have plucked from the street. Get working, really working, before I throw you back in the garbage where you came from. Are we clear?"

"Always, sir."

El Mago stopped the car. It was still raining, and they weren't anywhere near the apartment. Elvis stuffed the envelope inside his jacket, found the door handle and opened it, stepping onto the sidewalk.

"Try this word for the day: pawn," El Mago said, before he rolled up his window and drove away.

In that brief sentence, said low and steady, Elvis read the most cutting scorn. It reminded him of his mother, who called him a useless burden, of the teachers who called him stupid, of the older American woman who had used and dumped him, and the cultists he'd befriended who saw in him nothing but free labor. It was all those hateful people and their barbs, distilled and concentrated into a single whole. And in that moment he felt a terrible, roaring anger, and his hands shook.

Water dripped down his back, under his jacket.

Elvis waited five minutes before he raised his arm and hailed a cab. It was still pretty early, so he went and had himself a coffee, then walked to the women's building, a cigarette in his mouth. He had no idea what Maite Jaramillo looked like, so he stood on the other side of the street and watched people stream out of the building, some of them with briefcases in their hands, some of them tugging a child behind them. Office workers, first. Then came the housewives, who were going to the market or taking children to school. When he deemed a prudent amount of time had passed and everyone who had a job or an errand had left, he tossed away his cigarette and crossed the street. He took out his lock pick and opened the front door. Then he walked up the stairs to Maite Jaramillo's apartment.

He knocked twice and had an excuse at the ready. But nobody answered. He let himself inside. A parakeet, in its cage by the window, stared at him across the dining room. It was only then, looking at the bird, that he felt a bit of apprehension.

He shouldn't have done this. El Mago had told him he needed to work together with El Güero and the Antelope, but he had headed here on his own, intent on doing the exact opposite, like a stubborn child, his gut burning with humiliation and a quiet rage.

"Fuck it," he whispered.

Elvis began looking around the apartment, glancing at the pictures on the walls. There was a diploma from a secretarial school showing a young girl in an oval picture. Hair parted in the middle, dark eyes, wide forehead. Nothing much to her.

He'd have to steal a picture of the woman. The others would need a form of visual identification. Maybe there was a photo album somewhere. Photos, photos . . . He also needed to see if this woman had Leonora's camera. He found nothing in the bedroom, only a cheap pink vanity with the usual makeup and random items you'd expect atop it, including a little statue of San Judas Tadeo. In the closet there were three suits, two in navy blue and one in gray, the sort of attire a secretary would wear, along with blouses and dresses.

Maite Jaramillo lived alone, and it was a modest living, by the looks of it. One toothbrush in the bathroom, a pair of nylons hanging from the shower rod, a pink bathrobe with a frayed hem dangling from a hook. It was all very ordinary.

The surprise was the room with all the books and the records. It quite impressed him, to be honest, all those shelves filled top to bottom with things to read and listen to. A lot of her music was in English, imported vinyl that cost more than the refritos by local bands. She was a collector.

On the turntable there was a record. Though he knew he shouldn't, Elvis let the needle drop onto the vinyl. "Blue Velvet" began to play. She had good taste in music, he'd give her that.

He found a stash of comic books, neatly tucked in boxes. He didn't read comic books and was a bit confused by the titles. Romance stories, that's what they were. He didn't even realize anyone printed those. What about her books? Lots of classics with nice bindings, all of them sensible purchases. An encyclopedia, which for some reason was missing the letter H. She also had an *Illustrated Larousse*. It was even the same edition he owned. He smiled, looking at the familiar cover, and then, remembering El Mago's taunt about the word of the day, felt like hurling it out the window.

He didn't dare. Gently, he returned the thick dictionary to the shelf.

Then he saw it, at eye level, the album. "Family Memories" was emblazoned in big, bold letters on the spine. He opened it and flipped through the pictures. It was like looking at those sped-up movies of flowers opening: a baby, a girl, a teenager, and then finally a woman. Maite Jaramillo, this was what she looked like now, with her hair still parted in the middle. Elvis grabbed one of the more recent photos and stuffed it in his pocket.

The cover of "Blue Velvet" the woman owned was really quite nice, and he played it again; he wanted to smoke a cigarette while he listened to it. But she might notice the scent of it. He wondered if the woman ever smoked and if she spent a lot of time in this room. It was dark, a burrow, even if the blinds were open.

He looked at the kitchen and the dining room. He was quick, though it was as pointless as the search inside Leonora's apartment had been. No camera, no film, and nothing that resembled communist literature in the least. If this woman was a pinko, she hid it well. But he doubted it. As far as he could tell, this was a nobody. He would have been tempted to think El Mago had asked him to look into her as a joke, but El Mago didn't joke with this shit.

Well, then he'd have to put a tail on her. The Antelope and El Güero would have to manage that, since he needed to see about La Habana.

As soon as he reached the street, Elvis lit another cigarette. He thought about what El Mago had said, pictured roosters with silver spurs.

11

SHE GOT UP for work earlier than usual and phoned Emilio Lomelí as soon as she reached her office. Instead of speaking to a secretary, she was connected to an answering service. This threw Maite off. She had been ready for a slightly different scenario, but managed to blurt out her message and left both her home phone number and her office number, explaining at what times she might be reached at each location.

As morning turned to noon, she found herself trapped behind her desk. She didn't want to go to lunch for fear the phone would ring and she wouldn't be there to answer it. Diana asked if she wanted to get a torta, but Maite shook her head no, and soon all the secretaries had streamed out of the building, eager for the chance to grab a bite or smoke a cigarette in peace.

Maite was hungry and thirsty. It was too warm inside—the tall windows regularly turned the office into a greenhouse—and they weren't allowed to open the windows because of the rumble of traffic. What she wouldn't give for an office with air conditioning. The lawyers had ceiling fans, but the secretaries were not awarded such a luxury. Maybe it would rain later and that would cool down the city and chill the building.

She pictured the ride back home, the crushing pressure of bodies against her own and the simmering heat of those bodies pressed together; the suffocating stench of the passengers. She wanted her car back, but she couldn't even think of showing her face at the mechanic. He'd start phoning soon, she thought. He'd start asking what the hell was taking so long with her bill this time around.

She didn't want to think about that. Better to think about Emilio Lomelí, about the possibility of a meeting with him.

Maite brushed a strand of hair back into place and took out a compact from her purse, examining herself in the mirror. There were lines under her eyes, but then they'd been there for a long time. Worry lines, sadness lines. She touched her neck; at least it was still smooth. She hated the wrinkled necks of old women: they looked like turkeys. She pictured herself ten, twenty years older. The thought depressed her.

"Excuse me, you're Maite Jaramillo, aren't you?"

She looked up at the man. She hadn't noticed him approaching her desk, and he caught her by surprise. "How do you know?"

"It says so right there on your desk."

Maite glanced at the little plaque with her name. She sighed and snapped her compact shut.

The man standing before her desk wasn't dressed like a lawyer or bureaucrat. You could always tell which one was which, the bureaucrats with their ugly ties and cheap-smelling colognes that boasted scents such as "English Leather," the more well-to-do lawyers recognizable by their imported cigarettes. This guy had a gray jacket and a striped dress shirt. He looked older than her by some ten years, though maybe it was the mustache that aged him.

She assumed he was a client. He was out of luck. The boss had taken the day off. "Mr. Costa is not working today. Do you want me to make you an appointment?"

The man shook his head. "I've come to talk to you, not him," he said.

"Me?"

"Yeah. I'm Mateo Anaya. Dirección Federal de Seguridad," he said and took out his ID, showing it to her.

Maite was poorly informed about many things. Politics, government, crime, she tried to ignore the world's ills. But even an idiot knew what the DFS was. And like any Mexican with two brain cells, Maite also knew it was a lousy idea to talk to the police. Cops were more fearsome than robbers—and sometimes they were robbers too. But the secret police! The secret police were *terrifying*.

She had always lived with one simple philosophy: keep your head down and stay out of trouble. Now here was trouble looking for her.

She licked her lips and managed not to stammer. "What do you need, Mr. Anaya?"

The man took off his jacket and tossed it on her desk, on top of her typewriter. On his index finger he wore a ring with a big green stone. "It's hot in here. Feels like you're a lobster being boiled, don't it? Well, I'll try and be quick. I'm looking for a missing girl. Leonora is the name. Now, I understand you're friends with her. You have any idea where she might be?"

He pulled up a chair, sitting down and leaning back, a grin across his face. Then he took out a box of cigarettes from the front pocket of his shirt.

"I take care of her cat," she mumbled as she watched him light his cigarette.

"Sure, but maybe you've talked to her and stuff. Maybe you know where she is right now. Because, like I said, the girl is missing. Hasn't been seen for days and days, and that's pretty worrisome. Help me out, would you know where she is?"

"Oh, no. I wouldn't know. I hardly know her."

"Maite, come on." The man took a puff from his cigarette, spreading his hands. "You're hanging out with people from Leonora's crowd. They're a rowdy crowd too. Not nice folks, like you. Because you look pretty nice. Good, stable job, no issues with the law. It's the way I like it. Those hippie kids? They're bananas, Maite."

"What?" she asked, so dumbly that the man chuckled.

"You've been seen in the company of subversive elements, darling, is what I'm getting at," he said, as if he were spelling a word out for a child.

"Subversive elements? I don't—"

"Rubén Morales? Ring a bell?"

"I'm not sure. I watch Leonora's cat."

"You're not sure?" the man asked. "Weren't you at a print shop recently, a shop where Morales works? And then, weren't you having coffee with him? Do you want the addresses where you've met him? I got them here somewhere in my jacket."

"No . . . I mean, yes. Yes, I've met Rubén."

"Then you do know Mr. Morales. Tell you what, Mr. Morales has a file. Soon you're going to have a file too. Unless you're friendly. I like friendly people. I'm real friendly myself. A real chatterbox. Or so my colleagues say. What do your friends say? Leonora's your friend, no? And Morales?"

"No! I barely know him . . . her. Both of them, I barely know her."

"Her sister said you know her."

"She's mistaken."

"Is she?"

He held the cigarette between thumb and middle finger and stared at her. She recalled, incongruously, that she'd once read an article in a woman's magazine that said you could determine a man's personality by the way he held a cigarette. But she couldn't remember the personality types. She noticed the yellow nicotine stains on the tip of his fingers and wondered if those could also hold a secret meaning, like a zodiac sign.

Anaya waved his cigarette in the air. "So you're telling me that you're a casual acquaintance of Leonora and somehow the both of you know Mr. Morales? It's a pretty big coincidence."

"It's because of the cat."

"What about the fucking cat?" he asked. He was still smiling. It was a mockery of a grin. Suddenly he leaned forward, stretched out a hand, and caught her right hand with his own, his fingers tight around her wrist. He might be a chatterbox, but clearly he was growing tired of her inane answers.

She began to babble. "I told you already, I'm watching her cat.

She said she was going on a trip and I should watch the cat. That's what I'm doing . . . it's a cat. That's all it was about, that's all we've talked about. I live in her building. I have no idea what she's up to."

She really didn't, and the more the man looked at her, the more her brain became a blank slate, the scant details she did know about Leonora erased from her mind. She stared at him. Her silence seemed to irritate him, and he twisted her wrist. She winced but didn't speak, and he waited, impatient, his fingers digging hard into her flesh.

"You sure you don't know her better than what you're saying?"

She shook her head no.

Diana and two secretaries walked in, laughing. Anaya released her hand and stood up, snatching his jacket and placing it under his arm.

"That better be the truth," he said. "If you're holding out on me, I'll know. See you around, Maite."

He walked out of the office. Diana and the others secretaries gave her curious looks. Maite stood up and with shaky legs managed to make it into the bathroom, where she sat on top of the toilet seat and waited for a good ten minutes. When she returned to her desk she fiddled with a stack of papers. She couldn't concentrate. She was famished and anxious.

"I'm not feeling well," she told Diana, after she gathered her things. "I'm going to head home."

"What's the trouble?"

"My stomach," she lied. "Can you cover for me? Just in case Costa phones and needs something, could you? I'll see you Monday."

"Sure."

Maite smiled and left before Diana could ask about the fellow who had been speaking to her earlier. On Monday, if Diana still remembered him, she'd invent a lie.

When she reached the street, Maite looked everywhere, fearing Anaya might be around, watching her. But she saw no one suspicious. Of course, that didn't mean anything. Surely secret agents didn't dress like in the James Bond movies, with a full tuxedo. Anaya certainly didn't resemble Sean Connery. An agent could look like practically anyone.

What nonsense is that Leonora mixed up in? Maite wondered. It had to be something bad if DFS agents were looking for her.

She needed to hide somewhere in case they were following her. She needed to think. She went into a café de chinos and ordered a bistec and a soda. She rubbed her wrist, feeling the place where the man had dug his fingers into her skin, and wondered if she'd have bruises in the morning.

There, seated at a table and with the soothing noise of a radio playing "Bésame Mucho" softly in the background, she was able to calm her nerves. Maite took out the issue of *Secret Romance* she was carrying in her purse and flipped through it, looking at all those lovely faces and the sentences suspended in speech bubbles. She'd already read the issue, but she read it again.

She gazed at the face of Pablo, the playboy with a heart, and folded and refolded a paper napkin a dozen times absentmindedly. She needed to do something with her hands when she was like this.

A long time passed before she tucked the comic book back in her purse and paid the bill. When she opened the door to her apartment the telephone was ringing. She grabbed it and spoke loudly into the receiver. "Yes? What is it?"

"Miss Jaramillo?"

"Who is this?"

"It's Emilio Lomelí. Sorry to bother you at home, but I called your office and they said you were gone for the day."

She dumped her purse on the kitchen counter and opened her mouth, not knowing what to say. It was him! With Anaya's intrusion and the excitement of the day she'd forgotten about Emilio. She'd hoped he'd call, and now he had. It was such a wonderful moment; she closed her eyes.

"It's no bother, Mr. Lomelí."

"It's nice of you to say that. Anyway, I got your message, and I'm phoning you back. You needed to speak to me?"

"Yes. I was hoping in person, but if you're busy I can understand. I'm sure you—"

"That shouldn't be a problem," he said, interrupting her, and she could feel him smiling through the phone line. "Why don't you stop by my place tomorrow? Say around noon?"

Maite's breath was a ball of fire, caught in her throat, burning bright. She held it there until her tongue felt as though it had been scalded and she spoke. "Yes, yes, of course."

"Do you have a pen?"

She grabbed the pad by the refrigerator and the pen, scribbling the address. When she was done he said a polite goodbye and hung up. She stood there with the receiver in her trembling hand and slowly returned it to its place.

12

EL GÜERO AND the Antelope were not too pleased to learn they had to tail a woman. They had been blissfully enjoying their downtime at the apartment, and now it turned out they needed to do real work, and it wasn't even fun work, like breaking bones. It was the tiresome old watch and report.

"I got a molar aching and need to visit the dentist," the Antelope said. "Was hoping I could go soon."

"You always have a tooth aching when there's surveillance to be done," El Güero muttered. "Take an aspirin and fuck off." Then he turned to Elvis. "Who's this bitch, anyway?"

"I don't know," Elvis said. "It's tied to some other woman who's got the pictures El Mago wants."

"And we're supposed to babysit her."

"El Mago's orders."

"Surveillance is a crock of shit," the Antelope intoned glumly, and he rubbed his cheek, where his molar was aching.

Elvis couldn't deny that. There was nothing fun about spending hours in a car, pissing into a Coca-Cola bottle and watching someone's door. But there was nothing Elvis could do about that, and he shrugged.

"You grab the first shift, then let the Antelope take the next one," Elvis said.

"Where you going?"

"I got something else to take care of."

El Güero and the Antelope needed the car, so Elvis hailed a cab and asked the driver to drop him off a few blocks from the Café La

Habana. It was located on Bucareli and Obregón, therefore assuring itself a steady stream of journalists from the nearby papers, all of them wannabe Hemingways with dubious pedigrees who, on payday, drank too many beers and stumbled home to sleep away their hangovers. There were also Spanish refugees nursing old wounds, wannabe novelists and poets, and plenty of pinkos lured by the specter of Che Guevara, who had once sat in a corner with Fidel Castro and planned a revolution.

As Elvis rounded the café, he noticed the agents watching the building. There were always people keeping tabs on that place due to the clientele. He supposed it was almost a game: every patron knew they were being watched, but the constant watching also ensured a certain safety net. Better to be watched here than to have an asshole putting on binoculars and trying to peep through your window. Maybe it was force of habit. Someone's got to spy on someone.

Elvis had never been inside. It wasn't his type of haunt, and El Mago made them keep a low profile. But there he was. It was a large café, the ceilings were high, the tables were small. Black-and-white pictures on the walls spoke of the charm of Old Habana, perfumed with the stench of cheap cigarettes and stale dreams. In a corner there were excited chirpings about Allende, who they said was transforming Chile, and in another corner someone spoke reverently about José Revueltas, who'd been jailed in Lecumberri a while back—he was a hero! But the mood was somber, and the sound of the dominoes slapped against the tables couldn't hide the plain truth: lots of people were still spooked about the stuff that had gone down on June tenth.

Spooked or not, the place was packed. No matter what was happening outside, people needed a drink, and the reds drank as much as anyone else.

Elvis spotted the guy he was looking for pretty quickly, cigarette tucked behind his ear like El Mago had said, and a notebook on the table. Next to the notebook, a pack of Faritos, a glass ashtray, and a cup of coffee. Elvis had imagined that the man would be one of those fossils who wander around the universities all the time. Long in the tooth for a student and obviously enrolled for the sole purpose of beating activists. But the fellow didn't really look like a fossil; he was baby-faced, with horn-rimmed glasses and attired in a nice but not too flashy plum-colored velvet jacket. As far as informants went, this one had, at the very least, a little taste, and Elvis felt immediately a bit shabby in his old leather jacket and his hair slicked back with too much Vaseline.

"You Justo?" Elvis asked.

The man had been scribbling in his notebook, but now he looked up at Elvis. "Yes. And you are?"

"Elvis. An associate of El Mago."

"I know the guy. So what?"

"I also know El Gazpacho," Elvis said, trying that line.

The young man frowned. "Why isn't he with you, then?"

"He was shot. I dropped him off at the doctor's place. Not sure where he is now."

"Which doctor?"

"Guerrero," he said, which was the name of the colonia where the doctor's office was located, not the actual doctor, but Justo nodded slowly, as if he knew who he was talking about.

Elvis pulled out a chair and sat in front of Justo. He pointed at the pack of cigarettes. "Can I bum a cigarette off you?"

"Go ahead."

Elvis grabbed a cig and lit it. Fuck, he was also hungry. He'd hardly had anything at all that day, running from one place to the other. On the table, a waiter had left a menu. But he didn't intend to make this a dinner. Justo closed his notebook, resting both hands atop it.

"What's up?"

"I need help."

"Help isn't free," Justo said, sliding his notebook across the table.

Well. That was different than the usual handing of envelopes. Elvis took out several large bills and tucked them inside the notebook and slid it back across the table. Justo placed his hands atop the notebook again.

"El Mago says you're familiar with this thing called Asterisk."

"I know the people there. You need info?"

"I need in. Where are they at?"

"You want to go there? No, man. It wouldn't do. The people running that have gone paranoid."

"Jacqueline," Elvis said. "She's the one who runs that place."

"That's right."

"They're supposed to be artists, no?"

"Sure. Painters and photographers and things like that. Jacqueline has always been into politics so naturally it's always had a political bent. Leaflets, reciting poems. Just this little nothing of a group, but I think they're trying to get in bed with the Russians now."

"What, you mean Russian agents?"

"Yeah, man. KGB. Didn't you hear? Three months ago a bunch of Russian diplomats were ordered to leave the country. They were spying and trying to support MAR. Of course, we couldn't kick everyone out. Jacqueline says she knows one of the agents who managed to stay behind. She's tired of painting pictures. She wants to join the armed struggle."

"Wannabe guerilla groups."

"They're crawling out of the rocks these days," Justo muttered and shook his head. "What are you doing here worried about Asterisk, anyway? I'd thought all of you Hawks would be running for cover. El Mago is toast."

"What you talking about?"

"Anaya's out for him."

"Am I supposed to know who that is?"

Justo scoffed and shook his head in disbelief. "Anaya. Secret police, man."

Ah. One of *those* dudes. The Hawks were a thing apart, not secret police, not regular police, and in the case of El Mago's boys, they were that: El Mago's boys. Despite maintaining his distance from the secret police, Elvis had a clear impression of them. They were abusive pigs who walked around as if they had dicks as big as King Kong. El Mago didn't like them. Elvis concurred.

"What about him?"

"He's had a long beef with El Mago, but El Mago's got a magic shield. Everything slides off him. People can't touch that dude. Except now they say he's fucked up and Anaya is going to bury him."

"Who says? Bury him how?"

Justo held both hands up in the air and chuckled. "Look, that I don't know. I talk to people and people talk to me. But Anaya is one fucking asshole, and it's not as if bastards like Anaya ever loved the Hawks."

Elvis grabbed the glass ashtray and pulled it closer to him, tapping his cigarette against its edge.

"What's the deal with you? If you're talking to secret dicks then you're not with El Mago."

"Didn't say I was. If you want to get technical, I'm DGIPS." Justo chuckled and took another sip of his coffee. "I know what you're gonna say: you look like a kid, but that's the trick, isn't it? Well, if you want to get any traction around these activists and shit."

DGIPS. Swell. A pencil pusher. Intelligence service. The DGIPS was always at odds with the DFS. It was an old rivalry. Each side thought the other was redundant. The DFS called the DGIPS pansies. The DGIPS said the agents of the DFS couldn't even fucking read, much less speak Russian or English.

The Hawks were too low for either side to bother with, just a group of hired punks.

"You should apply."

"Apply what?"

"Apply to join the DGIPS. What else? There's no future for the Hawks. Even if Anaya doesn't bury El Mago, it's all toast, and you've got the right look for this line of work," Justo said. "We can always use young blood."

Young blood, yeah. That's what everyone was after. Men who could pass as students, as protesters. If you had something a little bit extra you could get to the top of the heap. Like El Gazpacho, with his Spanish accent, that little seseo. Everyone thought all Spaniards in Mexico were commies, and that meant El Gazpacho had a nice cover.

What Elvis had was a decent face for the job. El Mago had once told him that everyone looks like a character in a play or a book, that we are all someone's doppelgänger. Elvis didn't know what doppelgänger meant, but El Mago had explained it meant a double. Elvis then asked El Mago who he looked like. He was hoping he'd say Elvis Presley, because Elvis had a twin who died at birth, but El Mago had said Hamlet, Prince of Denmark. Elvis didn't think he could be prince of anything, except maybe of paupers, but El Mago had smiled and said, "The Devil hath power to assume a pleasing shape. You look like a kid who dances to Presley's records and watches foreign films."

And when Elvis had told him, confused, that this was what he did, El Mago had chuckled and told him, "Exactly. That's the trick."

A prince was no king, and Presley was the King, but it had all sounded pretty good to Elvis, and from then on he understood he had the right look and this was like currency. With his face and his training, his stock had to rise.

Unless something really bad happened. Unless El Mago was about to get fucked, which meant they were all going to get it.

"How do you know it's all toast?"

"Man, it's logical. They're going to get rid of the Hawks."

"You can't know that," Elvis said quickly, slamming his cigarette against the ashtray, putting it out with one fierce motion.

Justo seemed amused. He grabbed his cup of coffee and took another sip. Both men stared at each other.

They couldn't shut down the Hawks; they'd never! El Mago would have given them advance warning. But what if it was true? What would he do then? Elvis had been saving his money. He had a bank account under a fake name. Fake names and fake IDs were as easy to come by as one, two, three. But he didn't have a fortune in cash; it wasn't like he could retire. If he wasn't a Hawk, then what could he do? He really didn't want to be an agent of some dipshit place like Justo was suggesting, but he also had no interest in bouncing back to his mom's house. Plus, there was no guarantee the DGIPS would want him, good face or not. Elvis hadn't even finished high school.

Pawn, he thought, remembering El Mago's words.

The noise of dominoes, of people talking and laughing, the scraping of chairs against the floor and the radio by the counter loudly playing Victor Jara all mixed together, threatening to give Elvis a headache. He rubbed a hand against his cheek and felt the stubble there. Shit. El Mago hated it when they weren't clean-shaven and well-dressed. No untucked shirts with him. But Elvis had been up since early. He'd hardly had time for proper grooming.

"I'm not trying to bust your balls. I say it how I see it," Justo smiled, all friendly-like. Elvis suspected he wasn't as chirpy and fun as he appeared, that it was all a cover and he was fishing for info or wanted to trick Elvis in some way. But if that's the game he played, let it be.

Maybe he was a clown. Maybe not. You couldn't trust these guys. But it didn't matter if he was Bozo if he had the info he needed.

"Sure," Elvis muttered. "You know a girl from Asterisk called Leonora? She's pretty, an art student."

That was why he was there, after all. To find that woman. Not to worry about El Mago or the Hawks.

Justo nodded. "A Bohemian. She has money, but likes to pretend she's slumming it. Her uncle pays her bills. Jackie used her as her little piggy bank for a bit there," Justo said. It was his turn to reach for a cigarette. He took out a little book of matches and lit his cigarette, dumping the match in the ashtray.

"How so?"

"Jackie lives in a shitty vecindad with her family. She hasn't two pesos to rub together. So she depends on other folks to get anything done. You know, if they need to get food for a meeting or drinks. Leonora pitched in for a bunch of things. Even paid Jackie's rent one time, I think. I heard people talking about that."

"Then they're good friends."

"I guess so. Jackie's kind of bossy and Leonora can get on people's nerves easily. She's very anxious, very wishy-washy. Jackie's no-nonsense, you know? Leonora would skip meetings because she had a cold or because she hadn't slept well, or she had homework to do. Jackie doesn't believe in colds or lack of sleep. She's a fucking robot. Anything for the cause, you know?"

"The cause being a guerilla group."

"If she gets her way, sure. One day. But everyone wants that and no one can get really organized. They're amateurs. Guevarism ain't ever going to work in this country. Kinda sad, you know?"

"Does Leonora have any other friends?"

"She's friendly enough, I guess. There's a guy . . . Rubén. They used to date and she dumped him, so I'm not sure if they're friendly anymore at this point or if they try to keep it civilized. Let me think. There's a girl. Concha. Wears Coke-bottle glasses, short, has lots of freckles."

"I've got to get into Asterisk. You have an address for them?"

"I told you, Jackie's gone paranoid."

"Jackie could shoot bullets out of her ass, I still want to see what her band of friends is up to. You telling me or not?"

"Stubborn fucker. What do I care? If you want to see Jacqueline you should wait until tomorrow. They have meetings on Saturdays, around five."

Justo reached into his knapsack, which was hanging from the back of his chair. He rummaged inside it, taking out a black-and-white flyer and handing it to Elvis. "The address is there, and if you have one of those, they'll let you in. Tell them Carlito handed it to you. He talks a lot and is always half baked. He won't remember if he talked to you or not."

Elvis folded the flyer and tucked it inside his jacket. "Thanks. I have one more thing to ask."

"What, you want me to sneak you into Palacio Nacional now?"

"Man, I'm not trying to be rude. I'm trying to figure stuff here. And I mean . . . you're friends with El Gazpacho, no? I'm friends with him too. He is . . . was my unit leader."

"Yeah, I'm friends with him. Why else do you think I'd talk to you?"

"Good. Because I was hoping you can find him. He's left the unit and I don't know where he's gone. It's not like El Mago's gonna tell me, and I want to make sure he's all right. Plus, all his stuff is back at the apartment."

"You want to mail him his nail clipper and shoes? And you think I know where he lives or something?"

"Well, I sure don't know. But you being DGIPS and all, and being El Gazpacho's friend and everything . . ."

Elvis took out a few bills and stuffed them inside Justo's notebook. "I'd be more interested in knowing what your boss wants with Asterisk than your cash," Justo said.

"I ain't telling."

"And after I'm being nice to you, you little shit."

Elvis took out two more bills and stuffed them in the notebook. "Nice my ass. You're trying to jack up the price. Take the money or I'll look for another crooked asshole who'll find out."

Justo seemed amused. "Kid, you have an attitude. But you're lucky: I'm in need of petty cash. Come back in a couple of days," Justo said as a goodbye.

Elvis nodded and stepped out, feeling cheery. It didn't last.

He ate at a random tortería and stared at the calendar taped behind the counter featuring a corny Hawaiian dancer, paper flowers strewn around. The dancer's eyes reminded him of Cristina. Elvis didn't believe in losing his head over a girl, but that was now. A few years back, he'd gone and joined a fucking cult for one, hadn't he?

Yeah, he had, like the ass he'd been. In his defense, Cristina had been real pretty and she'd also seemed interested in him. Not like Elvis had been interested—he'd been neck-deep—but he also hadn't imagined the whole thing. The problem was she'd gone hot and cold and then hot again. Sometimes she wanted to leave Tlaquepaque, sometimes she wanted to stay forever.

She fucked Elvis, sometimes, yeah. But it always felt like a favor, and he didn't like it when he saw her with their leader or some of the other men around the complex. Complex! A rickety building with a few sad chickens and goats. Elvis working under the searing sun, Elvis feeding the damn chickens or trying to fix a piece of furniture. The others were lazy and assigned most chores to him. Every time he thought about quitting, though, she'd soothe him with a couple of kisses.

He liked that and he also didn't like it. It reminded him of the older American woman who'd kept him as her lover. In her eyes he read a definite indifference. He knew he was replaceable.

When Elvis left, it was because he couldn't stomach any more of that merry-go-round of emotions. In the months after, he'd thought of writing to Cristina, and then he'd figure it was pointless. But sometimes he still got the urge to go back. To see what she was up to.

He didn't want to live like a hippie, much less with that idiotic cult. But the money could be enough to rent an apartment, and they could install themselves somewhere nice and cozy.

Though God knew if Cristina was still in Tlaquepaque. And he hadn't spoken to her in years. It was stupid. He didn't even know why he was thinking of her. He supposed it was because Justo was making him nervous, talking about that man Anaya.

Elvis tried to force himself to imagine a different life from the one he led, maybe a life with Cristina. Or maybe he'd try to be an agent, like Justo had suggested. It couldn't be that hard. Maybe they'd throw him in cells with activists so he could pose as a fellow revolutionary and inform on them. Sometimes they used former real activists for this. People who had been hauled to Lecumberri and decided to become collaborators and squeal. Áyax Segura Garrido had squealed, and that's how the courts had found him innocent. He was now in the pocket of the DFS.

But none of that was what he really wanted. It was all a bit seedy. None of it resembled El Mago's life. He wanted El Mago's place, with his bookshelves and his car and his suits. It wasn't the things El Mago owned. It wasn't the silver cufflinks on his shirts or the fine cigarettes. It was the way El Mago spoke, the way he looked.

He worried that he'd never have that now. Not only that, but El Mago would disappear from his life. Just like El Gazpacho had disappeared. It was crazy to think people could be gone with a snap of the fingers.

God damn Gazpacho. Where'd he headed?

Elvis finished eating, gave the Hawaiian girl one last, longing look, and went back to the apartment. It was empty. El Güero was supposed to be completing his first shift. He supposed the Antelope had gone to relieve him.

Elvis opened the door to El Gazpacho's room and stood in the doorway, looking at the bed, the closet, the little desk in the corner. El Gazpacho kept his room neat and tidy, with a minimum of things. In a corner he had a poster of *Yojimbo*, a movie that Elvis had never seen but El Gazpacho had described in detail. Elvis stood in front of the narrow closet and looked at the shirts and trousers and what El Gazpacho jokingly called his "civilian" jacket: an avocado-green jacket with yellow patches.

It's what El Gazpacho wore to the movies. Elvis didn't know why he liked that ridiculous outfit, but he did. Then again, El Gazpacho didn't complain when Elvis put on his sunglasses at night or tried to comb his hair like James Dean or Presley, and when Elvis didn't know how to say a word in the dictionary El Gazpacho never laughed.

Although he didn't like either El Güero or the Antelope, he

suddenly felt very lonely and wished they were in the apartment with him.

Elvis went into his room and rummaged among his records. He found his copy of "Blue Velvet" and held the record up to the light, looking at the grooves. Elvis had the version by Bennett. He put the record on and sat down on his bed.

He thought about the woman who owned the Prysock cover, Maite Jaramillo, and as the record began to spin he felt a little less alone. She was probably playing the same song now. And if she was, if they were both repeating the same motion in two different places, somehow it felt like they were doing it together. Which meant he wasn't really alone.

He pictured two dust motes spinning in concentric circles. Maybe it was like that everywhere, for everyone. There was always someone doing the exact same thing. Like a shadow or a mirror image, like the doppelgängers El Mago talked about. People simply didn't know it. Could be you were cutting vegetables with your left hand while it rained in Japan and a woman in Puebla was doing the same thing, and you both looked up at the sky at the same time and saw a bird fly by.

Elvis lay back on the bed, stretching up his arms until he got hold of the headboard, and he hummed to the music. He didn't know what the words meant, but he knew what they sounded like: it was the sound of sadness.

13

SHE DECIDED TO wear the yellow print dress with the bow at the neck. The color was vibrant and brightened her face, but it looked a little young. When she'd bought it, the dress had been perfect on the rack, but as often happened with Maite, when she put it on at home she had an entirely different opinion of the garment. It was garish, it exposed her knees, and no matter how hard she rubbed a pumice stone against her knees they always looked dirty.

She hadn't worn it, stuffing it into the back of her closet. But it really was the nicest dress she owned and the most modern one. The rest of her wardrobe consisted of her drab office outfits, and her scant weekend wear was nondescript.

She clipped the tag off the dress, ruefully noting the price—my, she had spent too much on that. Then again it was a special-occasion dress. The problem was she didn't have enough special occasions to wear it.

She carefully ironed the dress and hung it up while she busied herself with her makeup and her hair. Again the fear of artificial youthfulness assailed her. She didn't want to look like a sad matriarch who rubs too much blush on her cheeks. Not that she looked exactly like a matriarch.

Thirty is not fifty, she told herself firmly, but in the back of her mind she remembered bits of conversation from some of the other office workers in her building, conversations she caught while seated at the counter of the nearby lonchería. Young men complaining a certain bar was filled with hags with saggy tits.

Where could the trim, young cuts be found? And Maite, sinking in her seat, staring at her reflection in the mirrors behind the counter.

Thirty is not fifty, she repeated as she did her hair. At least she had good hair, even if her aunts had both gone partially bald at an early age. Would she face the same fate? Maite inspected her hairline.

Stop being silly, she whispered and continued with her preparations. She still needed to feed the cat in Leonora's apartment, and she didn't want to be late.

Cristóbalito had liked her hair. Tumbling down her back, so long it almost reached her waist in those days. When she lay naked in bed with him it could cover her breasts, as though she were Lady Godiva. Who'd want to see her naked now, though? Her skin was dry and her thighs—

No, she wasn't going to be upset today. Today was a good day. Today was a day when things would happen, even if nothing ever happened to Maite. She was merely a weathervane, tossed from one point to another by indifferent winds, but now something was happening to her, and it wasn't only the lunch with Emilio Lomelí, it was Leonora's mysterious disappearance, Rubén asking her for assistance, it was the whole of it.

She was part of a story.

She must hurry. Maite decided not to feed the cat. She'd be late if she did. She was already late as it was. She'd worry about the cat later. It's not as if she'd be gone for hours and hours.

She dashed out of her apartment and down the stairs. It would have been easier if she could take a cab, but she needed to watch her expenses and so it was public transit and a bit of a walk.

Emilio Lomelí lived in Polanco. She'd seldom been in that part of town. It was a neighborhood that had been for a number of years now the favorite destination for upper-crust Jewish families, American and British diplomats, and a growing contingent of affluent Mexicans who wanted to enjoy the delicatessens, European-style bakeries, and coffee shops not far from Chapultepec

Park. This was the kind of place where you could order corned beef and red wine to be delivered to your home, or stop at Frascati's for paella. Women attended fashion-show luncheons and charity benefits.

Everything was new in this area: there was no sign of moldy colonial palaces and old tezontle. Everything was beautiful. It was a pageant of prosperity, so far removed from the neighborhood where Maite had grown up that she might as well be a tourist on another planet.

Emilio Lomelí's house was painted white, looking deceptively simple from the outside. Emilio opened the door and showed her in, and Maite swept her gaze up and down. The ceilings were extremely tall, and the walls were paneled in dark, rich oak. The space was very open, as though the architect had forgotten the meaning of the word *wall*, the dining room flowing into the living room. Acrylic bubble chairs, a long, beautiful red velvet couch, a table big enough for eight, green glass vases filled with flowers . . . it all seemed plucked out of a catalogue. Maite's atelier, which she'd thought quite adorable, now became shabby in comparison.

Emilio was like a jewel in a beautiful setting. He almost sparkled against the expensive furniture, his hair artfully slicked back, looking a bit like David Janssen in *The Fugitive*. Only Emilio was much more handsome.

To keep from gawking at him, she set herself to admiring the photographs on the walls. These were all very large black-and-white images, close-ups really, of body parts, in silver frames. A woman's eye, lips, a manicured nail. She couldn't know if this was one woman or different women. The style of the photos anonymized them.

"Are these your photos?" she asked.

"Yes, it was a whole series. I exhibited it a few years ago," he said, moving his arm and pointing from one end of the house to another. "I have my own darkroom upstairs."

She glanced at the stairs. She wondered if he'd decorated the second floor with those same pictures, a multitude of eyes, ears, and lips. She wondered what his room looked like, whether the photos in there were bolder. Pictures of nipples and tongues and vulvas above the bed. Leonora's nipples could be rendered in shades of gray. Her eye might be staring at Maite from that photo on the wall, the pupil completely dilated.

It was an odd thought, but it was the word *darkroom* that conjured it, which suggested secrets and the cover of the night. It meant nothing, and yet her mind leaped at it and was filled with the strangest, most fantastical thoughts when she heard certain words.

"The lunch is cold cuts and cheeses, I'm afraid. I have a cook come in a couple of days a week, but on weekends I keep it simple," he said, carelessly gesturing toward a side table that was prepped with several plates.

"Oh, anything is fine, really," she said and meant it. She was too nervous, wouldn't be able to get down a single bite with him looking at her.

"Can I fix you a martini?" Emilio asked.

"Oh . . ." Maite said. She wasn't the type of person who had a three-martini lunch. She'd never taken to drinking, and it wouldn't have done at her office to come in plastered. Besides, as with the food, she wondered if the taste wouldn't sit with her.

Emilio must have noticed her panicked expression. He smiled. "Would you prefer mineral water?"

"Yes."

"Thanks. I was starting to feel like a terrible host," he said, opening a bottle of Perrier and filling a glass for her.

Emilio had a smoothness about himself . . . the way he spoke and handed her the glass, like she'd seen men do in the movies and never experienced in real life. And his eyes! Amber-colored, like two jewels, matching his light brown hair with its few strands of gold glinting in the sunlight.

"Thanks for coming over, by the way. You said something about Leonora's camera in your message? Did you find it?"

"It's a little bit more complicated than that," she said, holding the glass with two hands and peering down at it. "Leonora has gone missing, and I think it's because of that camera."

"What do you mean?"

"She hasn't come home. I have reason to believe she had some pictures which would have been . . . compromising. Pictures of the Hawks."

She looked up at him, trying to gauge his response. He didn't appear surprised. "Did she talk to you about that?" he asked.

Rubén had told her not to mention him, so she nodded.

"What else did she say?"

"She only said that. Nothing more. I don't know what it means. I'm worried, and I was thinking maybe you might be able to explain what's happening."

Emilio sighed and sat down on the velvet couch while Maite carefully sat on one of the bubble chairs, leaning forward, grasping her glass tight as she took a sip. She wondered if he liked her dress. Maybe it was too short. Maybe she looked like an idiot. She discreetly tugged at the hem with her free hand, attempting to pull it down a little and cover her knees.

"It's hard to explain. Last week Leonora told me she was thinking of visiting a journalist friend of mine who lives in Cuernavaca. She doesn't have a car, so she needed a ride. But I was busy and couldn't take her, and in the end she didn't truly seem interested in going, so I thought that was the end of that."

"But then you went to see her last weekend and she wasn't around," Maite said.

"Yes. That's when I realized she'd gone to see Lara after all. She must have obtained a ride from someone else."

"You came for a camera. Did you know it had compromising photos?"

Emilio nodded gravely. "That's why I wanted it. Because I was afraid of what Leonora might do with it. I was afraid she'd change her mind and visit Lara."

"And she did."

"She must have."

"What's so terrible about the pictures?"

"I haven't seen them, she wouldn't let me, and she was cryptic about them, but what she did mention worried me. It's a dangerous climate out there, and Leonora . . . Leonora doesn't understand how dangerous it is, and those friends of hers . . . well, they're very dangerous too."

"You mean Jackie?"

"You know her?" Emilio asked.

Maite traced the rim of the glass with her index finger. "No. I haven't met her. But I know she's an activist."

"An activist. That's a nice way of putting it. We have a problem in Mexico. You only have to look around for five minutes to see that. Poverty, instability, corruption. I agree with that. A lot of people do. We need change. Jackie and people like her want to solve these problems through an armed revolution. She's read Guevara and Marighella. You remember a few months ago, they captured those terrorists who attacked a bank in Morelia? That's what Jackie wants to do."

"I'm not sure what that has to do with Leonora."

"Leonora idolizes Jackie. It's Jackie this and Jackie that. Leonora has an uncle who was in the military. He's a well-connected guy. And I think through him she got those compromising pictures of the Hawks and wanted to give them to a journalist, to Lara. But I told her to reconsider."

"Why?"

"Because it could get her into a lot of trouble. What if someone came after her? What if she was painting herself into a target? I said she needed to be ready for this. I actually worry about her. Unlike Jackie. She'd have Leonora go into a ring with an angry bull."

She didn't know what to say. She gulped down her water instead. Finally, she managed a few words. "Sounds like you don't believe in Jackie's cause . . . in . . . in this change."

Emilio smiled charmingly and shook his head. He stood up

and took her empty glass from her hands. Their fingers touched for a moment, then he was placing the glass back on the side table.

"Change should come peacefully. We need a more educated nation, we need to come to agreements. President Echeverría has said he is willing to have conversations. He's different from Ordaz, he's more open. Conversations can't take place when you have folks like Jackie trying to kidnap businesspeople and rob banks. I don't trust Jackie."

Emilio leaned back against the table and crossed his arms, grimacing. "God knows what she might have told Leonora to do," he muttered.

"You care a lot about her?" Maite asked softly. She wondered if she disappeared, if anyone except her pet bird would care. Her mother would probably shrug and say she must have done something wrong. Her sister would be equally unmoved.

"Yes," Emilio said. "I do."

How she wanted someone to care about her! A thick, destructive yearning flamed inside her chest, and a flicker of emotion must have shown on Maite's face because he chuckled and quickly added, "It's not love. Not like that. We broke up."

"Yes, I heard," Maite said, playing with the bow on her neck, trying to seem nonchalant even as she felt herself blushing. "What . . . may I ask, what happened there?"

"Nothing special, diverging interests. She's young, I'm not."

"But you're not old," she protested.

"I'm twenty-eight, Leonora is twenty-one. When you're twenty-eight you begin to get serious about life, you begin to think about things like a family, to plan for a real future. She wasn't ready for any of that. I mean, I was a founder of that art collective she's a member of, so I understand the impulse to want to leave your mark. But there's more to life than that, don't you think?"

"I'm not an artist," Maite said, smoothing down the bow at her neck.

"You should consider yourself lucky. Art is a constant torment. I still take a few pictures, but my business takes up most of my time now," he said and pointed at one of the photographs on the walls.

"Antiques?"

"Yes. I own a beautiful shop. Not flea market merchandise, either. Genuinely enchanting pieces. I have gorgeous Chinese porcelains and a Louis XV chair right now. Leonora is not much for antiques. That was the other thing. New, new, new. Everything had to be new."

"I can't say I know much about antiques, but I do appreciate the value of an old heirloom. It seems to me something that has been preserved for a long time acquires a certain gravitas."

"I'd agree. It's the same with people: age refines us."

She liked that thought. That she was refined. It was like an alchemical process. From coarse lead one could bring forth precious gold. A man of the world, such as Emilio Lomelí, would be able to discern that. She observed him carefully, taking in the curve of his smile.

"It's very good of you to worry about Leonora, you know?" Emilio said. "Some people wouldn't care if their neighbors lived or died in this city."

She remembered the money the girl owed her and how she desperately needed to fix her car, plus the delight she obtained from her thieving escapades, the delight she was feeling now sitting in this living room.

"I suppose I'm old-fashioned. Always have a cup of sugar handy and all that," she told him and looked down at the floor. She'd heard you can tell a liar by their gaze, and for a minute she thought maybe he'd look into her heart and discern all her untruths.

He sighed. "I wish we knew where she's gone."

"Would that journalist, Lara, know?" she asked.

"I could phone and ask. Would you let me know if you hear anything?"

"Of course," she said, raising her head and looking at him again.

"I'd also like to ask you . . . if by any chance you do happen to find those photos, please, bring them to me. I don't want anyone else getting in trouble because of them."

"You shouldn't worry about me."

"I admit I am a little concerned."

Concerned! About her! Maite almost undid the ribbon, her fingers clumsy. He was sweet! Then, for a second, she remembered that scary man who had come to her office, and she wondered if it wasn't sweetness, if it was merely levelheadedness and she was a fool. Shouldn't she be a little frightened, after all? She had been, the previous day. But now his proximity intoxicated her, now she felt like she was in one of the issues of *Secret Romance*.

The phone rang. Emilio excused himself and picked up, smiling apologetically at her. "Yeah? No, I have a visitor. No, there's no word on that . . . We'll be done soon, yes . . . I wish you wouldn't." He turned his back to her for a moment, muttering something into the receiver before hanging up.

"Everything okay?" she asked.

"Work," he said, glancing at his watch. "I'm needed at the store."

"I'm so sorry, I didn't mean to take so much of your time. You didn't even have a chance to eat your lunch."

"It's fine. I'll grab something later. Besides, I'm glad you stopped by. We'll be in touch?"

"Of course," she said.

It wasn't until she was almost home that she realized she had somehow pledged assistance to two entirely different men. It was a contradictory, impossible task. She'd told Rubén she'd help him find Leonora. She'd now told Emilio the same. And by keeping Rubén's involvement in this quest quiet, she had perhaps endangered her nascent friendship with Emilio. He might be upset if he found out she'd gone to see him at Rubén's insistence. And there was that man Anaya. She had no idea what she was going to do about him. She hoped he wouldn't bother her again.

It was all turning into a mess.

Angrily she remembered that she still didn't have her car back. And the cat! She must feed the cat.

As Maite walked down the street, toward her apartment, she was so distracted that she didn't notice the man stepping out of a car and following her until he touched her arm.

14

"WHAT THE FUCK are you doing this far away? Can you even see a damn thing?" Elvis asked as he sat down in the passenger's seat. He'd brought a bag of peanuts and a couple of sodas. Elvis was going to take a short shift so El Güero could head back to the apartment and get a little shut-eye.

El Güero snorted. "I ain't blind, like others, Mister Magoo. I can see the door of the building fine from here. Besides, I can't park any closer. Too fucking obvious, and someone else's already staked out the prime spot."

"Meaning what?"

"Meaning we're not the only ones watching this building. Can I have some of those?"

"Stuff yourself," Elvis said, handing him the bag and craning his neck. "Who else's watching?"

El Güero tore the bag of peanuts open and tossed a couple into his mouth, chewing loudly. "Like I know? Can't very well go asking them, can I? But I can tell."

"DFS, maybe," Elvis muttered, remembering what Justo had said about the dude named Anaya.

"Not *those* fuckers, damn it. What they want?"

"I'm not sure."

"There she is. Finally," El Güero said as Maite Jaramillo stepped out of the building.

"Follow her."

El Güero sighed. It seemed his naptime would have to be deferred. The woman was easy enough to tail. Elvis was more worried about the car ahead of them that also seemed to be tailing her, though once they reached Polanco, the driver either noticed Elvis's car behind them and decided to split or simply changed his mind. Either way, by the time they parked, it was only El Güero and Elvis following the woman.

Elvis noted the address the woman went into, scribbling it in a tiny notebook. He opened his soda and they waited. Often, when they had to watch someone, Elvis brought a crossword puzzle or a book, to keep the boredom at bay. But he hadn't bothered with that this time; he'd been too tired to remember. He hadn't forgotten the word of the day, thank God. It was *dilated*. The way Elvis tried to memorize the words was to use them in everyday conversation, but El Güero thought he sounded like an idiot when he did.

Dilated, he thought, looking at his reflection in the rearview mirror. *The pupil is dilated.*

El Güero crossed his arms and closed his eyes, dozing off. Elvis let him, feeling kind. Besides, that way he didn't have to talk to the guy. They'd never gotten along and they weren't going to start now, especially if the Hawks were done for and they wouldn't see each other again.

Not that Elvis knew the Hawks were done for, but that shit Justo had mentioned hadn't gone down well with him.

He lit a cigarette and, having nothing better to do, began thinking about the woman they were following. She reminded Elvis of someone. Bluebeard's wife. Well, the way he pictured Bluebeard's wife in one of the few books he'd owned as a child, a volume of fairy tales. Each story had an illustration. With "Jack and the Beanstalk," it was Jack throwing the seeds on the ground and a tiny sprout emerging: that was his favorite story.

In Bluebeard's case, there was a woman in a long dress, bending down to look through a keyhole. The way the picture had been drawn, you couldn't see the woman's face that well, her long hair partially obscuring her features, but you could see the eyes. The resemblance was in the eyes, and it seemed to him that if she had turned to look at the reader directly, the woman would have looked exactly like Maite Jaramillo.

The eye is dilated, he whispered.

It was the expression on Maite's face, slightly lost and scared in all those pictures he'd found of her in that photo album.

Well, at least she had good musical taste, and he couldn't fault her on the account of books either. She had books by Caridad Bravo Adams and he'd never read her, so he had no idea if that was a decent author or not, though he recognized the name from a soap opera. But Maite also owned a bunch of volumes from the Sepan Cuantos collection, and also a fair amount of Brontë and Austen and a fine edition of *El Quijote*, all of which pointed to class and sensibility; the sort of stuff the university students bought. He admired a gal with class. He wasn't sure what to make of her taste in comic books. He'd never been one for those, and if he ever flipped through them at the newsstand, he flipped through Westerns.

He began humming "Bang Bang (My Baby Shot Me Down)." Did Maite have any Nancy Sinatra in her collection? Chances were yes.

After a while, the woman came out, and Elvis nudged El Güero awake. They followed her back to her building, where she was intercepted by a young, long-haired man. He looked like a standard-issue hippie. They exchanged a few words and got into his car, making El Güero groan in frustration, because now they needed to tail her somewhere else.

They wound up in Tacubaya, going into the same building Elvis was supposed to visit that afternoon. Well. That was a mighty big coincidence.

"Asterisk," Elvis said.

"What did you call me?" El Güero asked angrily.

"Shut up. It's a meeting place for students. I'm gonna go in," Elvis said. In his jacket Elvis was carrying a fake driver's license, a few bills, a pack of cigarettes, the flyer, the bits of metal he used to pick locks in a pinch, and his screwdriver, all pretty innocent.

Well, maybe not the screwdriver, but it wasn't a knife or a gun, and even if the commies were paranoid they probably couldn't say much about that. And he was dressed for the part; all he needed was to mess up his hair. He could pull it off.

"You gonna go alone?" El Güero muttered, skeptical.

"It's easier that way. You get back to base," Elvis said, looking at himself in the rearview mirror. He untucked his shirt.

"Don't have to tell me twice."

"Later."

Elvis got out of the car, and El Güero drove away. He waited a little, eyeing the gray building. Didn't look like much, some old dump, but then there could be five hundred reds with rifles inside. And wasn't the Cuban embassy nearby? And the Soviets too. Maybe everyone liked to keep it nice and cozy and close together. Kind of stupid for Asterisk to set up shop near them, though. It would arouse suspicion.

On the ground floor of the building there was a shoe repair shop, but there was a little black door and an intercom with business names. Number three corresponded to "Asterisk Gallery." It wasn't five yet, not by far, but he wanted to see what the woman was up to. He pressed a button.

"Who's that?" someone said over the intercom, taking his sweet time to answer.

"Carlito told me I should stop by. Something about a meeting Saturday."

Elvis was buzzed in, and he went up the stairs. When he reached the third floor he saw a red door with a sign affixed to it that read "Asterisk Art Gallery and Cooperative." He knocked. A young man opened.

"Who are you?" the man asked.

"Carlito told me to stop by," he said, showing the man his flyer.

Elvis was ushered in, no other questions asked. Like Justo had said, these guys were amateurs.

The gallery space consisted of a very long room with tall ceilings and few windows. On the walls there were photos and paintings with tiny pieces of white cardboard affixed next to them indicating the name of the artist. There were a couple of doors; one said "Office" and the other "Bathroom." Foldable chairs had been piled in a corner. The air was a cloud of tobacco and marijuana smoke.

There were maybe a dozen people in attendance, but he didn't spot the woman or her companion. They were probably in the office. Or they could even be on another floor. He wasn't sure about the setup of this place.

He walked around, pretending he was eyeing the paintings, which were, in his limited opinion, a crock of shit. There was a picture of a chacmool. He recognized it from a visit to a museum he took with his class before they kicked him out. He stood before it for a couple of minutes before resuming his walking.

He saw a girl standing by one of the few windows, cigarette in hand. She had a lot of freckles that covered her skinny shoulders and went down to the top of her breasts, easily visible with the clothes she was wearing. Her Coke-bottle glasses and her hair tied in a bun made her look like a clueless school teacher who had been stuffed into a tiny crocheted top and a mini-skirt. Concha, standing all alone and looking bored.

On a plastic table there were pamphlets and a few bottles of soda. He grabbed one and opened it with the screwdriver, aimlessly walking toward the woman.

"Hey, got a light, girl?" he asked her, opting for the tone of a down-to-earth student, but avoiding the intonation that would identify him as someone from Tepito. He'd learned, while working for El Mago, at least to hit a bland, middle-class way of talking. El Mago's posh, smooth voice and vocabulary were still not quite within his grasp, mostly because he got nervous and flubbed it when he spoke to the man.

It took more than a word of the day to pin that down, to be a gentleman.

The girl opened her morralito made of yute, searching until

she produced a pink plastic lighter, and he bent down, pressing the tip of his cigarette to the flame.

"Thanks," he said.

"No problem."

"Nice shirt," he said, pointing at her garish crocheted top. His comment pleased her immensely, and she gave him a huge grin.

"Thanks!" she said, placing the morralito back on her shoulder. "I made it myself."

"That's nice. Not much going on?"

"Not yet. It's kinda early."

"Guess so. If I'd known I'd have stopped for a couple of quecas."

"Gosh, nothing ever starts until six," she said and then, as she held her cigarette between two fingers and tilted her head flirtatiously, "I haven't seen you around before."

"First time," he said, with a fake smile that mimicked her flirtation, since that seemed to be her line.

"Really?"

"Yup. To be honest with you, I'm not even sure what I'm doing here. I got an invite from a friend who said I should stop by, said things were hopping here but can't say it looks like anything's hopping."

"Not now," Concha said with a sigh. "It used to be fun. I came to so many parties and openings. But Jackie's really dull these days. She says it's no time to party and I get it, but also, man, it can't all be super serious, can it?"

"Agreed."

He offered her a sip of his soft drink, and she took it, smiling again. "I don't think I see my friend," Elvis said. "I'm wondering if she's coming."

"What's her name?"

"Leonora."

Concha touched his arm, squeezing it dramatically, and gasped. "Leonora? You don't expect *she'll* be here!"

"Why not?"

"Well . . . not after what happened. Why, Jackie has practically excommunicated her."

"I don't know what happened. I haven't spoken with her in a couple of weeks."

"I really shouldn't be telling you this, but you seem all right," Concha said, now running her hand down his arm, giving him an even bigger, more flirtatious smile.

He responded by resting his palm against her hip for a few seconds, close and cozy to the girl, but casual too. "You seem all right too. Why don't you tell me?"

She spoke in a whisper, obviously relishing the chance to gossip despite her mock secretiveness. "Jackie thinks Leonora is the mole."

"The mole?"

"Yeah. Someone's been talking to cops, telling them every little thing that's going on here."

"How'd you figure that?"

"I'm not sure. But even if Jackie's wrong, it doesn't matter much, does it? Luz never liked Leonora, when push comes to shove Sócrates falls in line with Jackie, and Carlito is kissing Jackie's butt, so it's a done deal. Rubén objected, but you know, he can be easily overruled. Are you good friends with Leonora?"

"Not really. She lives in my apartment building," he said, because he felt it was safer than saying they had taken classes together. He'd played the role of student before well enough, but right now he wanted to distance himself a bit from Leonora, seeing as she was *persona non grata*. That was a term he'd learned from El Mago. He quite liked it.

"You're friends with her?"

"I guess I was," Concha said thoughtfully. "But she's been very mysterious lately. I think because she was back together with Emilio and she didn't want others to know."

"Emilio? Why would that bother anyone?" he asked innocently.

"Oh, you know, Rubén's still sore about what happened. Leonora dumping him for Emilio. And then they broke up anyway! She's silly like that, sometimes. I mean, obviously she's my friend, but . . . well, you know Leonora. She's always burning bridges. I think the only person who still likes her now is Sócrates. I think he has a thing for her. But of course everyone has a thing for Leonora."

"Popular girl," he replied. Leonora had a bunch of associates, but they seemed to have let her down. Jackie had turned on her for some reason, and Leonora hadn't gone back to the priest for help. Could be she was hiding with Emilio, Sócrates, or Rubén, but the last two were apparently Jackie's underlings. Nevertheless, Rubén had objected, and Sócrates might be a fan of the girl. What Elvis needed was to figure out the coordinates of those two.

And Emilio Lomelí . . . El Mago had said he, like the girl's sister, was a dead end. But was he? Anyway, why had El Mago been so adamant about keeping him and the sister out of this? Sure, he'd said Emilio was money and also PRI, but that didn't quite explain everything. And Leonora's file was so thin, like El Mago was trying to hide half of the girl's life. It didn't add up, and though it didn't have to add up for Elvis to do his job, he was getting curious.

"You think Sócrates would be her type?"

"Why, you're also waiting in line for her?" Concha said, scoffing, and she flicked her cigarette out the window and rolled her eyes.

"I'm curious, that's all," he said, his hand resting against her hip again.

"I don't know. He's Jackie's right-hand man these days, so I don't think he'd go there even if he could, what with everything. But he did have a crush on her for a while. He tried reading poems to her. It was goofy."

He nodded. And then, just as Elvis was smiling charmingly at the girl and wondering if he couldn't squeeze a few more drops of information from her, the door to the office opened and out walked several people. Three men and a chick. One of the guys was the fucking Jesuit priest they'd beaten up a couple of days before. His head was all bandaged, and he had dark purple bruises around his eyes. Looked like hell.

Before Elvis had time to duck or hide, the eyes of the priest fixed on him, and he let out a hoarse scream.

Elvis ran. He pushed aside the people in his path and yanked the door open, rushing down the stairs like a man who had been set on fire. Before he reached the ground floor, someone slammed him against a wall. Elvis elbowed the person away, tripped, and fell the last three steps, landing at the foot of the stairs.

The street was a few paces from him, but Elvis didn't have a chance to get up and slip out, because the same person who had slammed him against the wall now pressed a knife against his neck.

"Stay still," a man said.

15

SHE SPUN AROUND, startled by the man's touch. For a moment, she was afraid, thinking of what Emilio had said, that she might be in danger, and recalled Anaya. But she was greeted by a familiar face.

"Hey," Rubén said.

Maite slid a hand down the strap of her purse. "What are you doing here?" she asked with a frown.

"You told me to come see you around lunchtime."

She'd completely forgotten about that. She'd been too busy thinking about her meeting with Emilio, the stupid cat, and financial matters to even remember what she'd told him.

"I'm sorry," she said, quickly changing her tone of voice. "Were you waiting for me?"

"Not too long. You already ate?" Rubén asked.

"I haven't."

"Then wanna go get a bite? Jackie lent me her car," he said, pointing to a sad-looking red Chevy.

From the car's mirror dangled two pine-shaped air fresheners and in the back Maite spotted a couple of cardboard boxes. It wasn't a carriage, but it was something, and Maite bitterly remembered her own car, still at the mechanic. Even a student had four wheels.

"Where would you like to go?" Rubén asked.

For a moment Maite thought of all the expensive restaurants she'd read about in the newspaper. Focolare and La Cava and Jena. The one place that had really caught her imagination was the

Mauna Loa, which was over on Hamburgo Street. The menu promised "Oriental" delights and the décor was supposed to be inspired by the South Seas. It was the sort of restaurant that excited her imagination. It made her think of the island in *Secret Romance*, the pulsating lure of drums, adventure, and romance.

But she couldn't afford such a venue, and she doubted he could either.

"Wherever you want to go," she muttered.

They ended up at a lonchería with plastic chairs, red plastic salt shakers, and plastic plates that offered the sort of cheap, unassuming fare you'd expect at such a place: tortas and more tortas, washed down with Coca-Cola and Sidral Mundet. She worried about dirtying her dress. She didn't particularly like it, but it had to be dry cleaned. All she needed was to have to pay another dry cleaning bill.

"Did you talk to Emilio, then?" Rubén asked as they sat down in a corner with their drinks. There was no waitress at this joint. You paid at the cash register and someone barked your order. It was so different from Emilio's house that she began to feel glum, deprived of what to her had been an Edenic delight.

"I just came back from seeing him," she said, suppressing a sigh and looking at the sleeves of her dress. Under the harsh lights inside the lonchería she thought her hands looked ugly and rough.

"What did he say? Does he know where Leonora is?"

She hid her hands in her lap, clasping her purse tight. "He doesn't know where she is. She wanted to go see a journalist last weekend, but Emilio couldn't drive her there, and he's not sure if she ever made it. He's worried about her."

"So am I," Rubén muttered.

Maite looked around the lonchería. It wasn't busy, and the cashier was far from them, behind the counter, looking up at the television set. They were broadcasting an old movie with Miroslava. Still, Maite leaned forward and spoke in a whisper.

"A man came to speak to me at my office yesterday. He was also looking for her, and he mentioned your name."

"He mentioned me?" Rubén asked, frowning.

"Yes. He said he was from the Dirección Federal de Seguridad. He said you were a . . . a 'subversive element.' What does that even mean? You wouldn't be, right?"

"The government calls everything subversive," he said. "A poster of Mao Tse-tung is subversive. They can accuse you of promoting social dissolution and jail you because you went to a rally. They'll spy on you if you're a journalist who writes the wrong sort of columns."

"Sure, but Emilio said something about terrorists. But you aren't terrorists, right?" Maite insisted.

"We should eat our food and then pay Jackie a visit," Rubén said.

"What for?"

"If someone from the DFS is going around looking for you and me, then she needs to know."

A teenager yelled their order number. Rubén stood up, went to the counter, and returned with two plates, placing one before Maite. While they ate, she kept glancing at Rubén. Discreetly, of course. Or as discreetly as she could.

Rubén hadn't answered her question. That could mean he was really a terrorist, after all. One of those radicals the papers mentioned. If only she paid more attention to that sort of news. But Maite was forever skipping the front pages. And yet, he didn't fit with her, albeit limited, knowledge of those people. If there were guerillas, they were in the countryside, in places like Guerrero.

Bandits. That's what one of the papers had said one time. Bandits in Guerrero.

Was she having lunch with a modern-day Robin Hood or someone more sinister? A cold-blooded killer, a kidnapper, a lurid, cartoonish monster. A villain! She shouldn't be messing with villains, bad guys who tied women up with rope that scratched their soft wrists. And the villain's lair . . .

The thought of meeting Jackie, of seeing the place where these people hung out, excited Maite. Maybe they were cigar-chomping outlaws with rifles. She wondered what would happen if there was a guerilla in *Secret Romance*. Funny, she'd never pictured such a thing. This turmoil was impossible. The island of her comic books was replete with melodrama, but distasteful reality didn't intrude there.

"You didn't tell the guy from the DFS anything, did you?" Rubén asked.

"As if! I grew up in the Doctores. You don't ever tell cops anything, it makes it worse," Maite said, and she sipped her soda.

He seemed surprised by that answer. "That's good," he said.

"It's not like I know anything, either. Will you have to blindfold me when we go to see Jackie?"

He chuckled. "No need for that. It's not top secret."

The building Rubén took her to was quite ordinary. There were no sentries, no vicious dogs barking to announce their arrival. They went up the stairs and into a gallery space that appeared equally mundane—a little sign on the door proclaimed this "Asterisk Art Gallery and Cooperative." An art gallery. Not Maite's sort of place. She'd gone to the National History Museum on school trips a couple of times but never set foot in an art gallery.

There was a party at the gallery, judging by the number of young people milling around, drinks in hand. Maite wondered if there were parties every weekend. Maybe Leonora attended these events regularly, together with Emilio.

A couple of women glanced at Maite. She wondered what they must think of her, in her too-young yellow dress. Fussy. She looked fussy. Maybe they weren't looking at her, maybe they were looking at Rubén.

"Where are we going?" she asked him.

"Told you, we're looking for Jackie," he said, glancing around the room.

"You sure she's here?"

"She should be. She must be in the office. Come on."

The gallery's office came with the expected contents: paintings leaning against bookcases, small sculptures on shelves, a tall pile of boxes. Two desks had been placed together in the center of the room with two typewriters on them. Rickety tables and chairs were scattered all around. The room was hot, even though the window was open and a fan whirred in a corner. It was also smoky from many cigarettes, five people crammed inside smoking for god knew how long. Three men and two women.

One of the women sat behind a desk and was busy going through documents while the other one was standing in front of the fan, trying to cool off. Two of the men were sitting on the other side of the desk. One of them had recently been in a serious scuffle. He had two black eyes, and his arm was in a sling. It was an alarming sight.

"Hey, this is Maite, that friend of Leonora's I was telling you about," Rubén said as they walked in and the five people in the room stared at them.

Maite nodded. The woman who had been sitting behind the desk stood up. She wore a white shirt with flowers embroidered around the neckline. Over this she had a vest; its pockets were also embroidered. Her hair was in a messy braid. She didn't look much like a revolutionary. None of them did, and they were all very young.

"I'm Jackie. That's Luz," the woman said, pointing to the other woman in the room, who gave Maite a tiny smile. "This here is Sócrates," Jackie continued, placing a hand on a young man's shoulder. He wore a bandana and was drinking from a pocillo, which he put down to wave at her.

"Hey," Sócrates said.

"And this here is Casimiro."

The man with the arm in a sling nodded at Maite. Jackie didn't introduce the fifth person in the room, the man in a suede jacket and a turtleneck sitting in the back, smoking a cigarette, his legs stretched out.

Maite smiled at them, the smile tense, trying to keep the corners of her lips from wavering. "It's nice to meet you."

"Maite talked to Emilio earlier. Tell them what he said."

When she hesitated, Rubén gave Maite a reassuring pat on the arm. "He didn't say much," she began. "He hasn't seen Leonora. She told him she wanted to meet with a journalist who lives in Cuernavaca. Lara. But Emilio couldn't give her a ride. That's all he knows."

"You know any journalists called Lara?" Jackie asked, turning to Luz.

The young woman shook her head. "Doesn't ring a bell."

"Anything else?" Jackie asked.

"Maite caught Emilio poking around Leonora's apartment."

Maite turned to look at Rubén, aghast. "I didn't say that!"

"You said he was looking for a camera."

"But he wasn't really poking. He was worried. He was worried that Leonora was getting into a mess," Maite said. "And you've got to admit he's right, what with that man from the Dirección Federal de Seguridad talking to me and all."

"Wait, what man?" Jackie said, whipping her head up and looking at Rubén. "There's a guy from the DFS involved?"

"That's why we stopped by. We thought you ought to know."

"Shit," Jackie said, rubbing a hand against her forehead and shaking her head. "Does this guy have a name?"

"Anaya," Maite said. "He wanted to know where Leonora was, but I have no idea. I told him so. But somehow he knew I'd talked to Rubén, and he mentioned you too."

"They must be watching her," Sócrates said. "It was a mighty fine idea to bring her here, Rubén."

"Oh, shut up," Rubén muttered. "It's no big secret where you can find me. Where you can find all of us."

"I'm saying maybe you shouldn't leave a fucking trail of bread-crumbs for them to follow, asshole."

"We get it," Jackie said, shushing Sócrates and pressing her hands together, resting the tips of her fingers right beneath her chin as she sat down again on the chair she had been occupying when they walked in. "Emilio was looking for a camera, but he didn't find it. Are you sure? Did you look through Leonora's apartment?"

"There was nothing there," Maite said. "Leonora phoned me and wanted me to take her cat and a box to her, but the box is garbage."

"You went through it? You're sure?"

"Yes. You're welcome to go through it too."

"Maybe Lara has the pictures," Rubén said. "Leonora could even be with that journalist, in Cuernavaca. She could be hiding there."

"If there's a journalist," Jackie muttered.

Rubén tensed immediately. He had been leaning against a bookcase, but now he stood up straight, his eyes fixed on Jackie. "What are you saying?"

"She's saying none of us have seen those pictures," Sócrates replied, setting his pocillo down atop a pile of books.

"Then where the hell is Leonora? Why is the DFS interested in this? There're pictures, I know it. You can't think . . . she's not the mole, Jackie!"

But Jackie didn't seem convinced, and the rest of the people in the room gave Rubén equally dubious glances.

"Fuck, Jackie, not that again," Rubén said with a sigh. "You don't even know for sure there's a mole."

"I know," Jackie said.

"How?"

"Look, it doesn't matter," Sócrates said, interrupting them. "We have more important stuff to worry about now."

"What's more important than finding Leonora?"

"Someone, maybe from the DFS, treated Casimiro like a punching bag."

"Yes, and they could be beating the living shit out of Leonora right now. And there're the photos to worry about too."

"Leonora was never trustworthy," Luz pointed out.

"That's not true."

"Just because you slept with her doesn't mean she's really our friend," Sócrates piped up.

"You should talk," Rubén said, raising his voice. So did Sócrates. Then it was a jumble of back and forth pronouncements and recriminations that Maite couldn't even begin to follow.

"Fuck!" Jackie said, lifting her hands in the air dramatically, then letting them fall and resting them against her knees. "Sócrates, why don't you and the others let me chat with Rubén and his friend for a bit? There're too many damn people in the room."

They obeyed. Out went Luz, Sócrates, then finally Casimiro and the man in the suede jacket who had not spoken a single word. He tossed his cigarette in an ashtray, and when he walked by Maite he gave her a wink.

Rubén moved to stand by the window, arms crossed, looking outside. He was frowning.

"I know what you're thinking, but it's not my fault she's missing," Jackie said.

"She was supposed to meet you. You were supposed to keep her safe," Rubén replied.

"I did meet her. And then she said she couldn't give me the photos after all, that she wasn't sure. She jumped out of my car, Rubén. I didn't make her do that."

"You told her she was the mole."

Jackie raised her chin, her eyes hard. "I told her it was time she proved herself. She didn't."

"I need to borrow the gun," Rubén said coolly. "Maite and I are going to pay that journalist a visit."

"I don't want you getting in trouble."

"We're all in trouble already. We need to recover those photographs. If agents from the DFS are out there looking for them too, then I better be prepared."

Jackie frowned, but she grabbed a set of keys from her vest's pockets and unlocked a desk drawer. She took out a gun and held it in her hands, looking carefully at it.

"What if she destroyed the pictures?"

"You've got to have more faith in people, Jackie."

"I suppose you want faith and my car for the weekend, on top of my gun."

"I'll have everything back to you Monday."

She handed the gun to Rubén, who nonchalantly grabbed a paper bag that was sitting on a corner of one of the desks and stuffed the weapon in it, as though it were his lunch.

The door opened, and Luz rushed back in. "Arkady caught the guy who beat Casimiro the other night! He was here!"

"Here? Where?" Jackie asked.

"Here, right here! Arkady is taking him to the storage room."

"Let's go," Rubén muttered, grabbing Maite by the arm.

"What's wrong?"

Maite looked over her shoulder at the women who were talking excitedly, but Rubén was leading her out of the office at a quick pace. Rather than exiting the way they had come, he pulled her to the back of the room, where there was a door that led to a narrow set of stairs.

Rubén moved so fast Maite almost tripped and fell. She protested, but he didn't relent. They got in the car. He tossed the paper bag on the dashboard, and she asked him what was wrong again, but he didn't reply.

The idea of villains who tied women with a thick rope returned to her, perversely knotting itself around her brain. She eyed the paper bag and bit her lip, turning her head to look out the window.

16

IF IT HAD been one of the bozos from the art collective with a knife, Elvis would have chanced it and tried to fight him off, even with the threat of a close-range attack. But when Elvis got up and raised his hands, he realized three other young men had come running down the stairs.

"Come on, son of a bitch," one of the men said, and Elvis allowed himself to be taken to a storage room, because he could do basic math and one against four guys and one of them with a knife would have been stupid, especially when the fucking knife was pressed against his neck. A knife against your neck wasn't negotiable.

Once they reached the storage room, one of the men told him to take off his jacket, which Elvis did, and the other two ordered him to sit down and tried tying him to a chair. They had no idea how to do it, and Elvis almost chuckled at their fumbling fingers as they pinned his hands behind his back.

Meanwhile, the guy who had been expertly holding the knife against his neck began emptying the contents of Elvis's jacket and carefully setting them on a table with a lonely radio. Something about his bearing, about the way he worked—cool, composed, while the other two were still trying to tie a knot—seemed out of place.

The storage room was full of boxes. There were no windows. Once Elvis was tied, the man with the knife tucked his weapon away.

"I want to talk to him alone," the man said. "Step outside and don't let anyone bother me until I come out."

The men closed the door behind them. Elvis could hear the muffled sound of music and loud stomping coming from the floor above. He looked up at the ceiling, frowning.

"Dance studio," the man said, still looking at Elvis's possessions. He was holding up his driver's license. It was a fake, of course. "You dance much?"

"Not really."

"No, I didn't peg you for a dancer, and I don't think you're here for the art gallery. So, what's your angle?"

"Sorry?"

"Your angle," the man said, putting the driver's license down and turning to Elvis. "Who do you work for? DFS? Or you a judicial?"

"Who do *you* work for?" Elvis shot back. "You speak Spanish like you learned it from a Spaniard, but you're not from there."

"How would you know?"

"I knew a real Spanish dude," he said, thinking of El Gazpacho.

"There're several regions in Spain, you know. Not everyone sounds the same," the man said, swiping a newspaper from a tall pile and opening it, his eyes scanning the contents instead of focusing on Elvis. "But I'll give you a point for being observant. And maybe I'll even tell you where I'm from if you answer my questions. What's your name? Your real name."

"Elvis."

"Your real name, I said."

"It's as real as it gets."

It was true. There's nothing that Elvis loved more than being Elvis. The loser he'd been before was best forgotten. Elvis wasn't a code name, like it might have been for the others. Elvis was him. His interrogator must have appreciated the honesty in his voice, because he nodded.

"You can call me Arkady," the man said. He was tall and

dressed nicely in a suede jacket and a turtleneck. Sharp, but not overly fussy. His shoes were of shiny patent leather. With that fashionable outfit he could as easily fit in at a trendy cocktail party or a hippie's birthday bash.

"Sure, Arkady."

The man plugged in the radio. "Who do you work for, Elvis?"

"It's all the same garbage. What difference does it make?"

"Ah, you think you're clever, don't you? Answering my questions with questions. Well, I can't waste all my day with a sloppy man like you."

"Sloppy," Elvis repeated.

"The way you beat Casimiro was sloppy. Too messy. I can't stand messy interrogations. You probably are messy all the time," the man said, raising his hands in the air and sighing. "Three guys to beat a skinny priest? You couldn't do it on your own?"

"You handle it any better in Russia?"

"How'd you figure that one out?" the man asked. He didn't sound surprised. Just pleased that Elvis had caught on quickly. Maybe he'd assumed Elvis was a fucking idiot and he wouldn't even guess right.

"You sure aren't from Peralvillo. Arkady's a Russian name. It's from *Crime and Punishment*."

"Are you studying literature?"

Elvis chuckled. "I like to read."

"Good. Everyone deserves an education. Now, what's your angle?"

"I'm guessing that yours is to try and scare me by telling me you're KGB and then waving your gun at me."

He probably had a Makarov somewhere on him, fucking commie spy.

The man smiled and switched on the radio, turning up the volume pretty damn high. "White Room" was starting to play. He rolled up the newspaper he was holding, his hands tight around the paper. "No, by keeping it simple. Not sloppy. Simple."

Arkady whacked him in the face with the newspaper, like Elvis was a damn dog. And shit, it fucking *hurt*. Arkady whacked him again and again and again. Elvis tried to focus on something else. That's what El Mago told them when they were hurt, focus on something else. But there wasn't much to focus on in that gray storage room filled with boxes.

"Scream if you want, by all means," Arkady said. But of course the radio was blasting, and who the fuck was going to hear Elvis anyway? Better to bite his tongue instead of whimpering like a baby.

He thought of the woman. Maite. With her startled eyes, the face like Bluebeard's wife. The way she'd craned her head that morning when the hippie had been speaking to her in front of her building, before they got into the car. Her dress was yellow with a flowered print.

Elvis blinked, looking up at Arkady. The man had stopped hitting him and was now looking down at him, still smiling. His teeth were very white. He probably brushed them after every meal, the fucker. Combed his hair very nicely, made sure not a strand of it was out of place. Even now after hitting Elvis eight times in a row he looked pristine.

"Who do you work for?" Arkady asked, now tapping Elvis on the shoulder with the newspaper. A tiny tap. Elvis flinched and swallowed, the taste of bile coating his tongue. He'd once read about an asshole who beat a dog to death with a newspaper and wondered if you could do the same with a man. He wasn't about to find out.

Reveal what you must, conceal the rest. That's another thing El Mago always said. He decided to try that avenue. "DFS," he muttered. A lie, but it sounded real enough. He was thinking about the DFS quite a bit lately, and it was safer to say he was with DFS than a Hawk. Even a KGB orangutan would think twice about putting a bullet in a DFS man. It would cause too much trouble.

"What do you want here?" the Russian asked.

"I'm guessing the same thing you want," Elvis muttered. "An art education."

"You mouthy idiot. What. Do. You. Want."

Each word was followed by a blow and the rhythmic wah-wah of Clapton's guitar until Elvis croaked a name. "Leonora," he said, figuring what the fuck. He had to say *something*.

"Ah, Leonora. The girl with the pictures. Do you have any good leads?"

"My only lead brought me here, so it's not much."

"No, it's not," Arkady agreed. "Who's your boss?"

"Some dude."

Arkady hit him again. Half a dozen whacks to the face. Elvis's mouth was bleeding. But if he answered too quickly, the man would know he was faking it. So he thought about Maite again, the picture he'd stolen from her apartment. The dark eyes captured in that snapshot, that quivering of the mouth, frozen in time.

Upstairs, the people were dancing again. The tap-tap-tap of their feet seemed to mark each blow. He couldn't recognize the music. It sounded distorted, muffled by the radio in the room. Danzón, maybe. For all he knew, a tango. Yeah, probably a tango. He couldn't dance. Put music on and he'd stand firmly in place, ramrod straight.

A fucking tango was taking place above his head, Los Hooligans were on the radio now that the song by Cream was done, and the damn Russian was striking him with indifferent, methodical blows while Elvis swallowed blood.

Another half dozen blows and Elvis spoke. "Anaya," he sputtered. "It's Anaya."

It sounded honest, and Arkady seemed satisfied, though he still smacked him across the face with the newspaper one more time before stepping out.

Elvis waited a few minutes before testing his bonds. It was a good thing the men who had tied him up were nitwits because Elvis had never learned the finer points of undoing knots. He relied on stretching the rope and wriggling out of it in a rather clumsy manner, but it worked. He managed to untie himself.

Quickly Elvis put on his jacket and stuffed his possessions in his pocket. Then, curious, he looked into one of the many cardboard boxes around the room. It was filled with black-and-white flyers. The flyer said "UNITE!" in big letters. "Wake up to the struggle!"

The door to the storage room was garbage, and he jimmied his way out using his screwdriver; he didn't even have to actually pick the lock. A couple of quick, efficient strokes and the door opened.

The Russian was gone, but outside the storage room was one of the men who had tied him to the chair. He looked quite startled by the sight of Elvis. Elvis paid him back by slamming him against the wall and kneeing him in the balls, then punching him once he was groaning and doubling over.

Elvis would have liked to pluck out the asshole's fucking eyeballs, he would have liked to have found the damn Russian and slammed his screwdriver into his ear, but there was no time to waste. The storage room was on the ground floor, behind the stairs, and he sprinted his way to freedom.

Once outside, he kept running and didn't stop until he was out of breath. His lungs were on fire, sweat dripped down his brow, and his hands were trembling. He didn't know what to do. His training had taught him how to beat people and how to spy on them, but not much of this stupid game he was caught in.

El Güero was going to make fun of him, he knew it. He was going to say, you sad little fucker, getting beat up. And the Antelope wouldn't be much better. El Gazpacho would have known what to do now, would know how to piece together all the info and deliver a report, cool and composed, but Elvis had no idea what was what.

Fuck, he'd been tortured by a damn KGB agent.

He found a public telephone in front of a tlapalería. He wiped his mouth with the back of his jacket's sleeve. Copper. His mouth tasted of copper.

He grabbed the receiver, tossed a coin, and dialed El Mago's number.

"Yes?" El Mago asked.

"Something happened, I need to come in," he said. El Mago didn't normally have any of them at his place—it was a rare treat—but he figured this was a special occasion.

There was silence.

"See you in half an hour," El Mago said. "Bell number twelve, ring four times."

Elvis hung up. Two streets from the tlapalería he hailed a cab. His face ached, and he rubbed his jaw.

He had almost forgotten El Mago's address, and for a moment he panicked, thinking he wouldn't be able to find it. But in the end he managed fine and rang the bell El Mago had indicated, four times. El Mago buzzed him in without a word.

Elvis climbed the stairs rather than using the old elevator. He didn't need to knock. El Mago opened the door and let him in. El Mago took one look at Elvis and turned away from him.

"You need ice," he said. "Come to the kitchen."

The kitchen was as fabulous as the rest of the apartment, and despite the pain in his jaw he let himself admire it. The counters and cabinets were done in a dark wood, very classy, with silver knobs, and there were blue-and-white tiles on the walls. Nothing to do with the dirty linoleum and rickety furniture of Elvis's childhood.

El Mago took out a few ice cubes and wrapped them in a kitchen rag. "What happened to you?" he asked, handing him the rag.

Elvis pressed it against his face. "I followed that woman, Maite, to Asterisk. I figured I'd go in there and do some talking with those artists, see what I could find, maybe even chat with her myself. Well, that shit priest we talked to the other day was also there. He recognized me and raised hell. There was a motherfucking Russian with him. He beat me up."

"A Russian. Really?"

"No joke. And what's worse, I still don't know where this chick is. It's like she's vanished. Oh, and DFS? They're on the same path as us."

"How do you know that?"

"We're not the only ones watching that woman's building. There were other folks there. I can't say who they were, but the name Anaya ring a bell? Justo said he might be into this whole thing."

"Anaya." El Mago shook his head. "Yes, I know Anaya. He is a nosy bastard who wants to climb up the ranks using my bones to lift himself up. Dirty thief."

"Thief?"

"He has a side business smuggling stolen American cars into the country. It came out a little while ago, and it's gotten him in a bit of trouble. That wouldn't have been tolerated in my day, but now!" El Mago made a fist. "He believes if he can make me look bad, he can make himself look good. If he gets those pictures before I do, it's all over. It is over for me and it is over for *you*. You understand?"

Elvis nodded. "I told the Russian I worked for Anaya. Figured it was better than saying I worked for you. And maybe he'll go and stab that fucker instead of us, if he feels like it."

Elvis switched the rag with the ice from one cheek to the other. El Mago crossed his arms, deep in thought, then began walking toward the living room. Elvis followed him. He glanced at the pictures above El Mago's upright piano. There were two little girls in several photos. A younger El Mago with other family members.

"Sorry if I didn't tell you over the phone, but I was trying to follow procedure," Elvis said, and he had been. Keep chatter to a minimum over the phone, that's what El Mago told them.

"You were scared," El Mago said. "You are still scared. Scuttling around in fear. Well, you cannot. This was a minor incident."

It didn't feel very minor to Elvis with his jaw throbbing. "Sure."

"What did you find out about Asterisk? Aside from the fact that they seem to have a Russian friend."

"They think Leonora is a mole. And there're a couple of people she might have turned to for help. Emilio and, yes, I know you said not to dig there, but also a dude named Sócrates. I didn't get much chance to ask anything else."

El Mago walked toward where Elvis was standing, by the piano. He lifted the lid and ran his fingers over the keys, playing a simple melody. "I can give you a file on Emilio. But you need to be cautious with him. He is no dissident."

"If he's hiding the girl, maybe he is."

"Doubtful."

"You have anything on Sócrates?"

"I have something on every member of Asterisk. Wait here."

El Mago exited the room, and Elvis leaned down, looking at the piano keys. Then he straightened up and glanced around the room, at the beautiful books, the beautiful shelves, the antiques and decorative items. What a perfect, precious place this was. If only he could live like this instead of having the crap beaten out of him in a storage room.

He'd never wanted this, the fucked-up job he had, the fucked-up people he lived with, the fucked-up assignments watching folks when he didn't give a damn if they were red or not—Jesus, what was the big deal about that? He needed the money. Needed the gig. If he wasn't a Hawk he'd be a damn delinquent, a thief, a nothing. He needed the hope that at the end of the tunnel there was a place like this, safe and cozy. A little apartment with a piano and beautiful furniture and pictures in silver frames.

El Mago came back with two folders and handed them to Elvis. "Should we still be watching the girl's neighbor?"

"She was at Asterisk, which is apparently a den of KGB spies these days. She spoke to Leonora. That woman must know something she is not telling us yet. Keep tabs on her."

That was that. El Mago told him to go back to the apartment and clean himself up. When he reached the street it had started to rain. An anemic rain, but it felt good on his face.

17

"YOU NEED TO get Lara's address from Emilio," Rubén told her.

"He was going to his shop when I saw him earlier."

"I know where that is."

Maite thought it was rude to drop by uninvited, but there was a gun in a brown paper bag sitting on the dashboard. They were past the point of pleasantries. It scared her a little, but she also enjoyed the electric frisson it conjured. It was like one of her comic books. Except Rubén didn't look much like a comic book hero, in his t-shirt and driving that ratty car. Would his appearance improve at all in a tuxedo? Who knew.

Emilio. So she'd get to speak to him twice in one day. She opened her purse and began digging inside of it, trying to see if she'd packed her lipstick. But she hadn't. She pulled down the side passenger mirror and smoothed back her hair, trying to at least fix that.

Her reflection showed her all the little imperfections of her skin. She closed her eyes.

Rubén let her out exactly in front of Emilio's shop, but he told her he'd park around the corner. She stepped out of the car, grasped her purse with both hands and looked at the sign, which said "LOMELÍ ANTIQUES" in large letters. In the window display there were porcelain vases and dishes, and one could see the glint of crystal and lacquered furniture in the background.

It looked like a very nice shop, as he'd promised.

She walked in, a silver bell ringing as she opened the door. The shop was charming, but a little crammed, and she had to walk carefully by a display with porcelain dolls. A young woman was sitting behind a counter, reading a magazine, her long, pink fingernails tapping a picture. Maite wound her way through the shop and clutched her purse tighter, wondering what she should tell the girl.

When she reached the counter, Maite placed her purse upon its glass surface. "Is Mr. Lomelí in?" she asked.

The young woman looked up at Maite. "He's doing inventory. Do you have an appointment?"

"No. But I'm a friend of his. Maite. My name is Maite."

The employee gave her a thin, skeptical smile. "I'll see if he's available."

The young woman stood up. She was wearing a miniskirt and perilously tall heels. She swept a red curtain aside with a hand, stepped behind it, and closed it again.

Maite wondered if that was the way Emilio liked women. Slim, hair cut short, looking a bit like Twiggy, balancing atop shoes that were more like stilts. But no, Leonora didn't look like that. Her hair was long. Yet she was also beautiful.

Maite glanced down at her yellow print dress, her sensible shoes, and her ugly knees.

Emilio opened the curtain. He had rolled up the sleeves of his shirt so his arms were visible up to the elbow, the collar of his shirt open. He looked very nice in this more casual look.

"Hey there, we meet again. Come around to the back."

"I'm sorry I didn't phone," Maite said, quickly rounding the counter.

"It's fine. You can drop by anytime."

"That's very kind of you."

"I'm sociable."

He walked her into a well-kept little office. On his desk he had a lamp with a dark green shade, and on the walls there were antique engravings. She pictured him at the small desk, relaxed, going over figures and ledgers.

"What do you think of my shop?" he asked.

"It's nice. Very different from your house."

"Well, that's home and this is work. Truth is, this is my father's shop. I was more interested in photos and art galleries, but that was when I was younger," he said, dismissively waving away his early twenties with one hand. "Anyway, I'm guessing you're not here looking for a nice bronze sculpture?"

"I came to ask you for the address of that journalist friend of yours."

Emilio leaned against his desk and cocked his head a little. "You plan to pay Lara a visit?"

"Someone must know something about Leonora's whereabouts. Lara's house might be a good place to start looking for clues."

"Are you turning into a detective, Maite?" Emilio asked, but playfully, and then he turned around and began flipping through his Rolodex.

"I'm worried."

"Aren't we all? I'm not sure if Lara's home, though. I phoned earlier, no answer. But I suppose you could be luckier than me. She doesn't always pick up the phone if she's on deadline," he said, pulling out a card and copying the information onto a small slip of paper. He handed it to her. "Keep me informed, will you? I meant it when I said you can drop by anytime."

"I'll call as soon as I get back."

Emilio smiled. He had a wonderful smile. Good teeth, like the porcelain in his shop. Good hair, good eyes, good everything. *Why can't the world be full of men like this?* she thought, remembering the nobodies and losers she'd gone out with. One of the worst ones had been that bank clerk who liked to collect floaty pens—by tilting the pens one could move a boat down a river or make a Hawaiian dancer glide in front of a backdrop of palm trees—but there was also the man from the insurance company who chewed with his mouth open.

And Cristóbalito. She had loved without restraint, and he'd left a stain upon her soul, Cristóbalito. He'd been a portent of things to come, the beginning to a litany of bitterness.

She left the shop quickly, slipped back into the car. "I've got the address," she told Rubén.

"Great. We can go back to your place and look at that box before we head to Cuernavaca," Rubén said, glancing at his watch.

"You're thinking of going to Cuernavaca today?"

"Or early tomorrow. Did you have any stuff you had to do this weekend?"

She shook her head, wishing she could tell him she had prior engagements. That she'd have to check her calendar.

When they reached the apartment, the first thing she did was feed Leonora's irritating cat. If the girl didn't come back, she wondered what she'd do with the animal. Something might have happened to her, after all. Or maybe nothing was wrong. Perhaps the girl was holed up with a friend. Leonora seemed to have many friends. She also had money. For all they knew, she was sunbathing in Acapulco.

After feeding the cat, Maite showed Rubén the box Leonora had left behind, and he began taking all its contents out, spreading them on the dining room table. There was nothing of interest there. Old newspapers, papers, magazines. Junk meant for the trash heap.

Maite let him dig through the box and put on a record. The notes of "Somos Novios" spilled out of her atelier. She went into her bedroom, looked at the mirror atop her vanity, once again examining her face. Under the subdued lights of her apartment the face looked somewhat prettier. She grabbed a tiny perfume bottle, another one of the stolen items from her collection, now displayed atop the vanity along with other trinkets, and dabbed a bit of perfume on her neck.

She'd stolen the perfume bottle, which had already been half empty anyway, from her mother, and it brought her great pleasure to wear it. But she only did on special occasions, rationing it. She supposed it was a special occasion. She seldom had any men in her apartment.

She walked back to the dining room, watching him as he sighed and put a newspaper down.

"There's nothing here," he said, rubbing his forehead. "Unless there's a cryptic clue hidden in one of these old newspapers."

"You look tired."

"I was up late, working."

"Want a cup of coffee?"

"Sure."

She slid into the minuscule kitchen and put the kettle on the burner. She'd always wanted a nice kitchen. This one was falling apart. Peeling linoleum and sagging counters. But the landlord would never fix it.

She prepared two cups of coffee and brought out the sugar bowl. She was very proud of the dainty sugar bowl. It was real porcelain. She'd bought it at La Lagunilla, haggling until the woman selling it brought down her price. It wasn't very ladylike to haggle, but Maite would bicker over a miserable peso like a furious wolf if it was necessary. It often was.

Maite placed the cup of coffee before him, and he smiled. A couple of days before she'd thought about inviting this man to her apartment, and there he was. And of course now that he was here, sitting in her dining room, she wasn't sure what to say to him, although in her imagination she had asked him to fuck. Easily and plainly. Just because she could.

Maite was boring, and she was tired of being boring. But she couldn't, didn't quite, want to go there.

She wouldn't be any better than the man with the floaty pens, who also collected pictures of pinups, his hungry eyes classifying every woman alive, measuring her, sliding her into the drawer of his memories. Their legs, their breasts, their torso. He'd been a sleaze, but she was somehow worse.

You're perverse, she thought. *Deep down, you're a monster of perversity and you know it. All you have is cheap fantasies.*

"How long have you been working at the print shop?" she asked.

"A couple of years, part-time. It'll take a while to find something else. I dropped out of university so it's not that easy getting a decent job."

"What did you study?"

"Literature."

Better than poetry, she thought grimly. Though not by much. Maybe he'd spend the rest of his life in that print shop, growing bent and grayed.

"Where do you work?" he asked.

"I'm a secretary at a law firm."

"You like it there?"

"I hate it," Maite said honestly, stirring her coffee and taking a sip.

"You could quit."

"The pay at another job wouldn't be any better."

"It might be more fun."

How odd, she thought. To think of a job as "fun" or "not fun" when a job was simply a paycheck. She supposed it was his youth that made him think like that. Ten years in the trenches, and he'd burn through those ideas.

Youth. All he had was his youth. He wasn't attractive; he was too hairy for her taste and not nearly as sophisticated as she might have wanted. Still, he'd dated Leonora, and Leonora was beautiful. Maybe that's how it went for men. It didn't matter if you were the Hunchback of Notre Dame, you still had a chance to romance Esmeralda.

"How did you and Leonora meet?" she asked.

"At Asterisk. I've been designing flyers for them for a while, helping Jackie out like that and with other stuff. Leonora started showing up and we got to talking and we had a lot of stuff in common, so we started going out together."

"For how long?"

"Over half a year. She'd just arrived in the city. She was a bit provincial, but not for long. And she was eager to make friends, to meet people, and everyone wanted to meet her. She has a glow about her, as you know."

Maite didn't know. She didn't know this woman at all. She thought of the island in *Secret Romance*; she pictured the girl writhing on a stone altar.

"I felt I'd hit the jackpot, you know? I was crazy about her. I took her out, drove her wherever she needed to go, we talked for hours."

"What happened?"

He grimaced a little, as if he were picking at a scab. "Emilio happened. Every weekend he'd come to Asterisk, looking for an easy fuck. He sleeps with anything that moves, and I guess he thought it was a good place to pick up girls. Lots of young people to snack on."

"And he met Leonora."

"He met Leonora," Rubén said, nodding and drinking his coffee. There was a pause; he scratched his wrist. "The thing is we used to make fun of Emilio. Leonora and I, we thought he was another bourgeoisie pig looking for a thrill. He was stuck-up, thought so much of himself simply because his money had helped start the collective. Every time he walked into a room, he was wearing sunglasses, and he'd whip them off, like a cheapo movie star. It was funny."

"But obviously she thought he was nice," Maite said, a little angrily. She didn't like Rubén talking about Emilio like that. Emilio was classy, and Rubén was being bitter about the whole thing. As if anyone could blame Leonora for trading up.

Rubén looked at her, frowning. "Yeah, well, I don't know what bullshit he told her, but she believed him. She dumped me and they started going out. She did it nicely, told me she didn't want to cheat on me. Like she was doing me a favor, you know. Very gently. And I'm not even sure she *didn't* cheat on me."

"Oh," she said and wondered if the girl had ever received Rubén with the scent of her other lover still on her crimson bedsheets. Or if she'd been more careful, if they'd only met in the safety of Emilio's home. In distant places where prying eyes couldn't reveal their secret.

"She was very sweet to me toward the end, and the thing is, when Leonora is sweet it's because she's making up for something. She feels guilty. That's Leonora's problem. Guilt always catches up with her; it weighs her down and she suffocates. She must have cheated on me."

She pictured beautiful Leonora tearfully telling Rubén it wasn't her fault. It had just happened. They could remain friends, and she was *so* sorry. In her mind, Leonora's tears streamed down her face, under her large sunglasses, lips parted. Like in the comic books. But it hadn't been a comic book. It had been real. Like Cristóbalito had been real.

"But you still like her," Maite said, almost accusingly.

"Yes, well, ain't that the thing? No one said I was smart," he told her with a chuckle. "Just because someone stops loving you, it doesn't mean you stop loving them."

She felt bad for him. He was a loser, like Maite. Both of them a couple of dumb fucks sitting in the silent dining room—the music had stopped playing.

"I felt like that about a boy, once," Maite admitted. "He broke my heart and still I wanted him back. I'd sit at night and cry my eyes out. I thought I'd die when he left. I wanted to die. I would have, if I weren't such a coward."

If this was a comic book, she thought, there'd be a panel flashing back to a distant point in the past. And Maite, holding her heart out in her hands, like a maiden in an Aztec sacrifice.

But Rubén didn't seem to be listening to her; he wasn't looking at her. "I want her to come back. To be safe."

She stretched out her fingers, patting his hand, which was resting by the cooling cup of coffee, but even then he didn't seem to realize she was there. He let out a sigh and smiled a little, and then she pulled her hand back, resting it in her lap.

She felt more lonely, sitting in front of this man, than she'd felt in ages.

"I guess I'm a little tired after all," he said, pinching the bridge of his nose. "Maybe we should go in the morning. I don't think I'm up for a long drive. Do you have a blanket I can borrow? I can take the couch, no problem."

"You want to stay here?"

"I don't want to scare you, but someone beat up our friend, and that someone was also around Asterisk today. Maybe it's the guy from the DFS who went to your office, maybe someone else. Either way, I don't think you should be alone."

She wished to laugh. This young man was inviting himself into her apartment. How funny. That he should fulfill her wish, now she didn't really want him around. He'd made her sad.

"I have a blanket," she said, and she went to her room and brought it out to him.

It was too early to sleep, but he had already taken off his shoes and was lying horizontal on the couch, an arm over his eyes. She put the blanket on him, and he thanked her, his voice sounding muffled.

It was early, so she sat in her atelier, carefully turning the pages of an old issue of *Secret Romance* while Lucho Gatica sang about his one and only love. She thought of Emilio Lomelí, who looked like one of the beautifully drawn characters in the comic book, and Leonora, who resembled the heroines who cried their way through such publications. And then she thought of Rubén, sleeping in her living room, with a gun in a paper bag at his side, who didn't look like anyone except maybe the blurry faces in the background of a panel. And Maite, who wasn't even a blurry face, who wasn't included in any issue.

18

THE SKY WAS gray when they left the apartment, yet it didn't rain. It was like the whispered broken promise of a half-hearted lover.

They spent most of the journey in silence. Maite wasn't sure how to treat Rubén. They were not friends. No, not quite, she thought, watching him as he sat behind the wheel. In her lap there was a copy of *Secret Romance*, which she flicked through aimlessly.

She rolled the window down. She flipped through another page of her comic book. All the while she kept thinking she didn't know Leonora, she had no business in this car, with this man. Maite had enough problems with her debts, her broken vehicle, her family, to be taking on anyone else's problems. To become involved with a bunch of commie kids who were being watched by DFS agents.

She resolutely stared into the rearview mirror and told herself she wasn't going to give in to mundane concerns. Not that day. Come tomorrow, yes, she'd dress in her office clothes, grab her purse, and take the bus to work. Right now, though, she didn't have to consider any of that.

Besides, she hadn't gone on an outing in so long. It was always work or worry; maybe the movie theater if they had a good film. At least she was leaving the house. She was going somewhere. Anywhere would do.

"I hope you slept well," Maite said after a while, because she wanted to at least pretend they might be friends. "The couch isn't very comfortable."

"It was fine. I was really beat. A marching band could have come into the room and I wouldn't have known. Are you a morning person?"

"Pretty much. All I need is a cup of coffee and I'm out the door."

"I wish I was like that. I get up in stages."

"In stages, really?"

"Yeah, first roll out of bed, then roll onto the floor. That sort of thing. Leonora is the same. No, she's worse. She's terribly lazy. You won't see her out of the bed until noon. She's always late to class. When I tried to wake her she would always say, 'No, five more minutes!' Five was not five. More like fifteen."

He smiled. She pictured Leonora, looking adorable with her messy hair and her rumpled clothes. The disarray would enhance her beauty. When Maite woke up she looked a mess. No man would have been charmed by that sight.

Prettiness is currency, she thought. *All doors open for you if you're pretty*.

"What are you reading?" Rubén asked.

"Oh," she said, looking down at the magazine in her lap. She'd tightened her grip on it. "*Secret Romance*. Comics, you know."

For a moment she expected he would beam at her with interest, maybe ask her about the artist who drew the illustrations. After all, he was an artist of a sort. He spent his time with painters and poets and people in that milieu. You'd expect someone like that, someone with a sensitive soul, to understand her pursuits. But he chuckled.

"Really? Like what, like for kids?"

Maite glanced at him, felt herself blushing.

"These are not for kids. They're like novels. Except with pictures. Just like novels," she said, smoothing the page of the magazine with her palm and trying to keep her tone level. It wouldn't do to pick a fight in the car, halfway to Cuernavaca. If they fought, maybe he'd toss her out. She'd be left to walk by the side of the road.

"I think my mom reads stuff like that. Nurse romances, yes, that's it."

Maite had read plenty of nurse romances, and she supposed this was similar. But it annoyed her to think that he was comparing her to his mother. She wasn't *that* old. Her palm slid harder against the paper, the cheap ink smeared against her hand.

"What's that name . . . Barbara . . . Barbara Cartland! Doesn't she write that syrupy stuff?"

"It's not syrupy. This one has an adventure. The hero is in a coma and now the heroine is going to have to rescue him. At least, I think she will. It's not syrupy."

"No?"

"There's a scene. A scene with an Aztec sacrifice," she said.

"That sounds different."

There wasn't, was there? No. The Aztec sacrifice was something Maite had dreamed. A stone altar and a woman lying upon it. Why, then, had she said that? It had been so lifelike, for a moment. That image. She even knew what the heroine was wearing: white, so the splash of blood upon her chest would be more vivid.

"It's not kids' stuff!" she said, her voice high-pitched, almost breaking.

He looked at her in surprise, and she felt mortified. She looked at her fingers, dark with the ink.

"Sorry. I wasn't trying to be rude."

"No, no," she said. "It's fine."

She squeezed her eyes shut and turned her face toward the window. Red and white. She saw red and white behind her eyelids, and when she opened her eyes again there was the gray sky. They sank into silence after that.

They arrived at Lara's house at noon and rang the bell. A woman in her thirties, a scarf knotted around her neck, opened the door. She was wearing khaki trousers and a white blouse. It gave her the look of a European hunter on a safari. Her hair was pulled back into a ponytail.

"Yes?" she asked.

"Hi," Maite said. "We're looking for a journalist. For Lara."

"I'm Jessica Laramie," the woman said. "Everyone calls me Lara. And you are?"

"I'm Maite. And this is Rubén. Emilio Lomelí gave us your address." Maite felt his name alone was like the key to a magical kingdom, which would open any door, but the woman looked at them curiously. Maite's fingers were still a bit dirty from the ink, and she felt like placing her hands behind her back, hiding them.

Her dress didn't have pockets so she couldn't slide her hands into them and tuck them out of sight. It was an ugly dress, too. The journalist's clothes looked simple but chic. Maite's dress was dark navy, the collar reached her chin. Her mother had gifted it to her the year before. She had no idea why she'd worn it, and now . . . ah . . . her horrid hands.

"Everything's all right with Emilio?" Jessica asked.

"With him, yes. But we were wondering if you'd talk to us for a few minutes. It's about a friend of ours, and he thinks you might be able to help us," Rubén said. "Please, we've come all the way from Mexico City. Do you have five minutes?"

The woman tilted her head, probably trying to figure out what was up with them. The young man in a wrinkled t-shirt and blue jeans and the secretary who looked exactly like a secretary, wearing her prim dress. The journalist probably thought they didn't seem like Emilio's usual friends. No, Maite imagined Emilio's friends as a crowd of glittering people, very fancy, very smooth.

"Come on in," Jessica told them.

They followed the woman into a small living room with rattan furniture and a multitude of cacti. There was a bookcase with ceramic figurines and pots made of barro negro, and another bookcase with stacks of magazines and books. The woman sat in a low chair, and they took the rattan couch.

"So who's your friend?" the woman asked, grabbing a box of cigarettes that was resting on a circular coffee table and taking one out.

"Leonora. She came to see you. Now she's disappeared. We're worried about her," Rubén said.

The woman lit her cigarette and pressed it against her lips. "I see. I'm not sure why you're here, though."

"You're one of the last persons who spoke to her, and maybe you know where she might be."

"Aha. She didn't leave me an itinerary, you know."

"Perhaps if you told us what you talked about?"

The woman shook her head. On the circular table there was also a glass, half empty, and the woman raised it to her lips, the ice clinking against the rim. "We talked about a possible story. I can't discuss the particulars with you. You've made a long trip for nothing."

"We know about the photos," Maite ventured, wondering if that might get them anywhere. She clutched her hands tight before her. No one would be able to see the stains on her hands if she maintained that pose.

The woman set the glass down again, then crossed her legs and rested her elbow on her knee, leaning forward. She had long fingers, a good manicure. The tips of her nails were white halfmoons. "You've seen them?"

"No. But we have a good idea of what's in them. Anyway, we need to know what you talked about," Rubén said. "We're Leonora's friends, we swear to god. You can phone Emilio and ask him if he knows us."

Jessica didn't reply. She kept looking at them.

"We're trying to find out what happened to her," Maite added. Now she clutched her hands harder. Now she was a supplicant.

The journalist sighed. "I imagine the same thing that happens to everyone that goes missing these days. You want to know what Leonora and I talked about? Exactly that. The disappearance of activists, the wiretapping of phones, the massacre in San Cosme on Corpus Christi day."

"You were there?" Rubén asked.

"No. But plenty of my colleagues were."

"Who do you work for?"

"I'm a freelancer. I've got stuff in *Time* and a bunch of other places. I've been covering Mexico for two years. Before that, I was in Peru."

The woman took another sip of her drink, another puff of her cigarette. Practiced, elegant motions. She had little wrinkles around the eyes and her skin was dull, but the journalist was still attractive. Maite recalled what Rubén had said—Emilio slept with anything that moved—and she wondered if this was another one of his conquests. Maybe Emilio had a picture of her manicured pinkie in his house, or the eye, blown up, magnified, until it didn't look like an eye.

"You talked about the attacks in San Cosme. What else?"

"Your newspapers are saying the students were armed, that they instigated this. *El Sol de México*, many other places, they're taking the government line. They're trying to wash the government clean. Leonora wanted to change that. She said she had access, through a family member, to pictures which proved the Hawks attacked the students and they were doing so with presidential orders. Not only that, the CIA helped train them."

"The CIA," Rubén repeated.

"That's what she said. It would make quite the story. The problem was that Leonora didn't carry any evidence with her. No pictures, nothing. She told me she was keeping the negatives in a safe place but wouldn't say where."

"Maybe she didn't know if she could trust you."

Jessica chuckled and grabbed an ashtray made of barro negro, tossed the cigarette into it. "Maybe. Maybe she was getting cold feet. She kept insisting that she didn't want the names of certain people in the story. She wanted to make sure no one in her family would be identified."

"What did you tell her?" Maite asked.

"I couldn't promise her that. If what she was telling me was accurate, then that family member of hers was a top-ranking military man who recruited and trained Hawks. His name was bound to come up."

"What happened in the end?" Rubén asked.

"In the end, she said she needed time to think about this. I gave her my phone number, told her to call me. She didn't."

"And you heard nothing from her at all?"

"No. Frankly, I didn't think she'd cooperate. You get a feeling for this stuff. The people who're willing to talk and the ones who won't give you anything. She gave me very little. It was a great story, but there was nothing solid behind it to make it stick. I figured I'd pursue other channels."

"But you think she did have the photos?"

"Probably. She was scared. Very scared. Can't say I blame her. There's a reason why I live in Cuernavaca: it's harder to be placed under surveillance outside of Mexico City."

They were quiet. There was a low hum. Air conditioning, perhaps, for this was a nice house and it was cool inside. The journalist was not a starving one. If she'd had the chance, Maite would have loved to steal something from this place. A little figurine from the bookshelf, or the ashtray. But she was clasping her hands together, and it was impossible considering where she was sitting.

"Did Emilio tell you Leonora would be visiting you the day she came?"

"He had mentioned something about a girlfriend of his who had a story I might be interested in, but no. We didn't speak that day."

"Afterward, did you talk to him?"

"I didn't. I've been busy."

Maite looked at Rubén, frowning, wondering why he was asking about Emilio. He'd had nothing to do with this.

"Was there anything Leonora said that struck you as odd?"

"Aside from the fact that she was being secretive and nervous?

Come on." The journalist smiled and grabbed her glass again, letting out a low chuckle.

"We're trying to look for any clue that might allow us to find her."

"You might ask the man who dropped her off here. After all, he was driving your car."

They both stared at the journalist, too stunned to reply. Finally, Maite licked her lips and spoke. "Our car?"

"Or one that looked very much like it. I'm pretty sure it's that one, though. It was red, at any rate. The man didn't come in; he waited for her and then they drove off together."

"Can you describe him?" Rubén asked.

The woman nodded. "Yeah, a little. I got a quick look. He was young. Brown hair, glasses. He was wearing a bandana and had on a blue jacket. Does that help?"

"It does," Rubén said, getting up quickly. "Thanks. We should head back."

"Wait, let me give you my card," the woman said, standing up and going to the bookcase, where she took a business card from a plain, white cardboard box. "If you find your friend, tell her to call me. I can help get this story out."

"Sure," Rubén said, stuffing the card in his pocket.

"Tell Emilio I say hi."

"We will."

Rubén placed a hand on Maite's back and ushered her out of the house, the gesture insistent.

When they were back in the car, Maite turned to him. "How could it be this car? Isn't it Jackie's car?"

"Yeah, but she lends it to us when we need it."

"Then it could have been anyone from Asterisk?"

"Oh, she doesn't lend it to everybody," Rubén said, turning the key in the ignition. "It's a handful of people. And Sócrates is the only man with glasses and a bandana in our group."

She recalled that young man from the previous day. He seemed to be friendly with Jackie and all the other people there. He had even gotten into a bit of a verbal sparring match with Rubén.

"But then that means he didn't tell you he drove Leonora to Cuernavaca."

"Yep," Rubén said.

"What do we do?"

"We head back into the city and ask him why he had the sudden memory lapse."

19

BY THE TIME Elvis returned to their apartment, El Güero was foraging for snacks in the kitchen. When El Güero saw him, he grinned.

"You've got blood on your shirt. What happened? They figure you out?"

"Bad luck," Elvis muttered, opening the refrigerator door and taking out an aluminum ice-cube tray. Rather than carefully prying the cubes he slammed the tray against the sink, and the cubes bounced out. He wrapped them in a rag.

"You must be real upset that they messed up your hairdo."

Elvis didn't reply and pressed the rag against his cheek. Let El Güero chuckle if he wanted. It's not like one could expect solidarity from that piece of shit. Never had and never would.

"That's what happens when you don't carry a gun, marshmallow boy," El Güero said, waving a fried chicken leg in Elvis's face.

"El Mago says no guns."

"Sure, sure thing. And you're such a good little kiddie you do everything El Mago tells you."

Elvis elbowed El Güero away. "We're up at five sharp. Morning call."

"Fucking five? What for?"

"Morning call, I said. Go switch places with the Antelope, then come back at midnight, and at five you're up again."

"Fuck you. You've got us round the clock!"

"Whatever El Mago needs. Unless you want to complain to him. I'll even dial the number for you. Want to?"

El Güero didn't reply, instead gnawed at his chicken leg.

"Good," Elvis said, tossing the rag with the ice cubes into the sink.

He locked himself in the bathroom. The warm shower was a damn blessing on his aching muscles. Eyes closed, chin pressed against his chest, he let the water slide down his body. *How the hell did you get yourself involved in this shit?* he asked himself. But the truth was he was going to get involved in bad shit of one kind or another. He didn't know any better and could admit it. And like El Mago said, no sense in wallowing. Keep your priorities simple and stick to the rules.

The rules were El Mago was the boss and he'd assigned him a job. He was there to fulfill it.

After a long time Elvis closed the tap and stood before the mirror, wiping it with the palm of his hand and examining his face. He had to admit the Russian was good. He'd beaten Elvis thoroughly but didn't leave many marks. For that, he was grateful. He wasn't terribly handsome, but Elvis didn't want to lose the few points in his favor.

He grabbed the clothes he'd tossed on the floor. The t-shirt was useless, and the jacket also had bloodstains. He tried washing the blood out and hung the jacket to dry from the shower rod.

He ran his hands through his hair and stepped back into his bedroom, plucked a record from the stack by his bed, and let Sinatra soothe him. He opened the folder El Mago had given him.

He scanned Emilio's file, which consisted of a bunch of snapshots and the usual dry information. Age, height, full name. He recognized his address as soon as he saw it: it was the same place where the woman had gone, that house in Polanco.

Elvis considered that tidbit. Maite was now paying visits to Emilio Lomelí, the boyfriend of their missing girl, and she was also at Asterisk. Was Emilio worth checking out? He was going to pay either Emilio or Sócrates a visit the next morning, and although a rich kid wasn't his usual target, he was willing to change things around if that's what it took.

But Emilio looked dry. Nothing sticky he could find. His record was clean. A wannabe artist with no teeth. His associates were writers, journalists, cultural critics, other photographers, but none of them were the sort that attracted the attention of the authorities. They worked for papers toeing the official line. He wasn't palling around with agitator cartoonists like Rius; instead he had dinner with editors of *El Nacional* and was good friends with boot-lickers like Denegri.

He turned to Sócrates, pulling out the pages from the report and checking it line by line. In his short twenty-one years of life Sócrates had had several run-ins with the police, all because of his activist leanings—he'd marched in several demonstrations, distributed dissident leaflets, that sort of stuff. If anyone could be harboring the missing girl, it would be a lefty radical like Sócrates. Plus, Sócrates and his buddies were hanging around with Russians.

That, then, would be their next target. Elvis took out his dictionary and flipped through the pages, looking for a good word to encapsulate the next day.

Maite had a Larousse, like the one he owned. Lots of people had such dictionaries, but it made him pause and consider the woman again.

He grabbed the picture he had stolen from her house and held it up, wondering if it wasn't time to have a talk with the little lady too. But El Mago hadn't said anything about intercepting her.

He kind of wanted to talk to her, though. He wondered what her voice sounded like. Bluebeard's wife, with her startled eyes. Sometimes, when they were watching someone, marking their comings and goings in a ledger and snapping pictures, Elvis got bored and tried to build a profile of the targets via the details he knew about them. It was fairly easy and often accurate. He imagined their voice or pictured their kitchen drawers.

He'd been inside the woman's apartment, so there was no need to imagine her surroundings, but the voice nagged at him. Would she have a nice voice? Or would it be squeaky, high-pitched? Or lower? Would the voice match the face, or would it be one of those wild tricks of nature where the voice is a sultry delight and the person is as plain as rice?

Cristina hadn't had anything close to a nice voice. But she'd been pretty as hell, and Elvis was a sucker for a pair of dimples and a smile.

He wondered about the woman and thought about asking her out sometime, for kicks. When all this was over. Maybe.

Sinatra sang about the foolish things that remind you of a lover, and the record spun.

He liked crooners because he thought they sang the truth. And he liked Elvis because Elvis was simply fun. A true rock-and-roll hero, with music in his blood. Back when he'd lived with Sally and tried his hand at the guitar, he half believed he could make something of himself like that. Singing in lounges or bars. But they'd closed the singing cafés down, and it wasn't like he'd ever had any talent, anyway.

Elvis picked the word *necrology* and went to bed. In the morning, he tucked a large knife in his jacket because they had business that day, and you can't scare anyone with a screwdriver.

The Antelope was still on watch duty over at Maite's apartment, so El Güero and Elvis caught a taxi. The traffic hadn't reared into motion, and they reached Sócrates's neighborhood quickly, paid their fare, and installed themselves across from the building, tucked behind a low cement wall surrounding an empty lot. A stray cat stared at them as they leaned against a withered tree and lit their cigarettes.

It was drizzling. Elvis repeated the word of the day in his mind, then drummed his fingers against his thigh, to the rhythm of silent music. Presley, singing "Can't Help Falling in Love." Half note, half note, sweet as honey. Life should be a slow song, affection should be a melody. The word of the day was *necrology*, and he was thinking about fate and lovers.

He hoped Sócrates didn't take long. His body ached, and there was the danger someone might spot them, though they might assume El Güero and Elvis were simply a couple of homeless men camping in the lonely lot. Still, it was chilly, and the drizzle was turning into full rain.

Around eight Sócrates exited the apartment building, and they began tailing him. He didn't go far, sliding into a coffee shop and sitting at the bar. After he'd sat down, Elvis and El Güero walked into the establishment. Elvis took the stool to the left of Sócrates and El Güero grabbed the right. Sócrates still looked half-asleep, and Elvis had to practically jab him in the ribs to get his attention.

"Huh?" he muttered.

"Come on, buddy, we're going back to your place for a talk," Elvis muttered.

"What?"

"It's a fucking knife I've got here; get up and get walking and don't you dare yell or I'll slice an artery so fast you won't even feel it."

That seemed to do the trick. Sócrates jumped to his feet, giving Elvis a worried look. He opened his mouth and groaned but didn't speak, as if, at the last second, he'd suddenly remembered there was a knife pressed against his body.

They walked out together while El Güero took out a few coins and tossed them on the counter, paying for the coffee the young man had ordered. The three of them walked back toward the building, Elvis next to Sócrates and El Güero ahead of them. This way, there was nowhere for the guy to run to, but he wasn't a runner. Elvis could tell.

"Who are you? What do you want?" Sócrates whispered.

"Don't matter much," Elvis said. "You live alone? Is there anyone back at the apartment?"

He was hoping there wasn't. It would make things easier. The man shook his head, glanced at El Güero and back at Elvis. In no time they were walking into the young man's apartment, which was on the top floor of the building. No elevator.

It was a studio, crammed with books and boxes and a hot plate on a table instead of a proper kitchen. On a shelf Sócrates kept cans of Choco Milk, a jar of Nescafé, and cans of sardines next to piles of papers and more books. If you sat on the bed, you could see the bathroom, which lacked a door. Instead, a curtain made of wooden beads served as a divider. There was no couch, and the room smelled of incense and also the faint sweetness of marijuana.

Elvis motioned for Sócrates to sit on the bed, and when he did the bed creaked, as if uttering a complaint. For a moment Elvis felt weird standing there with the young man staring at him. This room, this setup, wasn't so different from where Elvis had lived when he was younger, and it made him uncomfortable. Maybe it would have been better if he'd gone to see Lomelí. It might have been fun to slap a rich fucker around. Right now, he didn't feel too great about torturing this kid, just as he hadn't felt good about beating the priest, at least at the beginning.

But then he remembered how the priest's buddies had grabbed him and the Russian slapped him with the newspapers, and Elvis's sympathy was drained.

"Look around for the camera," Elvis told El Güero, and then he turned to Sócrates. "You try anything, I cut off your dick." He traced an arc in the air to emphasize his words. Sometimes people were real stupid and needed visual aids, a fucking diagram to tell them what was what.

Sócrates raised both of his hands. "I'm not trying anything. I know your type!"

"Do you, now? Well, Mr. Know-It-All, what do you know about Leonora then?"

"Leonora?" he repeated, staring at him stupidly, as though Elvis had spoken in Chinese.

"Yes, Leonora. You're friends, no?"

"Yeah."

"How good a friend are you?"

"We know each other."

"You recite shitty poems for everyone you know?"

Sócrates blushed. The hands, which had been in the air, came down to rest crossed against his chest. "Who told you that?"

"People say you have a hard-on for Leonora. Lots of people."

"They're exaggerating. It's not like that."

Which meant it was like that. Not that Elvis blamed the guy: the girl was pretty. Her friend, Maite, was not, although to be honest he found her more interesting than Leonora. It was the eyes that did the trick. There was a spark of pain in them, there was shock and something cloudy and lost. As if she'd been dreaming and had suddenly been awoken by the clapping of thunder. It made him curious.

But Leonora. Leonora was the one he needed to be focusing on, Leonora was the lost lamb.

"Would you hide her if someone was looking for her?"

"Hide her where? In the bathroom?"

El Güero smirked at that. "He's a joker," he said and kept fiddling with a pile of books by the bed, opening and closing them. "It's gonna be real funny when we stab you in the balls."

Sócrates was already nervous, but that seemed to do it. He flinched and almost jumped a little, as if they'd administered an electric shock to said balls. "Man, I am not hiding her! Damn. I already told Anaya, I don't know where she is!"

"Back up," Elvis said. "How do you know Anaya?"

"Fuck," Sócrates muttered.

"Fuck, yes. Talk. Fast."

"I mean, I wouldn't know where to begin, I mean, it's not—I can't tell you."

"Hit him," Elvis ordered.

El Güero turned around and slammed a book against Sócrates's head, then moved across the room to start browsing the contents of a bookshelf. Sócrates let out a high-pitched whine, almost like a cat, and pressed a hand against his ear, eyes closed. Elvis let him sit like that for a minute, then he tucked the knife inside his jacket's pocket and took out a cigarette. He lit it.

"I'm having a shitty week, and you don't want to make it any worse," Elvis said. "Talk before I get my friend to use every volume of your fucking encyclopedia on your ribs. How do you know Anaya?"

"I pass information to him."

"You're a rat."

"An informant," Sócrates said, still rubbing his ear.

A rat. A fucking squealer. A rat's a rat no matter if you've read a thesaurus and can call it something fancy. But if he wanted to call himself Goldilocks, it didn't matter to Elvis.

"You're with DFS, then?"

"No, nothing like that! They nabbed us one time distributing leaflets, and Anaya said if I didn't cooperate with him, didn't help him, he was going to make sure I was tortured for weeks. So I do, I cooperate. He asks me questions from time to time, and I answer them."

It wasn't unheard of. Ears were a dime a dozen. Justo had been sniffing around Asterisk for the DGIPS, and this bozo had been talking to Anaya, and there was some Russian fucker too, and for all Elvis knew the CIA and Santa Claus also had spies in that little commie nest. Overkill and lack of coordination. That was the problem. The DFS hated the DGIPS, thinking they were hicks, and the DGIPS thought DFS agents were stuffy pricks.

"Anaya asked you about Leonora. What did you tell him?"

"Can I . . . can I have a cigarette?"

Jesus! Bumming his cigarettes! But if it helped get this dipshit explaining, Elvis would give him a whole pack. He took out one and lit it for the man. El Güero was whistling "La Cucaracha" and had gone into the bathroom.

Fucker, Elvis thought. He couldn't stop giving him grief for one damn day.

Sócrates took a puff, then licked his lips. "I drove Leonora to Cuernavaca last weekend. She went to meet a journalist."

"A friend of yours?"

"No. A friend of Emilio, her ex."

"Did she have the pictures with her?"

"No." Sócrates reached for a dirty glass sitting on a table by the bed and let the ash from his cigarette fall into it. "She didn't know if she could trust the journalist. I drove her because I wanted to know if she'd tell me more about the photos, if maybe she'd show me where she kept them. On the way back, I asked her a few times, but she clammed up and asked me to drop her off at Casimiro Villarreal's house. She thought she'd be safe with him."

"Not with Emilio? Or with Jackie?"

"No. I guess they weren't the first people she thought about, and maybe she wanted to confess something to him. Religious stuff, you know? I tried to convince her she was better off staying with me, but I couldn't."

"Stay with you. So you could hand her over to Anaya?"

"She would have been safer. If Anaya knew where he could find her, he wouldn't have made such a fuss about this."

"You're such a good friend."

"Fuck you," Sócrates said, his teeth almost clamping on the cigarette for a second before he took a puff. "I was hoping I could get her to hand over the photos to me, and I'd hand them to Anaya. I thought that was the best thing to do. That's why I took her to Casimiro's house and not Anaya. I *could* have turned her over to Anaya. But then she vanished."

"Abracadabra, like a magician."

"No one's heard from her."

"And you didn't help her perform this magic act?"

Sócrates dropped the cigarette into the glass. "No. She has money. It's not like she couldn't have used it to go hide somewhere. And I've looked for her in all her old haunts. Nothing."

El Güero walked back into the room. "Can't find anything resembling a camera or pictures. Should we call it a morning?"

"I'm expecting someone in less than an hour," Sócrates said.

"But we're just beginning to know each other," Elvis said.

"It's Anaya."

"You lying to me? Because remember: knives cut balls."

"It's true!"

"Well, you're lying about something," Elvis said. He had no idea about that, but he decided to throw it out there. See what he got. It seemed to work, because suddenly Sócrates was rubbing his forehead and looking down. But he didn't speak. He pressed his lips together.

"You son of a bitch," Elvis said, and he grabbed the knife and pressed it against the guy's leg. "I'll slice you, one ball and then the other. How would you like that? It'll take me a minute, so no danger in running into Anaya."

And for a moment as he held the knife like that and stared at the dude's face, he wondered if he wasn't overdoing it—this had been El Gazpacho's role, and El Gazpacho was always a bit of a gentleman—and he even felt a little sorry for Sócrates, because the guy was about to shit himself while El Güero chuckled in a corner. But Elvis hadn't been lying when he said he'd had a lousy week and his body still ached, so he wasn't exactly in the best of mindsets.

"An ad! I said I'd put an ad in the paper!"

Elvis frowned. "What paper?"

"When I dropped her off at Casimiro's apartment building I told her you can't be too careful. I said, people might be after you . . . because, because of Anaya. Because I was scared. And I said if there's trouble and you have to lay low, do that, stay hidden, and then I'll put an ad in the paper letting you know if the coast is clear."

"Son of a bitch," Elvis said, stepping back and smiling. "You were trying to double-cross Anaya?"

"I was trying to keep her safe."

"Can't do that. Too many people are looking for the girl. What paper, and what is the ad supposed to say?"

"*El Universal*. In the classified section."

"Write down the message."

Sócrates sat there, stiff as a rod, but then Elvis angled the knife a little, and Sócrates grabbed a notepad by the bed and scribbled a few words.

"Have a good day," Elvis said, folding the piece of paper and putting it in his pocket. Then he motioned to El Güero, and they went down the stairs. It was still early and taxis were scarce on the street they were walking down, so they went looking for a taxi stand rather than attempting to hail one. Elvis didn't mind, even though it was still drizzling. He wanted to think.

He didn't have Leonora's location, but he did have the message that was supposed to tell her the coast was clear. Or at least he thought he did. It could be Sócrates had mangled the code, in which case Elvis and El Güero would have to go back for a visit. But he thought Sócrates had written down the real message. This meant Elvis could put it in the paper and see if he flushed Leonora out.

The problem with this strategy was that he wasn't sure where Leonora might go if she really thought the coast was clear. Immediately back to her apartment? Would she be that foolish? Or would she show up at her sister's house? Her ex-boyfriend's? Leonora hadn't trusted Jacqueline, and the people at Asterisk mistakenly thought she was the mole in the organization. This probably rendered all of her associates there null—including Casimiro and Sócrates. She wouldn't go to them.

Though if she trusted Sócrates's message, maybe that meant she trusted Sócrates? Definitely. Sócrates was a possibility. She might try to go back to her apartment—it was stupid, but also not unlikely if she truly felt safe. Elvis mentally cancelled out Emilio and Leonora's sister. El Mago had told him to keep his distance from them, and in the case of Emilio, Elvis felt that, though he'd supplied her with the name of a journalist, if Leonora truly had trusted him—or if he had wished to assist her—he would have taken her there himself.

Yeah, now that Elvis considered it, Emilio was probably a crafty bastard. He agreed to help his ex, but in a way that wouldn't get him into too much trouble. A simple referral to the journalist was no crime, while harboring her when the DFS and the Hawks were on her trail was another matter. No, that rich boy wasn't going to be of much value. The sister . . . well, Elvis couldn't say. He really didn't know anything about her, and if El Mago hadn't released info on her then that avenue was closed.

Leonora would either attempt to return to her apartment or she'd contact Sócrates. That was Elvis's conclusion. This meant he needed two damn lookouts. He had two men, but they couldn't watch a building for twenty-four hours. This was going to be complicated. Elvis figured if he put the ad in that morning, then it couldn't be in the papers until the next day. It might even have to go in Tuesday's edition. Either way, this gave him at least a little time to figure out their schedules. Maybe he could hire Justo to watch Sócrates's building. El Mago wouldn't like it, but Elvis didn't have enough manpower.

For now, Elvis and El Güero stood under an awning, shielding themselves from the rain, and lit their cigarettes. The owner of a newspaper stand had arrived and was beginning to open for business and arrange his wares at the corner. Elvis bought *El Universal* from him and circled the phone number of the classifieds' office with a pencil. He'd ask what they needed for a quick ad in a bit. But first, there were other matters to attend to.

He placed the newspaper under his arm and walked to a pay phone, then phoned El Mago to give him an update. It was early, but El Mago answered at the first ring, and he didn't sound sleepy.

"Found the mole," Elvis said. "It was Sócrates, feeding info to Anaya."

"Anything else?"

"Nothing worth repeating now. I've got to look after a few things," he said and hung up, following procedure. Keep it quick and simple, that's what El Mago said. Anyway, he couldn't discuss his concerns with El Mago over the phone. He'd have to ask to meet again, and he was leery of doing that. He didn't want to seem like a helpless buffoon who ran to him for everything. Elvis was team leader, after all. He could figure this out.

Elvis whacked El Güero's arm with the newspaper. "Come on, let's get going."

20

THEY HAD TACOS de barbacoa on the way back from Cuernavaca, in a little eatery on the side of the road.

This is what people do on their weekends, she thought. *They go out with their friends.*

Rubén wasn't her friend, and they weren't hanging out together because they enjoyed each other's company; he was merely hoping to find his ex-girlfriend. Still. Maite was going to tell Diana she'd visited Cuernavaca with a date. A new beau. Diana would look at her in admiration, since she rarely went anywhere alone. She traveled, as if a part of a troupe, with her mother and sisters.

Rubén was nice to her during their lunch too. He paid for the tacos and their Cokes, and they had a pleasant, simple conversation. When they got back to the city, Rubén went straight for Sócrates's building, but as much as he pressed the buzzer, no one came down.

"Maybe he's at Asterisk," Rubén said, and they walked around the corner, to a pay phone. Rubén called, but Sócrates wasn't there either.

"What now?"

"We come back tomorrow morning."

"Tomorrow's Monday. I've got work tomorrow. Don't you?"

"Damn it, that's right," Rubén muttered. "I'm sure I can take off early. What about you? Can you get off around one p.m.?"

He looked at her eagerly. "Yes," Maite said, thinking she could always make up an illness. She hated Mondays, anyway. *Secret*

Romance was the reason she got up some weeks. There had been days when she could have stayed in bed forever. It's not as if she would have missed anything.

The lawyers never came in on time, and they often cut their days short. She figured if they got away with such unprofessional behavior, she could invent a flimsy excuse without a shred of guilt.

"I can pick you up outside your office if you give me the address; that way we can get here faster. Hey, I need to stop by my place to get clean clothes, do you mind? It'll take five minutes," he said.

"Why do you need clothes?"

"I figure I can crash on your couch again, for your own safety. But I'll have to change in the morning."

"You can't live on my couch eternally."

"Maybe until we talk to Sócrates. I don't know, I don't feel right about leaving you alone."

I'm always alone, she thought. But . . . again, why not? Why shouldn't he spend another night over if he wanted to? She could cook something. She could pretend she was making dinner for a good friend. It probably wasn't a big deal for him, this popping up in a random woman's house and spending the night there.

They drove to the guesthouse where he roomed. Rather than wait for him in the car, Maite went with Rubén, curious to see where he lived, though the moment she walked in she thought about stepping outside again, because a couple of young men were walking their way and greeted him, throwing her a perplexed look.

She probably didn't look like the sort of person who visited the guesthouse, not in her prim, ugly dress. She didn't look like Leonora, who was pretty; she didn't even look like Jackie, who seemed interesting. She looked like a finicky aunt.

"This way," Rubén said, and she followed him down a hallway and into his room.

It was very small and plain. By the bed Rubén kept a cheap bookcase piled high with thick tomes. There was no bathroom and no phone, though he told her the landlady sometimes let them use the phone in the living room if they promised to be quick about it. He had a window, but the view was of a low, damaged brick wall circling the property next door. The neighbors had a chicken coop, but all she could see was a single sad rooster sitting outside of it, all alone.

She wondered if Leonora had ever been in that room. Rubén's bedspread was green and orange, and she ran a hand across it. Did Leonora sleep here? Did she bump into some of the men they'd seen before in the hallway? Did they also stare at her, looking perplexed?

"Have you lived here long?" she asked.

Rubén opened a drawer and tossed a shirt into a canvas bag. "Almost since I moved to Mexico City. The rent's fair, and the landlady's cooking's decent too."

"Where are you from?"

"Guerrero," he said, folding a pair of trousers.

"You ever think about going back?"

"Maybe. There're guerillas there. Real guerillas."

"Are there? Isn't it all bandits?"

"You really don't read the papers, do you?" he asked. He didn't sound scornful, surprised maybe, but it made her frown all the same. "They're in the sierra. They can't get them there. Genaro Vázquez Rojas, he's the real deal. And Lucio Cabañas. They're going to change the country; they'll overthrow these bastards of the PRI."

"You'll end up in jail if you keep talking like that."

He laughed. "So you don't know anything about anything, but you know that?"

"Everyone knows that."

"You're probably not wrong, but what's the other option?"

"Does Leonora want to join a guerilla and live in a place like that?" Maite asked, and she remembered Leonora's apartment, her pretty dresses, the red sheets and expensive bottles of wine.

But he hadn't heard her or didn't bother answering, instead tossing a couple more things into his bag. "Ready," he said. "All packed."

In no time they were back at her apartment. She went to feed the cat. Rubén asked her why she didn't bring the cat into her apartment, so she didn't have to be walking into Leonora's place three times a day.

"It'd be easier. But I don't know. I don't like cats," she admitted.

She supposed if Leonora didn't return soon she'd have to do something about the damn animal. At least Rubén was the one who paid for the cat food when they stopped at the supermarket to get a few grocery items. She preferred buying her fruits and vegetables at the tianguis because you could haggle there, but there had been no chance of that, so they ended at a Superama.

"Maybe I can bring the cat over here in the morning, I don't know," she said wearily.

"You don't have to. It was a suggestion."

She took off her shoes and sat on the couch, rubbing her feet. She felt tired, although they hadn't done much that day. It was the excitement of the trip, she supposed. He'd sleep there that night, then they'd talk to Sócrates . . . and then what? This situation couldn't go on forever. Chasing after some girl . . . and there was that man, Anaya, and whoever had beat up Rubén's friend from Asterisk. Anaya might show his face around her office again. That might be embarrassing. Or dangerous.

"I'm going to put on a bit of music," she said and went into her atelier.

Rubén followed her, looking at Maite as she fiddled with her records, unsure of whether she should pick an old-fashioned bolero or attempt something newer.

"You have a huge record collection."

"It's not that big," she replied, a little defensively, because that was the same thing her mother said when she complained about Maite's lifestyle: "Maite, you spend all your money on records and books and comics and nonsense."

He bent down and grabbed a copy of the comic book she'd left on her chair. "*Secret Romance*."

"Oh, yes," Maite muttered, feeling even more flustered and clutching her hands together as he flipped through the pages. "Let me put that away."

He handed her the issue. "Does this one have the Aztec sacrifice in it?"

"No, it's not the one."

Maite tucked the comic book away and put on "No Me Platiques Más," not because she felt particularly like she wanted to hear Vicente Garrido's romantic lyrics, but because she couldn't make up her mind. She wanted to impress Rubén with her taste, but she also suspected it would be futile.

"I wanted to say I'm sorry, by the way."

"Sorry?"

"Yeah. I've been a bit rude, you know. Saying you don't read the papers or know anything. Saying you read syrupy stuff—"

She didn't want him talking about her reading habits. *Nurse romances*, that's what he'd said, like it was very funny. And so what! What if people wanted a bit of romance once in a while? A bit of fantasy? Didn't he fantasize about things? People? Maybe about Leonora?

"I suppose you read *important* books, being a literature major," she muttered, even though her instinct was to shut her mouth. Speaking would invite further commentary.

"Not lately," he said.

Rubén had moved from one side of the room to the other. He stood by the window and looked out, even if there wasn't anything to look at. Just another building, very much like her own. The blinds traced dark lines over the worn square of red-and-white carpet she'd bought from a Lebanese shopkeeper. She told herself it was a Persian rug, but knew it was not. It was a fancy she had, like calling this room the atelier.

"It might be dangerous, getting involved with those people in Guerrero."

"Better than being dragged to Lecumberri and rotting in a cell there," Rubén replied with a shrug. "And don't doubt it, we'll all be dragged one day, over nothing. I'd rather be running from the cops around Guerrero than ending up a political prisoner."

"It can't only be those two options."

"That's what people like Emilio say, but trust me, in the end you either fight or lie down to be trampled."

"But what does a print shop worker know about guerillas?"

"There're all kinds of people with the guerilla. Lucio Cabañas used to be a teacher. You might say, what does a teacher know about revolution? Hell, what did Emiliano Zapata know about revolution when he organized a bunch of peasants?"

"I guess I can't see how you'd change anything. It all feels complicated. And the cops! We all know what the cops might do to you." She took a couple of Elvis Presley records from the shelf and flipped them over, looking at the song list. "Love Me Tender." She slid her nail along the record sleeve.

"You're direct."

"I'm not trying to be cruel."

"Nah. You're good at hiding your head."

"There's nothing wrong with that! If more people minded their own business the world would be a better place."

"I strongly disagree."

Maite brushed a strand of hair behind her ear and bit her lip. She quickly switched her record, putting on "Piel Canela" and flipping up the volume, then she sat down on her corner chair and crossed her arms, her foot moving to the music.

"You mind if I have a smoke?"

"Not here," she said, not so much because she didn't like cigarettes but because she wanted to punish him. He was irritating.

Nice one moment and then annoying the next. No wonder Leonora had dumped him.

"Whatever you say," he muttered and stepped out of the room.

After a couple of songs Maite also left the atelier and peeked into the living room, to see if he'd taken refuge there, but no. He was leaning in the doorway of her apartment, his head turned toward the hallway.

She thought to tell him that there wouldn't be cigarettes in the sierra, that he wasn't nearly as interesting as he thought he was, and his little fantasies about guerillas and guns and revolution weren't any more solid than her own daydreams. But then she didn't know if there was a point in bickering, and she suddenly felt very tired.

The way he stood, he also looked tired, and something about the way his shoulders were slumped made Maite guess he was thinking about Leonora.

Maite fed sunflower seeds to the parakeet while watching the young man.

21

IT WAS TOO early to drop by La Habana and talk to Justo, so Elvis went by Maite's building and gave the Antelope a chance to rest for a few hours. He had already sent El Güero back to the apartment after they'd stopped to place their ad in the paper. Alone in the car Elvis dismissed one station after another, settled on Stereo Rey as he usually did, and smoked cigarettes, patient, drumming his fingers against his thighs. "Dream a Little Dream of Me" was playing.

A few songs later, Maite stepped out and into a car with the same man he'd seen her with before. The hippie with the unibrow. Elvis followed them, but after a good fifteen minutes he lost track of them when a taxi veered to the right and blocked his path. Fucking drivers! You couldn't shadow someone properly in this city, not with the multitude of fucking cars and buses and taxis and pedestrians, although the truth of the matter was that maybe Elvis wasn't cut out for this shit.

Maybe El Güero was right that he was a marshmallow, a softie, and he couldn't measure up to El Gazpacho.

Damn it! The woman. Where could she have gone? For a minute he panicked, thinking maybe she was meeting with Leonora, but then he calmed himself down. No, Leonora was still in hiding; she wouldn't read the ad in the newspaper until the next morning. Could be the woman was visiting Emilio Lomelí again. That's where she'd gone the last time. He remembered his address quite clearly, along with other details in the file.

Or maybe they were driving to the art collective? He doubted it, judging by the direction they'd taken.

Fucking shit. He was too tired and too tense, that was the problem. He still ached from the beating, his muscles screaming about the mistreatment inflicted on them. In particular his back, his spine, they burned like holy hell, and it was getting worse, as if every nerve ending was waking up to the reality of the situation.

He stopped by a pharmacy and bought a bottle of aspirin, then drove back to the apartment. It was one o'clock. Still a while until he could hit La Habana, and he needed a rest. All of them needed a rest if they were going to manage tomorrow and for the next few days. That's when they must be alert. So he decided to get some shut-eye, just like the others.

The boys were napping, but they'd be up in a couple of hours. He pinned a note to El Güero's door telling him he had the next shift and it started at five. Then at eleven the Antelope should take his place. He wasn't sure who he wanted watching Sócrates and who he wanted watching the woman.

The woman. She wasn't much, and yet there he was, thinking about her again. He supposed it was because he couldn't have a normal life and therefore almost any woman would catch his interest. Not that he'd ever had much of a normal life, first living with that older American lady and then with that weird cult.

He was in bed, on top of the covers, smoking a cigarette with the lights off and trying to lull himself to sleep. He knew he shouldn't do this, that chain-smoking was already bad, but doing it in bed was a recipe for waking up with third-degree burns, but he did it anyway when he felt acutely empty.

Cristina, Cristina. Dimples and long brown hair flowing down her back. He remembered her naked, laid out on a narrow bed, humming a song. He liked to remember her like that, naked, next to him.

The woman didn't look anything like Cristina, who had been exactly his type. Petite, pale, with a pretty, kissable mouth. That's the way he liked them. But he was still smoking in the dark, wondering whether, under different circumstances, it wouldn't be possible for him to bump into Maite in the street and meet her that way.

Hundreds of people met every day, after all. It was the easiest thing to chat up a girl on the bus or in line for the movies. And he wasn't interested in her in a perverted way; it was all very innocent. He was simply curious.

He kept wondering what her voice sounded like. He'd seen her from afar, stared at her photo, read the information El Mago had provided, but he couldn't imagine her voice. It probably wasn't anything special, but he wanted to have a full picture of the woman. He wanted to ask her how many records she owned and whether she listened to "Blue Velvet" late at night and swayed to the music, all alone, while the city slept.

He couldn't imagine her with others, certainly not with that hippie with the bushy eyebrows. She existed in isolation, standing in front of a stark, white background.

Some people are made to be lonely.

He put out his cigarette and slept.

When he woke up it was late in the evening. His body still ached. He winced as he put on a jacket and headed to La Habana.

At that time of the day it was packed, with old men shuffling their dominoes and the literary types crowded around the tables. He saw Justo sitting near the back. He had his pack of Faritos on the table and his coffee, and was immersed in a book or doing a good job at pretending that was the case. His baby face was neatly shaved, and he gave every appearance of being a young, eager student taking a break.

You'd think him newly baptized, that's how innocent he looked.

Elvis took a seat in front of him. Justo turned the page. Waiters in black trousers and black vests walked around carrying orders of molletes on round trays. The scent of coffee beans and cigars mingled together. People spoke with accents in this place. Spanish, Cuban, some Chilean.

"Back so soon. Keeping busy?" Justo asked, but he didn't look up.

"Sure, I guess," Elvis said, not knowing how to begin. Now that he was here, he was thinking his idea was pretty dumb. After all, why would this guy want to lend him a hand? And even if he did, how was he going to pay him? Elvis had his stash of money in the cigar box, but he didn't want to spend it like this.

The young man bent the corner of the page he was reading and set his book down. "I might as well tell you right away: your friend's dead."

Elvis heard what he said, but at first he didn't understand. He was still thinking about the stakeout he needed to conduct, and the words flew by. But Justo kept staring at him from behind his horn-rimmed glasses, looking serious, and then Elvis got it.

El Gazpacho.

He meant El Gazpacho.

"He can't be dead."

"I did some quick checking around and found him, saw him with my own eyes. He's definitely dead."

Elvis shook his head. "You've got it wrong."

But Justo was now looking at Elvis with bemused pity, and Elvis knew he didn't have it wrong. He thought of El Gazpacho, drenched in blood, and the sounds he made as Elvis drove the car to the doctor. Maybe he'd been too slow or too clumsy transporting him. Maybe it was his fault. His mouth was dry.

"Where'd you find him?"

"They picked him up in a ditch near Ciudad Satélite. He was strangled," Justo said, and he took out a matchbox and lit his cigarette. He offered Elvis one, but Elvis did not move.

Elvis stared at him, watching as Justo tossed the match into a cup.

"Strangled," he repeated. "No, he had a bullet wound, and I dropped him off at the doctor's place."

Justo chuckled and took a drag, sliding the box with cigarettes closer to the center of the table, inviting Elvis to pick one with a gesture of his wrist. "Your boss doesn't like bullets."

Elvis almost laughed at that. What a prick. To say that. To even *think* it.

"It wasn't El Mago."

"Who, then? El Coco?"

"Fuck—" Elvis said, and he pressed his hands hard against the table with such force that Justo had to steady the damn thing so it wouldn't flip over.

"Sit down, you imbecile," Justo muttered, and in that moment, his face contorted with anger, he didn't look as young as before. There were tiny creases on the sides of his eyes, and his mouth was stern. "I liked El Gazpacho. He was an okay dude. That's why I bothered looking for him and then bothered to tell you. I could have just taken your money. El Mago is no saint, you should know that by now."

"Why would he kill him, huh? He was a Hawk."

"How the hell should I know? He wouldn't be the only dead Hawk this week."

"Makes no sense."

A man had won a game of dominoes. He laughed, and the murmur of a radio in the corner drifted across the café. Violeta Parra was singing about being seventeen and innocent again. Elvis stared at his hands. He wanted to grab a cigarette, but he was afraid his fingers would shake, so he sat there, stiff and afraid and trembling inside instead while men laughed.

"Look," Justo said, lowering his voice until it was nothing but a whisper across the table, "They're disbanding the Hawks, trust me on that. Things are way too hot and El Mago is up to his neck in problems. He fucked up—people are going to pounce on him. You ought to get yourself away from him now. The clock's ticking for that guy."

"Clock's ticking for everyone."

"He killed El Gazpacho."

Parra spoke of the chains of destiny and strummed a guitar.

"I heard you the first time," Elvis said. "But there're others who could've done it. CIA, for one."

"CIA? You kidding me?"

"They trained some of the Hawks. Maybe they got nervous," he said, realizing he sounded as stupid as the Antelope when he got into one of his conspiracy streaks. "Fuck, I don't know. El Gazpacho was one of El Mago's boys, so you can't peg it on him."

El Gazpacho. Poor, smiling, Gazpacho with his love of Asian films and his good-natured jokes, saying brother this and brother that. And it didn't mean anything, except it did. Brother. He'd never had a friend like El Gazpacho, a friend who really cared, someone who wasn't there just for himself.

El Gazpacho was there for all of them, but mostly he was there for Elvis.

He squeezed his eyes shut for a second, just a damn second. He felt a black rage in his body, bile coating his tongue. He crammed a cigarette into his mouth.

"What'll happen to the body? Is someone claiming it? He had family. A sister."

"You know her name?"

"No," Elvis muttered. "I don't know his name or hers. Maybe you could find out?"

"I did enough finding him. You owe me for this, motherfucker."

"You sure it's him? If he really wanted him gone, wouldn't El Mago have cut off his head or something? To prevent identification?"

"Why? He doesn't have a name."

Elvis wouldn't even be able to go to church and have a mass said for the dead man because he had no idea who El Gazpacho had really been. Just a guy. An anonymous dead guy. If Elvis dropped dead tomorrow, he'd be an anonymous dead guy too. A fucker from the gutter El Mago had found and discarded, lower than El Gazpacho or the others.

Elvis wasn't sure his mother would give a fuck even if he was identified. He hadn't seen his family in years. They liked it like that.

His real family were the Hawks. El Mago, El Gazpacho, even those fuckups El Güero and the Antelope. That's what he had.

Elvis let the cigarette dangle from the corner of his mouth, his eyes unfocused.

"You've got company tonight," Justo said.

"Where?" Elvis asked, raising a hand, slowly holding the cigarette between his fingers, his voice made raspy with pain. Tears pricked his eyes, but he squeezed them away.

"Behind, to the right, table near the door."

Elvis opened his eyes, but he didn't look. Instead he fiddled with one of Justo's books, pretending he was reading it. "What does he look like?"

"Tall, brown hair. Suede jacket and turtleneck."

"Anaya's man?"

"Couldn't swear on it, but I'd said no. They usually travel in twos, and he doesn't look like a gorilla. Snappy shoes, this one."

"Fucking prick," Elvis muttered. He'd bet an eyeball it was that Russian shit-eater again, with a Makarov tucked in its leather holster. It had to be a Makarov. What the hell did he want? He'd already given Elvis a good beating. His back was still tender from the damn newspaper he'd swatted him with.

"Not a friend?"

"No."

"Who?" Justo asked, curious.

"Another player," Elvis said, because he didn't think it was a good idea to be revealing it was a damn KGB agent. He didn't really know Justo. His whole idea to ask him for help was stupid.

He didn't know what to do. Head back to the apartment and pretend everything was normal? Forget that El Gazpacho was dead?

God fucking damn it, El Gazpacho was dead. El Mago had killed him. El Mago had fucking killed him. Or maybe not. No sense into leaping to conclusions.

It better not have been El Mago.

"Is there a way out the back?"

"Past the bathrooms. Remember, you owe me, so if I ever need—"

"I know how it works," Elvis muttered.

Elvis stood up. He walked at a normal pace, like he wasn't worried, and wound his way out the back. He darted past a couple of waiters who were having a smoke break, leaning against the wall in their black vests and starched shirts. It was dark now outside.

He walked faster, began running. He ran until he was out of breath.

Brother.

22

WHEN SHE ARRIVED at work on the dot Monday morning, Maite told Diana that she'd gone to Cuernavaca for the weekend, but in her version of events it was with a new suitor. Diana seemed impressed when Maite said he'd be picking her up in his car. She asked if Diana could cover for her.

"Do I get to meet him?" Diana asked.

"Not today," Maite said. "But later on, maybe."

"What's his name?"

"Rubén," she said proudly.

"Is he good looking?"

"Very."

They continued in that vein for a few more minutes, before the arrival of their co-workers made it necessary to retire to their desks. Maite smiled. Not only did the latest issue of *Secret Romance* show Jorge Luis waking up from his coma, but the lies she'd told perked her up. Besides, she'd leave the office early and in a car, no need to ride the stinking bus this time.

That's not to say that the morning didn't have its hiccups. Twice the phone rang, and she nervously picked up the receiver, fearing it might be that dreadful man from the DFS. But first it was a wrong number, and then it was Maite's mother calling to say that the mechanic had phoned her and how dare Maite give out her number and why was Maite always suffering from money trouble. Maite really hadn't had any money trouble other than with the mechanic. The reason she'd given her mother's number was because she needed a guarantor when she bought the car, and then the mechanic had also asked for an emergency contact. Most women put down their husband's name, but since Maite didn't have a husband, she was subject to this extra layer of scrutiny.

Maite told her mother she couldn't speak because she was at work, but then her mother threatened to phone her at home that night. Maite hoped she forgot to do it and almost considered asking her sister if she wouldn't get her mother off her case.

Around eleven a.m. Maite made up a migraine and said she needed to go home early and explained Diana had promised to finish her work. Her boss didn't seem pleased, but he said fine, and at one o'clock she took the elevator downstairs and waited for Rubén to show up.

She smiled, thinking if Diana poked her head out the window she'd see her getting into the car.

"Good day at work?" Rubén asked.

"Fine. And you?"

"Work was all right. But worms keep coming out of the woodwork to prop up the president. Look at Octavio Paz and Carlos Fuentes, that couple of boot-lickers. And you should have seen *Excélsior*: they had a letter signed by José Luis Cuevas, Rufino Tamayo, Ramón Xirau, and all that lot, praising the president. Intellectuals and artists with Echeverría! Fuck them! You hear people saying it's 'Echeverría or fascism,' like there's no other choice, and you can't trust anyone these days. Changing things from the inside! The bullshit they spout. And we . . . even we are not immune to this crap."

Maite frowned. "I'm not sure I understand."

"Asterisk," Rubén said, "it's winding down."

"It's closing?"

"I went to see Jackie before I picked you up. She says it's too dangerous to keep meeting like we have."

"She's probably right."

"There are so many opportunists waiting for their slice of cake. Political dilettantes. I feel helpless."

Rubén gripped the wheel. He looked young and haunted; it was easy to feel sorry for him.

When they arrived at Sócrates's apartment building, he still wasn't home or was pretending he couldn't hear the buzzer. Luckily they managed to slip into the building when a couple of people were leaving and walked up the stairs to the apartment, which lay at the end of a hallway.

The door was open a crack, and they walked in.

"Hey there, are you home?" Rubén asked.

On a messy bed someone had left a cup filled with cigarette butts. The light was on in the bathroom. Rubén walked ahead, brushing aside a curtain with wooden beads.

A young man, stripped down to his underthings, sat on the toilet, his chin pressed against his chest and his hands on his lap. Maite immediately noticed the little round burn marks on his skin and the rope binding his feet. He wasn't moving.

"Is he dead?" she whispered.

Rubén didn't reply; instead he stepped forward and placed a hand against the young man's neck. "Yes," he muttered.

"Oh, my God. What—"

"Let's go," Rubén said, grabbing her by the hand and pulling her out of the tiny apartment.

They rushed down the stairs. Their escape was so loud she feared the whole building heard them, but no one poked their head out the door.

"We need to phone the police," she said when they reached the car and Rubén fumbled with the keys. He looked up at her, his eyes sharp.

"No."

"But he's dead. He'll have to be buried."

"Get in."

Maite obeyed, but as soon as she was in the passenger's seat she spoke up again. "We can't just leave him there."

Rubén started the car. "What do you think they'll do to us if we tell them, huh? You want to end up at Lecumberri? With my history—"

"What history?"

"I've been arrested. I've had my run-ins with the pigs."

"But he's dead!"

"I know he's dead, and we'll be dead soon if we call the cops."

Maite laced her hands together tight, resting them against her lap. Rubén reached into his jacket pocket and took out a cigarette. When they stopped at a red light, he lit the cigarette and turned to her.

"I'm going to drive around for a bit. Then we'll go back to your apartment."

"You're going to let a man rot in a bathroom."

"Better him than me."

She tried to think of something, anything to say, but as she squeezed her eyes shut, the image of the dead man haunted her, and she forgot how to utter words. When they reached her apartment, still mute, she decided to boil water for a coffee, but she fumbled with the tin and ended up dropping it in the middle of the kitchen. Grains of coffee spilled across the laminate floor.

She grabbed the broom. The phone rang. She guessed it must be her mother and considered letting it ring, but knowing her, Mother would simply phone again in ten minutes and then get even angrier at Maite because she hadn't been there to answer the first time. She propped the broom against the wall and took a deep breath before lifting the receiver.

"Yes?" she asked and closed her eyes, already imagining the harsh recrimination she was going to have to endure. *Maite, you can't handle money. Maite, you can't handle anything.* She pressed her back against the refrigerator and waited.

"Hello? It's Leonora," a woman said, her voice soft.

She clutched the phone cord, astonished, her eyes snapping open. "Where are you? We've been looking all over for you!"

"I was reading the early edition," the girl said, and then something else Maite didn't catch; the girl was talking in whispers.

Rubén, who was sitting on the couch, raised his head and stared at her. "Who's that?"

"It's Leonora! It's so good to hear you. What about the early edition?"

"You have the cat? And the box?"

"Yes, and yes. When can we see you?"

"Tell her to hang up."

"Huh?"

Rubén stood up, whip quick, and rushed toward Maite. He pulled the phone from her grasp, shoving her away. Maite lost her balance and stumbled down. "Hide! It's not safe!" he yelled into the receiver and hung up.

Maite stood up, holding on to the kitchen counter. "Are you crazy? We've been trying to find her for days!"

She rubbed her knee, but he glared at her, as if she'd pushed him and it hadn't been the other way around.

"That was before Sócrates wound up dead. She can't come back. She's in real danger now."

"She can't hide forever," Maite said. She took a few steps out of the narrow kitchen and into the living room, then turned to look at him and stepped back into the kitchen. "What about Jackie? Can't she do something?"

"What's Jackie going to do?" Rubén muttered tiredly, rubbing his jaw.

"I don't know! You said she'd help. What about Emilio?" Maite snapped her fingers. "That's right, we'll phone Emilio."

She grabbed the phone, but Rubén immediately took it from her hands and hung up. She stared at him, mouth open.

"You can't tell anyone she called."

"Why not?"

"Don't you get it? It's not safe. You can't trust anyone."

"Why should I trust you then? I don't even know you. Step away from the door. I'm going to see Emilio."

"Calm down."

"You step away! It's my house!"

"I'm telling you to calm down. Someone is going to start banging on the door asking what the hell is going on if you keep this up."

"I don't care!"

She stomped toward her atelier, and when she walked in she cranked the volume up and let the needle fall upon a record, the music like a clap of thunder, so loud, making the whole room tremble. "Will You Still Love Me Tomorrow" began playing.

"For God's sake, Maite, don't be doing this," he said and turned the volume down with a swift flick of the wrist. "You want to make it worse? Don't you see we're in a mess?"

But all she could see right then and there was the dead man again. Slumped over, with the horrible burn marks on his legs, and his neck bent and his eyes—for a quick second she had seen those eyes, glassy and open, staring back at her.

She felt so lost, so utterly alone, and wanted to clutch something. She turned to him and grabbed onto his jacket with both hands. But she was also furious, the anger boiling up because none of this was her fault, it was all that girl's fault, that girl she didn't even know, and it was Rubén's fault too. He had allowed her to get involved in this reckless quest.

Maite lunged up and bit him hard, on the mouth. He stepped back, startled, pressed a hand against his lips and stared at her, drawing back. His fingers were stained with blood.

He grabbed her face between his hands and bit her back. For a moment they both froze, stunned by what was happening, and there was this pause, like the crackling of a record.

"You should fuck me before I change my mind," she said.

She meant it, too. She had fantasized about a similar encounter but never dared, she had even pictured herself with this man in a fit of boredom. And there she was now and there he was, and for all of Maite's deficiencies, he seemed willing and interested in her.

The music was a low hum as she undid his belt buckle and he pulled up her skirt, pressing her down against the cheap red-and-white carpet. Wary, perhaps, that she might bite him again, he did not attempt to kiss her. It was not as if she felt in the mood to be kissed. Kisses were for the pages of *Secret Romance*, they were for sweethearts, and this wasn't an episode that belonged in any of her magazines.

They were both angry at the world, that was why this was happening. It was a kiss of scorpions, both heavy with poison. Both weary too. The tension and excitement of the past few days was the kindle they required.

Still half-dressed, Rubén thrust into her. She wondered, for a brief, flickering second, how she might compare to the beautiful Leonora, and she drew him closer to her, pressing her face against his neck so he wouldn't look at her.

It had been so long since she'd had a lover, she feared she'd forgotten how human bodies worked, but they found a rhythm, something between sorrow and delight.

She felt his tongue, wet and warm, sliding against her neck. She thought about Emilio, handsome, cultured, interesting Emilio, and let herself play-pretend for a minute, imagining it was him with her. Then she thought it was one of the men of her comic books, that perhaps both of them were taking turns having their way with her. Rubén grunted something, lifted his head, and she looked at him and the fantasy was broken.

She came a few minutes after that; it caught her by surprise. It was a brief, low tremor, like a butterfly brushing its wings against her skin, not a precipice of pleasure, but at least he'd had the decency of waiting for her. Some men didn't care.

He thrusted once, twice, then lay still above her for a couple of minutes before rolling aside. Music was still playing, but it was a different song and faster tempo. She closed her eyes, and when she opened them again he was staring at the ceiling. She felt nervous, wondering what he was thinking, whether he felt guilty.

"I'm jumping in the shower," she said, lifting the needle from the record player as she headed into the bathroom.

She didn't take long, vigorously scrubbing her stomach and legs, washing off the sweat and semen, removing any makeup. She stopped in front of the mirror to contemplate her face, free of any adornment, flushed with the warmth of the hot shower, and, in the aftermath of lovemaking, somewhat pretty. When for a split second, the face was angled in the mirror, it even seemed almost beautiful.

Perhaps it was merely her imagination, merely the need to be desirable, but it was a nice illusion.

When she walked back into her bedroom in her ratty pink robe, she saw that Rubén had settled on the bed. He leaned on his elbow and looked up at her as she toweled her hair, then ran a hand across the objects arranged on her vanity, her little treasures—like jewels snatched from a shipwreck. She caressed the statue of San Judas Tadeo and the bottle of perfume. She thought about faceless men wielding sacrificial knives and maidens bound upon stone altars.

"You all right?"

"Hmmm?" she replied.

"You look worried."

"Aren't you?"

"Of course. But I'd like to not think about it before I take a nap. Fuck, I'm tired."

"I can't stop thinking about things, ever. Sometimes I look at a word in a dictionary and I wonder, how did that word come to have this meaning? How did hot mean hot or cold mean cold, and why some words sound the same but mean different things. Then I also think about how things might be and how they aren't."

He looked at her curiously, as if she were singing in an unknown language.

"You're not like that," she said. "You don't overthink."

"I suppose it depends who you're asking."

"Leonora, what does she say?"

She assumed he would be upset if she mentioned the girl, but Rubén merely shrugged. Maite opened a drawer and took out her nightgown. It had buttons going up the front and ruffles on the wrists. Holding it up, she realized how hideous it looked and felt a bit embarrassed to be wearing it, but she changed into it and slipped under the covers.

Rubén took off his clothes but did not bother getting changed into pajamas. He also didn't shower. She wondered if he had even brought pajamas. Perhaps he slept naked. He and Leonora together, the apartment musky with their scent.

"I still think we should let Emilio know." Maite turned her head and looked at him. "It would be selfish not to tell him she's okay."

"Emilio is a rich junior who is in the pocket of the PRI, I've told you that. There's no reason to dig deeper there."

"You're so annoying," she muttered. "Where's the gun, anyway? If an assassin walks in here now, he'll shoot you dead. You'll die without underwear."

"You do overthink things," he said, but he was smiling. "It's not a bad way to die, having had a good fuck and sleeping in bed. If I do end up in the damn sierra with the guerilla, I'll remember you fondly."

It wasn't quite a declaration of love, but she liked that. She wondered if she'd been wrong and Rubén might have the raw material to be a hero from a comic book, after all. "Soldier" sounded exciting. She supposed if he was the member of a guerilla it wasn't quite like being a soldier, but close enough. A rebel with a cause.

23

MONDAY AT EIGHT a.m. Elvis and the Antelope parked their car in front of Sócrates's building. Elvis had slept little, in fits and bursts. First he'd told himself that Justo was lying, that El Gazpacho was alive. But sometime near dawn he'd admitted the truth. El Gazpacho must be dead. Whether El Mago had a hand in it, he couldn't tell. He also couldn't phone El Mago and ask if he'd murdered a man.

The Antelope chewed bubble gum and took a nap. Elvis looked at the crossword resting on his lap and couldn't fill in the missing letters. He hadn't picked a word of the day. In one pocket of his jacket he had his screwdriver and in the other he carried a pack of cigarettes, but he'd forgotten his lighter.

Around one-thirty p.m. the Antelope nudged him. "Isn't that the woman we've been tailing?" he asked.

It was Maite, walking together with her friend, that same man he'd previously seen her with. They made a mismatched pair. He looked like a student, his hair too long, and she was prim and proper in a suit. Elvis wondered who the man was and what they were doing there. They went in, but came out rushing like the devil was after them.

"Follow them," Elvis said.

"I thought we were watching this building."

"Change of plans; when someone runs like that, you follow."

However, rather than leading them to an interesting location, the couple simply returned to Maite's apartment building. Elvis parked the car, and they found El Güero, who had been keeping watch all this time alone and rolled his eyes when he saw them.

"Finally! Ready to relieve me?" he asked.

"Not yet," Elvis said. "Anything happening here?"

"It's dead. The woman just came back home."

"Yeah, we bumped into them at the other location."

"So what now?" the Antelope asked. "Do we stay here?"

Elvis wasn't sure, but he didn't want to say that because then they'd think him indecisive, weak. El Güero solved his problem by speaking up. "I'm starving, man. Let's get a decent meal and come back."

"Fine. Antelope, stay here in the car and wait. We'll be back in twenty minutes," he said. Now that El Güero mentioned it, Elvis needed to grab a bite. He had a damn headache. Maybe he could stop at the pharmacy too.

A couple of blocks from the apartment building there was a park and around its perimeter a little tianguis, where office workers and low-tier government functionaries clustered around food stalls, drinking soft drinks and eating tacos. Everyone preferred a comida corrida and the comfort of a chair and a beer, but sometimes it was hard to make ends meet, and tacos de canasta served as well as anything else.

Elvis and El Güero stopped at a stall selling barbacoa, where a woman deposited two bowls filled with meat in front of them. Elvis salted his food and ate slowly, sitting on an overturned bucket that served as a chair while a little radio played "Are You Lonesome Tonight," and for a moment he didn't mind sitting there, squeezed between El Güero and a stranger, with a scrawny dog circling around them, waiting for scraps.

For a moment the music smoothed the edges of everything away and he felt like in those movies, when the lens is blurry and a halation—that's a word he'd learned from his handy dictionary—distorts the light.

Then some prick changed the station, and they were playing "Surfin' Bird." Elvis frowned and took a sip of his soda. That's when he noticed the four men standing on the other side of the food stall. They were wearing suits and ties, but those were no bank tellers or office workers—he could recognize trouble when he saw it.

He nudged El Güero, asking him for a light. El Güero took out his lighter, and Elvis lowered his head and pressed his cigarette against the flame, eyes down on his bowl of barbacoa. "Four fuckers right across."

El Güero put away his lighter and pressed a napkin against his face. "I've seen that fucker on the right, he's been watching the building. These assholes must be DFS."

"Figures."

"What the fuck do they want?"

"Guess they're marking their territory, like dogs pissin' on the sidewalk."

"You got the gun? Take it out."

Elvis shook his head. "Don't have it. What you got?"

"Pocketknife."

"Let's get the fuck outta here. Follow me."

They stood up slowly and began walking between the stalls. The men matched their pace. When they reached the edge of the park, Elvis made a sharp right, and they dashed across the street. It was a performance worthy of marathon runners but it did them no good; they couldn't shake those motherfuckers off. Elvis veered into an alley behind a laundry; the smell of detergent was strong, spilling out of an exhaust pipe. He eyed the door to the laundry, wondering if he could pry it open quickly. But the men were right on their heels. Four at one end of the alley and two on the other end, blocking their way.

El Güero took out his pocketknife. Elvis bent down and picked up a wooden plank that had been left on the ground; there was no point in trying to do much with the screwdriver. His palms were sweaty. Six against two. The Hawks beat people, but it was usually defenseless students, not trained agents. He wished he had a real weapon.

One of the agents charged toward Elvis, and he swung the plank, hitting him hard and sending him staggering back. But that meant that another two rushed forward and tried to land a punch. Elvis whacked one of them in the face, but the other son of a bitch was like a ninja from a movie, and within two moves he had twisted Elvis's hand and pulled away the wooden plank.

Elvis fell to his knees and then he tugged forward, pulling the agent down. For a minute he thought he had the upper hand as he punched the fucker in the face, but then the man he'd whacked with the plank decided to get revenge by kicking Elvis in the ribs. Quick as that, the fucking ninja had pinned him down and was choking him into oblivion.

Elvis managed to raise an arm and hit the son of a bitch on top of him with his elbow, stunning him for a second, and coughing and wheezing, he leaned on a pile of crates and pulled himself to his feet.

Meanwhile, for all his strength and his knife, El Güero didn't seem to be doing too hot either. A man was hitting him in the face with the butt of a gun. "Fuck, leave him alone! What do you want?" Elvis yelled, and the guy beating El Güero turned to Elvis and pointed the gun at him.

"Easy there, don't shoot them."

A man who had been leaning against a wall, arms crossed, now stepped forward. He made a motion with his hand, flashing a ring, and the man with the gun put his weapon away. El Güero slumped down. His face was painted crimson, and Elvis was pretty sure he'd lost several teeth. As long as he didn't swallow them, he'd live. Or so he hoped.

"Hello, hello, how are we doing today?" the man with the ring asked. He sounded chipper.

"Well, our lunch got fucked up," Elvis said, spitting on the ground, "so not that great."

"Sorry to hear that. But you deserve it."

"What the hell you talking about?"

"My name is Mateo Anaya. I'm with the DFS."

"I know who you are."

The man ran both hands through his hair and adjusted his cuffs. "Good. Then you know what this is about. You interrogated one of my agents. I want to know what he told you."

"Why don't you ask him?"

"I would. Turns out he's dead."

"I didn't kill him."

"Liar."

"He's telling the truth," El Güero said, his voice raspy. "It wasn't us."

Anaya cocked his head and frowned, like he was trying to figure out whether they were hiding an ace up their sleeves, but it was plain as day that the beating would have taken the liar out of any man. "It doesn't matter," Anaya said finally. "I want to know what he told you."

Elvis wiped his mouth with his sleeve. "He told us he spied for you."

"And?"

"Told us about the girl, Leonora, and said he had a way to contact her, through an ad in the paper. But we haven't seen her, she hasn't shown her face, so maybe he was lying."

"That's it?"

"What the fuck else should he have told us? He said he was a rat."

"Told you. Carrion peckers. They don't know shit," the man with the gun muttered.

A teenage boy holding a pack of cigarettes in one hand opened the back door of the laundry and stared at them in astonishment. Elvis rushed forward, pulling El Güero with him by the arm, and they shoved the boy aside and made their way into the shop.

Many shirts, suits, and dresses hung from the ceiling, wrapped in plastic. It was a veritable labyrinth of clothes, and Elvis yanked some coats away, dragging El Güero until they reached the front of the store and stumbled out. Then it was a mad dash back to the Antelope and the car. When they reached him, the Antelope was happily chewing gum. He stared at them, mouth open.

"Open the fucking door!" Elvis said, and the Antelope fumbled with the locks until Elvis was able to shove El Güero in and jumped into the car. "Drive!"

The Antelope turned the key, turned the wheel, obeying with a quick nod of the head, and they were off. The big man moaned pitifully while Elvis attempted to get a better look at his injuries. El Güero had lost teeth and his nose was a mess, but the thing that worried him was the eye. The right eye was probably busted.

"Antelope, let's go to Escamilla's place," he said. That was the same doctor they'd visited when El Gazpacho was injured, and El Gazpacho maybe died in his fucking office, but Elvis didn't know any other doctor that could help them.

The doctor lived in La Guerrero, which wasn't exactly next door but was close enough by car and besides, they didn't have much choice, whether it took twenty minutes or fifty-five to drive there depending on the fucking traffic.

Escamilla's ratty office sat atop an ugly, peeling yellow building a few blocks from La Lagunilla and right next to a gym where boxers trained. When they walked in, with El Güero oozing blood from everywhere, the doctor was standing in the reception area, a cup of coffee in his right hand. He looked at them and stirred his coffee with a plastic spoon.

"Hello, gentlemen, come over to the back," he said, like it was no big deal to have a man without teeth stumble into his office. And maybe it wasn't, with so many boxers in that neighborhood, plus the assorted unsavory characters who needed bandages.

The doctor told El Güero to lie down on the examination table while he washed his hands in a tiny sink. Then he shone a light in El Güero's eyes, checked the inside of his mouth. The doctor moved away from the patient, opened a cabinet, and began pulling out gauze, bandages, cotton swabs, and disinfectant with slow, methodical fingers.

"Might be an orbital fracture," the doctor said, raising his head and looking at Elvis. "You can step out. This'll take a few minutes."

Elvis obeyed. A young man in a gray smock had materialized and was mopping the floor, cleaning the blood that had dripped onto the linoleum. He didn't look at either Elvis or the Antelope. Elvis sat down on a plastic chair, and the Antelope took the other chair. Between them there was a tiny table with a pile of old *Reader's Digests*.

"You going to tell me what happened?" the Antelope asked.

"DFS happened," Elvis said. "They found Sócrates dead and wanted to pin it on us."

"That little shit we saw Saturday?"

"That shit."

"Pricks. Who do you think killed him?"

Elvis shrugged. For all he knew, Sócrates's commie friends had wised up and killed the traitor, or maybe it had been that big fucking Russian—after all, he'd followed Elvis to the Habana. Or, hell, maybe it was Leonora, or Maite and that hippie. After all, they'd run out of the building real quick. He definitely didn't like that hippie.

The doctor wandered into the reception area. His white coat was splattered with crimson, and he was wiping his hands on a rag. "How's he doin'?" Elvis asked.

"I gave him painkillers and cleaned everything up, but he's going to lose that eye if he doesn't have surgery. I can make the arrangements."

"Can I have a word about that with you, doc?"

"Come on," the doctor said, and they went into a second examination room. There was a bowl filled with mints in a corner atop a mini refrigerator and one of those charts with all the human bones on the wall.

"I'm not letting you take El Güero anywhere. The last team member I brought here ended up in a ditch, strangled."

The doctor stared at Elvis. "That's not my business."

Elvis grabbed the doctor by the collar of his shirt and slammed him against the wall, his mouth a snarl. "What happened to him?"

"I don't know. I released that man, and he was supposed to head back to his apartment," the doctor said, and Elvis had to give it to him, the doctor had balls, because he didn't flinch and he didn't yell, speaking instead like he was dictating a prescription.

But Elvis supposed the doctor didn't have to be afraid. The people he worked for, they must make sure he didn't get in any trouble.

Elvis released him and stepped back. The doctor rubbed the back of his neck with his hand and glared at Elvis. Elvis went into the examination room where El Güero was sitting. "Let's go," Elvis said.

"The doc said he was getting an ambulance."

"No he ain't."

They went down the stairs real quick and got into the car. Elvis wasn't sure what to do. In the end, he told the Antelope to drive to a Cruz Verde. El Güero wasn't too happy with that idea. He was still going on about the ambulance.

"Look, things are fucked here left and right," Elvis said. "Check yourself in and lay low. It's the best chance you got."

"I don't get it."

"El Gazpacho's dead and you saw the DFS is out for us. So, stupid fuck, lie low and get your damn eye fixed. Find us in a few days."

El Güero looked at Elvis suspiciously, but he grunted a "fine, fucker," and when they reached the hospital, he got out of the car and didn't ask any more questions.

"Where to?" the Antelope asked.

"Back to our apartment, then to the girl's place."

The Antelope took out a stick of gum and unwrapped it. "You weren't joking about that shit, about El Gazpacho being dead?"

"I'm not sure."

"We're not calling in El Mago? About this stuff?"

"Later tonight," Elvis muttered. "Right now we better go get the fucking gun."

24

MAITE HADN'T LIED when she told him she thought too much. After a brief nap, she'd woken up to find Rubén snoring next to her, and quickly her mind jumped to everything that had happened to them so far, like unspooling the reel of a film and looking at it frame by frame. And then, of course, she started worrying about the whole situation and wondering about the police and what they might do to them if they connected them to the dead man in the apartment.

Unable to lie still, Maite got up and went to the atelier. She couldn't play her music for fear of waking Rubén up—he looked like he was enjoying his sleep—so instead she sat down and leafed through old issues of *Secret Romance*. She'd reached the panel where Jorge Luis kisses the heroine for the first time when he cleared his throat and she looked up to find him by the doorway.

He was still naked, standing there, hair tousled and eyes fogged by sleep. She glanced down at the floor, feeling embarrassed. She'd fucked him, but she hadn't really looked at him.

"I thought you were gone for a moment," he said.

"Where would I go?"

"I don't know. I thought you might still be mad at me. I guess I should say I'm sorry. I shoved you away but I needed you to hang up. I wasn't thinking right. I don't want Leonora to wind up dead."

"She wouldn't wind up dead by talking to us."

"She could. We can't meet with her. She needs to lie low, until they move on to something else. We should lie low too."

Maite stood up and placed her comic books back on the bookshelf. Then she touched the cuffs of her nightgown and brushed her hair behind her ear and looked at him. The stupid nightgown did her no favors, and she was sure he was comparing her to Leonora. Who wouldn't? Maybe he was laughing at her dismal performance.

When she'd pictured an encounter with a stranger, it was sexy and intriguing. But if she replayed the scene with Rubén in her mind, it all seemed tawdry. She wondered if he was going to complain about it, but instead he yawned.

"Want to get a bite to eat? I'm starving," he said, scratching his belly with his left hand. He was slim, his stomach was flat, a bit of muscle there and also in the arms, perhaps from lifting boxes around his job. Or else he played a sport.

"It wouldn't be . . . you know, dangerous?" Maite asked.

"It's probably safer outside," he said. "It's harder to kill someone in the middle of a restaurant. I'll take the gun, just in case."

"Can you even shoot it?"

"It's not that hard."

They headed back to her room, and she quickly picked a blue dress with a paisley print that she thought flattered her. Or at least wasn't one of her dismal office outfits. He followed her and scooped up his shirt and jeans from the floor.

"Do you?" she asked, as she buttoned her dress, half-hiding behind the dresser's door. She didn't want him looking at her as she changed, noticing her imperfections: the annoying curve of her belly, her dry skin, the stretch marks left from puberty crisscrossing her ass. Maite's mother had varicose veins, and she feared she'd have the same one day, to make it all worse.

"Do I what?" he replied.

"Know how to shoot."

"Sure I do."

"Where'd you learn?"

"Jackie taught me," he said nonchalantly.

She watched him sit down and put on his jeans. "Why were you arrested? You didn't shoot anyone, did you?"

She was merely curious, not really concerned about the possibility of spending time with a killer. He zipped up his jeans and looked at her, and then he laughed merrily. "As if!"

"Then?"

"I joined a protest, which is enough to get you labeled as a member of a 'criminal conspiracy.' That's what happened three years ago, in Tlatelolco. That's what the president said. That all the students protesting were criminals and agitators, subversive elements. Same as always, I guess."

"Were you there? At Tlatelolco?" she asked. That had been a huge mess. Some political activists escaped the country after that. It was the sort of thing that was so big, no one could keep a lid on it. Even Maite had seen the pictures of the tanks and the soldiers and people screaming. Still, that hadn't stopped the same thing from happening again.

"No way. If I had, I'd probably be dead now. That wasn't my scene yet. After that, that's when I got into this whole activism thing. You couldn't ignore what was happening and so I went to meetings, printed leaflets. I got thrown in jail for a night for the leaflets and then got caught at a protest another time."

"Why didn't you stop?"

"What do you mean?"

"If I'd been thrown in jail twice, I wouldn't do anything like that again."

"That was nothing, a bit of time in a cell. I was lucky. They torture people, Maite. They kill. What happened at Tlatelolco, what happened with the Hawks? That shit is going to keep on happening if we don't stand up and defend ourselves. That has to end. We need to rise up in arms."

"I suppose so, but that's war."

"It's already war."

He stared at her. Maite didn't know what to say, and he'd gone quiet too, pulling his shoes on and tying the laces.

They drove to a restaurant where he said they made very decent milkshakes and they also served great burgers. As they sat there, waiting for their order, she tossed a coin in the jukebox sitting in a dusty corner and "At Last" began playing.

She felt like swaying to the music. If she'd been at home, she would have done it, her bare feet against the floor, her arms wrapped around an invisible lover. Because there was never a real lover for Maite. No flesh-and-blood man.

Except there was a man with her now, sharing her booth. She touched the back of her neck, her fingers sliding down to brush the top button of her dress.

The waitress came by with their food, and Maite busied herself with her hamburger; she'd ordered the same thing he had, feeling it was the safest choice. One time she'd ordered a pineapple carved and filled with shrimp at a restaurant, and Cristóbalito had chided her because it was the most expensive item on the menu. Between taking sips of her soft drink, she glanced at Rubén. He still had feelings for Leonora. He'd said as much. But he'd slept with her, and now they were sitting there together, all friendly-like.

She didn't want to ask, but she had to. She took a breath. "You're not sorry?"

"About what?"

"You know. About sleeping with me."

He blinked, confused. "Why would I be sorry about that? I told you, it'll make a nice memory."

"Oh, don't joke like that."

"Overthinker," he said, tapping his head with his index finger and smiling. He had a decent smile, all warm.

She blushed again and figured by now he thought she was a complete fool. But it wasn't like she did this regularly. She was angry at herself for not having the composure of the women in the stories she read, for not being the sophisticated lady. Instead, she was a stupid, blubbering spinster.

He took out a cigarette, lit it, and leaned an arm against the back of the booth as he took a drag. "Can you call in sick tomorrow?"

"Why?"

"For one, I'm still a bit nervous and don't want to have you out of my sight in case, you know, that DFS agent tries to speak to you again. Second—"

"I can't skip work all week because of that."

"I know. But you didn't let me tell you the second thing."

"What's that?"

"Second, you're pleasant and I don't mind spending time with you," he said, reaching for the ashtray and placing it in the middle of the table. "I've been so stressed I thought I'd have a damn heart attack, but I feel relaxed around you."

"Do you, really?"

"Yeah. I'm not sorry at all."

He stretched a hand and caught her own, his thumb rubbing circles against her wrist, and he was looking into her eyes with such interest Maite felt herself blushing again, like a girl. With her free hand she touched her neck, a finger pressed against the hollow of her throat.

"So you want to lie low tomorrow?"

"Yeah," he said. "What, is that really bad? I can teach you how to shoot too."

"In my apartment? Are you crazy?"

"Without bullets, of course. Or maybe how to punch a guy. I bet you don't know how to make a fist and throw a punch without breaking your fingers."

"It sounds like you want me to become a guerilla fighter," she said. "I take dictation."

"Well, you never know."

He wasn't astonishingly handsome like Emilio, nor enthralling like Cristóbalito, but Maite figured he was something. Right? He was at the very least courageous. She could picture him with a machete, deep in a jungle, carving a path through the greenery and leading his men.

There wasn't a jungle in Guerrero like the ones in *Secret Romance*, lush and filled with toucans, but there was some vegetation. Mountains, caves, rugged trails. And if they did connect them to the dead man, then that definitely would be a better location than Mexico City, rugged trails or not.

She imagined herself as an outlaw, far from civilization, while the moon, like a single unblinking eye, stared down at her. A man stood up and picked a song from the jukebox. "Blue Velvet." She adored that song. The music made her wish to dance, again, while wearing a long velvet dress.

Maite raised her chin, glancing at the man who had thrown a coin into the jukebox, and he looked back at her—his eyes were black, not the blue of the song, but they did resemble the soft velvet upon which you could pin jewels. No one ever looked at Maite for too long, but the man was staring at her. He had a cigarette in hand, but he wasn't smoking; instead he leaned an arm against the jukebox, looking terribly thoughtful, and he slowly pressed the cigarette against his lips and smirked, his lips curling a tad, before he smoothed his expression and walked back to his table, breaking eye contact.

The song was brief, filling the diner for three short minutes, before the place plunged back into silence.

Maite frowned and opened her purse, looking for a coin. When she found it, she stood up and walked to the jukebox. She went over the song list, nibbling on a nail. Maite picked "Can't Help Falling in Love." As she walked back to her table, smiling at Rubén, the young man's black eyes turned toward her for the briefest moment before he looked down and pressed his cigarette against the bottom of an ashtray.

25

THEY DROVE BACK to the apartment, and Elvis pocketed El Gazpacho's gun and stuffed a bunch of bullets and the speedloader in a worn leather messenger bag. Then he went into El Güero's room, looking for *his* gun and ammo, because even if he wasn't allowed to have one, Elvis was sure El Güero secretly kept a firearm in there. He found it pretty quickly. El Güero had hidden it in a tin box in the closet. He handed it to the Antelope.

"Those bastards from the DFS have firepower."

"We'll show them next time, put a couple of bullets in their ass. I never get to shoot anyone," the Antelope replied. He blew a bubble of gum and popped it, making a mocking motion with the gun, as though he were shooting across the room. "And I feel like shooting someone today."

"Man, don't play with that," Elvis muttered.

"Chill. I know weapons," the Antelope assured him, and he blew an even bigger bubble.

He wasn't in a mood to lecture anyone. If the Antelope shot himself in the dick by accident, so be it. Elvis went to the bathroom, cleaned up the new scrapes he'd acquired, and washed his face. When he was done, he tried phoning El Mago, but the old man didn't answer. Elvis didn't want to swing by his place unannounced a second time, so he told the Antelope that they were going back to the woman's apartment building, to keep watch as usual.

"You sure about hanging 'round that building? You know, those guys could come back and grab you again," the Antelope said.

"I'm pretty sure they have what they want. And that's why we've got the guns. Bullets up their ass, like you said." He wasn't confident about anything, but he also wasn't going to tell the Antelope that.

"First chance I get I'm shooting them trice. For El Güero, you know. Poor fucker's gonna lose an eye, I bet."

"We'll see."

"I mean it," the Antelope said. He had a hungry look on his face, like he sometimes got when they were beating someone, and Elvis knew he was for real. He was out for blood.

"Yeah. I get it."

The waiting game went as usual. Apparently Elvis had been right and the DFS agents had what they wanted, because they didn't show their faces. Elvis chain-smoked, since there wasn't anything else to do, and listened to the radio. The Animals strummed their guitars while he blew smoke rings and the Antelope chewed his bubble gum. He still hadn't picked a word of the day, and it bugged him.

When the woman and the man exited the building, they followed them into a restaurant. The Antelope and Elvis grabbed a table, ordered a couple of beers and a couple of daily specials. There was a jukebox in a corner, and the woman stood up and picked a song. It was "At Last," and he mouthed a line from the song. He knew this song, he knew what it meant. Outside it was starting to rain.

They were too far away from the woman's table to hear what she was telling the man, but he was leaning forward and smiling, and she blushed.

Elvis wondered how people did this. This being normal and going out together. He couldn't remember going out with many girls. Fucking, yes, and chasing skirts in the noisy, wild way boys from his neighborhood did. But he hadn't gone out much with the older gringa—he was private entertainment—and with Cristina there were always the other members of their fucked-up cult milling around. It wasn't ever him and a girl, together, out like this, drinking and eating while the jukebox played its tunes.

He didn't even know why he was thinking about this since the woman he was looking at wasn't particularly pretty, not the kind of woman to inspire a man to fantasize. Yet there was something about her. It was that air of tragedy, that's what it was, the way she sat, with one hand constantly pressed against her neck. And her eyes were dark and deep, slightly lost and unfocused.

He wondered if he had met her in another way, in another place, whether she would have accepted an invitation for coffee. If Justo was right, there weren't going to be Hawks soon anyway. He didn't know what he'd do then. Join another group of goons? Fuckers who hungered to shoot someone, dogs who had acquired a taste for blood. The more he thought about that, the more he hated the idea. But he wasn't sure what else he'd do.

And what if Justo was right and El Mago had killed El Gazpacho?

"No fucking way," he muttered.

"What?" the Antelope asked.

"Nothing," Elvis said, and he stood up and walked to the jukebox. He tossed a coin in and picked "Blue Velvet" as a joke, a little secret chuckle lodging in his throat, and turned his head to look at the woman.

She raised her head and looked at him, her eyes fixed on Elvis for a few precious seconds. She seemed a little confused. When the song ended, she stood up, walked daintily toward the jukebox—as if she could not let him have the last word—and picked another song: "Can't Help Falling in Love." Her lips curled into a tiny smile. When she smiled she looked almost pretty, like someone had struck a match and lit a veladora and the light was streaming out, but the glass colored it. Made it yellow or red or blue, like you could see the colors of her soul.

There he was thinking stupidities again. Elvis put out his cigarette and hoped the Antelope hadn't noticed he'd been staring at the woman. But the Antelope had glued his gum under the table and was cutting into a bistec, terribly indifferent to anything that wasn't the meat in front of him.

They drove back to the apartment and watched the couple walk into the building arm in arm. Elvis pushed the car door open.

"Where you going?" the Antelope asked.

"Gonna try to get in touch with El Mago again," Elvis said. That was true enough, but he also wanted to walk. He felt irritated from being cooped up in the car, and his body ached. Plus he was a little pissed off because that fucking hippie put his arm tight around the woman, all romantic, and meanwhile the Antelope kept blowing his bubble gum and popping it. It was annoying.

It was raining, and he walked with brisk steps toward a public telephone booth, tossed in a couple of coins and waited.

"Yes?" El Mago said.

Elvis braced himself against the plastic wall of the booth and pressed the receiver close to his mouth. "It's Elvis. We need to talk."

"Where are you?"

"Girl's place."

El Mago mentioned the name of a nearby intersection and told him he'd drive by in half an hour, which was more than enough time for Elvis to walk back, tell the Antelope he was meeting El Mago, and then head to the intersection.

He was running low on cigarettes, so he wandered into a pharmacy and bought another pack. He stood under the green glow of the store's sign for several minutes, thinking of nothing, watching the rain trickle down the awning. Persistent, this rain. All day long it had fallen slow and steady.

El Mago was punctual, and as soon as he rolled around the corner, Elvis tossed his cigarette away and hopped into the car, setting his leather bag on his lap. For a couple of blocks Elvis didn't say anything, hypnotized by the back-and-forth of the windshield wipers.

"What is it?" El Mago asked.

"The mole knew how to get in touch with the girl with a code in the classifieds, so I used that, thinking I might flush her out. But nothing so far."

"You have a new scrape on your brow."

"Yeah," Elvis said, touching his forehead and glancing at the rearview mirror. "Sócrates is dead. Anaya and his buddies thought we did it, so they gave us a beating. El Güero was pummeled pretty bad and I had to take him to the doctor. Everything else is pretty much the same."

"There is no sign of the girl?"

"No. But as you can imagine, I'm a little short-staffed right now," Elvis said, trying to keep a very formal, straightforward tone about the whole thing. It made no sense to wriggle like a worm in El Mago's presence. It would make it worse.

"What, did El Güero lose a hand?"

"Almost lost an eye. He's too mangled, can hardly move. Maybe you could get El Gazpacho back to us?" he asked, managing to maintain that same neutral tone. He sounded casual.

El Mago frowned. Elvis stared straight ahead, looking at the big billboard with a picture of a woman inviting everyone to drink a tall glass of Jugo V8.

"El Gazpacho has his walking papers."

"But this is a special situation. El Gazpacho—"

"El Gazpacho is not part of this."

Elvis watched the raindrops slide down the windshield and thought about Gazpacho's body in a ditch. But maybe Justo was a liar. Maybe he'd made all that up. Still, Elvis didn't get why El Mago wouldn't bring him in to assist them if it was necessary.

"What about one of the other Hawks? El Topo or El Tunas?" he asked, remembering two of the other men they'd sometimes collaborated with. Men who were also under El Mago's watch.

"Damn it, Elvis. You cannot see what is happening?" El Mago asked, surprising Elvis by the way he raised his voice. The light ahead of them turned red, and El Mago hit the brakes so quickly Elvis was jolted forward and had to grasp the dashboard to steady himself.

El Mago muttered something under his breath and turned a corner, parking the car in a random street, in front of a stationery store that was closing its doors. For a while they sat there, in front of a sign that clearly said "no parking," both of them watching the rain slide down the glass and listening to it pound on the roof of the car. In the distance there was the rumble of thunder, slowly rolling closer.

"You know how the Hawks came into existence? It was the mess of '68. Students wanting to vandalize the new subway line, painting graffiti, organizing protests. And after Tlatelolco, we decided you could not break down protests with military men. It was a task better suited for other kinds of people. But the problem is that everyone is always thinking small.

"Thugs. That is what they wanted. Thugs who could beat and who could spy on young students, but not much more. What use is teaching a man to beat another one if you are not going to aim higher, I say? So I asked to lead a few small units that had more refined personnel. But people like Anaya do not like that sort of thinking, they do not like you stepping a little higher. They abhor competition, they need to own the whole ring. You get it?"

"Kinda," Elvis mumbled.

"There is talk about a new unit, this time under the command of the DFS. A 'special brigade.' " El Mago snickered. "Special. Younger, that's what they mean. Young idiots leading other young idiots. Anaya is thirty years old."

"They're thinking about replacing the Hawks with that brigade?"

"Now you're getting it."

"But we've done what they wanted."

"It is a turf war. On many levels. The president was probably killing two birds with one stone: flexing his muscles and showing the lefties who's boss, and kicking Alfonso Martínez Domínguez out of the way by pinning this on him. Meanwhile, people like Anaya see a chance to cut a few heads and gain a bit more power. With the Hawks gone, he and his men will swoop in to deal with the radicals once and for all."

"But it's not fair!"

"I think this is what I like most about you, Elvis, how you are still, at times, capable of being such a child. A big, giant baby. I wonder how you do it, that you can look at the world and manage to think there is a speck of fairness to it when all that the eye can see is garbage from here until forever. What a fool you are."

Elvis stared at El Mago's reflection in the rearview mirror. The man looked older that night, the wrinkles under his eyes were deeper, and even with his round, black-rimmed glasses, he did not resemble a retired professor. He looked like a bitter, worn soldier.

El Mago smiled a crisp, small smile, his eyes fixed on Elvis in the rearview mirror, as if he could guess what he was thinking.

"It is just us, dear boy," he said. "Just us. There is no cavalry. If we can solve this mess, if we can find the girl and get those photographs, then I might be able to save our hides and steer us into a safe harbor. Anaya thinks he has me, but he does not have shit."

It's not like we have shit either, he thought.

"Get me something," El Mago said. "Get me anything."

There was something raw and desperate when El Mago spoke, and Elvis almost felt like laughing.

It was his cue to exit. Elvis opened the car door and got out, clasping the leather messenger bag tight, feeling the weight of the gun and the bullets tucked inside. He ended up thinking about the woman again so he wouldn't think about what the fuck he was doing, so he wouldn't think about El Gazpacho bloated and purple in a ditch.

26

SHE WAS HAPPY, and it occurred to her this was an unusual and unforeseen state.

The morning was lazy, spent in bed, oversleeping. Normally she banged her palm against the alarm clock and got up quickly, but since she wasn't going to the office there was no need for that. She simply lay under the covers, feeling the warmth of Rubén's body against her own.

It was strange resting like that, with no worries or obligations, no papers to file or notes to type. Of course, she still had obligations. Her job would be there tomorrow, and her car was still at the mechanic's, and she had to get up and feed Leonora's cat. But for now, for a precious, brief now, there was the cocoon of the bedsheets and curtains pulled tight, preventing the sun from sneaking into the room.

She wondered if this was how Rubén lived. Maybe he didn't work every day, maybe he worked when it pleased him. If he really went to Guerrero, he'd have to wake up at the crack of dawn. She pictured revolutionaries performing exhausting daily drills.

When Rubén finally woke up, it was close to noon. She asked him if he wanted to have lunch, but he seemed uninterested in food and asked her if she wanted to fuck before he showered. So they did that. He was enthusiastic, and it pleased her immensely to be desired in such a raw way, with minimal preamble and no need for the hollow, useless conversations she had had to endure on previous occasions with other men. No lies, either, like the ones Cristóbalito whispered into her ear about loving her forever.

I've been doing it all wrong, she thought.

They showered and eventually ventured out, to a café where Rubén wolfed down a sandwich and she rested her chin on her hand, watching him and wondering if Leonora was ever coming back, and if it mattered at this point.

They stayed out for a while doing nothing of importance and went up the stairs arm in arm. It was dusk, and the apartment lay in shadows. They headed straight to the bedroom. Rubén took off his jacket and tossed it away. He had removed his shoes, unbuckled his jeans, and taken off his shirt before they even reached the bedroom's doorway. She thought they might end up fucking on the floor again.

Maite laughed, her palm against the wall, trying to find the light switch. Instead, Rubén caught her face between his hands and kissed her, and she bumped into her vanity, and there was the noise of things being knocked down as his tongue found her mouth.

Laughing again, she turned on the light and there, on the floor, was the broken statue of San Judas Tadeo. It had cracked neatly in half, and two film canisters had spilled out of it, like treasure from a galleon run aground.

Maite bent down and picked them up, holding them in the palm of her hand. She looked at Rubén. "It's the film," she whispered.

"What?"

She held the canisters up, for him to see. "The film . . . Leonora's photos. You couldn't find them because they were in here."

"You had them all this time?"

"I . . . I took the statue from her apartment. I didn't know."

Rubén stared at her, and then he launched himself into the kitchen. He was in his underwear and socks. Maite watched as he grabbed the telephone and dialed a number. He tapped his foot impatiently and cursed under his breath.

"Jackie? Yeah, that's right. Listen, I need you to get Néstor over to Asterisk," Rubén said. "What do you mean he's not around?

Fine. Then get any photographer. I don't know! Anyone who knows their way around a darkroom."

Rubén checked his watch. "Forty minutes. Yeah. Bye."

Rubén hung up, and then he was rushing back to the bedroom scooping up his jacket from the floor. Maite was still carrying the film canisters in her hands.

"We've got to get the film developed."

"Now?"

"It's what I'm going to try to do. Put those in a purse or something, will you? Where's my shoe?" he asked, his voice like sandpaper.

"Oh . . . oh, yes." Maite grabbed her purse, which she'd dropped in their dash to the bedroom. "I had no idea," she added. "I thought it was garbage she'd thrown out."

It was true. It was not like she ever stole anything that mattered. And even if she did, even if she was a consummate thief, he didn't have to know that. But the way he was looking at her, the way he frowned, she didn't like it.

Maybe he could tell she was dishonest. Maybe it was the way her voice trembled.

But he shook his head. "Don't worry. It's fine. But we've got to see what's in those pictures."

He found his shoes, found his belt, and she watched him as he sat on the bed and dressed again; watched him as he inspected the gun he'd borrowed from Jackie before tucking it in his jacket's pocket. She ran a hand through her hair.

"What happens after we develop the film?"

"We take it to the papers. Not every journalist is a coward. And even if they are . . . I don't know, we'll figure something out."

"Will Leonora come back if we do that?"

Rubén tied his shoelaces. "I'd like to think so."

Maite didn't know if she agreed. The thought of returning to the dull normality of days past suddenly frightened her. Rubén looked at her. "What's the matter?" he asked.

"I guess I was getting used to you being around."

"Are you looking for a new roommate, Maite?"

"Don't tease me."

He chuckled and stood up, buckling his belt as he looked at her. "I didn't realize you liked me that much."

"I don't, but maybe you could grow on me."

"Yeah," he agreed. "Maybe I could."

She leaned forward and kissed him. It wasn't something that she'd normally do, too worried about what a man would think of her, whether he'd like it or not, whether she was his type or was completely off base. But she figured what the hell. If she pretended she was bold long enough, maybe she could actually be bold.

He kissed her back, and then he said they should go, and they were walking down the stairs and into the car. It was raining outside, and traffic was heavy. By the time they reached Asterisk, the streetlights had bloomed into life.

Familiar faces awaited them in the office. Jackie, sitting behind a desk; the man who had been in the background last time was also there, smoking, sitting by the window. And Emilio Lomelí: he was leaning against Jackie's desk, bending down to tell her something.

The notes of "The Girl from Ipanema" drifted from an open window on another floor.

"What's he doing here?" Rubén asked gruffly, pointing at Emilio, who simply quirked an eyebrow at them.

"You said you needed a photographer," Jackie told him. "This is what I could do on short notice. He's fast, he knows how to use the equipment. What did you want, a first-year student?"

"Fuck, Jackie, are you serious? Him! Of all people!"

"I've financed this space so I think I'm allowed to step foot in it," Emilio said. "Besides, I also want to see what's on the film."

"This jackass will sell us out for five cents."

"Unlike you, I don't need five cents, thanks."

"Yes, rub it in, rub all your money in our faces."

"Not all of us can be deadbeats."

Emilio chuckled, and then Rubén jumped forward and threw a punch, just like that, no warning, straight to the jaw, and Emilio yelped, his back hitting the desk. Rubén attempted another punch, but Emilio moved and the young man missed. And then it was Emilio throwing a punch and hitting Rubén in the belly.

It was like watching two orangutans fight in the jungle. Maite had never been to the jungle, but there were orangutans in her comic books, and when they snarled, they looked like these men, their eyes narrowed and the mouths savage. She almost expected them to beat their fists against their chests and start biting each other.

Jackie yelled at the men, telling them to stop it, to stop being stupid. In his corner by the window, the man in the suede jacket observed the spectacle with amusement, but did not seem interested in stopping it. Maite merely clutched her purse and pressed herself against a bookcase, far from the brawlers.

"What do you two think you're doing?"

Maite turned her head. Four men had walked into the office. She recognized the one who had spoken. He was the fellow who had visited Maite's office: Anaya. He stood with his hands in his pockets, looking puzzled. The men standing next to him had their guns out and had pointed them at Emilio and Rubén.

"Hands up in the air," one of the men ordered.

Everyone was silent. Emilio and Rubén slowly stood up and raised their hands.

"You too, in the back."

The man in the suede jacket shrugged and obeyed, raising his hands up high. The altercation between Rubén and Emilio had not interested him, and this didn't seem to ruffle him either.

"Let's give up all the guns," Anaya said. "All the guns, or everyone is going to get shot."

Rubén slowly took out his gun and tossed it onto the floor.

"Is that it?" Anaya asked. "If I find you have a gun, you fuckers, I'm going to shoot it up your ass. Line up. Come on."

They lined up. Rubén stood next to Maite. She wanted to clutch his hand but didn't dare move; she was holding her purse tight. Bossa nova was still playing nearby.

"Now where's the film?"

"How do you know we've got the film?" Rubén asked.

"We heard you mention a darkroom, you idiot. The line was bugged," Anaya said. "Now do you want to try and get smart with me again? All of you, empty your pockets. Everything, come on. And you, your purse."

Anaya was stuffing his hands into Rubén's jacket and found nothing but a pack of cigarettes. Then he turned to her. Maite stared at the man, not knowing what to do. Her lips trembled.

"The purse," Anaya said. "Open it up, come on."

She wanted to. She really did. She didn't mean to be brave or stubborn. Fear had rendered her mute and made her dig her fingers into the cheap purse, feeling that it was the only thing keeping her safe. What would they do if they found the film inside? What would they do to her? Would she be hauled to jail? Tortured and branded a dissident?

"Lady, the purse."

Her hands shook, and she fumbled with the clasp.

"Come on!"

And then the guy in the suede jacket kicked one of the men and slammed him against the ground. At the same time, Rubén jumped at Anaya. He threw himself against him, like an angry bull, no finesse in the attack. It was brute force. Jackie grabbed a green table lamp and swung it at one of the men.

"Run!" Rubén yelled.

There was a gunshot. Maite screamed. She didn't know who shot who, because Emilio grabbed her hand and pulled her with him, and they ran to the other end of the office. By the windows, to the left, there was the door that led to the back stairs.

They made it onto the street and into Emilio's car, which was parked behind the building. From an open window the sound of samba drifted onto the street, a plaintive saxophone bidding them goodbye.

27

ELVIS WAS STARTING to believe his life was an unending circle, because they were back at Asterisk. The woman and the hippie had gone into the building. God knew he would have preferred it if they had driven back to the diner of the previous evening. At least there he might have ordered a coffee and picked a song from the jukebox.

Elvis readied himself for a few more boring hours of his ass stuck inside a car, watching the rain droplets slide across the windshield, when he saw a bunch of men jump out of two vehicles and head into the building. He counted seven of them. Elvis didn't need the binoculars to know these were DFS men and that Anaya was with them.

"Son of a bitch," the Antelope whispered. "What's that all about?"

"The film's inside," Elvis said.

"What? You sure?"

"Why else would they be here, all of them at once?"

"To arrest people."

"Same story."

Elvis took out his gun from the messenger bag. The Antelope gave him a weary look. "What're you doing?"

"We can't let them grab the film," he said. The film, yes. Though, for a second, the thought flashed in his mind: the woman was in there. The woman with the sad eyes. And these assholes had beaten El Güero. El Güero wasn't his buddy, but he was part of his team. Maybe they had even killed El Gazpacho.

He would bet that's what happened, yeah. It hadn't been El Mago, it had been Anaya and his goons. They had murdered his friend. It would be their style. He was sure of it.

"There're seven of them. We don't know if anyone inside is armed," the Antelope said.

"Seven means we have to kill three each and hope one of them pisses his pants and runs off."

"Well, that's damn easy, no? You're crazy."

"El Mago's fucked—we're all fucked—if we don't get those pictures. Come on, are you a wimp? Do I have to do it alone?" he said, his voice a blade, thinking of all the times El Güero had called him a marshmallow and the Antelope had snickered in agreement.

But not today, no sir, and ultimately the Antelope was the kind of man who did what he was told, and Elvis was . . . well, he wasn't sure what kind of man he was, but he knew he was going into that building. He wanted blood and he wanted that film because, fuck it, they'd been working at this too long to let it go and it was a night for death.

"You're all machín when it comes to shooting imaginary motherfuckers and American gangsters, but what happens when it's for real, huh? Did your balls shrink?"

"Fuck you," the Antelope muttered as he took out his gun and patted the pocket where he was carrying his ammunition. "I have better aim than you, you prissy fucker. I'll put three bullets up their ass, like I promised. I bet you can't hit one of them, you fuck."

"Up yours."

They went into the building and up the stairs carefully and quietly, the way El Mago liked it. Elvis poked his head through the open door of the gallery. Three men stood near the entrance to the office, at the other end of the room.

Because the gallery space had little in the way of furniture and because it was essentially one long rectangle, there would be few if any places to take cover, though there was a small nook in the wall right in front of the gallery's entrance.

At the same time, three men standing like that, a little distracted, were three men in the open ripe for the picking. Elvis stepped back into the hallway and whispered what things looked like to the Antelope, who frowned and nodded.

"So three in the gallery. Where're the rest of them?" the Antelope asked.

"Probably in the office, maybe torturing someone."

"What do we do then?"

There was the sound of a gun going off and a shrill scream. "Let's roll," Elvis ordered. No time for elaborate plans.

They ran into the gallery. The Antelope shot dead one of the men standing by the office door with his first bullet and ran straight toward the nook, kneeling down and then peeking around and shooting again. No luck this time, he missed his target. Elvis ran behind the Antelope and also took cover behind the nook.

"I'll cover you and you run across, back to the entrance," the Antelope said. "Draw them out."

"Like hell."

"You think I can't cover you? You wanted to come in here in the first place. We can't hide in the corner. We need to move, fast."

"Fuck it," Elvis muttered.

Shots rang again, shattering glass, and Elvis gritted his teeth. He sprinted across the gallery, back in the direction of the doorway. When he reached the entrance, he spun around and crouched low. One of the men had taken the bait and was headed in his direction. Elvis shot and missed, but the Antelope did not. He got the agent square in the back. When the man spun around, in the Antelope's direction, Elvis shot again. This time he made the target.

The Antelope motioned to Elvis, pointing toward the office, and they both sprang forward and aimed their guns in the direction of the remaining agent, who was taking cover behind a large statue. For a few minutes the fucker managed to tuck himself safely there, like a snail, before the Antelope got tired of this bullshit.

"Cover me," the Antelope said.

Which Elvis did, although there wasn't much need for this, since the Antelope essentially unloaded his gun and the agent didn't have time to scream, much less shoot back.

The Antelope reloaded his gun and grinned. "Pretty neat, no? Told you I was a better shot than you. Three down. That's half, no?"

"Nearly half," Elvis muttered, looking at the blood on the floor.

"Come on, let's get it over with," the Antelope said and rushed into the office.

Elvis followed, but had not taken more than three steps when the Antelope staggered back into the gallery space and slumped onto the floor. Elvis pressed himself against the wall and eyed the door to the office.

There was yelling and the sound of broken furniture and someone had shot the Antelope dead. Or was he dead? Elvis needed to check. He couldn't leave him there on the floor.

Fuck, fuck, fuck.

Elvis dashed forward and pulled the Antelope by the arms, dragging him away from the spot where he'd fallen. He checked his pulse, pounded on his chest.

"Come on, you prick!"

The blast of a gun and the piercing sting of a bullet hitting him smack in the arm made Elvis yelp. He raised his hand and shot back at the agent standing by the doorway. He didn't even aim properly, just pulled the trigger and hoped he hit someone.

The agent stumbled back into the office.

Elvis took a breath and reached for the messenger bag dangling from his shoulder, fumbled with the speedloader for a second, and reloaded his gun. He winced as he held up the weapon with both hands.

He thought the agent would be back to fill him with lead, but the doorway was empty.

He walked into the office. The agent who'd shot at him lay flat on his back, with his mouth open. Gone.

He spotted two more agents on the ground. Maybe they were dead too, Elvis wasn't one hundred percent sure. A woman, her mouth filled with blood and missing a few teeth, stared at Elvis from behind a desk. She had a broken lamp in her hands. The hippie Elvis had been following was slumped in a corner. He couldn't see Maite, but there was an unexpected spectacle: the fucking Russian who had given him a beating was fighting with Anaya, both of them struggling over a gun. Anaya seemed to be winning, though Elvis wasn't sure if he was playing fair—the Russian had been wounded. He was trailing blood down his leg, and by the gash on his trousers it was a knife injury, which could be very bad news.

He took a deep breath, trying to decide if he should intervene. This was like watching Godzilla versus King Kong, and he didn't know if he should be cheering for the lizard or the monkey. Probably neither, but he also didn't feel it was right to shoot both of them while they were distracted.

Anaya gave the Russian a fierce blow to the head and grabbed the gun; then the fucker turned his head, saw Elvis, and pointed the damn weapon at him. Elvis couldn't even duck. Jesus Christ, not again! He was going to get shot a second time in the span of three minutes.

The bullet hit the shelf next to Elvis, steered off its course by the Russian, who had smacked Anaya in the arm, making the agent miss his mark. The gun went flying through the air, and the Russian clutched his leg, grimacing.

That did it. Elvis shot Anaya in the leg. Not because the asshole had tried to kill him, but because it definitely wasn't fair to have one man bleeding out all over the floor. Let the two assholes face each other in equal conditions.

Anaya yelped and stared at Elvis in surprise. The Russian took advantage of the chaos and confusion to jump on top of Anaya and slam him down against a desk. Papers and pencils and splinters went flying through the air as Anaya's body hit the cheap piece of furniture and he was toppled backward.

The Russian didn't waste time. He jumped on top of Anaya, punching him in the face two, three times. Anaya responded by roaring and punching back. Both men rolled across the floor, smashing into chairs and boxes.

The Russian reached for a telephone and yanked its cord, wrapping it around the agent's neck from behind. Anaya's eyes opened wide, and he tried to elbow the Russian in the ribs, to no avail. The Russian held the cord tight against the man's throat until he stopped moving. The Russian winced as he released his hold on the cord and let Anaya's body flop against the floor. He was breathing hard as he looked up at Elvis and pressed a hand against his leg again.

"Thanks. I thought you were DFS," the Russian said.

"We both know that was bullshit."

"I don't like Hawks any more than I like DFS agents."

"And I don't like Russians, but you just saved me from a bullet to the head."

"I guess that makes us even."

Elvis had assumed if he ever saw this son of a bitch again he'd beat him with a hammer, or the Russian would kick his teeth in. He didn't think they'd take it easy with each other, but the Russian had his share of cuts and bruises, and Elvis thought that, yeah, it was as even as it would get.

"Where's the film?" Elvis asked.

"Your guess is as good as mine."

Elvis walked toward the hippie slumped in the corner. The woman with broken teeth had retreated to the opposite side of the room, but she yelled at him. "Leave him alone!"

Elvis knelt next to the man and pressed a hand against his neck. His eyes were closed but he had a pulse. And two bullet holes in his body. Elvis slipped his hands into the man's jacket pockets. Nothing. He stood up. "You better phone him an ambulance," he told the woman.

She stared at him, then stretched a shaky hand toward a telephone and began dialing.

Elvis walked to the door.

"Hey! Where are you going?" the Russian asked.

"I'm guessing if the film's not here, then it's with his lady friend," Elvis said, pointing at the hippie with the two bullet holes.

"Pretty big guess."

"I've got to find her."

"And get your film."

Maybe he wanted to find her, period. Elvis's shoes were stained with blood, and his hands were shaky. He was tired and spent. Just damn fucking spent. Every last bit of him gone. He couldn't do this shit.

"You know where to start looking?" the Russian asked.

"I've got a hunch."

"Wait a minute, I'll go with you," the Russian said, limping toward Elvis.

"Why the fuck would I let you go with me?"

"You look like shit. You're left-handed, no? They fucked your stupid arm. I'll drive."

"Someone stuck a knife in your fucking leg."

The Russian shrugged. "I'll bandage it in the car."

"What car?"

"My car. Unless you have a first aid kit in yours."

"Fine. Fuck it," Elvis muttered. What did he care if the whole KGB was tagging along. He had a damn bullet in his arm and the Antelope was dead. Maybe Elvis would be dead too, and he supposed going out at the hand of a Russian agent was more interesting than getting killed by those pricks from the DFS or being knifed in Tepito, which was the way he originally thought he'd go.

The Russian's car was a piece of shit Volkswagen—it needed a paint job and to be washed sometime this century—which he'd left around the corner. It also reeked of pot and cheap booze. The Russian drove a few blocks from Asterisk and parked the car. He took a sip from a silver flask. Then he turned around and pulled a box from the back seat and handed it to Elvis. Inside Elvis found the promised bandages and gauze. He tried winding them around his arm and failed, so the Russian gave him a hand and a sip from the flask. It contained mezcal, of all things. He'd expected vodka.

When Elvis's bandage was in place, the Russian slapped several layers of gauze on his leg, tied it all up, and took another swig of mezcal. Then he opened the glove compartment and reached for a gun, which was tucked under a map of the city.

"Smith and Wesson," Elvis said and scoffed. "You own a Smith and Wesson."

"Model sixty. You got a problem with that?"

"No, no problem," Elvis said, wanting to break out in laughter. Another one of his teammates was dead, and he was in a beat-up car with a Russian who didn't even own a Soviet weapon. "You gonna shoot me?"

"If I wanted you dead I'd have killed you back at Asterisk. Don't get paranoid. I figure it might come in handy since I'm not sure where the fuck you're taking me. So. Where to?"

Elvis gave him the first set of directions. He wasn't going to blurt out the address. If the Russian wanted to murder him, he'd have to wait until they arrived at their destination.

28

SHE ALMOST BROKE down when they arrived at Emilio's house. She had been able to keep herself in one piece until then, but the moment they walked into his living room she took a deep breath and then another, and she started shivering, her eyes brimming with tears.

Emilio didn't look too thrilled about this. He quickly poured whiskey into a little glass and shoved it in her hands.

"It'll steady your nerves," he said.

"We shouldn't have left. They're probably dead."

"We'd be dead if we hadn't left."

"But someone should call an ambulance!"

"I'm sure the cops are there. Someone must have heard the gunshots."

"We shouldn't have left," Maite repeated. "We have to get the pictures to the papers, like Rubén wanted."

"I would if I knew where they are."

"I have them," Maite said, and she spilled a little of her drink as she tried to open her handbag. Her hands were trembling. "I've had them all this time."

"All this time?"

She looked up at Emilio, who was frowning. Clumsily she sat down on an acrylic bubble chair and put her drink on the floor. She opened her bag and took out the film canisters, showing them to him before quickly stuffing them back in her purse. "I didn't know. I swear. I . . . she put them inside this little statuette . . .

I swear I didn't know. Shouldn't you develop them? You have a darkroom."

"I'm not sure I should touch the film rolls."

"But we need to see what's inside."

Emilio grabbed the bottle of whiskey and filled a glass for himself, topping her off in the process. "It depends. The newspaper might want to do it, to make sure we don't tamper with anything. I know an editor who might be willing to publish them."

"Really?"

"I'll give him a call. Wait here. Drink up." he said, downing his whiskey. "Liquid courage for the both of us."

He disappeared up the stairs, and Maite was alone, in the large room of paneled oak, sitting in front of Emilio's black-and-white photographs. A gigantic eye stared at her from a frame, and she drank as he'd suggested.

She wondered if the others had escaped the building. It was possible. If they had, she had no idea where they might have gone. Aside from the hospital, that is. She supposed it depended if they were badly hurt or not. If Rubén was alive, she promised herself she'd waste no time finding him and nursing him back to health. And then they would leave the city together. She could become a modern adelita, caring for the sons of revolution, the guerilla fighters deep in the mountains. Rubén would have scars from this night, but he would wear them proudly.

The eye stared back at her, unblinking and cruel.

She raised the glass to her lips, hit her teeth in the process and winced. Emilio came walking down the stairs just then.

"He'll be here right away. No later than half an hour, he said. He lives nearby."

"Does he? That's good. What's his name?"

"José Hernández. He works for *El Universal*."

"He'll publish the pictures?"

"If there's anything to publish, he will. You want something to eat?"

"I don't think I could eat anything. I'm so nervous."

"You've been very brave."

"I don't think so," she whispered. Her purse was on her lap. She clutched it with one hand, not letting go of it for an instant. If she let go, she feared she'd lose what little composure she possessed. Somehow the purse and the film canisters held the tears at bay.

Emilio sat in front of her, in a matching chair, and solicitously offered to refill her glass. She accepted but didn't take another sip. Her mouth tasted sour. He then offered her a cigarette, and she declined. He shrugged and lit one for himself, leaning forward a little as he smoked. Their conversation dwindled as the smoke rose.

The bell rang. She almost dropped her glass, startled by the noise, but Emilio smiled.

"It's probably José. Give me a second."

She heard a muffled greeting and then Emilio was walking back into the room, still smiling. "I was right. José, this is Maite, the young lady I was telling you about."

The man who walked into the living room in the company of Emilio was older and distinguished, dressed in a good camel coat. He was also terribly familiar. Maite knew that face. She'd seen it before in the house belonging to Leonora's sister. It was Leonardo, the uncle in military uniform, whose photo sat proudly in a silver frame.

Maite glanced down quickly at the floor, trying to conceal this flash of recognition.

"Maite. I'm glad to meet you. Emilio was saying you've kept some important photos safe."

She nodded and licked her lips.

"Have you developed them?" the man asked.

"We haven't had the chance. We thought perhaps you'd like to do that," Emilio said.

"Of course. Even though you haven't developed the film, perhaps Leonora told you what was in the photos? Did she, Maite?"

She wanted him to go away, to leave her alone. The purse felt heavy on her lap. She shook her head again, no.

"But you've been keeping the film safe for her all this time. You must have done it for a reason. You must have an idea of what's in there."

"I didn't know," she muttered.

She looked up at the man. He had a hand in one coat pocket. A casual detail, unimportant. Except he might be concealing a gun. She stood up. "Excuse me, I drank too much and I need to use the bathroom. Where is it?"

"Oh, that way," Emilio said, raising a hand and pointing in the right direction.

Maite tried to walk without a hurry, her purse slung over her left shoulder. Multiple eyes, rendered in black-and-white, watched her from the walls. As soon as she stepped into the bathroom she locked the door. It was a large bathroom, spotless, with plush towels and expensive looking fittings. If she'd had more time, Maite would have admired it and carefully gone through all of Emilio's prescriptions and toiletries. She would have stolen a memento. But she didn't have time. She pulled the shower curtain aside and stepped into the shower.

There was a window there. It was high up. She grabbed a stool that was tucked by the sink and stood on it, attempting to pry the window open. It remained stubbornly jammed. As she stood there on her tiptoes there was a knock on the door.

"Open up," the man said.

She didn't bother replying. Maite looked around in a panic, but there wasn't anything she might use as a weapon; she tried to wedge the window open, pressing her hands against the glass. There came a sonorous crash, and the door slammed open and the old man walked in. She stood in the shower, stunned, not knowing what to say or do while he reached forward and pulled her with him.

Maite reflexively grabbed on to the shower curtain, and when the man yanked her by the arm, she yanked the shower curtain in turn, ripping it off the shower rod. Silver shower rings fell onto the floor, rolling across the tiles.

"Let go of me," she said.

The man did not reply. Although he was old, he was still strong, and soon he had hauled her back into the living room, where they almost collided with Emilio. He stared at them and stepped back, mouth open.

"You recognized me. How do you know me?" the old man asked, shoving her until her knees hit the back of one of the chairs and she was forced to sit down.

"Leonora's graduation photo," Maite said quickly.

"Really? How unfortunate. Now, give me the film."

She sat in the bubble chair, one hand on the strap of her purse, and looked at Emilio, waiting for him to intervene. To say something. Anything.

"Do what he asks," Emilio muttered at last.

"Why?"

"Because otherwise I'll wring your neck," the man said simply.

She realized that Rubén had been correct about Emilio all along. He was nothing but a rich kid who was out for himself and himself alone. He wouldn't raise a finger to protect anyone, least of all Maite.

"Did he send you to find the film? That first time we met, when you were trying to get into Leonora's apartment?" she asked, staring at Emilio.

Emilio lit another cigarette and avoided her gaze. "No. He got in touch with me later."

"But the people at Asterisk are your friends. Leonora is your girlfriend."

"I'm becoming impatient," the man said.

She touched her mouth, thinking of Rubén. He was probably dead. And then she didn't know what got into her, what needless idiotic impulse flashed through her brain, but she tried to run. It was useless. The man was old, but he wasn't decrepit, and he caught her in a swift few steps and slammed her against a wall, the back of her head hitting one of the black-and-white photographs.

Rather than surrender the prize, she tried to scratch him, but he slammed her back, harder. She heard the crunch of glass and winced. Her hands trembled.

The man snatched the purse from her and opened it, taking out the canisters. He began pulling the film out of them, exposing it to the light.

Nothing. Rubén was probably dead over nothing.

She slid against the wall, clumsily trying to step away, toward a door.

"Don't move," the man said, as he continued unspooling the film. "I still have business with you."

Her head ached. He'd hit her hard, and she didn't want to be hit again, so she stood stock still until he was done and he looked at her, tossing the useless negatives on the floor. In a second he had erased the truth. A second was all it took.

"Where's my niece?" the man asked.

"I don't know."

"You fraternize with terrorists. You keep Leonora's precious photos. I'm pretty sure you know more than you're saying."

"I didn't mean to. I stole the film by accident. I didn't realize—"

He punched her in the stomach. She was left breathless, bending over, and then he grabbed her again, sinking his fingers into her hair, and pulled her head up. He slapped her face so hard she knew he'd leave bruises.

"Come on, there's no need for that," Emilio said.

"Pull up a chair and look at the wall," the man ordered.

"What?"

While still holding on to Maite with one hand, the man took a gun out and pointed it at Emilio. "I said pull up a chair and look at the wall."

Maite couldn't move away, she couldn't turn her head, not with him gripping her hair, but she heard the scraping of a chair against the floor as Emilio obeyed. The man released her and took a step back. His gun was pointed in Emilio's direction, but his eyes were on her.

"My niece. I need you to tell me where she is."

"You're going to kill her," Maite mumbled.

"I will kill *you* if you don't talk."

"I told you. I don't know! I really don't know!"

The man hit her on the head with the gun, and it hurt so badly. The other blows had hurt, but not like this. She was going to weep. Blood trickled down her forehead, staining her lips.

"I haven't done anything," she swore, but the gun came down again, making her scream.

She thought that she'd been wrong. That Leonora was not the maiden who would be offered as a sacrifice. It was her, it was Maite, who must have her heart carved out. From the very first page, the very first line, the very moment this began.

He pressed a hand against her mouth, as if to muffle her scream, and she responded, fueled simply by furious instinct, her teeth sinking into his fingers. He made a yelping sound, like a dog, before brutally punching her. She tumbled to the floor, clutching her stomach, tasting blood. She didn't know if it belonged to her or to him.

"Stop that," a man said.

Maite swallowed the blood and stared at the two strangers who had walked into the house.

29

THEY PARKED THE car outside the little white house. Even in the dark he recognized the other car parked right ahead of them, by the house's gate. He would have known it anywhere: El Mago's vehicle. For a minute he stood there dumbly, in the rain, until the Russian coughed.

"What's the matter?"

"I think my boss is here," Elvis said.

"Nice. A reunion. You've got the keys to this place?"

"No, but I can pick the lock," he said, and he plumbed the pocket of his jeans for the two little strips of metal. It wasn't a difficult lock.

They walked into the house, followed the sound of voices. He heard screaming, and they picked up the pace, reaching a large room with a very long table and many pictures on the walls.

El Mago was beating the woman. Elvis had never harmed a woman in his life. That was for scum. For lowlifes. And Elvis was a thug, sure, but he wasn't scum. It surprised him to see El Mago doing such a thing. He'd never imagined he could. So he spoke quickly, without thinking twice, using a tone of voice he had never dared to employ with El Mago until that day.

El Mago was his boss, after all. El Mago was their leader. El Mago was everything that Elvis ever wanted to be. El Mago was the King.

"Stop that," he said roughly.

A man was sitting in a chair staring at the wall. He winced

when they walked in, but he didn't say anything, and when Elvis spoke he lowered his head and pressed his palms against his eyes.

"You've made it. Who is that with you?" El Mago asked.

The woman's eyes were huge, and there was blood on her lips. Those were the eyes of Bluebeard's wife when she opens the door and finds the chamber filled with corpses.

"It's the Russian asshole," Elvis said, looking away from the woman and at El Mago. El Mago's eyes were calm. He'd done this, or something similar, something worse, many times before. Elvis thought El Mago was a gentleman, a cut above others, but he really was another little shit.

A shit like all the other shits Elvis had ever known. Somehow he'd never realized that. Even when El Mago scared him, even when El Mago exuded danger instead of mirth, always, absolutely always, Elvis felt he was in the presence of a superior species.

And Justo had accused El Mago, but Elvis wouldn't believe it. He had pushed his doubts and his sorrow deep down, and he didn't let himself dwell on it.

"Have you switched sides already?" El Mago asked.

"No. Arkady might actually shoot us both in the next five minutes."

On the floor Elvis saw strips of negatives. He bent down to look at the pieces of film. El Mago snickered. "They're exposed. So if your Russian friend wants to start shooting, he can now. There's nothing to see here."

Elvis brushed his fingers against the film. "Then why are you hitting her?"

"Because I need to find my niece," El Mago said, reaching for the woman and pulling her up, close to him.

"I told you. I don't know where Leonora is," the woman said, but softly. Her voice trembled.

She looked at Elvis, and Elvis stared back at her, into those tragic eyes of hers, now brimming with tears.

"She said she doesn't know. Let her go."

El Mago shoved the woman aside and turned to Elvis. She

scrambled away from him, bumping into a side table, while El Mago straightened his coat, running a hand down a lapel then sliding it through his gray hair. In the other hand he clasped his gun. "It is not a good day to grow a conscience. Or to make new acquaintances," he said, his eyes measuring the Russian before he fixed them on Elvis. "You were supposed to solve my problems, not make them worse."

Elvis thought of all the damn work he'd done, all the spying and the beatings he'd earned himself and the bullet in his arm. The way El Mago spoke, it didn't matter. It was nothing. He should have known that would be the case. But he was dumb. A marshmallow, like El Güero said. Worse than that.

"You were supposed to find the girl."

"You never said the girl was your niece," Elvis replied, taking a couple of steps toward El Mago.

"It was not important. Family matters, if you will."

"That's fucked up. Killing your own family."

El Mago's fingers were like claws as he again ran a hand through his thinning hair. "I did not want to kill her. I wanted to save her from herself. She was a fool, placing her trust in an informant. Sócrates! She might as well have telephoned Anaya."

"Then it was you," Elvis said. "You killed Sócrates."

"One less rat in the world. It was not a great loss. At least you found out who betrayed her, who started this. You managed that much."

Elvis took another couple of steps. He had a knot in his throat. He slid his hands into his jacket pockets to keep them from trembling. "Did you also kill El Gazpacho?"

El Mago actually seemed a little surprised when Elvis said that. So far his composure had been impeccable. Even when he'd been beating the woman, there had been little emotion. Now he frowned, his voice wavering. "Who told you that?"

"Doesn't matter. He's dead, isn't he?"

El Mago didn't reply. But he didn't need to. Elvis chuckled and shook his head. He thought about poor Gazpacho, who loved Japanese movies and the songs of The Beatles. Dead. Tossed into a ditch like rubbish. People had to die one day, but not like that. Not by El Mago's hands.

"Fuck. Why?" he asked in a whisper.

"The order came to disband the Hawks, to disband my units. They're starting up something new."

His units. His boys. *Elvis, my boy*. How many times had he heard El Mago say that? *My boy*.

"Disband doesn't mean murder."

"You really think you get, what, a goodbye card in these cases? He knew things! Too many damn things, and I already had Leonora to worry about, to be also worrying about another damn loose end who could ruin me if he decided to cozy up to Anaya. I knew Anaya was out to hang me and I couldn't let him get hold of the rope. They think we don't understand how to deal with guerilla fighters. Shoot them like dogs, is what they say. Shooting alone doesn't fix things!"

"Says who?"

"These new shits! Shits like Anaya. And you know what they all want, don't you? To get into politics. Gutiérrez Barrios, he was with the DFS and now he's angling for something bigger. This is just a stepping stone for them, not a vocation. Or they want to steal, plain and simple. They're thieves or they want to traffic drugs; they're out to get what they can."

"And you're clean?"

"I'm no thief and no drug dealer either," El Mago said, sounding affronted.

"Anaya's dead," Elvis said dryly.

"Is he?" El Mago laughed. A good, full laugh. Elvis always liked El Mago's laughter. It was rare, but it was lavish, like the rest of El Mago. El Mago was so lavish, so big, so much. A god, not a man. El Mago wasn't a coward who murdered his underlings because he was scared.

El Mago was a figment of Elvis's imagination. But El Gazpacho had been real.

"Yeah. I guess we saved your ass in the end. You know, the Russian and I."

"The same Russian who will shoot us in the next five minutes," El Mago said, smiling; it was like a raw gash across his face.

"No," Elvis said. Now he was standing right in front of El Mago, and he looked him straight in the eye. "He's not shooting you."

His fingers curled around the screwdriver in his pocket, and he jammed it into El Mago's neck. The old man gasped, his mouth wide open, but no sound emerged. In his shock, he dropped the gun he'd been holding in his hand, the gun he'd been using to beat the woman.

El Mago was always telling them guns were a weapon of last resort, and Elvis had decided to follow his lesson plan, after all.

El Mago fell to his knees and made a motion, one hand fumbling, attempting to retrieve his gun. Elvis kicked the weapon away and bent down, pulling the screwdriver out. Blood welled like a fountain, and El Mago scrabbled at his neck, tried to press his hand against the wound, but it was too much blood. No way of stopping it.

He fell and lay on his back, his eyes fixed on Elvis's face, and Elvis wondered if he'd had the decency to look into El Gazpacho's eyes when he died. Elvis stared back at El Mago until he stopped shivering, then he dropped his own gun next to the screwdriver, on the puddle of blood that had formed by El Mago's head.

The woman wept, her tragic, lost face for once seemed to fit her surroundings, and in his corner the man who had been staring at the wall had pissed himself. Elvis looked at the Russian and wiped his nose with the back of his hand because he was also crying.

"So," Elvis said, "you gonna shoot me with that Smith and Wesson?"

The Russian shrugged. "What for?"

"To get even for your lost film."

"Killing you won't bring it back, will it?"

"No," Elvis muttered. "It sure won't."

"My professional advice is to get out of here and stay out of trouble."

"You'll leave the lady alone?" he asked.

"I have no problem with her."

"All right."

He looked at the woman again, and for a second he thought about saying something to her, but he didn't know what the fuck to say or even why he felt that impulse to speak, to murmur a nice word in her ear.

He wanted to tell her he'd seen her in a book about fairy tales once, when he was a kid, and he believed you could grow a beanstalk that might reach the heavens.

He did as the Russian said: he left. He had no car, so he walked. It was raining and the water was icy against his skin, washing away the blood on his hands and chilling his bones. But nothing was ever going to wash away the rest, to rinse the past clean.

He walked and let the rain kiss him.

30

HOW DO STORIES end? she wondered. With comic books it was easy to tell: the closing panels were clearly indicated, the words "final issue" were emblazoned on the cover. With life it was harder to figure out where anything begins and where it concludes. Storylines bled outside the margins of pages; the colorist didn't apply final touches.

She didn't know how it would end, that first night, and she didn't search for Rubén immediately. That first night, she went home. She was still afraid, and she had bruises and cuts that needed to be looked after. In the morning she called her job and told them she'd been in a car accident. Then she tried the hospital closest to Asterisk, and after a few awkward questions she got lucky: he was there.

She didn't know how he'd react when he saw her, but he seemed pleased, and even when she told him the photos were gone, he didn't appear too upset. She supposed since he had survived two bullets, other matters were, for the moment, much smaller issues.

"You did your best," he said. "It's not your fault."

"I still feel I should have done something *more*. Those pictures meant so much to you."

"Maite, you matter more than the pictures. They could have killed you if you didn't turn them over."

He looked at her with such tenderness that Maite let out a sigh. "Is there anyone I should phone for you? Any family members?" she asked, determined to assist him any way she could. She'd failed him once, but it would never happen again.

"God, no. Jackie already asked the same thing, but I don't want my mother to know. She's all the way in Guerrero, anyway. I don't want to worry her. I'll tell her later. Besides, I'm doing okay."

"It must be dreadful. The pain," she said and brushed the hair away from his forehead. But he smiled and simply raised a hand to touch her cheek.

"You don't look too hot, either."

"I know. I have to go to work tomorrow, they're all going to stare . . . but I'll come and see you after work. Do you need anything?"

"It's fine, Maite. I'm fine. Well . . . maybe you can get me a newspaper. I'm bored."

"I'll bring you half a dozen."

He chuckled. Although Maite had always hated hospitals, she lingered at his side even when the other patient sharing Rubén's room shot her a poisonous glance because she'd come to visit rather late in the evening and the old coot wanted to sleep.

Just as Maite had thought, her return to the office was odd. All the other secretaries wanted to know what had happened, and Maite lied, saying she'd been in her boyfriend's car when the accident took place. Her boss was merciful and told her if she didn't feel up to it, she could stay home for a week or two, though he was not so generous as to give her time off with pay.

So she took off early from work, bought a couple of newspapers for Rubén, and headed back to the hospital. She pulled up a chair and sat next to him as he turned the pages.

"Look," he said, pointing to a short news story with a small black-and-white picture.

Leonardo Trejo, the story said, had passed away peacefully in his sleep. The retired colonel had been sixty-four years old. His wake would be celebrated at Funeraria Gayosso. A time and address were provided.

"That's not how it really happened," she said.

"It's never how it really happened."

"I wonder how Emilio explained the corpse to the police. Unless he moved the body. But even then, the man was stabbed."

The last time she'd seen Emilio, the coward had been pissing himself, and she hadn't bothered asking how he was after that. He hadn't bothered phoning her, either. She didn't think he would drag a body out of his home.

"Maybe Emilio is involved with the Hawks, in which case he simply called another one of them. Or he phoned someone else with enough pull to get the whole thing sorted," Rubén said as he folded the newspaper.

"They won't come after us, will they?"

"Why would they? We didn't kill him and the pictures are gone."

"I can't sleep well," she admitted.

"It's over," he assured her, clasping her hand. "We have nothing they want."

Maite brought more newspapers the next day, but although they looked everywhere, there were no more stories about the dead colonel. She wondered who the two men had been who had walked into Emilio's house. She especially wondered about the man who killed the colonel and who saved her life.

He looked familiar. She tried to remember where she'd seen him before. She remembered his eyes, very dark, but little else.

"I feel like I've met him before."

"There's not much point in thinking about that," Rubén told her, and kissed her as if to erase any bad memories with that gesture.

She wondered if he'd move in with her. It was senseless to keep two places. Maite's mother would deem it all very inappropriate, to be living with a man, and a younger one at that, but Maite was frankly tired of listening to her mother.

Maite's bruises changed color. The one on her face, near her eye, was green and could now be covered with a sensible amount of makeup and wouldn't stand out. She spent endless minutes in front of the mirror, applying mascara and doing her hair. Then, in a fit of inspiration, she decided to buy Rubén flowers.

She realized it was unusual for a woman to get a man flowers, but his room was small and drab. She wanted to cheer him up, and since he still needed to spend a few more days in that sterile, cold hospital, she figured flowers couldn't hurt.

She picked a nice bouquet with daisies and a couple of yellow roses, which the flower seller tied with a ribbon for her, then rode the bus to the hospital. In the hallway outside his room she bumped into Leonora.

The women stared at each other.

"You're here. I . . . *how* are you here?" Maite asked. She couldn't think of anything else to say. She had not expected to ever see Leonora again. She was like a character from a story who has been written out, erased from the page.

This did not make sense. Yet, in certain melodramas, even the dead manage to rise from the tomb, cheating the afterlife.

"I saw the story about my uncle in the paper," Leonora said. True enough, she was dressed in respectful, mournful black.

Maite was stunned. Her mouth felt dry. "But how did you know Rubén was in the hospital?"

"I called Jackie and she told me. Rubén looks ghastly." Leonora grimaced. "Why are you visiting him?"

"Rubén didn't tell you?"

"He said you were both looking for me."

Maite supposed it wouldn't have been in good taste to simply blurt out the whole story. Still, it irritated her that Rubén hadn't even hinted that they were involved. "Yes, we looked for you. Where were you? You vanished. I waited for you with the cat."

The young woman crossed her arms, rubbing them and looking at the ground.

"I was going to pick up my things and the cat, but when I was headed to the print shop I noticed someone was following me. I don't know if it was my uncle's men or someone else, but I panicked. I managed to lose them and I left the city. I tried calling back when I thought it was safe to do it, but you hung up on me."

"Rubén hung up on you."

"Well, it scared me even more. Then I read the paper and I decided to come back to the city. I went to see my sister, and she said our uncle was dead and Emilio had phoned and was looking for me. He told me the photos were destroyed."

"Your uncle did that. It was all this fuss for nothing."

"Yes," the girl said, looking sheepish. "At least Rubén will be okay."

"Look, I'm sorry, but I was dropping these off for Rubén, I need to put them in water," Maite said, clutching her bouquet.

"Oh. Sure."

Maite walked past Leonora and went into the room. She was annoyed to hear Leonora following her inside, but she put on a smile as she approached Rubén's bed and showed him the flowers. He had a newspaper in his hands and tucked it away when she walked in. It was the evening edition. She wondered if Leonora had brought it in.

"Hello there, I hope you're feeling better."

"Maite. What, you bought flowers?"

"I thought they'd brighten the room, except now I'm realizing there's no vase to put them in. Do you think a nurse might have one?" she wondered, and she set the flowers on the night table. "Leonora, maybe you could find a vase?"

Once the girl stepped out, Maite touched Rubén's hand and smiled. "Feeling any better?"

"I'm getting discharged in two days," he said, sliding his free hand across his chest.

"So soon! But I suppose that's good. I was thinking . . . and it was thinking, but it's a good idea . . . at least I'm certain it's a good idea . . . Anyway, I was thinking you could stay with me. You're going to need someone to take care of you for a little while. Your guesthouse won't do."

He looked embarrassed. She'd never seen him embarrassed. He'd paraded through her apartment without a stitch of clothing and didn't seem to mind. Now he was blushing.

"That's nice of you, but I'll be leaving the city as soon as I can—"

"I thought you liked me," she said quickly.

"I do. But it's not like we have anything in common. You know how it is."

She shook her head. "No, I don't."

"Come on, Maite, you didn't really think . . . and Leonora and I . . . well . . ."

He trailed off and looked at her, as if the smile on his lips could do all the talking for him. They had reconciled, then. She supposed it was simple enough for people so young to blow hot and cold from one instant to the next. Maybe Rubén had portrayed himself as the wounded hero and that had reeled Leonora in. Or maybe he had been on her mind all along.

Maite felt her face growing warm with shame. He didn't say anything else, instead looking down at the newspaper on his lap.

She realized, with his silence, how inadequate and meager she was, and how utterly she had misinterpreted his every gesture. Yet she almost felt like laughing. There was something furiously funny about the situation.

Maite turned around and saw Leonora standing by the doorway. She realized that the person who had been written out of the story was her, not Leonora.

"Don't forget your damn cat this time," Maite told her as she walked out.

Epilogue

MAITE'S FEET WERE sopping wet. She'd waited for the bus forever, but when it came at least it was half-empty, and she took a seat with a sigh and placed her bag with groceries on her lap. She glanced out the window, at the city lights and the water droplets sliding down the glass and thought of nothing, her mind as numb as her chilled fingers.

It was Sunday. Sunday she went to the movies. But not that Sunday. She'd gone shopping instead and bought chicken and a few vegetables. At the supermarket, not the tianguis, because she'd missed the damn tianguis again. She was planning on making consommé. It was simple enough, and it should last her for a few days.

Someone sat next to her. She slid a hand against the glass, traced a circle with her fingertips.

"I'm wondering if you'd go for coffee with me."

She took a while to raise her head and look at the man speaking, because she didn't think he was talking to her. But then she glanced at him and realized he was. And she knew him. It was the man from Emilio's house, the one who had killed the colonel.

"What are you doing here?" she asked.

"Following you," he said simply.

"Why?"

"Habit. You were under surveillance."

"By you?"

"Me and my teammates."

So she'd been right. She *had* seen him before the confrontation at Emilio's house. Up close she was able to place him: he'd been at the diner. He'd cocked his head a little, smiled at her while he lit a cigarette. Now she remembered.

"You played a song," she said and then she frowned. "Am I under surveillance again?"

"No. That's all over. Plus, it would be pretty dumb for me to talk to you if that was the case."

"Why *are* you talking to me?"

"I'm curious about you. And I told myself I would. Talk to you, that is. After it was all over."

It was odd how she wasn't nervous, sitting there, talking to a killer. Because the young man was a killer and God knew what else. Maybe she was tired. She felt old, as if life had drained out of her body, and her soul was as numb as her cold hands.

"Who are you?" she asked.

"I was a Hawk. I'm not anything in particular now."

"I meant what's your name."

"Oh. That. I suppose it's Ermenegildo," he said.

"Suppose?"

"Yeah. I could tell you. Over coffee. It's kind of cold in this bus."

"I'm headed home."

"I know."

She looked ahead. The bus was slowly rolling down the avenue. The man took out a cigarette and offered one to her. She shook her head. He lit his cigarette, took two puffs.

"There's a café over there," he said, pointing at the street corner coming up ahead. "It's nice. Or you want to hit that joint of yours with the jukebox?"

"I'm going home."

"You scared of me?"

She didn't reply. He smoked his cigarette and leaned forward, resting his forearms on the seat in front of him. "I saw your record collection in your apartment. It's impressive."

"You were in my apartment."

"Told you: surveillance."

She pictured him and his buddies going through her drawers, sitting in her atelier and sliding their hands over her books, her records. Her meaningless, dull life laid bare to strangers.

"Anyway, I was wondering why you've got the Prysock cover, not the Bennett."

"That is what you want to know? That is why you followed me onto this bus?" she said, her voice suddenly tinted with anger.

He turned his head and looked at her. His hair was shaggy and wet with rain, water droplets sliding down his neck, and his eyes were twin black abysses. They were painted with ink, like the eyes of a comic book character.

"I don't know what I want, don't know who I am," he said, and the smoke curled up from his mouth. "I don't know anything. But I can't stand being alone right now."

She thought of the jungle, as she'd seen it in those cheap romance stories she liked to read. The quality of that jungle sky came back to her. That's what his eyes were like: the night on the printed page. Blacker than the night outside the bus, the real and tangible night awaiting them here—because in the city there were lights from buildings and cars. But the night in the comic books was smeared on the page and did not allow any light. Even the moon did not provide illumination: it was a circle, the size of a coin. The absence of ink but not the presence of light.

The moon did not glow.

"I'm getting off at the next stop and I'm going back to that café," he said. He sounded tired too. Like her.

She clutched her bag and pressed her lips together. The bus neared the curb, and the young man climbed off it. The semaphore light was red. She saw him, with his cigarette in his mouth, standing on the sidewalk for a moment, before the light changed and the bus stuttered forward.

He was mad. That was clear. Who else but a madman would come looking for her like this? Who would look for her at all?

Crazy killer, crazy man standing back there, in the rain, walking back to his café. Maite thought of the safety of her apartment, of the parakeet in its cage and her collection of stolen trinkets. She thought of playing "Strangers in the Night" and sinking into the shadows of her living room and dancing alone, dancing on her own, as usual. As she should.

At the next stoplight she jumped off the bus. The rain fell slow and steady, making music of its own. She stood in the middle of the sidewalk with her umbrella in one hand and her grocery bag in the other, looking down the street in the direction of the café.

She wondered what would happen if she started walking there, if she did not head immediately home.

She wondered what kind of story started like this.

She saw a figure in the distance, hazy, and he waved at her. Maite held her breath.

Afterword

THE TELEGRAM THAT opens this book is a real message sent by the CIA. One Thursday in 1971, a shock group funded and organized by the Mexican government attacked a group of students marching through a large avenue in Mexico City. The Hawks (Los Halcones) had been trained by Mexican authorities with support of the CIA in an effort to squelch communism in Mexico and suppress dissent. Hundreds of protesters were injured or killed during what became known as El Halconazo or the Corpus Christi Massacre. President Luis Echeverría and local authorities, including Mexico City's regent, Alfonso Martínez Domínguez, denied the existence of the Hawks or shifted the blame.

As a result of this attack, simmering guerilla action in Mexico increased, as incensed students decided that one could not reason with the authorities. Meanwhile, the Hawks were disbanded. However, repressive action against activists and guerilla fighters did not cease. Through a group known as the Brigada Blanca, the government abducted, tortured, incarcerated, and murdered Mexican citizens during the decade of the 1970s. This was known as the Dirty War (Guerra Sucia).

Music debates had been heating up in Mexico for years. In upper-class neighborhoods, government approved "singing cafes" could play the music the government sanctioned, harmless covers of American songs. But by the late sixties, most of these venues had closed down. The government claimed they fomented rebellion and anti-nationalist values. A few months after the Halconazo, the Festival de Rock y Ruedas de Avándaro took place. It was called the "Mexican Woodstock." Subsequently, President Echeverría outlawed rock concerts, and the government demanded that records played on the radio be free of content that offended morality. In response, young people of the lower classes organized clandestine reunions called "funky pits," but the rock scene suffered greatly.

Backlash against rock music and live performances was a symbolic way for the government to tighten its grip on the nation. There would not be another Halconazo during the 1970s, but of course the reigning PRI party would never give people a chance to march together again: the Brigada Blanca made sure to exterminate any opposition.

The more daring, innovative bands of the 1970s did not survive the inhospitable conditions for music making. None except for one: El Tri, which began as a cover band called Three Souls in My Mind. They had played at the legendary Festival de Rock y Ruedas de Avándaro and began writing original songs in Spanish, not just playing covers. In the mid-seventies, El Tri recorded the first explicitly anti-government rock song: "Abuso de Autoridad." They obviously did not have a major label behind them.

Nobody was ever punished or found guilty for the Halconazo, which echoed a previous armed attack in 1968—the Tlatelolco massacre. In 2006, ex-president Luis Echeverría pleaded guilty and was put under house arrest for his participation in the Halconazo. He was later exonerated and charges against him dropped. None of the men who led the attacks against activists during the Dirty War ever did any jail time, either. Many of them have now died quietly in their beds of old age. Some went on to have successful political careers: Alfonso Martínez Domínguez became the governor of Nuevo León.

In 2019, President Andrés Manuel López Obrador released the archives of the Federal Security Directorate, which contain information about the Dirty War and the political persecution of activists by the Mexican government.

We'll never know the exact number of victims of the Dirty War. My novel is noir, pulp fiction, but it's based on a real horror story.

The Author's Playlist to *Velvet Was the Night*

LISTEN ON SPOTIFY at randomhousebooks.com/VelvetWasTheNightPlaylist

1. "Todo Negro" by Los Salvejes
2. "Jailhouse Rock" by Elvis Presley
3. "Dream Lover" by Bobby Darin
4. "Can't Take My Eyes off You" by Frankie Valli
5. "Eleanor Rigby" by The Beatles
6. "Abuso de Autoridad" by Three Souls in My Mind
7. "Run for Your Life" by Nancy Sinatra
8. "Quiero Estrechar Tu Mano" by Los Ángeles Azules
9. "El Día Que Me Quieras" by Carlos Gardel
10. "Smoke Gets in Your Eyes" by The Platters
11. "Love Me Tender" by Elvis Presley
12. "Satisfacción" by Los Apson
13. "Sin Ti" by Los Belmonts
14. "Lost in My World (Perdido en Mi Mundo)" by Los Dug Dug's
15. "Blue Velvet" by Arthur Prysock
16. "Shain's a Go Go" by Los Shain's
17. "Bésame Mucho" by Antonio Prieto
18. "El Cigarrito," 2001 Digital Remaster, by Victor Jara
19. "Bang Bang (My Baby Shot Me Down)" by Nancy Sinatra
20. "Cuatro Palabras" by Juan D'Arienzo
21. "White Room" by Cream

22. "Agujetas de Color de Rosa (Pink Shoe Laces)" by Los Hooligans
23. "Somos Novios" by Armando Manzanero
24. "Kukulkan" by Toncho Pilatos
25. "Solamente Una Vez" by Lucho Gatica and Agustín Lara
26. "No Me Platiques Más" by Vicente Garrido
27. "Piel Canela" by Eydie Gormé and Los Panchos
28. "Dream a Little Dream of Me—with Introduction" by The Mamas and the Papas
29. "Volver a los Diecisiete" by Violeta Parra
30. "Will You Love Me Tomorrow" by The Shirelles
31. "Are You Lonesome Tonight" by Elvis Presley
32. "Surfin' Bird" by The Trashmen
33. "At Last" by Etta James
34. "Can't Help Falling in Love" by Elvis Presley
35. "The House of the Rising Sun" by The Animals
36. "The Girl from Ipanema" by Stan Getz, João Gilberto, and Astrud Gilberto
37. "Strangers in the Night" by Frank Sinatra
38. "Pobre Soñador" by El Tri

Acknowledgments

A BIG THANK you to my agent, Eddie Schneider; my editor, Tricia Narwani; and the production team at Penguin Random House. My interest in music was fueled at a young age by my father, who waxed on nostalgically about certain bands. Noirs have a proud tradition in Latin America. The first noir writer in Mexico was Rafael Bernal, who published *El Complot Mongol* in 1969. So thanks to Rafael and the other writers of old noirs.

READ ON FOR A SNEAK PEEK AT

THE DAUGHTER OF DOCTOR MOREAU

by Silvia Moreno-Garcia

A dreamy reimagining of *The Island of Doctor Moreau* set against the backdrop of nineteenth-century Mexico.

Enjoy this special preview!

1

Carlota

THEY'D BE ARRIVING that day, the two gentlemen, their boat gliding through the forest of mangroves. The jungle teemed with noises, birds crying out in sonorous discontent as if they could foretell the approach of intruders. In their huts, behind the main house, the hybrids were restless. Even the old donkey, eating its corn, seemed peevish.

Carlota had spent a long time contemplating the ceiling of her room the previous night, and in the morning her belly ached like it always did when she was nervous. Ramona had to brew her a cup of bitter orange tea. Carlota didn't like when her nerves got the best of her, but Dr. Moreau seldom had visitors. Their isolation, her father said, did her good. When she was little she'd been ill, and it was important that she rest and remain calm. Besides, the hybrids made proper company impossible. When someone stopped at Yaxaktun it was either Francisco Ritter, her father's lawyer and correspondent, or Hernando Lizalde.

Mr. Lizalde always came alone. Carlota was never introduced to him. Twice she'd seen him walking from afar, outside the house, with her father. He left quickly; he didn't stay the night in one of the guest rooms. And he didn't visit often, anyway. His presence was mostly felt in letters, which arrived every few months.

Now Mr. Lizalde, who was a distant presence, a name spoken but never manifested, was visiting and not only visiting but he'd be bringing with him a new mayordomo. For nearly a year since Melquíades had departed, the reins of Yaxaktun had been solely in the hands of the doctor, an inadequate situation since he spent most of his time busy in the lab or deep in contemplation. Her father, however, didn't seem inclined to find a steward.

"The doctor, he's too picky," Ramona said, brushing the tangles and knots out of Carlota's hair. "Mr. Lizalde, he sends him letters, and he says here's one gentleman, here's another, but your father always replies no, this one won't do, neither will the other. As if many people would come here."

"Why wouldn't people want to come to Yaxaktun?" Carlota asked.

"It's far from the capital. And you know what they say. All of them, they complain it's too close to rebel territory. They think it's the end of the world."

"It's not that far," Carlota said, though she only understood the peninsula by the maps in books where distances were flattened and turned into black-and-white lines.

"It's mighty far. Makes most people think twice when they're used to cobblestones and newspapers each morning."

"Why did you come to work here, then?"

"My family, they picked me a husband but he was bad. Lazy, did nothing all day, then he beat me at night. I didn't complain, not for a long time. Then one morning he hit me hard. Too hard. Or maybe as hard as every other time, but I wouldn't take it any longer. So I grabbed my things and I went away. I came to Yaxaktun because nobody can find you here," Ramona said with a shrug. "But it's not the same for others. Others want to be found."

Ramona was not quite old; the lines fanning her eyes were shallow, and her hair was speckled with a few strands of gray. But she spoke in a measured tone, and she spoke of many things, and Carlota considered her very wise.

"You think the new mayordomo won't like it here? You think he'll want to be found?"

"Who can tell? But Mr. Lizalde's bringing him. It's Mr. Lizalde who's ordered it and he's right. Your father, he does things all day but he never does the things that need done either." Ramona put the brush down. "Stop fretting, child, you'll wrinkle the dress."

The dress in question was decorated with a profusion of frills and pleats, and an enormous bow at the back instead of the neat muslin pinafore she normally wore around the house. Lupe and Cachito were giggling at the doorway, looking at Carlota, as she was primped like a horse before an exhibition.

"You look nice," Ramona said.

"It itches," Carlota complained. She thought she looked like a large cake.

"Don't pull at it. And you two, go wash your faces and those hands," Ramona said, punctuating her words with one of her deadly stares.

Lupe and Cachito moved aside to let Ramona by as she exited the room, grumbling about all the things she had to do that morning. Carlota sulked. Father said the dress was the latest fashion, but she was used to lighter frocks. It might have looked pretty in Mérida or Mexico City or some other place, but in Yaxaktun it was terribly fussy.

Lupe and Cachito giggled again as they walked into the room and took a closer look at her buttons, touching the taffeta and silk until Carlota elbowed them away, and then they giggled again.

"Stop it, both of you," she said.

"Don't be mad, Loti, it's just you look funny, like one of your dollies," Cachito said. "But maybe the new mayordomo will bring candy and you'll like that."

"I doubt he'll bring candy," Carlota said.

"Melquíades brought us candy," Lupe said, and she sat on the old rocking horse, which was too small for any of them now, and rocked back and forth.

"Brought *you* candy," Cachito complained. "He never brought me none."

"That's because you bite," Lupe said. "I've never bitten a hand."

And she hadn't, that was true. When Carlota's father had first brought Lupe into the house, Melquíades had made a fuss about it, said the doctor couldn't possibly leave Carlota alone with Lupe.

What if she should scratch the child? But the doctor said not to worry, Lupe was good. Besides, Carlota had wanted a playmate so badly that even if Lupe had bitten and scratched, she wouldn't have said a word.

But Melquíades never took to Cachito. Maybe because he was more rambunctious than Lupe. Maybe because he was male, and Melquíades could lull himself into a sense of safety with a girl. Maybe because Cachito had once bitten Melquíades's fingers. It was nothing deep, no more than a scratch, but Melquíades detested the boy, and he never let Cachito into the house.

Then again, Melquíades hadn't liked any of them much. Ramona had worked for Dr. Moreau since Carlota was about five years old, and Melquíades had been at Yaxaktun before that. But Carlota could not recall him ever smiling at the children or treating them as anything other than a nuisance. When he brought candy back, it was because Ramona asked that he procure a treat for the little ones, not because Melquíades would have thought to do it of his own volition. When they were noisy, he might grumble and tell them to eat a sweet and go away, to be quiet and let him be. There was no affection for the children in his heart.

Ramona loved them and Melquíades tolerated them.

Now Melquíades was gone, and Cachito slipped in and out of the house, darting through the kitchen and the living room with its velvet sofas, even stabbing at the keys of the piano, ringing discordant notes from the instrument when the doctor was not looking. No, the children didn't miss Melquíades. He'd been fastidious and a bit conceited on account of the fact that he'd been a doctor in Mexico City, which he thought a great achievement.

"I don't see why we need a new mayordomo," Lupe said.

"Father can't manage it all on his own, and Mr. Lizalde wants it all in perfect order," she said, repeating what she'd been told.

"What does the mister care how he manages it or not? He doesn't live here."

Carlota peered into the mirror and fiddled with the pearl necklace, which, like the dress, had been newly imposed on her that morning to assure she looked prim and proper.

Cachito was right: Carlota did resemble one of her dollies, pretty porcelain things set on a shelf with their pink lips and round eyes. But Carlota was not a doll, she was a girl, almost a lady, and it was a bit ridiculous that she must resemble a porcelain, painted creation.

Ever the dutiful child, though, she turned from the mirror and looked at Lupe with a serious face.

"Mr. Lizalde is our patron."

"I think he's nosy," Lupe said. "I think he wants that man to spy on us and tell him everything we do. Besides, what does an Englishman know about managing anything here? There are no jungles in England, all the books in the library show snow and cold and people going around in carriages."

That was true enough. When Carlota peered into books—sometimes with Cachito and Lupe looking with interest over her shoulder—magic lands of make-believe spread before her eyes. England, Spain, Italy, London, Berlin, and Marseille. They seemed like made-up names to her, jarring in comparison with the names of the towns in the Yucatán. Paris especially surprised her. She tried to say the name slowly, the way her father did. *Paree,* he said. But it wasn't merely the way he said it, it was the knowledge behind it. He had lived in Paris, he had walked its streets, and therefore when he said Paris he was invoking a real place, a living metropolis, whereas Carlota only knew Yaxaktun, and though she might conjugate her verbs correctly—*Je vais à Paris*—the city was never real for her.

Paris was the city of her father, but it wasn't her city.

She did not know the city of her mother. An oval painting hung in Father's room. It showed a beautiful blond woman wearing an off-shoulder ball gown and sparkling jewels around her neck. This, however, was not her mother. This was the doctor's first wife. He'd lost her and a baby girl; a fever took them. And then, afterward, in his grief, the doctor had acquired a lover. Carlota was the doctor's natural daughter.

Ramona had been at Yaxaktun for many years, but even she could not tell Carlota her mother's name or what she looked like.

"There was a woman, dark and pretty," she told Carlota. "She came by one time and the doctor was expecting her, he received her and they talked in the little parlor. But she came round only that one time."

Her father was reluctant to paint a more detailed picture. He said, simply, that they had never wed and Carlota had been left with him when her mother went away. Carlota suspected this meant her mother had married another man and had a new family. Carlota might have brothers and sisters, but she could not meet them.

"Listen to your father, who gave you life, and do not despise your mother when she is old," her father said, reading the Bible with great care. But he was both mother and father to her.

As for her father's family, the Moreaus, she knew none of them, either. Her father had a brother but he lived across the sea, in distant France. It was the two of them, and that was enough for her. Why would she need anyone but her father? Why would she want Paris or her mother's town, wherever it might be?

The one place that was real was Yaxaktun.

"If he brings candy, I won't care if he's nosy," Cachito said.

"The doctor will show him the laboratory," Lupe said. "He's kept himself there all week, so he must have something to show them."

"A patient?"

"Or equipment or something. I bet it's more interesting than candy. Carlota is going into the laboratory. She'll tell us what it is."

"Are you really?" Cachito asked.

He had been pushing an old wooden train across the floor, but now he turned to Carlota. Lupe had stopped rocking her horse. They both waited for an answer.

"I'm not sure," Carlota said.

Mr. Lizalde owned Yaxaktun; he paid for Dr. Moreau's research. Carlota supposed that if he wanted to see her father's lab, he would. And they might show it to the mayordomo, too.

"I am. I heard the doctor talking to Ramona about it. Why do you think they got you in that dress?" Lupe asked.

"He's said I might receive our guests and walk with them, but nothing is certain."

"I bet you get to see. You have to tell us if you do."

Ramona, walking down the hallway, paused to look into the room. "What are you still doing here? Go wash your faces!" she yelled.

Cachito and Lupe knew when their merriment was at an end, and they both scampered away. Ramona looked at Carlota and pointed a finger at her. "Now don't move from this spot."

"I won't."

Carlota sat down on the bed and looked at her dollies, at their curly hair and long eyelashes, and she tried to smile like the dolls smiled; their tiny mouths with a cupid's bow looked perfectly pleasant.

She grasped the ribbon in her hair, twisting it around a finger. All she knew of the world was Yaxaktun. She'd never seen anything beyond it. All the people she knew were the people there. When Mr. Lizalde chanced to appear in their home, he was, in her mind, as fantastical as those etchings of London and Madrid and Paris.

Mr. Lizalde existed and yet he didn't exist. On the two occasions on which she'd glimpsed him he had been but a figure in the distance, walking outside the main house, talking to her father. But during this visit she would be up close to him, and not just to him, but to the would-be mayordomo. Here was an entirely new element that would soon be introduced into her world. It was like when Father spoke of foreign bodies.

To soothe herself she took a book from the shelf and sat in her reading chair. Dr. Moreau, wishing to cultivate a scientific disposition in his daughter, had gifted Carlota with numerous books about plants and animals and the wonders of biology so that, in addition to the fairy tales of Perrault, Carlota could be exposed to more didactic texts. Dr. Moreau would not tolerate a child who only knew "Cendrillon" or "Barbe Bleue."

Carlota, always agreeable, read everything her father put in front of her. She had enjoyed *The Fairy Tales of Science: A Book for Youth*, but *The Water Babies* scared her. There was one moment in which poor Tom, who had been miniaturized, met some salmon. Even though the book assured her salmon "are all true gentlemen"—and even though they were more polite than the vicious old otter Tom had previously run into—Carlota suspected they would eat Tom at the slightest provocation. The whole book was full of such dangerous encounters. Devour or be devoured. It was an infinite chain of hunger.

Carlota had taught Lupe to read, but Cachito stumbled over his letters, jumbling them in his head, and she had to read out loud to him. But she had not read *The Water Babies* to Cachito.

And when her father said Mr. Lizalde would be visiting, along with a gentleman, she could not help but think of the terrible salmon in the book. And yet, rather than turn away from the image, she stared at the illustrations, at the otter and the salmon and the horrid monsters that inhabited its pages. Though they were all getting too big for children's tales, the book still fascinated her.

Ramona returned after a while, and Carlota put the book away. She followed the woman into the sitting room. Carlota's father was not much for fashion, so the furnishings of the house had never concerned him, and they consisted mostly of the old, heavy furniture that the previous owner of the ranch had brought, supplemented by a few choice artifacts the doctor imported through the years. Chief among these was a French clock. It struck a bell upon the hour, and its sounds never failed to delight Carlota. It amazed her that such precise machinery could be produced. She pictured the gears turning inside its delicate, painted shell.

As she stepped forward into the room she wondered if they could hear her heart beating, like the song of the clock.

Her father turned toward her and smiled. "Here is my housekeeper with my daughter. Carlota, come here," he said. She hurried to her father's side, and he placed a hand on her shoulder as he spoke. "Gentlemen, may I present my daughter, Carlota. This is Mr. Lizalde and this here is Mr. Laughton."

"How do you do?" she said, automatically, like the well-trained parrot that slept in its cage in the corner. "I trust your trip has been pleasant."

Mr. Lizalde's whiskers had a bit of gray in them, but he was still younger than her father, whose eyes were bracketed with deep wrinkles. He was dressed well, in a gold brocade waistcoat and a fine jacket, and dabbed at his forehead with a handkerchief as he smiled at her.

Mr. Laughton, on the other hand, did not smile at all. His jacket was of brown and cream wool tweed, with no embellishments, and he wore no vest. She was struck by how young and dour-looking he seemed. She'd thought they'd get someone like Melquíades, a man balding at the temples. This fellow had all his hair, even if it was a bit shaggy and untidy. And how light his eyes were. Gray, watery eyes.

"We're doing well, thank you," Mr. Lizalde said, and then he looked at her father. "Quite the little princess you have there. I think she might be of an age with my youngest child."

"You have many children, Mr. Lizalde?" she asked.

"I have a son and five daughters. My boy is fifteen."

"I am fourteen, sir."

"You're tall, for a girl. You might be as tall as my boy."

"And bright. She's been schooled in all the proper languages," her father said. "Carlota, I was trying to assist Mr. Laughton here in a matter of translation. Could you tell him what *natura non facit saltus* means?"

The "proper" languages she'd learned indeed, though the smattering of Mayan she spoke she had not obtained through her father. She'd learned from Ramona, as had the hybrids. She was, officially, their housekeeper. Unofficially she was a teller of tales, an expert in every plant that grew near their house, and more.

"It means nature does not make leaps," Carlota replied, fixing her eyes on the young man.

"Right. And can you explain the concept?"

"Change is incremental. Nature proceeds little by little," she declaimed. Her father asked questions such as these frequently, and the answers were easy, like practicing her scales. It soothed her fragile nerves.

"Do you agree with that?"

"Nature, perhaps. But not man," she said.

Her father patted her shoulder. She could feel him smiling without having to look at him.

"Carlota will guide us to my laboratory. I'll show you my research and prove the point," her father said.

In its corner the parrot opened an eye and watched them. Carlota nodded and bid the gentlemen follow her.

PHOTO: MARTIN DEE

SILVIA MORENO-GARCIA is the *New York Times* best-selling author of the critically acclaimed speculative novels *Mexican Gothic, Gods of Jade and Shadow, Signal to Noise, Certain Dark Things,* and *The Beautiful Ones;* and the crime novel *Untamed Shore*. She has edited several anthologies, including the World Fantasy Award–winning *She Walks in Shadows* (aka *Cthulhu's Daughters*). She lives in Vancouver, British Columbia.

silviamoreno-garcia.com
Facebook.com/smorenogarcia
Twitter: @silviamg
Instagram: @silviamg.author

About the Type

This book was set in Walbaum, a typeface designed in 1810 by German punch cutter J. E. (Justus Erich) Walbaum (1768–1839). Walbaum's type is more French than German in appearance. Like Bodoni, it is a classical typeface, yet its openness and slight irregularities give it a human, romantic quality.